TEQUILA VIKINGS

D0878547

J.E. Park

Mailing List Sign Up for Newsletter and New Release Info: https://jeparkbooks.com/

Follow me on Facebook at
https://www.facebook.com/JE-Park-100409961692113

Twitter handle: @JEPark94519501

Email at: jeparkauthor@gmail.com

Cover design by DAMONZA.COM

Table of Contents

PROLOGUE

Randy Green did not look like a monster. He was short, barely five and a half feet tall, and skinny, struggling to tip the scale even a hair beyond one hundred and ten pounds. With his red hair, freckles, and "aw-shucks" Kentucky demeanor, he seemed to be some harmless hillbilly Howdy-Doody. Once he got home and into his bourbon, however, he tended to go after his wife and her son as if he were a miniature Mike Tyson.

There was a time when I sympathized with the man. We were in the same duty section aboard the *USS Belleau Wood* and Randy often sat with us in the radar repair shop, voicing his regrets over marrying a Filipina bar girl. The man would drive himself crazy, wondering what his wife was up to when he was not there.

When Rafaela started wearing black eyes like poorly applied mascara, and Manny suddenly became an exceptionally accident-prone five-year-old boy, my empathy for Randy evaporated, replaced by intense loathing. Raised by a man just like him, I was fully conscious of what that bastard was capable of. I knew what he would eventually do to that family, even if they had yet to develop a clue themselves.

I tried to warn him. When I first suspected what was going on in the Green household, I made it a point to describe to Randy in very graphic detail how my father murdered my family. I also let him know what I would do to anyone that I suspected was a danger to his own. Having heard about the things I occasionally did for my master chief deep in the bowels of the ship, Randy had to have known that it was no idle threat.

Still, he did it anyway. I was not surprised. I learned from experience that people like my father and Randy Green couldn't help themselves. They would never stop until someone eventually stopped them.

When I heard Randy Green broke his stepson's arm so that the boy's mother would unlock the door that she was hiding behind, I was oddly relieved. Rafaela and Manny were alive, and I was sure that the courts would finally deal with that son-of-a-bitch. After I learned that Randy's wife concocted a story that got his charges dropped, though, I was furious. Not at her, as I knew the methods that fiends like Randy used to keep their women in line. My fury was targeted squarely upon the shoulders of Petty Officer Green, right where it belonged.

I did not wait for Master Chief Darrow to come to me this time. I went to him. Finding him alone in the Electronic Materials Office, the EMO, I took a seat in LT Howe's chair and told him I thought Randy Green was about to have an accident.

Darrow grinned and leaned back in his seat, putting two heavily tattooed arms behind his head while a burning cigarette dangled from his lips. "Yeah, you'd be surprised how many people have come talking to me about that clumsy little fucker."

A few days later, the master chief was standing before the division at roll call, announcing an upcoming zone inspection by the captain. He demanded that all of the division's spaces sparkle, the Nixie Winch Room in particular since that was what got us gigged last time.

The Nixie, or officially the SLQ-25, was the ship's protection against a submarine attack. Located at the *Belleau Wood*'s stern, a Nixie "fish" looked like a miniature torpedo that was hooked up to a long transmissible cable and towed a couple of hundred feet behind the vessel. When energized, the device duplicated the ship's electromagnetic signature to fool incoming torpedoes into hitting it instead of us.

TEQUILA VIKINGS

The winch room, which housed the equipment used to deploy and retrieve the fish, was a challenging space to maintain. Located in a remote area with a deck made of metal grates, it was impossible to sweep. We needed to sponge down virtually every square inch of it, a task as labor-intensive as it was time-consuming. "Do you need any assistance down there, Petty Officer Murphy?"

I grinned, knowing what the master chief was really asking me. "It's a big job. We could always use help."

With a nod, Darrow said, "No problem. Petty Officer Green! You're helping out the radar guys in the Nixie room today. Understand?"

Randy's voice cracked as he answered, "Yes, Master Chief." He knew what was in store for him. Judging by the way the rest of our division fell silent, they did too.

*****

Despite his reservations, Petty Officer Green showed up right on time, looking every bit the part of a condemned man. He was sweating, trembling, and stuttering over his responses to my questions, acting like a twitchy Chihuahua trying to suppress the symptoms of a methamphetamine overdose. I was as friendly as possible, smiling when I spoke to him and cracking jokes as I loaded his arms full of cleaning supplies. I even offered him a cigarette. That made him even more uneasy, considering I had not given him the time of day for months. Finally, when there was nothing left to make him carry, I opened the door and let him lead the way below.

We descended the first three flights of stairs in silence. Hitting the fourth, Green turned to me and whimpered, "You know Doyle, I'm not the kind of man your father was."

Oh, but you are. You even have the same podunk accent. You're a loser. A coward. A weakling. The world is going to beat you down, and you'll take your frustrations out on your family. Then, one day, you'll snap. You'll grab that shotgun just like my old man did and start with her. Then you'll go after the little boy and...

Images of my family flashed through my mind, making me wince. They were always so vivid, even though I never actually saw the bodies. Had I been there, my father would undoubtedly have killed me too. My imagination spared no detail when playing the carnage back for me. I saw every piece of gore, smelled the blood and spent gunpowder, and heard the screams. I could even feel my mother's grief as she watched her children blown to pieces before her, powerless to stop it.

I never hid what happened to my family. I wore it like armor to show people how tough I was, and it never bothered me when the subject came up. Until now. Listening to Randy Green attempting to separate himself from my old man was infuriating. He was trying to minimize what he did to his family by comparing it to what happened to mine. Sensing that was not working, Green switched tactics and started blaming his wife.

"...I wasn't myself, Doyle. I thought she'd been hanging around the Trophy Lounge with her friends. No, I *knew* she was! She's picking up other men, bringing them into our house...into our fucking bed for Christ's sake!" It sounded like Green was trying to convince himself of his wife's infidelities far more than he was me.

Although Randy was never more than an arm's length from my ears, he started to sound far away, almost as if he were underwater. My heart started racing, and I could feel my sweat pores opening up. All were surefire symptoms that one of my episodes was coming on. Usually, I would hide in my radar dome until it passed. This time, though, I couldn't. I would lose the opportunity to ensure that Green got what was coming to him.

Randy kept droning on, unaware of what was happening to me. "...she made me this way! If only she'd not go out when I was on duty! If only she looked at me as something more than a ticket to the United States! I know! I know! Some of it's my fault! I should've never married a whore but..."

From behind, Green even started to look like Liam Murphy. He grew a few inches. He started limping a little on that left leg. The blue dungaree shirt he wore transformed into a grease-stained denim jacket, and his shoulders slumped forward. Randy was starting to cry, though, and that was something I never saw my father do.

"...I didn't mean to break Manny's arm, Doyle, but she wouldn't come out of the bathroom! I was only trying to make him scream, so she'd open the door, you know? But it snapped like a twig! He was so fragile. I never thought it would break like that! I swear..."

As we approached the winch room, I reached for my keys before remembering that Kevin Dixon and Claude Metaire, two of my radar techs, went there ahead of us. The entrance was already open, inviting us into that dark and lonely space.

Up until he stepped through that hatch, it seemed as if Green had resigned himself to his punishment. Once he caught sight of Dixie and Metaire, though, he lost his nerve. Randy dropped everything he was carrying and turned to run, only to find me blocking his escape route.

Unable to flee, Green's survival instincts incited him to fight. Trying to knock me out of his way, he cranked his right arm back and threw his fist against my jaw with everything he had. It would have been a debilitating blow had I been a ninety-pound Filipina woman, but that was something I most decidedly was not.

My composure, which was little more than the thinnest of façades at that point, completely melted away, and I let my episode take over. Usually, there was nothing I could do during my flashbacks but despair. This time, however, I had something tangible that I could fight back against other than macabre hallucinations. I had a surrogate for my father. Instead of being paralyzed by grief, I exploded with rage.

When I finished with him, Randy spent the rest of his life suffering for what he did to that little boy. I nearly did too. When Metaire and Dixie finally pulled me off of Petty Officer Green, there were only a few almost imperceptible heartbeats keeping me from spending decades behind bars.

Up until then, my life in the United States Navy had been somewhat charmed. Our days may have been full of tedium and monotony, but once we were pumped full of liquor and set loose on liberty, we morphed into the maritime marauders of old. We were Tequila Vikings, seeking glory through sexual conquest, tavern combat, and other forms of mayhem and misadventure. We even had it tattooed on our arms.

I did not join the Navy to spend six years bar brawling my way through life with a blood alcohol level spectacularly exceeding my IQ, but I was pretty happy with the way things turned out. At least I was up to the point where I nearly beat Randy Green to death. That was when I discovered how effective being investigated for attempted murder could be in persuading a man to reassess his lifestyle choices.

*****

CHAPTER 1

"**H**OLE-leeee SHEEEE-it!" For a cautionary tale of what happens when wealth has more to do with earning a commission in the US Navy than fitness to lead, one needed to look no further than Ensign Whitaker. Officers needed to be even-keeled and cool under pressure. Whitaker was neither. He was a high energy, low aptitude Texan lacking tact, a verbal filter, and other critical social graces.

"Hey!" Whitaker yelled while looking over the side. "Murphy! Check out this guy coming up the pier! He looks like one of your dance partners!"

A couple of months before, I took quiet pride in my role as one of Master Chief Darrow's bruisers. When under an active investigation, however, a reputation as a hooligan becomes far more of a liability than it ever was an asset. The last thing I needed was some moron like Whitaker reminding everyone within earshot of what I was capable of.

I joined the Officer of the Deck more to get him to shut up than out of any genuine curiosity. Still, I was impressed by what he pointed out to me.

The closer our mangled seaman got, the worse he looked. His left arm was in a sling across his chest, bound in enough gauze to make it twice its usual size. The medics wrapped his broken ribs, but there was little covering the man's face, which was bruised and swollen to macabre proportions. Angry red patches of bare skin covered his scalp, where it appeared his hair had been ripped right out of his skull. It was gruesome. Shaking my head, I returned to my podium.

"Hey, where ya goin'?" Whitaker asked. "You suddenly squeamish over the sight of a little blood?"

"I'm calling medical," I told the OOD as I reached for the IC line. "We need to get a corpsman up here for this kid."

As I was dialing, the seaman's Master-at-Arms escorts helped him up the three flights of steps to the top of the gangplank. After crossing over to the quarterdeck, he presented his ID and requested permission to come aboard. Whitaker granted it before stepping closer to get a better look at his injuries. "What's your story, son?"

I always found it amusing when ensigns called young enlisted men "son." Whitaker was twenty-two, the same age as me. According to his ID card, Seaman Corey Baker was twenty-four. He was older than both of us. "You get beat up?" the OOD inquired when the seaman did not answer fast enough. Whitaker was never one to pass up an opportunity to ask a stupid question.

"I got attacked in Tijuana, sir," Baker mumbled through puffy lips. "By the cops."

"For what?"

"For nothin'. They got pissed because some guys they were chasing got away, so they grabbed some random squids off the street to take their frustrations out on. I didn't do a goddamn thing."

After ending my conversation with the duty corpsman, I turned to the seaman and asked, "Who got you? The local dicks or the *federales*?"

"How the hell should I know? Whoever that fucker Hulagu belongs to."

"Hulagu?" Whitaker asked. "What kind of name is Hulagu? That doesn't sound like a spic name to me."

Ensign Whitaker's parents bought him an expensive education, a future of privilege, and an insufferable sense of superiority, not to mention a vast array of prejudices to go along with all of it. He was a silver spoon on a paper plate.

"Hulagu isn't a Spanish name, sir," I told him. "It's Mongolian."

"Mongolian? Why the hell is Mexico hiring Mongolian cops?"

7

I sometimes wondered how Whitaker kept from drooling on himself. "It's a nickname, sir. Hulagu was the grandson of Genghis Khan. He razed Baghdad and killed a half million people. Legend has it that Tijuana's Hulagu has that same sunny disposition. Hence the moniker."

I turned back to our battered shipmate. "I thought Hulagu was an urban legend. You always hear about him through a friend of a friend. Nobody ever runs into the guy on their own. You saying you saw the man in person?"

"I saw way more of him than I wanted to," Seaman Baker told me.

"Yeah? What's he look like?"

"He's tall and fat. Big bushy mustache. Brutal right hook."

That was a new description, but then again, they all were. I came to believe that Tijuana cops were randomly calling themselves Hulagu just to raise the fear factor when roughing up *gringos*.

It did not take long for the duty corpsman, HM1 Bateman, to emerge from the passageway that led to the mess deck. Prancing is not how one would typically describe any service member's gait, but Bateman was one of the most effeminate men I had ever met. He practically danced when he walked.

In 1992, being gay was one of the quickest ways to get tossed out of the Navy. Despite that, Bateman put little effort into concealing his inclinations, causing many of us to wonder how his career survived so long. Getting decorated for bravery while serving as a medic with the Marines probably helped. You did not question a combat veteran's man card, no matter how prissy he was acting.

Bateman's medical knowledge was so dependable that *Belleau Wood* sailors often trusted his diagnosis over the ship's doctor and routinely sought him out for an unofficial second opinion. Even as hostilely homophobic as the military was then, we went to Bateman if we wanted something done. Except for maybe prostate exams. For that, the men always hoped for HM2 Lippincott, a notorious womanizer, despite his reputation for having ridiculously fat fingers.

"Well, well, well," the corpsman said as he reached the quarterdeck, making Whitaker cringe. "What've we got here?"

"A victim of *federale* hospitality." I passed the corpsman the report that the Master-at-Arms dropped off with the patient.

TEQUILA VIKINGS

"Can you walk, or do you want me to get you a stretcher?" the medic asked Baker, ignoring me. Bateman was the man who saved Randy Green's life, so he was not my biggest fan. I didn't blame him for it.

"I can walk," Baker answered, recoiling as the corpsman grabbed his arm to lead him away. Looking back towards Whitaker and me, the expression on the seaman's face suggested the young sailor was afraid of becoming Bateman's date instead of his patient.

"Don't worry, you're in good hands," I reassured him while resting my forearm on the .45 automatic hanging from my hip. "Since you spent the night in a Mexican jail, you're going to want a man with tender fingers doing that anal cavity check. I can assure you, no one's fingers are more tender than Petty Officer Bateman's."

"Anal cavity check?!?" the seaman gasped, looking at the corpsman in abject terror.

"Of course," Bateman cooed, going along with the joke despite his personal distaste for me. "We have to make sure you're not carrying any contraband. The Navy also likes to know if your cell mates filled up your dance card while you were waiting to post bail."

Whitaker busted out laughing, his sophomoric sense of humor finding our little joke far funnier than it actually was. He was still giggling when he heard a familiar voice clear his throat behind him.

The ensign swung around towards the gangplank, dropped his jaw, and screamed, "ATTENTION ON DECK!" Then, snapping rigidly to the position of attention, he rendered a crisp salute to the ship's captain as he stepped onto our quarterdeck. I suspected Whitaker might have peed a little too.

After saluting the captain myself, I walked over and powered up the 1MC, the ship's public address system. Striking the bell beside the microphone four times, I then announced, "*Belleau Wood*. Arriving."

"Do I make you nervous, Ensign?" Captain Stephen J. Fleming asked as he approached the Officer of the Deck.

"N-n-no, sir." Whitaker's lie was blatant. Beads of sweat were forming on his forehead though it had yet to crack forty degrees out.

"Good," The captain said, always entertained by a jittery junior officer. Turning to me, Fleming then asked, "How about you, Petty Officer Murphy? You nervous today?"

"I've been nervous a lot lately, sir."

"I know you have, son." Fleming stepped over towards my podium. "Murphy, I'd like you to come to my office once you're relieved from watch. Right away. Understand?"

"Aye aye, sir." I then rendered the skipper another salute, which he returned before leaving.

Once the captain was gone, Ensign Whitaker walked up and stood beside me. Still frazzled by the old man sneaking up on him like that, he said, "Man, it sucks to be you."

"Why's that?"

"Most people don't get called to the old man's office to get good news."

"Maybe you don't," I said. "In my situation, though, if I was getting bad news, it wouldn't come directly from the captain. It'd be delivered by a couple of NIS agents putting me in handcuffs."

*****

For the commander of an American warship, Captain Fleming was disarmingly personable. Rarely seen without a smile on his face, Fleming was quick to laugh and had a way of effortlessly putting you at ease. With his white hair and cheerful demeanor, the captain reminded me of a cleanly shaven Santa Claus. Unlike Saint Nick, however, the captain did not drop off little lumps of coal to those who misbehaved. He delivered a horde of screaming leathernecks, napalm fireballs, and a rain of disfiguring shrapnel instead.

When I stepped into his office, the captain told me to relax and take a seat. Once I did, he leaned forward, clasping his hands together in front of him. "Are you still nervous, Petty Officer Murphy?"

Though I was reasonably confident I was getting good news that day, I was not entirely sure. "You have no idea, sir."

"I think I do." Fleming picked up a report from his desk. "The NIS came across this from the San Ysidro Police Department while investigating the Green affair. I would love to hear your side of it."

I instantly knew what it was. There was only one report about me from the border area. Caught off guard, I had to clear my throat. "Sir, that happened a couple of years ago. We weren't charged with anything. In fact, we were…"

"I know, I know." Fleming cut me off by waving his hand dismissively. "You're not in trouble for this. I just want to hear your account because I doubt…" The captain lifted the police report to scan it for a name. "…I doubt that Officer Linda Miller has the same flair for storytelling that you do."

I swallowed hard. If the captain wanted to listen to one of my mildly amusing anecdotes, I had little choice but to tell him one.

"Well, sir, ET3 Dixon just reported aboard the ship, and Dan Jasper, who was running behind, brought him down to Tijuana to meet the rest of us. I made E-5 that week, so the guys got me pretty loaded and I ended up getting sick all over myself. Dixie offered to take me back since he drove down there, and I wouldn't get in trouble if I threw up again on the trolley. Obviously, he did not want me to mess up his ride either, so after we crossed the border and got to his car, he stripped me down to my underwear and put me in the passenger seat, where I instantly passed out. He was going to clean my clothes in the bathroom at the McDonalds there, then dress me before we drove back."

I paused to take a breath. "Anyway, Dixie drives an old Lincoln with this monster trunk. He has cleaning supplies in there, but they're way in the back. Being as short as he is, Kevin had to crawl inside to get to them. Somehow, the lid came down on him, and he got locked inside with my clothes. No matter how much he screamed or pounded on the seatback, I wasn't waking up. Eventually, he fell asleep too.

"The next morning, I'm woken up by a female police officer knocking on the window asking for my ID. I'm all disoriented and still a little drunk, so I go to reach for my wallet and come up with nothing but a handful of my own ass. Because I couldn't identify myself, she ordered me out of the car."

"In your underwear?" the captain asked. "That must've been embarrassing."

"Sir, I'm a tequila drinker. I'm sad to say that that was not the first time I'd found myself in public in an advanced stage of undress. What was uncomfortable, though, was needing to use the bathroom and standing practically naked before a lady cop with a spectacular case of morning wood. She must have thought I was positively *delighted* to see her.

"Anyway, she starts asking me questions I don't have answers for and then eventually leads me to the back of the Lincoln, where Kevin's keys are still dangling from the trunk. She has me open it, sees Dixie in there, and then completely freaks out, drawing her weapon and ordering me to the ground."

"She drew her weapon on you?" Fleming asked. "What did she think you did? Raped and murdered your buddy, then stuffed his body in the trunk?"

I shrugged. "I guess so. I couldn't really blame her. For a moment, I thought I did too."

The captain laughed and then asked if I learned anything from the incident. I told him that no matter how excited the police officer is, never dive belly first onto a concrete parking lot with a raging erection. Taking a bullet probably hurts less.

"You know, you could have been shot, Murphy. That would've been a shame, considering what you've accomplished."

The captain set the police report down and opened my file. "You're a product of the foster care system. You know, the more I find out about your childhood, the more I realize you shouldn't be here. You should be homeless, on crack, and overdosing in some Detroit drug den. But here you are, a second-class electronics technician in the United States Navy. You taught yourself two foreign languages, French and Spanish, and I understand that you picked up a working knowledge of Tagalog in three months while working the mess decks. That's impressive."

"Thank you, sir. Learning languages is kind of my superpower. I'm studying Japanese now, trying to get ready for our change of homeport."

The captain smiled in approval. "That's great. I see that you were also sent on a classified mission to El Salvador right out of C School…"

I blushed. "Uh sir, that El Salvador thing was only classified because of something I saw there. It's not like I'm a Navy SEAL or…"

"It was a training mission. I know. I don't know what made it classified, but I know your C School command was impressed enough to send you."

"Sir, if languages are my superpower, electronics nearly became my kryptonite. I graduated at the bottom of my class during ET A School. It's why I drew a nearly obsolete radar like the SPN-35 as a C School. They only sent me to El Salvador because I could speak Spanish."

"Okay, even if electronics did not come easily to you at first, you still made it, and according to your performance evaluations, came to become one of the top technicians in your division. Murphy, what I'm saying is you have a lot of unrealized potential that was nearly extinguished by this unfortunate situation with Randal Green."

Fleming closed my file. "Well, I get to tell you that the NIS has officially concluded their investigation. The well deck camera clearly caught Green striking you first. Coupled with the fact that he came at you with a spanner wrench, you had a legitimate reason to believe that your life was in danger. The amount of force you used was justified. Once discharged from medical care, Green'll face court-martial for assaulting a senior petty officer. I'd rather hang him for what he did to his stepson, but he's still going to prison for a while."

I let out a long sigh of relief as an immense burden fell from my shoulders. "Thank you, sir."

The captain nodded. "Murphy, I'm going to leave a lot of things unsaid about what happened in the Nixie room. What I am going to say, though, is that the way you conducted yourself during the investigation was commendable."

In other words, thank you for accepting sole responsibility for what happened to Green. We are grateful that you kept your mouth shut and did not even hint that Master Chief Darrow, or anyone else in the chain of command, encouraged you to handle that situation with enough violence to cripple that sickening stain of swamp shit.

"Thank you, sir."

"Petty Officer Murphy, have you thought about your future in the Navy?"

You took care of us. Now we'd like the opportunity to take care of you.

"Until now, I was afraid my future in the Navy would probably be spent in the brig."

Fleming nodded. "Well, that threat's passed now. You're a smart guy. The fact that you taught yourself French and Spanish attests to that alone. Until Green attacked you, you also had a spotless military record."

Tapping the report from the San Ysidro Police Department, the captain added, "Officially anyway. Unofficially, you have one of the most entertaining collections of liberty stories I've ever heard. Given the right opportunity, I don't think there's a limit to where you could go. I'd like to give you a chance to earn that opportunity, son."

"Sir?"

"I would like to nominate you for the BOOST program—Broadened Opportunity for Officer Selection Training. It's a yearlong immersion into math and English followed by a four-year scholarship into any university with an NROTC program. When you finish, you'll be commissioned an ensign in the US Navy. How does that sound?"

I was speechless. The day before, the Navy was considering making me a prisoner. Now, they were offering to make me an officer.

"Well?" the captain asked, waiting for me to say something.

"I…uh…of course, sir…I…uh…what do I have to do?"

Fleming shrugged. "Well, for starters, I want to see you keep your nose clean for one year. It's well past time for you to grow up. I get a kick out of hearing your stories, but that's 'Old Navy' stuff. The service is changing. The 'New Navy' and *especially* the officer corps, demands professionalism and dependability. No more of this Tequila Viking stuff. Can you do that, Murphy? Lay off the booze and the shenanigans?"

"I already have, sir." I was sober for a solid month in the immediate aftermath of Green's beating. Since meeting my girlfriend, I drank on weekends, but far away from my friends on the *Belleau Wood*, who tended to encourage my more libertine impulses.

The captain nodded his approval. "Good. I want you spending less time in bars and more time in libraries. Mind the company you keep. I know how tight you and Petty Officer Dixon are, but the two of you tend to be trouble together. Spend more time with Chief Ramirez. He's a sharp guy who's going places. You understand what I'm saying?"

"Yes, sir."

"And one more thing. Don't take this the wrong way, as I have nothing but fondness for the man, but Master Chief Darrow's a relic. His methods no longer have a place in the modern Navy. I need you to pull yourself out from under his influence."

TEQUILA VIKINGS

I blinked in surprise. Master Chief Darrow was more than a boss to me. He was the closest thing I ever had to a father figure. "Sir?"

"You need to start keeping Darrow at arm's length. In his day, he was the kind of man the Navy needed. I see a lot of him in you. So does he. The aspects of your master chief's personality that made him a larger than life figure in the '60s and '70s, though…"

The captain paused and stared directly into my eyes to make sure that I was getting the point. "…they'll make you a prisoner in the Navy today. They already very nearly did. Son, I hope you realize that you got away with a big one here with this Green thing. You got away with a *really* big one. Do you understand that?"

"Yes, sir."

"Make no mistake, Petty Officer Murphy. You will *not* be getting away with another."

*****

CHAPTER
2

Master Chief Bradley Darrow was a legitimate combat veteran. Near the end of 1967, he was sent to Vietnam to provide technical support to a group of mobile radio stations near the DMZ that broadcast propaganda and American cultural programming into the north. The communists must have taken great offense to that, blowing three of them to smithereens in quick succession. Darrow admitted to me once that he was glad to see them go. "There's only so much Lawrence Welk a man can take," he slurred over his eleventh beer one night. He was more partial to Jimi Hendrix.

Darrow was about to set up the fourth station when the Americans decided to cancel the program. They figured going forward at that point would just be a waste of brand new equipment, as well as a barely used electronics technician.

As a result, in January 1968, Petty Officer Darrow found himself in Vietnam without a job. Ordered to the closest naval installation to await a new assignment, he landed in Khe Sanh thirty minutes ahead of the first barrage of incoming Viet Cong mortar fire that heralded the start of the Tet Offensive.

TEQUILA VIKINGS

Darrow was stuck at Khe Sanh for three months, fighting alongside the Marines in infantry operations until the 7th Cavalry broke through in April. Once evacuated, he landed in the Philippines while the Navy tried to figure out what to do with him. Almost by accident, he ended up assigned to the Armed Forces Police Department in Subic Bay for the next two years.

Though only an E-4, Khe Sanh prepared Darrow to deal with troublesome servicemen on the streets of Olongapo, even if they significantly outranked him. "I just spent two months fighting a battle-hardened enemy with guns, bayonets, and a couple of times, with my bare fuckin' hands," he once snarled at me.

"Once you've done that, you certainly aren't going to let some rear echelon galley rat act like he's more of a man than you just because he's got more stripes on his shoulder. When I have that badge on, I outrank everybody. If some supply lieutenant thinks he has the power to pull rank on me when I'm on duty, well, I'm going to show that poor bastard what real power fuckin' feels like."

By the time Darrow returned to sea duty in 1971, he had developed a fearsome reputation as a military lawman. He boosted his infamy by returning to the AFPD in Subic Bay two more times, earning himself the nickname, "Olongapo Earp."

My master chief was a polarizing figure. Half of the fleet considered him a career saver, the guy who could pull a good man out of a bad jam and keep him out of serious trouble. The other half thought him a mindless thug who got his rocks off using excessive force at the slightest provocation. With what I knew of the man, I guessed he was a little bit of both.

If you were a west coast sailor in the US Navy between the Vietnam War and Operation Desert Storm, you heard stories about Olongapo Earp. They could scare the hell out of you, particularly if you landed on his bad side, which was something ET3 Warren Macklemore regularly did. When I walked into the EMO after meeting with Captain Fleming, Darrow was just finishing up gnawing the fat out of Warren's derriere.

Unlike Randy Green, Mack was not a malicious man. He was just incompetent and had a particularly poor sense of hygiene. Darrow liked to get into the face of his problem children when screaming at them, but he always kept his distance from Crusty Warren, not wanting to worry about his gag reflex interfering with his volume.

"I am NOT going to talk to you about your goddamn body odor again," our master chief growled. "You know those two gunner's mates that sleep near you? Do you know how badly they're itching to teach you how to clean yourself?"

"Yes, Master Chief," Warren meekly answered. Mack was a sorry sight. His greasy hair was unruly and in desperate need of a trim. Remnants of Warren's last six meals were caked around his teeth, adding an extra nauseating layer to his dragon breath. His glasses were so thick that they magnified his eyes to inhuman, squid-like proportions, yet were so dirty I could barely see through them. I had no idea how he ever saw out.

"Do you know *how* they intend to teach you?"

We all did. They were promising to give Mack something called a GI Shower. The gunner's mates would hold him down under scalding hot water and scrub him with wire brushes and industrial abrasives. It was the preferred exfoliation treatment of aspiring fascists.

"If I smell this funk on you again, goddammit, I'm going to fuckin' unleash them! Is that clear?"

"Yes, Master Chief."

"Good! Now get out of here and go clean yourself up for Christ's sake!"

Not needing to be told twice, Macklemore bolted from the EMO. Once Crusty Warren was gone, Darrow shook his head in disgust. "Fuckin' place needs a field day now. God, it stinks in here!"

At the time, Darrow was trying to quit smoking. That meant instead of smoking his own cigarettes, he was smoking mine. After reaching into my dungaree shirt and helping himself to one of my Marlboros, Darrow put his arm around my shoulder. "You talked to the old man?"

I nodded. "I did."

"And what did he say?"

"I've been cleared. Between the camera in the well deck catching Green hitting me first and the fingerprints they found on the spanner wrench, the NIS determined that I acted in self-defense. Thank you, Master Chief. I don't think I'll ever be able to repay you for what you did."

The spanner wrench was Darrow's idea. It turned the incident from a fight that went bad to an assault with a deadly weapon. My master chief made sure Green got a good grip on the tool, leaving his fingerprints on it, before the corpsmen got there. Since I beat the events of that entire day out of Randy's memory, he could not convincingly refute coming after me with it.

Darrow looked surprised by my show of gratitude. "Repay me? This whole shit show was as much my fault as yours. I thought letting you square off against that son-of-a-bitch would help even the score for you, let you exercise some of those demons you got in your head. I fucked up. I'm sorry, Doyle."

The master chief walked back to his desk, taking a seat and opening up the porthole to air out the office. I sat down at our division officer's desk and lit a cigarette for myself. "I'm sorry, too. It won't ever happen again."

"You're goddamn right it won't. We're both done with this shit. No more doing things the old way. By the book now. Counseling chits, report chits, captain's mast."

I laughed and pointed my thumb towards the door. "You sure? I just heard you threaten Crusty Warren with a GI Shower."

"I didn't threaten him with anything. Gunner's mates aren't my problem. If they want to clean up Mr. Macklemore, let 'em. Those two clowns are dirtbags anyway. It'll give me an excuse to toss them off my ship and maybe motivate Mack to curb his reek as well."

Darrow spent a few moments in pensive silence. "You know, I can't begin to express how glad I am that this worked out. That first day, when you were getting worked over by the NIS, I was pretty worried. That's a lot of pressure to withstand. At the time, especially when we didn't know if Green was going to make it, you could've been looking at life in prison. It took a lot of balls to stick to your story like that. I'm not going to forget it."

I shrugged. "I just did what you told me to. I said Green hit me first and went after me with the wrench. I repeated it over and over again. Besides, you told me you were going to take care of everything. That would've been a lot harder if you were locked up next to me."

Darrow nodded. "Yeah, that's a fact. It was tough enough already. We were working on the fly, trying to arrange everything down there in the few minutes we had before they secured the scene. I'm sure we made mistakes; I just don't know where. Fortunately, the captain made sure that Third Fleet told the NIS what Green did to that little kid to keep them from looking around too hard."

"The captain? You had the captain involved?" I grinned. "You have something on the old man?"

Master Chief Darrow pointed his finger at me. "Knock that off right now. The captain's a good man. He was just doing the right thing."

Bullshit. You got something on the skipper. I wanted to press the master chief on it but knew better. When Darrow told you to drop the subject, you dropped it. "Fleming told me he was offering you something," he said. "What was it?"

"BOOST."

The master chief cocked an eyebrow. "BOOST? Really? You going to take it?"

"A four-year scholarship? Why wouldn't I?"

"You really want to be an officer? All high and mighty with the rest of those prep-school pantywaists? You're a little too comfortable in the gutter for shit like that."

"You know," I countered. "After I ended up in foster care, I knew I would never amount to anything. If I worked my way up from orphan to ensign, though? Christ, if I can do that, I can do anything. I could be Captain Murphy one day."

Darrow rolled his eyes. "Don't get ahead of yourself. To be an officer, you need a certain amount of refinement, you know, those pansy little manners they all have. You're a brawler, though, a combat survivor like me. That makes you twice the man of any commissioned puke. You…"

"I've never been in combat, Master Chief."

"My ass you haven't! From what you told me, you spent thirteen years fearing for your life. Hell, I was only in Khe Sanh for three months."

"It wasn't the same. It wasn't like I fought back. I was just scared all of the time…"

"You think I wasn't scared in Vietnam?" the master chief asked me. "I was fuckin' terrified. I fought because I had to. Doyle, if I could have stayed safe cowering in some foxhole somewhere, I would have. Do you want to know why I left the perimeter to go fighting with the Marines? Because the hooch next to me took a direct mortar hit. There was one survivor, and his dick got blown clean off. Fuck that. I'd rather get shot."

Darrow angrily stubbed out his cigarette. "Murphy, I've been in this Navy going on thirty years now. These officers, these paper men in epaulets, they think people like you and me are the coins they spend to buy their promotions. We're expendable. You're better than that, and you've proven it. You kept your mouth shut during this Green thing and protected your men. What you did was the legal equivalent of throwing yourself on a live grenade.

"Doyle, officers don't do that kind of stuff. That's goddamn *mafiosi* shit. It's we enlisted men who do things like that."

"You saying I should turn down the captain's offer?"

Darrow rolled his eyes. "You don't turn down things like BOOST. You find a way to disqualify yourself. Fail a math exam or something. What I'm trying to tell you is be a chief, where you'd be making a real difference.

"Doyle, I don't want to give you a big head, but right now, you own this division. Tony Bard is a damn fine LPO, and everyone loves Chief Ramirez, but the guys didn't see them nearly kill a man on a child's behalf. They didn't watch them stand up to the NIS to protect their men. They saw *you* do that."

Darrow helped himself to another one of my cigarettes. "Which brings me to my next point. I know you've been keeping a low profile lately. That's smart. It's time to come back to the reservation, though. You should've heard the men cheer this morning when I announced you were cleared. It's too bad you were on watch. They're throwing you a party on Friday at McDini's."

I drew in a long breath. "Master Chief, Hannah's coming down to San Diego on Friday…"

"Good! Bring her! It's about time we got to meet that young lady. That accent of hers has been driving the watches crazy. Everyone's curious just how far out of your league you're playing here."

I grinned. "I'll save you the mystery. It's pretty far."

Darrow nodded. "I'll say. Judging by her voice, I'm betting your girlfriend rates at least an eight."

My master chief took a long drag off of his cigarette, then told me, "And let's be real here. You'd be a soft six at best if we caught you on a good hair day."

*****

CHAPTER
3

As the work center supervisor of the *USS Belleau Wood's* Radar Repair Shop, I was in charge of five other electronics technicians. Of all my men, ET3 Todd Franklin had been there longest. Lazy by nature, Franklin had a reputation for pursuing spectacularly unattractive women just because he considered them to be less work.

ET3 Claude Metaire was born in French Guiana. Though he could understand, read, and write English flawlessly, he spoke it with such a thick Creole accent that he was usually unintelligible. Had I not taught myself French to impress a girl from Quebec when I was in high school, no one would ever know what he was trying to say.

ET3 Kevin Dixon had been my main drinking buddy. Once I was placed under investigation, though, I put some distance between us. Even though I saw him almost every day, I missed the guy and still considered him my best friend aboard the *Belleau Wood.*

Our star technician was ET3 Rick Hammond. He was a man who lived and breathed electronics and genuinely enjoyed his job. Hammond looked the part. He was thin, pale, and socially awkward. Surprisingly, Rick was the only married man in the shop.

TEQUILA VIKINGS

And then there was ET2 Gianni Palazzo. John used to be the supervisor of Radar Repair but had a debilitating addiction to pornography, storing boxes and boxes of it on the shop's test equipment racks. When the captain found it, he ordered it gone. Instead, Palazzo tried to hide it somewhere else but ended up getting caught. He talked his way out of losing a chevron for disobeying the captain, but Darrow demoted him from his position as our work center supervisor.

Having just been promoted to second-class, LT Howe put me in charge, causing Palazzo and me to be at odds ever since. He was the only one of my men who did not applaud when I first walked into the shop after being cleared. While everyone else stood up and congratulated me for being exonerated by the NIS, Palazzo seethed and stayed put, leaning back in my seat with his feet on my desk.

"It's really over?" Dixie asked, obviously relieved. When the NIS cleared me, the cloud of suspicion hanging over him and Metaire lifted by default.

Palazzo shook his head in disgust. "That's bullshit! Green's still in the hospital! You beat a man into epilepsy, and you didn't get court-martialed for it? No captain's mast, either? Did you even get yelled at?"

"Nope. It was self-defense." Just to rub Palazzo's nose in it, I added, "In fact, the captain offered to help get me into BOOST."

Palazzo's jaw dropped. "BOOST? You almost kill a man, and the captain offers you BOOST? What the hell's the matter with this command?"

"You worn't zhere," Metaire said. "We war. Eet was zelf-defanze lak Doyle zaiyz. Green heet heem forst!"

"Bullshit," Palazzo growled. "We all know what went down."

Dixie was sitting on the workbench along the forward bulkhead, dangling his feet above the deck. "What's the matter, Spanky? You worried about getting called to the Nixie Room if you get caught with any more smut?"

As if his pornography obsession was not bad enough, Palazzo also had a habit of getting caught masturbating. It was so bad that we were considering referring him for psychological help. Because of this, nearly everyone working in the island structure referred to Palazzo as "Spanky" behind his back. Except for Dixie, who called him that right to his face.

23

Palazzo bristled. "You threatening to take me there, Dixon?"

"Nobody's threatening anybody," I said.

"Because if you're threatening me, I'll fucking…"

"Look, that's enough." Trying to get the shop's mind back to work, I turned to Palazzo and said, "You've got maintenance checks due on the SPN-43, John. Get started on them. I need my desk."

"In a second. You hear me, Dixie? I said I'll…"

"John, get out of my seat …"

Palazzo was technically the senior petty officer. That was likely why he thought he could get away with telling me to fuck off.

Before I could stop myself, I threw my foot out and kicked the legs out from underneath the chair, spilling Palazzo onto the deck. It was an instinctive reaction that I regretted immediately. If I was serious about BOOST, I needed to start handling things differently.

Palazzo's fall knocked the wind out of him. Still, he gasped, "That's it! I'm putting you on report!"

I laughed. "For what?"

"Assault!"

"Assault?" I asked, laughing even harder. "You fell out of your chair."

"You kicked it out from under me!"

"I didn't see Doyle kick anything," Dixie said. "Did you, Claude?"

"No. I zaw no-ting."

"Me neither," added Franklin. Even Hammond, who tried his best to stay out of these things, shook his head.

"I saw you commit a pretty blatant act of insubordination, though, right before gravity made you its bitch." *Now* Dixie was threatening Palazzo.

"*Zhat*, I saw," Claude agreed.

Palazzo was shaking when he got up. "You guys think you're going to get away with shit like this forever? Sooner or later, this ship'll get a real captain that isn't going to tolerate it and you're all going to fuckin' burn!"

"John," I said as I bent over to pick up my chair. "Until then, you need to get out of my sight. Go do your maintenance."

"But…!"

"John! I don't want to hear another word out of you." That was what Master Chief Darrow said right before he fired Palazzo as work center supervisor. Spanky got exactly one word out after that, and Darrow took his job. Since then, it was an effective way to end pointless conversations with the man. "Go. Away."

John shot daggers from his eyes at everyone in the shop. As he stormed out of the space, our Leading Petty Officer stepped in, just to have Palazzo slam the door shut behind him.

*****

"What the hell was that all about?" ET1 Tony Bard asked.

"Not everybody's happy that I'm not going to be court-martialed, I guess."

Tony hauled off and punched me in the shoulder. "Well, buddy, I sure as hell am glad things worked out for you."

Bard was New Navy all the way. He would never condone corporal punishment, but, as far as he was concerned, Green crossed a big line when he broke his stepson's arm. Tony was firmly in my court. "It'll be good to see things get back to normal around here."

"No doubt," Dixie said. "Does this mean you're back to us, Doyle? We've got some catching up to do! Tijuana's waiting!"

"No shit!" Franklin chimed in. "I've only got five months left. I put my time in on this ship! I earned my TJ party!"

Within the CSE division, it was a tradition to take a man to Tijuana for his going away party as he was finishing up his enlistment. With our move to Japan, Franklin would be the last to enjoy that ritual.

"Don't worry," I assured him. "I'll be there for that, but otherwise, I've got to make some changes."

It was then, when I was talking to my men, that it started to sink in just how close I came to spending the best years of my life behind bars. If Green had died, or not been caught on camera hitting me first, or if Master Chief Darrow was not as connected as he had been, or had I been under the command of any captain other than Fleming, this all could have ended much differently.

Feeling overwhelmed, I leaned deeper back into my seat. "This was a really close call. I lost control down there with Green. I can't do that again. I'm curbing my drinking and learning to keep my hands to myself. As for our Nixie Winch Room counseling sessions, that shit's over."

Bard looked happy that we would no longer be putting him in awkward situations. Looking at my two henchmen, he asked, "You guys down with this? No more taking matters into your own hands?"

Metaire nodded enthusiastically. Physically speaking, Claude was a very imposing man, but he was no thug. He never participated in our Nixie Room beatings. He was just there to look tough.

Dixie shrugged, "I'm more than cool with that. I'm sensing Macklemore's getting too much of the master chief's attention lately, and I don't want any part of that."

"Somebody say something about hurting Mack?" I asked.

Dixie shrugged. "Not outright, but after the department head caught a whiff of Warren at quarters this morning, Kramer commented about giving him the scrub. The look Darrow gave Bill suggested that the option was not off the table."

Bard shook his head. "Darrow's not that stupid."

"No, he isn't," I concurred as I lit a cigarette. "Nobody's touching Mack. That poor guy makes his own life plenty damn miserable all by himself. He doesn't need any help from us."

"Yez," Claude began. "Heez going to 'ave enough prow-blums zoon. I haird zhat heez not going to Japan wiz us."

Bard raised an eyebrow. "Who told you that?"

"I ovairhoord a coople of zhee Yeomen talking about heem in zhee galley. One of zhem was complaining aboot zhe stink and zhe othair zaid not to wooray as zhey were going to sheep him out soon."

"Seriously?" Bard asked, exasperated by the careless conversation of the Administration Department. Turning to the rest of the shop, he said, "Guys, you *have* to keep your mouths shut about this. Mack doesn't even know it yet." Pointing at Metaire, he added, "Especially you, Claude!"

"*Oui*," Metaire replied, but we knew better. Claude was plugged hard into the ship's gossip mill, and considering how much he liked to talk about stuff like this, I assumed that there was little tradition of *omerta* in Guianan culture.

"Do you know where you're sending him yet?" I asked.

"Not really," Tony answered. "We're working on it. There's a billet open on the *Blue Ridge* in Hawaii, but nothing's final. We can't take him with us. He'll end up getting into serious trouble overseas."

TEQUILA VIKINGS

"And he won't on the *Blue Ridge*?" The *USS Blue Ridge* was the 3rd Fleet's flagship. It was the vessel on which the commanding admiral sailed. In that spit-and-polish environment, I knew Mack would be a blinding beacon of ineptitude. "They're going to eat that boy alive."

Bard shrugged. "The Navy's not going to waste resources to train him on another piece of equipment that he can break. We can only ship him somewhere that has the gear he's already been trained on. That's the *Ridge*."

Mack's tenure on the *Blue Ridge* would be, to steal a line from Hobbes' *Leviathan*, "nasty, brutish, and short." It seemed like there should be a better method of handling the man. "There's no way we can take him with us?"

Bard laughed. "God, no. Why would you want to? What do you think will happen to him when we get to the Philippines? He'll end up like Green, marrying some hooker who'll use him up until he snuffs himself."

I shook my head. Petty Officer Macklemore had his issues, but his intentions were good. "Think there's anything we could do to whip him into shape?"

"That we haven't already done? Christ, Doyle. We can't even get him to shower."

I thought for a moment. "I know we've given him the stick treatment for goofing up. We ever try offering him carrots for when he does well?"

"No. Mack doesn't really do *anything* well."

"You know, half of his problem could be that the guy takes every working party. He works like a beast and sweats up his dungarees. Maybe we can start by offering him a pair of coveralls if he can make it to quarters without inducing vomiting at fifty feet."

"You have a connection for coveralls?" Coveralls were a coveted item aboard the *Belleau Wood*. The Deck and Engineering Departments had a monopoly on them since they tended to do the dirtiest work. We ETs had to steal them. "Could you get me a pair?" Bard asked.

"I have a connection, but I'll have to take a couple of his mid-watches to score some. So no, I'm not doing it for everybody. I don't even have a pair for myself."

"What about a foul weather jacket? I'd perform lewd acts of a perversely sexual nature to get my hands on one of those," Tony confessed.

"I don't think so," I said. Then I realized Franklin and Tony were about the same size. Todd had a jacket from when the *Belleau Wood* was doing Law Enforcement Operations in the Bering Sea. "Hey Todd, you mind if Bard takes your foul weather jacket?"

"Not at all," Franklin answered. He was soon going home to Florida. He would not need it there. "It's in the fan room."

"Cool." Looking back at Tony, I told him, "We'd best get it before we forget and it disappears."

The equipment that generated the energy pushed out of the *Belleau Wood*'s radar antennae was located in Radar Room One, just down the passageway from our shop at the top of the island structure. It was full of very loud, heat-generating components that had to be chilled to keep them operational. The fan room at the back of Radar One was what kept the space cool. The division also used the fan room to store our personal gear that would not fit in our shops or lockers.

When I opened the hatch to enter the space and turned on the light switch, I caught a frantic flurry of activity out of the corner of my right eye. Startled, I jumped up and unleashed a loud stream of colorful adjectives.

After landing, I found myself face-to-face with Palazzo, whose pants were down and wrapped around his knees. Sweat was pouring down his brow, he was out of breath, and he had his swollen member gripped tightly in his left hand, pointed directly at me.

I was not entirely sure what to do next. The only thing that immediately leapt to mind was gun range safety protocol. In other words, I quickly stepped to my left and out of the direct line of fire in case there was an accidental discharge.

Neither Palazzo nor I were clairvoyant, but in a situation like that, there is a lot of conversation that can occur between two grown men using nothing more than their eyes. In this case, Palazzo telepathically conveyed to me, "Look, man, there's no sugar-coating this. It is what it is. I would prefer to be relieving tension in some other manner, but I'm entirely inadequate around women and don't have the same options as you do. So here I am.

"Now, I would love to just get this over with and go on with my day, but it's virtually impossible to concentrate with you staring at me like that. So, do you think you can come up with some reason to break this impasse and excuse yourself from the situation?"

I did. Out loud, I politely asked, "Could you hand me that foul weather jacket hanging off the angle iron to your left...?"

As Palazzo reached for it, I had to stop him. "...with your *other* hand, please?"

Having gotten what I came for, I backed out of the fan room before sealing the hatch behind me.

Bard could tell by the look on my face that something was amiss. "Are you okay?" he asked. "What's going on in there?"

Now, I realized that Palazzo had issues. I was not the kind of bastard that would compound the man's embarrassment by informing one of his bosses that I just caught him worm burping in the fan room during working hours.

I was more the type of bastard that would send the LPO in there to see it for himself.

*****

CHAPTER
4

I met Hannah Baxter while on duty as the Petty Officer of the Watch. She dialed the wrong number, and instead of connecting to the command operator to inquire about an upcoming tour of the 32nd Street Naval Station, she rang up our quarterdeck by mistake. Her Australian accent was irresistible.

It was a slow night, so the OOD let me talk to her as long as I wanted to. I offered to give her a private tour not only of the base, but of the fleet's finest amphibious warship as well. She took the bait and drove down from Los Angeles to meet me.

I have to admit that when I first saw Hannah, I was a little disappointed. Judging from her voice and accent, I had impossibly high expectations. In my imagination, she was tall, slender, blue-eyed, blonde, and capable of wielding a bikini to the point of inflicting cardiac arrest.

What I got was a girl a bit below average in height with a long mane of unruly brown hair, a slightly lazy left eye, and freckles. She could have pulled off the bikini but was far too self-conscious for that. Hannah was cute, but not stunning. Still, she was comfortably out of my league.

TEQUILA VIKINGS

I gave Hannah the tour of the ship I promised her and dragged it out as long as I could. We walked from bow to stern and several times from port to starboard. I showed off by doing pull ups on the 5-inch guns and even snuck her onto the CIWS machine gun platforms. Near the end, I took her down the ladder to the dome housing my primary radar, the SPN-35.

The SPN-35 was an old, nearly obsolete radar that had two large antennas. One moved up and down to detect the altitude of an incoming aircraft. The other moved side to side to detect its azimuth. It had this ominous, Death Star look to it that made it appear far more sinister than it actually was.

I sometimes told girls that the SPN-35 was a super-secret death ray and that I could get into a lot of trouble for showing it to them. It was a line that occasionally paid off with an athletic use of the hammock I kept in the dome for unauthorized napping. I considered trying that one out with Hannah, but instead just described it as the space with the best air-conditioning on the ship that I often used as my own personal apartment.

After the tour, we took the trolley into downtown San Diego and ate at Dick's Last Resort. It was there that I learned Hannah was from Brisbane, the daughter of a mine inspector and an English teacher. She was also an illegal alien, coming to the US on a six-month tourist visa, but overstaying it by about two and a half years. Hannah supported herself by working off the books as a nanny to the children of a train-wreck C-list movie actress. She detested her employer, but fortunately, the woman ignored her two daughters so completely that Hannah rarely interacted with her.

When she inquired about my family, I let her know right away that I was an orphan. When she tried to get the details about what happened, though, I asked if we could wait a while before wading into that subject. I told her that I was enjoying her company and did not want to dampen the mood with such a morbid tale.

Over the next couple of days, I discovered Hannah was into surfing, crystals, marijuana, environmentalism, and the occult. She desperately wanted to be a vegetarian but could not bring herself to give up huge chunks of cow meat cooked so rare that it still had a pulse.

Walking along Mission Beach after dinner, I looked into the Pacific and spotted a gaggle of wave jockeys bobbing about in the water. I made a casual comment about how fun surfing looked, and before I knew it,

Hannah had me in the ocean, freezing my ass off while getting pounded into the sand by five-foot swells.

That was just a couple of weeks after the Randy Green incident, and Hannah quickly became the oasis of tranquility that I desperately needed. I made a great effort to keep her separated from my military life. She was a modern-day flower child, and I did not want her exposed to my reputation as a seafaring hoodlum.

One of Hannah's friends made a fortune discretely selling dope to celebrities like Hannah's employer. Her name was Cheri, and she had a three-bedroom house just a few blocks off of Ocean Beach that she let Hannah use when she came down to visit. Cheri never had time to stay there herself, so she was happy to have someone stopping in occasionally to take care of the place. I found it funny how, in all the time I spent in her abode, never once had I ever laid eyes on the woman who owned it.

Within a couple of months, Hannah and I established ourselves at Cheri's place far more than Cheri ever did. Being able to surf just a few blocks from where we lived, we ended up with our own circle of friends drawn from Ocean Beach's under-culture. They were a motley collection of beach bums with tattoos, dreadlocks, and a peculiar scent formed by combining the aromas of surfboard sex wax, sea salt, and Sinaloan ditch weed. We surfed all day, partied by bonfire all night, and used Cheri's place almost exclusively for making love and sleeping.

When I mentioned the soiree my shipmates were throwing for me, Hannah seemed overjoyed to be invited. It was as if she passed some arbitrary romantic milestone. "I finally get to meet your mates!" she squealed.

The problem was more in my mates meeting her. Stereotypes may be the language of hate, but the reputation sailors enjoyed of being aspiring alcoholics prone to spontaneous acts of random nudity, vulgarity, and violence hit pretty close to the mark. I was not sure how my pacifist girlfriend would take it.

Considering most of my mates were already smashed before we even got to McDini's, there was little doubt I was going to find out.

*****

TEQUILA VIKINGS

McDini's was a bar in National City, second in notoriety only to the Trophy Lounge a few blocks away. Unlike the Trophy, which drew in sailors with married Filipina women looking to strike up a quick affair while their husbands were at sea, McDini's appealed to us with a comprehensive beer selection. "Around the World in Eighty Beers" was their tagline, and if you drank them all, they gave you a baseball cap.

From the moment we arrived, Melissa Hammond, Rick's wife, fawned over Hannah and immediately stole her from me. Already fascinated by her being from Australia, once Melissa discovered that Hannah worked for an actress, she was positively star-struck.

"Well, I'm not sure I'd call her a real movie star..." Hannah said, trying to tamp down Melissa's expectations.

"Who is she?" Rick Hammond asked.

"Lauren Kale."

"Wow! That's so cool!" Melissa gushed, though it was obvious she had no idea who Lauren Kale was. Rick asked what she starred in.

Hannah laughed. "You know, I couldn't give you the title of a single movie. Horror films scare me, and that's about the only parts she ever gets. She's usually the third female victim. She runs around a bit, falls down, and then gets murdered in some gruesome manner. She's perfectly suited for the part, though. She's a bloody good screamer."

I was standing with Dixie and Bard, watching Hannah being introduced to Chief Ramirez's wife, when I was grabbed from behind and lifted off my feet by Master Chief Darrow. "Ha! Ha! Ha! Ha! Haaaaaah!" he bellowed as he bounced me up and down off of my feet. "You got a hell of a turnout, young man! Every CSE guy who's not on duty is here, along with their wives."

Bard looked over the crowd and nodded in agreement. "Don't take this the wrong way, but doesn't this feel a little bit wrong to you guys?"

"How so?" Darrow asked.

"Doesn't it seem like we're celebrating getting away with essentially crippling a man?"

I turned to Tony and looked him right in the eye. "No, not even a little bit."

I walked away from the group to find a table where I could rejoin Hannah. As I left, I heard Darrow ask his LPO, "What the fuck's the matter with you?"

It took an hour for Hannah to get through all the introductions, but once she did, I got us a booth where I could describe my shipmates to her as we saw them.

"Who's that?" she asked, pointing to a blonde, pear-shaped man doing shots at the bar with two gunner's mates, Mike Deaver and Phil Crowley. They were the ones that wanted to teach Macklemore a hard lesson in personal hygiene.

"That's Bill Kramer," I told her.

"Oh! He's married to Donna. She's so lovely!"

"She is," I agreed. "Everyone loves Donna. We all think her husband's a prick, though."

"Really? Why?"

I took a drink of my beer and then handed Hannah my bottle so she could do the same. "Bill's kind of a bully. He picks on guys he knows won't fight back and recoils like a beaten dog when confronted by someone who will. He makes Macklemore's life a living hell."

"Oh my god! Macklemore! Is he here?" Hannah already heard all about the legend of Crusty Warren.

Looking about the bar, I spotted him behind me. Mack was standing by himself near the waitress station, totally obliterated. At first, I thought he was swaying to the beat of the music, but I soon realized he was just trying to keep his balance. Nobody's sense of rhythm was that bad. Warren was wearing a wrinkled shirt, half untucked, and a pair of unzipped jeans, giving the bar a revealing view of the once-white cotton briefs he wore beneath them.

A couple of girls at another table spotted Mack's open fly and were laughing hysterically about it. Seeing he was the object of their attention, Warren's shoulders sadly slumped. It was his experience that when women noticed him, it was never for something complimentary. He looked ready to slink away and make an escape.

Before Macklemore took two steps toward the door, a passing waitress handed him a slice of pizza he had forgotten he ordered. The sight of food made Mack forget the girls, and his face lit up as if he just hit the jackpot on a Reno slot machine.

"Bloody hell," I caught Hannah whispering to herself as she took in the spectacle. Right after she said this, we watched the pizza slowly roll from the paper plate while Mack was not paying attention and land cheese down upon the floor of the tavern.

Dixie caught us staring at Macklemore as he was walking our way. Frantically reaching to pull a roll of bills out of his pocket, he peeled one of them off and slammed it down on our table. Taking a seat, he called out, "Ten bucks says he eats it anyway!"

"Eeeew!" groaned Hannah. "That's revolting! He'd never actually eat..."

Metaire came out of nowhere and loudly smashed another bill on top of the first, "I'll make eet twenty!"

"You guys are evil!"

To back up her misplaced faith in even the most wretched of souls, Hannah reached into her purse. She was pulling out her pocketbook when I stopped her. "Don't take that bet."

We turned back to look at Macklemore again. He was standing there forlorn, staring at his pizza on the floor. Placing one hand against the wall to steady himself, he squatted down to pick it up but still fell to one knee. He then used his paper plate like a dust bin to scoop up his fallen snack. Miraculously, he got back up to his feet without keeling over onto his face, then scanned the room for a garbage can.

"See, you deviants?" Hannah said, feeling vindicated. "He's not that bloody disgusting."

Claude wagged his finger at my girlfriend. "Theese ees not ovair yet."

Dixie nodded in agreement. "Yeah, I've been around this guy enough to be able to name this tune in two frickin' notes. I ain't admitting I'm wrong until I see Mack's dinner tossed into the trash."

Before Warren found the garbage, he was interrupted by another waitress who asked him if he needed anything. They talked for a couple of moments, and we all laughed at him when he stared lustily at her backside as she walked away.

The waitress completely derailed Macklemore's train of thought. Warren's face beamed a broad, toothy smile then, completely forgetting that he had just dropped it, Mack picked up his piece of pizza and took a ravenous bite out of it.

As Macklemore devoured his food with an almost orgasmic exuberance, Dixie, Claude, and I roared in hilarity. All Hannah could do was shake her head and whimper, "Oh my god. Oh, my bloody god. He ate the feckin' pizza. He. Ate. The. Feckin'. Pizza. Jesus Christ."

*****

Around one a.m., Melissa Hammond stepped up to the bar to settle her tab. As she was waiting to get the bartender's attention, Bill Kramer slipped past Deaver to slide up to his wife's friend. "Hey, Melissa," he slurred. "You and Ricky ain't leaving yet, are you?"

"Yeah, we're going. It's past our bedtime."

Reaching over, Bill put his hand on Mel's back. "That's crazy talk. Come on, lemme buy you a drink."

"Maybe next time, Bill." As Melissa tried to squirm away, Kramer's hand dropped past the small of her back as he attempted to pull her closer to him. "What the hell are you doing?" she asked.

"I'm just trying to talk to you…"

"Bill, get your hand off of my ass…"

"Oops! I'm sorry, Melissa." Kramer's apology sounded insultingly disingenuous, and he cast further doubt on his sincerity by keeping his errant hand right where it was. None of this was lost on Deaver and Crowley, who both started giggling. Overly intoxicated and egged on by his drinking companions, it only took a couple of seconds for Kramer to join them in laughter.

My star technician's wife saw little humor in getting felt up by her friend's husband and did not hold back in letting it be known. "Bill!" she shouted loud enough for the whole bar to hear. "Get your hands off of me!"

As heads turned to look at what was going on, Kramer panicked. "Shhhh! Quiet down! You're making a scene! It's not like…"

"Hey!" Melissa's husband shouted, marching up to Kramer while his wife scurried away from the bar. "What the hell do you think you're doing?"

"Heeeey, Rickeeee. It's not what it looks like, man. I…"

TEQUILA VIKINGS

"You putting your hands on my wife?" Rick barked in a tone of voice that made it clear he was ready to do something about it.

Rick Hammond was no match for Bill Kramer, and Kramer was not about to let himself be called out in public by a pipsqueak like Rick. Bill knew he had a hundred pounds on the man and could put his lights out with a single blow. Recognizing this, he drunkenly slid off of his barstool, confident in the mismatch. "You think you could stop me if I was, you little prick?"

Rick stepped forward to take a swing at Kramer, but Bill thrust both of his hands into Hammond's chest and sent him flying onto his back, gliding across the floor of the bar.

Staring at Hammond sprawled out on the deck, Kramer and his goons started cackling again. They were not laughing long. Without warning, Bill was launched violently forward, crashing face-first onto the floor right beside Hammond. When he rolled over to figure out what had just happened, he saw Dixie standing above him with his fists clenched. "You wanna try that with me, motherfucker?"

"That's enough!" shouted the bartender. "I want all of you out of here right now before I call the cops!"

"You hear that, Kramer?" Dixie asked as he stepped forward and bent down to grab a handful of Bill's hair. "The bartender wants us out of here. Let's finish this shit up in the parking lot."

"Hey, asshole! Let him g…" Crowley leaped off his barstool to jump in and help his buddy, but Marty Pruitt laid him out with an authoritative thump to the nose before his feet even hit the ground. Pruitt was an Aerographer's Mate that worked next door to us. He was the nicest guy sober but loved a good brawl after a few drinks. That was when inflicting pain took on some sort of weird Zen aspect with him.

I was not aware anything was going on until I saw Dixie dragging Kramer outside. When I spotted Crowley sitting on the floor with his back up against the bar, woozily trying to stem the flow of blood pouring out of his nose, my heart sank. We were all drinking and I feared that, while caught up in the moment, my men were going to forget that we were all still under the captain's microscope. None of us, especially Dixie, could afford to let matters get out of hand. I rushed to try to break things up, but by the time I pushed my way through the crowd of gathering spectators, the combatants were already outside.

When I finally caught up, the mob was in the bar's back parking lot, hidden from the street. Pruitt, having already taken one gunner's mate out of the fray, was itching to brutalize the other and paced menacingly in front of GMSN Deaver as he waited for permission to pounce. Master Chief Darrow was between Dixie and Kramer, holding them apart as Rick explained what happened. Melissa and Hannah were each at Donna Kramer's side, trying to comfort her as two of her husband's shipmates were posturing to beat him senseless.

When Donna saw me pushing my way through the crowd to get to my guys, she broke free from her friends and ran after me. "No! No! No!" she cried as she hysterically grabbed for my arm. "Please, Doyle! Not you! Please don't hurt him!"

Caught off guard, I turned and tried to loosen her grip on my wrist. "Donna, I'm trying to stop this! Let me go!"

As I entered the center of the crowd, I heard Darrow turn to Kramer and say, "You made a pass at Hammond's wife?" Our master chief was incredulous. He dropped his arms and turned to Kevin. "Fuck it. Dixie, go ahead and do what you do."

Kevin grinned, clenched his fists, and was just getting ready to charge when I called out, "Dixie! No! Stop it right now!"

Petty Officer Dixon halted, then looked at me with a confused expression on his face. Usually, I would have been happy to stand back and watch Kevin take Kramer apart. Before he could protest my order, though, I yelled for Claude.

"Yez, Doyle!"

"Grab Rick and get him and Melissa back to their car. I want them gone!"

"Fuck that, Doyle!" Rick exclaimed. "He grabbed…"

"I can't afford to have you getting into trouble! You're my best tech! We'll take care of this. Get out of here."

Before Hammond could say another word, Metaire scooped him off his feet and hauled him away from the commotion like a groom carrying his bride over the threshold. It was a comical sight that defused some of the tension.

TEQUILA VIKINGS

"You too, Dixie," I called out. "Get lost."

"What?!?" Kevin asked, sounding exasperated. I knew him well enough to have a pretty good idea of what was going through his head. Dixon was like a German Shepherd being offered a chunk of raw steak, only to have it ripped away before he had the chance to taste it. " You've got to be kidding me! I…"

"Are you serious, Kevin?!? After what we just went through with Green, you're going to argue with me?!? Go home! That's an order! And take Pruitt with you!"

I turned to Marty and slapped him on the back. "Thanks, man. Let me take it from here. Go before you get in trouble."

"Aye aye, Doyle." As a parting shot, Pruitt shoved Deaver down onto his ass before he left. Despite the public humiliation, the gunner's mate looked relieved rather than offended. Deaver had seen what Pruitt was capable of. He knew he had gotten off easy.

Turning to the rest of the crowd, I shouted out, "Show's over everybody! All *Belleau Wood* people, go inside and pay your tabs. We're going home. The cops will probably be here soon."

Kramer tried to follow the crowd back into the bar, but Darrow stopped him. "Where the fuck do you think you're going?"

While the master chief occupied her husband, I asked Donna to take their car and go back to base housing. I told her I would do what I could to keep Kramer from getting hurt, but if he went home angry and took his frustrations out on his wife, I assured her that the men would eat him alive. Donna protested a bit, but I noticed she did not waste much effort trying to convince me that my concerns were unfounded. That lent a lot of credence to other suspicions I had about the piece of shit she was married to. After some token resistance that I sensed was meant more for her husband's eyes than mine, Donna allowed Melissa and Hannah to lead her away.

When everyone was gone, my master chief scowled at me and asked, "You ordering me home, too?"

"Nope." I pulled a pack of cigarettes from my pocket. Lighting one up, I said, "I just got rid of all the witnesses for you. Except for me, of course. You know I'll back you up no matter what you decide to do to this son-of-a-bitch."

Darrow grinned, letting me know that he liked the way I think. The master chief was quickly coming up on his thirty-year mark. I was banking on him not wanting to throw all that away to personally beat the ass of a pathetic young nobody like Bill Kramer.

Before Kramer could see it coming, Darrow reached out and grabbed him by the throat, slamming him against the wall of the bar so hard that Bill's head bounced off the bricks. Then the master chief started squeezing.

Kramer reached up to grab Darrow's arm, futilely trying to rip it away so that he could breathe again. As he struggled, Darrow leaned in close to Bill's face. "You getting off fucking with the wives of your shipmates, Kramer?"

"No!" Bill gasped, his face turning red.

"Bullshit," I said. "It's kind of your thing, isn't it? Do you remember Rebecca Benoit, Bill?"

Kramer nodded, but only slightly. Darrow had his hand around Bill's neck so tight that he could barely move his head. "We dated," he croaked.

"You did. She got married after you split up. That's why she turned down your offer for a quick tryst when you ran into her at the base club a few months back. You didn't like that, though, so you and your goons cornered her husband and publicly humiliated him with blow-by-blow accounts of what you used to do with his wife before she met him."

Kramer's eyes burned with rage. I was getting to him. That incident was not something he wanted our master chief aware of, especially when the man was choking off his oxygen supply. Guessing that Bill would have wanted his wife to know about that incident even less, I asked, "How are you going to feel when I tell Donna that little story?"

Bill's hands clenched into fists, so I stepped forward to be within striking range. If he tried to hit me, I wanted him to connect. That way, maybe Green and Kramer could be court-martialed for striking a senior petty officer together. "He looks mad, Master Chief. You want to let him go to see if he has the balls to do anything about it?"

Darrow smiled and released his grip. Kramer hunched over while drawing in a deep breath, then angrily pointed his finger at me. "You need to learn that you have no right to interfere with a man's family! Keep your fucking mouth shut!"

TEQUILA VIKINGS

I laughed and then flicked my lit cigarette at Kramer's forehead. "Or what?" Even though Bill could breathe now, his face turned even redder. I started mentally counting down to prepare for the blow I was about to take in three...two...one...

Realizing what I was goading him into, Kramer backed down. "Yeah, that's what I thought," I said. "Pussy."

"How do you know about the other girl, Doyle?" Darrow asked.

"I was on shore patrol that night and found Becky sitting on a bench near the parking lot, bawling her eyes out. We went through BE/E School together. Becky's husband was so mortified that night that he couldn't even look at her. He gave her the keys to go home, then walked back to spend the night on his ship."

"Master Chief," Kramer wheezed, trying to pull his boss's attention back to his current transgression. Bill felt he had more wiggle room to portray what had happened between him and Melissa Hammond as a simple misunderstanding than he did of explaining what went down with Becky Benoit and her husband. There was no way to get into that sordid story without revealing just how big of a douchebag Kramer really was. "This stuff tonight was an accident. I didn't mean to touch Melissa that way. My arm just slipped."

"Yeah, well, that excuse went flying out the window the moment you pushed Hammond onto his ass," Darrow retorted, entirely unconvinced.

"B-b-but I..." Kramer was interrupted when a squad car from the National City Police Department pulled into the parking lot and lit us up with their spotlight. After it rolled to a stop, a patrolman emerged from the vehicle, looking the three of us over. Observing that Bill was under a significant amount of duress, he asked, "Is there a problem here?"

Darrow smiled and faced the officer. "There nearly was, but we got everything under control."

"Did you?" the officer's baby-faced partner asked as he stepped out of the passenger seat, sounding a little too cocksure of himself.

"We did." Darrow was not used to being challenged by less experienced men. Though it was probably not intentional, the tone in the master chief's voice sounded very condescending, as if he was telling the cop to go away and mind his own business. That rubbed the officer a little raw, and he asked all of us for identification.

The senior officer read the name from the master chief's ID card. "Bradley Darrow. That sounds familiar. We had any run-ins with you before?"

Darrow shook his head. "Nope. I'm a friend of Lieutenant Farrell, though. Maybe we crossed paths through him."

The younger cop scoffed at the obvious name drop. "How do you know the lieutenant?"

"We worked together in the Philippines. He was an MP out at Clark Air Base. I was with the AFPD in Subic Bay."

The older officer looked like a light bulb went off inside of his head. "Bradley Darrow? Bradley Fucking Darrow! You're Olongapo Earp!"

"No shit?" the younger cop asked. "Really? That was you?"

"Yeah, me and Farrell go way back."

"You sure do." The older cop gave the master chief back his identification. "I'm glad to put a face to the name."

"Thanks," Darrow said, shaking the officer's hand. "Tell Mike I said hello."

"We sure will." The officers handed our IDs back to Kramer and me. "We've heard a lot about you. These two kids yours?"

Darrow slapped me on the shoulder hard enough to be considered assault. "I claim this one. That punk over there, though…" the master chief stuck his chin out at Kramer. "He needs a bit more work before I'll admit he belongs to me."

The corporal pulled out his handcuffs and dangled them in front of the master chief. "You want us to teach him a lesson for you?"

Darrow laughed. "Thanks for the offer, but I'm sure I'm capable of putting this drooling dipshit back on the right path."

The officers walked back to their squad car. "So we've heard."

As they drove away, I caught myself shaking my head in awe. While I had little doubt that Master Chief Darrow would one day leave this mortal coil, I had a feeling that Olongapo Earp would fucking live forever.

*****

CHAPTER 5

When Hannah was in town, our world revolved around Ocean Beach. It was where our waves and our friends were. The night after my party, we gathered around a bonfire in the sand where Hannah gave Dreadlock John and Space Kate, two melanin-deficient Rastafarian wannabees, a detailed account of the deviants she met the night before.

Eddie Wayne and Lupe Castillo were also with us. Neither of them surfed, but Lupe had a direct supply line to authentic sinsemilla through her people back home in Tijuana. She was very popular on the beach, OB royalty, so to speak, as long as she had pot to push. "He didn't!" Lupe gasped as Hannah told her story.

"He did! I couldn't feckin' believe it. He ate the bloody pizza."

Our group around the bonfire erupted into laughter. Having seen Macklemore do so much worse, I did not laugh myself, but I delighted in watching everyone else enjoy the story. I felt genuinely at peace for the first time in months.

I loved spending nights laying in the sand with these people, smoking dope, listening to bootleg reggae, and discussing the mystic forces that guided our journeys through the cosmos. Of course, because of the US military's fascist policy of random drug testing, I stuck to mezcal and beer, but it never detracted from the sense of belonging I felt among those who shared OB with us.

Generally speaking, Ocean Beach was not the kind of place where the pretty people came to play. The OB crowd was darker than those who preferred the sand north of Interstate 8. They looked tougher and freely wielded their profanity. Tourists were not particularly welcome down that way, and the place had a vibe to it that screamed, "locals-only," or, as Dreadlock John liked to say, "*locos*-only."

Ocean Beach contained an eclectic mix of Southern California counterculture. In addition to pale Rastafarians, surf punks, and dope dealers, OB boasted at least one motorcycle gang, the Devil's Coachmen, and several cliques of Mexican street hoodlums. There was also a single house full of holdover Hare Krishnas. At some point or another, we shared a bottle and a bonfire with all of them.

There was only one group I regularly saw there for whom I had no use. I crossed paths with them in Tijuana from time to time and knew they had few redeeming qualities. They were fraternity brothers from SDSU who would cruise the beach looking for dope. I spotted the hooligans earlier and kept an eye directed their way as Hannah described Macklemore to our friends.

The frat dicks usually traveled in a pack of about a half dozen guys and were led by a cocky rich kid whose name I never learned. I found his haircut hilarious, though, so I usually referred to him as the Hockey Mullet Frat Guy, or HMFG for short. The mullet man and his boys liked to relieve boredom through testing the limits of upper-class impunity, most often by picking fights with people far less affluent than they were. One would think that to be an excellent way to get a knife shoved in your gut, but the HMFG crew were more sociopathic than they were stupid and only struck when the odds were about six-to-one in their favor. They were in desperate need of instant karma, something I would have loved to impose on them if I was not trying so hard to turn over a new leaf.

"Doyle!" I heard Hannah call out, breaking me out of my trance. "Aren't you listening?"

"What? Were you talking to me?"

TEQUILA VIKINGS

"Yeah, Luv! I was! What're you lookin' at over there?"

"Over there?" I asked. "Nothing. Just that group of idiots walking down the boardwalk. See that tall guy over that way? The guy with the black mullet? He reminds me of Kramer. Total asshole."

Eddie turned his chin towards where I was looking and chuckled, seeing who I was talking about. "Yeah, you got that shit right, *amigo*. His old man's a lawyer or judge or some shit like that. His boys jumped a couple of surfers here a few months back and fucked them up pretty good. Of course, the cops didn't do a goddamn thing about it. A couple of weeks later, those two guys returned the favor in spades. They got a bunch of their buddies together and whipped all their asses. After that, the sheriffs rolled in and turned this place upside fuckin' down."

I shook my head. "I see them down in TJ all the time," I told Eddie. "If they ever cross you, let your girl have her people down there take care of them."

"They ain't crossing us," Lupe said. "I don't sell to those *pendejos*. Not after that shit. If I catch them in Tijuana, I'll see if my guys will sick Hulagu on them."

I threw back another blast of mezcal. "Hulagu? You know, I had a guy on my ship claim to have gotten his ass kicked by Hulagu this week."

"Really?" Lupe asked. "I doubt it was really him."

Lupe grew up in Tijuana. She also operated amongst the Mexican underworld, albeit at a very low level. Figuring she had more expertise on the subject than anyone else I knew, I asked, "Is Hulagu actually a real thing in TJ?"

Lupe took a hit off the joint that John passed her and nodded as she tried to keep it contained. While letting the smoke out, she said, "Yeah, he's real, but he's not going to bother shaking down *gringos*. Not unless you guys are rioting or something and they need to bring in the big guns. No, Hulagu works with drugs."

"He's a narc?"

Both Lupe and Eddie broke into laughter. "Oh, Doyle, you're so naïve sometimes. Hulagu isn't a narc; he's a *narco*. He works with the Arrellano-Felix brothers. *Los Hermanos*."

"Really? You know him?"

45

Lupe shook her head vigorously. "No, I don't know him. I know of him. Everybody on the street in Tijuana does. *Sargento* Francisco Martinez of the *federales*. He's a real bastard, that guy. You never want to get to know someone like that."

When the joint made its way back to Hannah, she turned the conversation back to my shipmates. "What's the deal with that bloody horse's arse Bill, anyway? His wife is stunning. A guy that dumpy should be worshipping the ground she walks on, but he treats her like rubbish. I didn't see him speak with her at all last night. He spent the whole time getting pissed with his boyfriends at the bar." In Australian English, the word "pissed" was synonymous with "drunk." That occasionally caused confusion regarding Hannah's emotional state around our bonfire.

"He's just a prick," I answered.

"Still, she adores him. Did you see how terrified she was when you stepped in to keep Dixie from beating him to a pulp? She looked positively terrified that you were going to…that you were…"

Hannah trailed off as she thought about what had happened. "Doyle, Donna was out of her mind about what you might do to her husband. Did that have anything to do with the trouble you got into?"

I sighed, not feeling like getting into that subject. "It could be."

"Doyle, it's over, right? Does that mean you can talk about that Green bloke now?"

Hannah was beginning to harsh my mellow. Still, I had to tell her what happened eventually. Then was as good a time as any. "Randy Green broke his five-year-old stepson's arm to get the kid's mother out of the bathroom so that he could beat her some more." After I said that, I saw both Lupe and Kate recoil in disgust. "He got away with it because his wife wouldn't admit what he did. Anyway, Randy sucker-punched me while I was supervising him during a working party, and he got hurt as I was fighting him off. The Navy suspected that we beat him up for what he did to the boy. The camera in the well deck caught him punching me plain as day, though, so I was cleared."

"How did you hurt him?" Hannah asked.

I shrugged. "People are fragile. Where this happened, the Nixie Winch Room, well, there isn't a soft surface in that entire space. The guy went down hard and hit everything there was to hit on his way to the deck. That happens during a fight."

"Were you hurt?"

Shaking my head, I told her, "No."

"Why not?"

"Well, for starters, unless he was up against a tiny Filipina girl, Green was not much of a fighter. It also helped that when I went down, my fall was broken by the only soft surface in the entire winch room: Randy Green."

"Doyle, did you mean to…"

"Look, Hannah…" I winced. "I'm not proud of what happened. I kept Dixie from beating Kramer's ass last night because I didn't want him to ever go through what I did. Can we please just drop this?"

"Of course, we can, darling." Hannah started rubbing my back to calm me, and I breathed out a big sigh of relief. I did not want to admit to her that I had premeditated the attack on Randy.

I did not want to admit it to myself, either. Green was getting court-martialed for what happened that day, going on trial for a crime I knew he did not commit. Though I was reluctant to acknowledge them, pangs of conscience would occasionally bubble up from the depths of my psyche about that. I suppressed them by rationalizing that though the Navy was charging Randy Green with assaulting me, whatever sentence they imposed on him would be for what he had done to that little boy.

As if beating the man into clinical epilepsy was not punishment enough.

*****

It was around two in the morning when things really got going at the fire. We drank all the beer by three—the tequila by four. By five, I was drinking a bottle of mezcal by myself while everyone else made the most of Lupe's seemingly inexhaustible supply of pot.

I was sitting on my knees, at times coming dangerously close to falling into the fire. Pointing up at the stars, I slurred something like, "Naw maaaaannnn. There's a place out there where science ends and God begins. As Avicenna put it, there has to be a 'necessary existent,' something that cannot NOT exist. Without it, existence itself would not be, and we would not be here to have this conversation."

"So, God is the necessary existent thing?" Dreadlock John asked.

I burped, almost got sick, and needed to wash the sour taste of mezcal and bile out of my mouth. Tragically, the only thing we had left to do that with was more mezcal. "Yeah, man. Except like, God isn't that big bearded dude reaching across the roof of the Sistine Chapel beckoning Adam to pull his finger, but more like a state of omnipotent knowledge, the well from which we all sprang. That's why I still consider myself an atheist."

Some random guy who joined us stared at me with rapt attention. I was not sure if he was a hippy or homeless. "Dude. You're like some sort of point break bodhisattva."

I laughed. "That's a good thing, right? 'Cause I thought those people in Mississippi were being nice to me when they 'blessed my heart,' but later I found out they thought I was a moron."

"No, dude. That's deep stuff. Did you learn it in the Navy?" asked Eddie.

"Nah," I answered. "I'm just into philosophy and read a lot. The military doesn't encourage its enlisted people to think too deeply. They don't want you questioning things. You can't afford to have the grunts second-guessing their orders because it could cost you a mission. And if you lose a mission, people die."

"So you have to be 'Rah-Rah! America!' all the time?" Dreadlock John asked.

"It doesn't hurt."

"You don't seem that way," Lupe said. "You have a very subversive feel to you,"

"Well, I've seen things that made me question my country's motives. Don't get me wrong, if the Canadian hordes come pouring across the border, I'm still going to fight them off. I don't have any choice. All my stuff's here. I'm not going to blindly march off and kill folks just because some officer told me it's the right thing to do, though."

After another belch that nearly went too far, I continued. "If I'm going to commit horrific acts on behalf of my country, I have to know they're acting in the best interests of humanity." I forgot I changed career plans that week and was going to try to become an officer.

TEQUILA VIKINGS

"Were you in Iraq?" Kate asked. Operation Desert Storm had finished just over a year before.

I shook my head. "No, I spent the Gulf War taking advantage of all the discounts they were giving us sailors in Las Vegas."

"So, where did you see the stuff that has you questioning your country's motives?" Hannah asked, suddenly interested.

"I got sent to El Sal…" I stopped myself from blurting it out just in time, but letting my mind wander to that place during a mezcal bender was not a good idea. I fell silent, thinking of the girl I had gotten killed a couple of years before. Just like with my family, I did not actually see her die. I just heard the Salvadorans carry out the execution.

That fleeting thought was all it took. I felt myself descending into the underwater world where my episodes tormented me, and I started to panic. *No! I can't do this here! I gotta shake it!*

"Are you all right?" I heard Kate ask, sounding like she was miles away, although she was no more than six feet from me.

I was fighting hard to stay on the beach, trying to focus on my friends. As cold as it was, I was sweating like crazy. "Doyle…" Dreadlock John asked while snapping his fingers in front of my face. "Hey, man. What's going on?"

I tried shaking my head to get the cobwebs out. "Man, I'm really fucked up. I need to go home." I flinched again, hearing another gunshot. It was not the report of the pistol in El Salvador this time. It was the shotgun my father used. Instinctively, I brought my hands up to cover my ears. "Oh, no. Uh oh. I gotta go."

I stood up without saying goodbye and started speed-walking off the beach, ignoring Hannah's cries for me to wait up. I needed to get home before the screaming started.

It was a tough walk. Every little noise around me sounded like another explosion. Afraid I would not be able to maintain my composure for long, I sprinted back to Cheri's house as soon as I was out of sight of the bonfire.

Once inside, I ran to the bathroom, locking the door behind me. I was burning up. I ripped off my baja and tee-shirt, then pressed my bare chest against the cool bathroom floor. I still felt like I was underwater, but the soothing sensation of the tiles against my core calmed me down before the gunfire started again.

49

BLAM! I saw my mother's head explode as my old man hit her point-blank with a barrel full of buckshot. BLAM! BLAM! Rhiannon was running through the house, trying to get away. BLAM! Dad hit her in the kitchen, the blast lifting her off of her feet and sending her flying across the dining room. That one must have hurt. Rhiannon was always daddy's little girl.

I heard Conor crying in his crib, too young to understand what was happening but born with enough instinct to know he was in mortal danger. BLAM!

Conor abruptly fell silent, but somewhere in the distance, I heard Hannah yelling, "Doyle! Open the bloody door! You're scaring me!" BLAM! BLAM! BLAM! I could not differentiate between the gunfire in my head and the pounding on the bathroom door.

BAM! That was a new one. It was the sound of my right fist crashing into Green's cheek as I straddled his chest. BAM! That was the sound of my left, flattening his nose and sending blood splattering across his forehead. BAM! This was my right uppercut, breaking Randy's jaw.

As I beat Randy Green's face into an unrecognizable bloody mess, the bathroom started spinning on me, and I sensed a bitter taste again rising into my mouth. BAM! BAM! "Doyle! Goddammit! Let me in!" Hannah was closer now, clearer. I tried to answer her, but everything was whirling past me too fast. BAM! "DOYLE!"

My stomach convulsed and I lunged for the toilet, vomiting so violently that my testicles hurt. Then I threw up again. And again. After the fourth time, I was back, and just like that, all was normal. Well, as close to normal as it could be after drinking a fifth of Monte Alban nearly by myself anyway.

When I finished, I flushed the toilet and crawled over to unlock the door. I then fell onto my side and tried to catch my breath. Hannah walked in, quite shaken up. "Doyle! Are you okay? You've got us all worried sick!"

I smiled in relief as I felt myself surrendering to a state of alcohol-induced unconsciousness. "I'm much better now," I told her, right before passing out.

*****

CHAPTER
6

Lieutenant Jeffrey Howe was our division officer, the man above Master Chief Darrow in my chain of command. He was prior-enlisted, had passed his thirty-year mark, and with just weeks to go in his military career, he was basically calling it in. He was happy to stay out of Darrow's way and let him run the division however he saw fit.

Some things could not be delegated, though. We were eight months away from a change of homeport. It was Howe's responsibility to decide who went to Japan, who got discharged early, and who transferred to another command. To help, Howe wanted every supervisor's input and called us all to the EMO to hear us out.

Looking over the room, the lieutenant asked, "Is there anybody eligible to go to Japan who should not? Besides Macklemore?"

"Macklemore's not going?" I asked, doing my best to sound surprised.

Howe raised an eyebrow. "Do you think he should?"

I shrugged. "Well, Mack's not much of a sailor, but it's nice having him around to do the grunt work. It frees up our techs for the important stuff."

"No way," Darrow replied without hesitation, showing us all that as far as Macklemore was concerned, he had already made up his mind. "Our mission as a forward-deployed war vessel is not only to deter potential aggressors but to project a positive image abroad. Petty Officer Macklemore is hardly an asset in either endeavor. He looks and smells like shit, he's incompetent, and he's working on becoming an alcoholic. He's a liability that needs to stay here."

That was good enough for the lieutenant. "Anyone else?"

"Palazzo," I said.

Howe grinned. "Under what grounds? His over-active libido?"

The men in the EMO snickered, but Master Chief Darrow did not. "I think Palazzo's issues go beyond that, Lieutenant. We were seriously considering referring Palazzo for a psych eval. I don't think it's a good idea for him to go with us."

"Do we have another certified IFF tech?" Howe enquired.

"No," I answered.

"Then we don't have much choice." IFF stood for "Identify Friend or Foe." In 1988, the *USS Vincennes* downed an Iranian airliner over the Strait of Hormuz. In the immediate aftermath of that tragedy, the Navy blamed a faulty IFF transponder on the downed aircraft for identifying it as an aggressive warplane. We were only four years removed from that disaster, and no one wanted to go overseas short an IFF technician.

"Do you think Palazzo is a danger to the ship or its crew?" the lieutenant asked me.

"No." I did not think Palazzo had it in him to harm another human being. It was not that he was a pacifist. It was more like he was a coward.

"Is he a danger to himself?"

"I don't think he's suicidal if that's what you mean," I told Mr. Howe. "But he could experience some sort of catastrophic foreskin failure if he doesn't back it off a little."

Howe ignored my attempt at humor. "Is he lucid?"

"Yes."

The Electronic Materials Officer leaned back in his chair and clasped his hands over his gut. "So, tell me Murphy, is Palazzo crazy or just really horny?"

"I can't say, sir. I'm not a psychiatrist."

"Well, until you can, you need to figure out a way to work with the little pervert. Just avoid shaking hands with the guy if you can help it."

TEQUILA VIKINGS

Darrow, Ramirez, and I exchanged a quick glance to reassure ourselves that we were all on the same page. Once confident we were, Darrow objected, "Sir..."

"Pick another battle, Master Chief. Palazzo is an embarrassment, but he's not going to hurt anybody. We're taking on a lot of inexperienced men right out of A School. The *Belleau Wood* is going to need sailors with sea legs who know what they're doing."

"Sir," I countered. "I could make a pretty good argument that Palazzo hardly knows what he's doing. He looks squared away, with his spit and polish, but it's all camouflage for some glaring deficiencies. Without a doubt, he's my weakest technician."

Howe scowled at me. He already made up his mind and was growing irritated by our resistance to moving on. "You know what, Murphy? By the end of the week, my replacement will be here on a familiarization visit. If you can convince him that Palazzo's embarrassing behavior trumps our need to deploy with at least one qualified IFF technician, he can put in the paperwork to leave Spanky on the pier. Understood?"

"Yessir."

"Anyone else?"

"Bill Kramer." I was surprised to hear Darrow throw that name out. "He's a detriment to unit cohesion. He's unable to control his impulses, tends to bully weaker crew members, and instead of guiding junior techs to enhance their skills, he discourages them with obstacles to their development."

"Yeah," Tony answered tentatively, caught just as off guard as I was. "Kramer's an asshole. If we get rid of him, though, Macklemore becomes our primary WSC-3 tech. If we're losing both of them, we have no one."

"We all learned the WSC-3 in A School," Chief Ramirez said. "If I had to choose between the two, I'd like us to retain Petty Officer Macklemore."

"That's closed, Ben," Darrow said.

"I'd like to reopen it," the chief retorted. Ben Ramirez was born in the Philippines but moved to California when he was thirteen. As a result, his accent was more akin to that of Los Angeles than Manila. Within our division, he was the Yin to Darrow's Yang.

"Sir, Macklemore doesn't have many strengths..." Ramirez started.

"He doesn't have any," Darrow countered.

"I respectfully disagree with you, Brad. He's a hard worker and has good intentions. I think getting Macklemore up to Navy standards would not only be good for him, but it would be a great opportunity for a supervisor who's thinking about applying for BOOST. I think Murphy could make him an asset to this command."

All eyes suddenly turned to me. "What? Are you serious? Macklemore's not even one of my guys!"

"I can fix that easily enough." Tony Bard was Crusty Warren's supervisor. "If you can clean Macklemore up, you can keep him."

"We're not keeping Macklemore," Darrow said, cutting off the debate. "I've already got him on the *Blue Ridge*. It's a done deal."

I breathed a deep sigh of relief. "Thank you, Master Chief."

"Don't go thanking me yet," Darrow said, leaning back in his chair and flashing the room one of his nefarious grins. "Ben's got a point.

"Cleaning up Macklemore would be a damn good exercise in leadership skills for someone with aspirations of becoming an officer. You know, there's a lot of high-ranking people on the *Ridge*. If they get a load of Mack, they might think that Fleming is running a loose ship over here. I don't think it'd be fair to our skipper to get him that kind of attention. Do you guys?"

Everyone in the EMO shook their heads in agreement. Everyone except me, anyway.

"Good," Darrow said. "Doyle, on Monday, Macklemore is all yours. Do us proud, Petty Officer Murphy."

I hung my head and shook it, not happy at all with the way things unexpectedly worked out. There would be no way to escape Mack's stench in Radar Repair, a space so small it was little more than a glorified equipment closet. Bard patted me sympathetically on the back. "Better you than me."

With that settled, the conversation went back to Kramer. Bard admitted that he was not particularly fond of the guy, but he successfully lobbied that losing both Kramer and Macklemore would leave Comm Repair severely short-handed. Howe agreed with him, and even Darrow had to concede that once you got past his cretinous behavior and laziness, Bill Kramer did a pretty good job keeping the WSC-3s in working order. They decided that Bill would make the move to Japan with us.

"Okay," the lieutenant called out after resolving the Kramer question. "Is there anything else?"

I had a few ideas but kept my mouth shut. Things were not breaking my way, so I feared speaking up would only result in another nuisance falling into my lap.

"All right then," Howe said, happy to check a task off of his to-do list. "You're dismissed. Turn to."

As we filed towards the door, Chief Ramirez grabbed me by the shoulder as I passed his desk. "You okay with taking Macklemore under your wing, Doyle?"

I shook my head. "Not really. I already have one problem child in my shop. What'd I do to deserve getting saddled with two?"

Ben grinned. "You showed potential. This isn't punishment, Doyle. It's me thinking that you're the right man for this job. Bard tried to get that boy up to snuff and failed. So did I. Hell, even the master chief got involved last week and wasn't any more successful than the rest of us. I think you can pull this off, though."

"Yeah?" I asked, unconvinced. "Why's that?"

"The two of you've got a lot in common, and of everybody in this division, I think you're the most likely to be able to connect with him. Have you ever really talked to the guy?"

Shaking my head, I said, "Not really."

Ramirez nodded in understanding. "Not many of us have. You know, Mack's childhood was tough, too. I don't think it quite rose to the level of horror that your upbringing did, but it was still pretty ghastly. He bounced from house to house, staying with whoever his alcoholic mother was sleeping with. It sounds like he was neglected and essentially had to fend for himself for as long as he could remember."

"He told you that? You'd think that would make him more self-sufficient. That's how it worked out with me."

Chief Ramirez shrugged. "Well, Doyle, we can't all be you. You might not have gotten a lot of emotional nurturing once you went into foster care, but at least you were fed and had a roof over your head. To hear Mack describe it, he was about a half step away from going feral. You know, after talking with him, I got the feeling that he's descending into a dark place. He's always been something of an outcast, and he's losing hope that things will ever turn around. I think he's desperate for someone to reach out to him."

I let out a long sigh. "If Macklemore wanted someone to reach out, maybe he should consider showering enough for us to penetrate that funky force field that surrounds him."

Ben scowled at me. "I'm not joking about this, Doyle."

"Neither am I, Chief," I countered, the tone of my voice showing a bit of my frustration. "Look, I don't have any animosity towards Mack, but I'm not going to feel sorry for him. His troubles are largely self-inflicted. He doesn't have friends because he's revolting. He doesn't get invited out because he's a sloppy drunk and a girl repellant. He doesn't get the respect of his shipmates because he doesn't respect himself."

Chief Ramirez looked disappointed. "So, you're not even going to try to help the guy out?"

I groaned and leaned back, taking a seat on the corner of Ben's desk. "Of course I'm going to try, Chief. I just want to manage everyone's expectations here."

"Doyle, my expectations are more in the process than the result. I want to see if you can lead through inspiration rather than coercion. I want you to try to empathize with Macklemore, showing him how you rose above your circumstances so he can rise above his. I would like him to emulate you, Doyle, not dread you."

"Dread me? Mack doesn't have anything to fear from me, Chief. I'm not the kind of guy who's going to hurt a man who's incapable of fighting back."

"Good," Ben said. "Keep in mind, though, not everyone shares your lofty ideals. I've heard rumblings that some of the men in the berthing area are considering giving Mack the scrub. He's too fragile for something like that. I also want him under your watch so the other guys will leave him alone."

"What makes you so sure he'll be safe under my protection?" I asked. "The men know the captain has me on a short leash."

Chief Ramirez shrugged. "It doesn't matter. After what you did to Green, no one's willing to cross you. The Master-at-Arms told me they haven't dealt with a domestic violence issue since they loaded Randy into that ambulance. You've become a wife-beater's bogeyman, Doyle."

TEQUILA VIKINGS

Ben reached out and patted me on the shoulder. "You know, I don't particularly agree with the master chief's methods when it comes to that stuff, but I have to admit, in some cases, they're pretty goddamn effective."

*****

RM3 David Miller was a squirrelly character. The radioman had a delicate appearance to him, something he tried to toughen up with an enormous lizard tattoo on his left forearm. When that didn't work, he started pulling rank to boss around Marty Pruitt, the bruiser that tried to take on two gunner's mates at my exoneration party. Considering that Pruitt was three times that kid's size, it was a hobby I expected would end poorly for Miller one day.

The radioman tended to get on my nerves, so I was irritated when he stuck his head through our door and startled me. "Hey, I uh, I think there's something wrong with one of your technicians next door."

"In the radio room?" I asked. "That wouldn't be one of mine. It would be one of Bard's men from downstairs. What's up?"

"He ain't moving."

That got my attention. As electronics technicians, we worked with high voltage and were often at risk of touching the wrong terminal and frying ourselves. When I barged into the radio room, I found Miller was right. Macklemore was lying on the deck, his head and shoulders buried beneath the bank of WSC-3 radios lining the forward bulkhead.

"What do we do?" Miller asked. "Pull him out?"

I shook my head. "No, keep your distance. If he's taking volts and you touch him, you'll start taking volts too." Electrically speaking, I doubted that Macklemore was hot. If he were, we would be smelling a lot more of him than we usually did.

I slid down onto my stomach to get a better look at what we were dealing with. Mack's hands were both tucked into the bottom of the radio transmitter, so I could not see if they were contacting anything dangerous. What I could see was the rise and fall of Warren's chest and the cigarette in his mouth that burned all the way down to the filter, spilling ashes across his cheek. It looked as if he just dozed off in the middle of whatever he was doing.

If Macklemore was asleep, it was vital that we did not wake him with power still flowing into the equipment. If we startled the guy, he might jump and touch something lethal. Being as careful as I could, I got back up and turned to Miller, shaking my head in disbelief.

"Is he all right?" the radioman asked.

"I think so." I did not know Miller very well, but he seemed like the type of guy who took the names of people misbehaving when the teacher was away. I doubted he would appreciate what I was about to do next. To get rid of him, I asked, "Can you do me a favor and run down the hall and get Petty Officer Dixon to give me a hand? He's probably in Radar Room One."

"Sure. No problem," Miller said as he walked out of the door.

As soon as my potential witness left, I walked over and pulled the safety interlock switch, killing electricity to the equipment. I then reached between Warren's legs and wrapped my fingers around his testicles. He immediately came to life, and as I squeezed my fingers together, he undoubtedly wished it was the electricity that got to him instead of me. At first, I was going for volume, tightening my grip as Mack thrashed about the deck, banging his head repeatedly between the floor and the transmitter racks as he tried to escape the confined space, screaming bloody murder. When I was confident he could not get any louder, I started to twist until Warren's voice reached the octave I was going for.

Once satisfied that I had Macklemore suitably tuned, I ferociously yanked him out from under the radio bank. Shocked, in a great deal of agony, and terrified, Mack went apeshit, spastically flailing his limbs about and gasping for air as he tried to figure out what was happening to him. He made quite a racket, but fortunately, the radio room was the loudest space on the 07 level. Nobody heard him.

"What the hell do you think you're doing?!?" I screamed at Warren once I had him upright and trembling at the position of attention. "Are you trying to kill yourself?!?"

Mack's eyes were darting manically about the radio room, showing me just how confused he still was. A split second before, Warren was serenely asleep, and everything was all kittens and sunshine. Then he was yanked back into reality, literally, by the balls. He was too disoriented to reply.

TEQUILA VIKINGS

Frustrated by his lack of response, I grabbed a handful of Mack's tee-shirt and pulled him in so close our noses were almost touching, bellowing, "ANSWER ME, GODDAMMIT! DO YOU WANT TO FUCKING DIE?!?"

Though nothing came out of Macklemore's mouth, the look in his eyes gave me pause. I did not get the impression that Warren was actively trying to take his life that day in the radio room, but the expression on his face made me feel as if somewhere in the back of that poor man's mind, it was an option he'd been keeping on the table.

*****

When we were back in my shop, I wrote out the report chit to send Macklemore to captain's mast. It detailed his gross safety violation and called him out for sleeping on duty. I explained to Warren that once I submitted it, he would probably lose his rank.

Since it was unlikely he was going to Japan with us, and there was no billet anywhere in the fleet for an E-3 ET with Macklemore's substandard evaluations, he would likely separate from the Navy.

I was hoping that would be a relatively painless way to put some distance between Mack and the stresses of military life that he struggled so hard to cope with. When I explained it to him, I spun it as an act of kindness, a temporary hardship to endure before he could return to whatever element he was most comfortable living in. I thought that he would see that I was doing him a favor. Instead, however, Macklemore burst into tears.

It was shocking how quickly my sympathy for the man turned to disgust. Macklemore was not facing prison. He would lose a little cash, drop a pay grade, and leave the Navy with an honorable discharge. No harm. No foul. Unlike most of us, Warren was not serving out an enlistment on the *USS Belleau Wood*. He was doing hard time, and I was putting into motion the process for his parole. There was no reason for him to be carrying on about it.

"Do you like being like this, Mack?" I asked. "Is this the way you want to go through life?"

Mack shook his head vigorously, making it look like his oily strands of unwashed hair were trying to wipe the acne off his forehead.

"Use your words, Warren."

"No!" Mack sobbed. He was inconsolable.

It took a while for Warren to get himself together, but once he did, he asked, "Can't we just go down to the Nixie and settle this like you usually do? Please don't throw me out of the Navy!"

I stared at him, baffled. Not only did Macklemore want to remain in the service, but he was also willing to risk being gravely injured to do it. "Seriously?" I asked him. "You want to end up like Randy Green?"

After sucking his snot back into his sinuses, Warren shook his head again. "No. I want to stay in the Navy."

"How?" I was incredulous. "Look at you! Warren, you still smell like you haven't showered in days. Your tee-shirt is stained yellow, your dungarees are full of grease, and your trousers are worn white around the knees. You're a fucking mess! We've been going through this for over a year now, and you haven't changed a bit. The Navy just isn't the place for you."

"It's the only place I have right now! Doyle, please! I've got a brother back in Alaska. He's staying with his friends, but they don't have much, you know? As long as I pay for his food and rent. He has a place to sleep. If I stop, they can't afford to keep him. They're good people, just poor. They'll have no choice but to send him to live with our mother and…and…"

Macklemore broke down again. When he regained his composure, he drew in a deep breath. "He's a smart kid. He graduates next year, the class of '93. I just have to make it that long. I want to give him a chance. I don't want him ending up like me."

I sat there staring at Macklemore for a moment while he struggled to calm himself down. "What's the story on your mother?"

Warren shrugged. "She's a drunk. She disappears for days at a time, leaving us to have to fish or hunt for whatever we eat. A few times, things got bad enough that we had to raid the dumpsters in town for food. Especially when we weren't getting fed at school."

Macklemore was a pathetic sight. Despite resisting it, I had a difficult time not feeling sorry for him, which led to an epiphany. I realized that

TEQUILA VIKINGS

Warren had developed eliciting pity into a survival skill and finally understood how he lasted so long in the Navy. He had a way of making people cut him slack because they felt so sorry for him.

It was not that Mack lacked sincerity. If there was one thing I learned about Warren, it was that he was no liar. He was just agonizingly aware of his shortcomings and learned to adapt by keeping expectations of him ridiculously low.

Macklemore got positive attention for being a hard worker when the assignment required nothing more than mindless labor. He knew how inadequate he was at his job and went to great lengths to avoid doing it. He got away with this because the work he took on instead was grueling, and his colleagues were happy to put in extra time on his equipment so that they would not have to fill his slot on one of the daily working parties.

It was the way his mind adapted to his weaknesses, and we were all enabling it. It had to stop.

I passed Macklemore the chit I filled out. "You need to sign this. You're officially on report."

"Please, Doyle, don't," Warren begged.

"Sign it."

"Please…"

"Or don't," I said, withdrawing the piece of paper and putting it back on my desk. "Signing it only signifies you understand why you're being written up. The captain can explain your violations to you. Then you can tell him why you refused to endorse it."

That got Mack to stand up and reluctantly step towards my desk. Trying not to breathe through my nose, I handed him a pen and watched him write out his autograph. "When are you going to submit it?" he asked.

I looked at my watch. "It's a bit late now, so probably Monday."

Macklemore hung his head.

"I'll wait until Tuesday if you can make it to quarters on time Monday morning looking inspection ready. That means showered, shaved, your hair cut and cleaned, uniform crisp and ironed, shoes shined, and your bunk squared away and odor-free. It's Friday, so you have the whole weekend to work on it. I wouldn't go drinking if I were you. You realize that you're being reassigned to Radar Repair next week, right?"

Macklemore looked up and nodded.

"Good, I expect you to show up on Tuesday morning the same way. On-time and inspection ready. If you can do that, I'll wait until Wednesday to turn it in. If you can repeat the process on Wednesday, I'll wait until Thursday. Do you see the pattern here, Warren?"

Mack's eyes opened a little wider as he nodded his head.

"Good. This is the end of the line for you." I held up the report chit. "If you don't do what I just told you, I drop this on Master Chief Darrow's desk. As far as I'm concerned, you're already gone. It's just a question of when you'll be leaving us. It's entirely up to you. Understand?"

"Yes, Petty Officer Murphy."

"Mack, you need to be in your rack by the time lights are out at 22:00. No more drinking on weekdays or the day before duty. Spend the weekend getting new uniforms and making them ready. Fail at any of this, and you're gone. Is that clear?"

After a nod from Mack, I added, "You're a part of Radar Repair now. That means if you need someone to show you how to do something, we'll help you. We're not going to do anything for you, but we'll show you how it's done. That includes me. I'm going fishing with the master chief tomorrow, but I have duty on Sunday and will be here all day. I'm not going to seek you out, but if you ask for help on anything, you'll get it."

I could see a huge weight lifted off of Mack's shoulders. Overcome with relief, he stood up and said, "Thank you! Thank you, Doyle! You won't regret…"

Macklemore looked like he was getting ready to hug me, but I stopped him before he took two steps. "No! Ew. Just no. Don't fucking touch me. Get out of here and go clean yourself up somewhere. Jesus Christ."

*****

CHAPTER 7

The *Pescado Grande* was a beautiful boat. A thirty-six-foot Bertram, it was the smaller of the master chief's vessels but able to comfortably accommodate the craft's captain, Miggy Salinas, and six guests. In addition to Darrow and I, with us that day were four of the master chief's friends, mainly men he worked with while doing one of his shore rotations billeted to some sort of policing assignment. The command master chief of the 32nd Street Naval Station, BMCM Andrew Cairns, was the exception.

Senior Chief Brian Mileski was currently the top enlisted man running the Master-at-Arms detachment on base. It became apparent he spent way too much time on shore duty when the coastline disappeared beyond the horizon, and Mileski ran for the side to get seasick.

Wilson Fitzpatrick was a Special Operations Supervisor with the US Border Patrol. He cut his teeth in law enforcement working alongside Darrow in Pearl Harbor. Deputy Sam Dreyfus was with the San Diego Sheriff's Street Gang Task Force and became acquainted with the master chief while investigating how the Posole Locos ended up with an active cell aboard the *USS Long Beach*.

Captain Miggy's favorite fishing grounds were well south of the Coronado Islands, requiring us all to purchase Mexican fishing licenses. From there, it was a short jaunt to where the yellowfin tuna ran, and I must admit that hooking into fish that big and powerful was some of the most fun I have ever had with my clothes on.

It was also a lot of work. The tuna we hooked were huge, running over one hundred pounds, and since it was virtually unheard of to see this type of fish running those waters in late January, we had them all to ourselves. Within two hours, our shoulder muscles were screaming at us, and we decided to head north for some easier bottom fishing off the coast of Tijuana.

Pulling into another of the captain's favorite spots, Miggy turned to us and said, "Make sure you all have your licenses available, guys."

"Why?" my master chief asked. "What's up?"

"We got a TJ harbor patrol boat up ahead of us at 11 o'clock."

Darrow stood up to take a look. "No kidding?"

"Is that a problem?" asked Deputy Dreyfus.

The master chief shook his head. "Naw. Not really. Everything here's all above board. It's just unusual. Right, Miggy?"

The *Pescado*'s captain nodded. "Yeah, it's no big deal. Just make sure you know where your licenses are. That's all."

Everyone reached for their wallets to do a double-check, but it was unnecessary. The harbor patrol seemed uninterested in what we were doing and made no attempt to check us.

Bottom fishing off the Coronado Islands was much different than angling for tuna offshore. Most of the time, we were just loading our hooks, dropping them into the depths, then reeling them back in to see if anything filched our bait. We had about a dozen sea lions swarming our boat from the moment we arrived, so our anchovies were getting stolen off our lines before they got halfway to where the fish were.

About thirty minutes into this battle, I heard Captain Miggy laughing while looking through his binoculars. Reaching down from the flying bridge, he handed them to Darrow and said, "Check out our Mexican friends over there."

Darrow climbed up and took a look, letting out a little laugh himself.

"What are they doing?" Master Chief Cairns asked.

"The same thing we are."

"Fishing?" asked Fitzpatrick.

"Yep."

"No shit?" I asked. "Who goes fishing on a harbor patrol boat?"

"Someone high enough up the food chain to not be worried about getting caught commandeering public resources for personal use." Fitzpatrick was the Border Patrol agent. He climbed up to the bridge and held out his hand. "Mind if I take a look?"

Darrow handed him the binoculars. "Be my guest."

After a couple of moments, Fitzpatrick started giggling himself. "Man, those guys have no shame at all."

"Who is it?" Mileski was getting better, but he still looked a little green.

"It looks like the Tijuana police chief, Marco Baylon."

While Fitzpatrick looked over our neighbors, Master Chief Cairns suddenly let out a cry of excitement. "Holy shit!" he yelled. "I got a big one! Bigger than those goddamn tuna!"

We all turned to look at him, and it appeared that he had. His pole doubled over, and instead of going below the boat, his line was stretching out toward the shore. He had something big. Really big.

"What is it?" asked Fitzpatrick, setting down his binoculars. Our boat had suddenly become more interesting than the Mexicans across the water.

"I don't know," Darrow said. Typically, the catch around the Coronado Islands was sea bass, sculpin, and rock cod. None are much of a fight. Cod can be massive, but they tended to swim straight down. Reeling them in was like pulling up a dead log. "Maybe he got a shark."

"Cool!" I fished with Darrow semi-regularly but never saw anyone catch a shark before. "How big do you think it is?"

As if to answer my question, the monster on the end of the line pulled hard, jerking Cairns right to the deck's edge. If Mileski had not been there to grab him, the fish might have caught Cairns instead of the other way around. Darrow laughed. "Whatever it is, it's huge!"

Our boat became a flurry of commotion. There were six hands on Cairns' fishing pole trying to keep him from flying into the drink. Fitzpatrick and I reeled in the rest of the lines to keep them from getting fouled. Things got really loud, really quick, and I saw that we caught the attention of the harbor patrol. They pulled anchor and idled over to see what was going on.

When they got within earshot, the Mexicans called out to us. Fitzpatrick looked up at Miggy and asked, "What are they saying?"

"Fuck if I know," Miggy said, mildly irritated by the assumption that because of his Latino name, he spoke Spanish. His family traced its lineage back to Barcelona, and his ancestors landed in California via Ellis Island, not Tijuana. He was no more Mexican than Fitzpatrick was.

"They're asking if they can help," I said.

"Help?" laughed Darrow. "How the hell are they going to help from over there?"

I shrugged. "They're just trying to be nice."

Turning towards the harbor patrol boat, I cupped my hands around my mouth and yelled out, "*Muchas gracias amigos pero todos es bueno!*" I let them know that at least for the moment, everything was fine.

The men on the boat laughed, and I caught one of them saying something like, "Ha! The white boy speaks Spanish!" He used the term "*wedo*," though, which was derogatory enough to earn the patrolman a look of rebuke from the police chief.

"What did he catch?" asked the pilot of the harbor patrol boat.

I shrugged my shoulders, exaggerating the movement enough so that they could see it over the distance. "I don't know!"

But then we did. The beast Cairns was fighting so hard leaped above the water with an impressive splash and then let out a pitiful cry of distress. The command master chief had hooked a harbor seal.

My heart sank. The Mexicans erupted in laughter. The seals had been stealing their bait all day too, and seeing us hook one made them feel like they were inflicting a bit of revenge for all their lost anchovies.

Miggy stepped down from the bridge and patted Cairns on the shoulder. "Bummer. Tough break, man. You know what you have to do when you hook a seal, don't you?"

"No. What?"

Miggy grabbed the pole. "You land the bitch!" Placing his foot on the rail for leverage, the *Pescado's* captain then put his shoulders into reeling the seal in while the guys on the harbor patrol boat cheered.

TEQUILA VIKINGS

I winced and looked over at Darrow. "Master Chief, this is kind of messed up. Can't we just let it go?"

"We will, but we have to get the line cut as close to its mouth as we can. If we don't, it'll get tangled up in the kelp and drown."

It took about twenty minutes for Miggy to pull the seal in, clip the line, and release it. By then, the Mexicans were right beside us. "I hope you're all going home with a little more than that!" the police chief laughed. I translated for the rest of the men on our boat.

"Don't worry! We are!" Darrow assured them.

"So are we!" the police chief boasted. He then reached into a cooler and pulled out a lunker sand bass that looked at least ten pounds.

We nodded to show we were all impressed. It was big for a sand bass. Darrow motioned for Fitzpatrick and me to follow him to our hold. When the three of us hoisted up the one hundred and fifty-pound yellowfin we caught near Ensenada, the chief's eyes got as large as dinner plates. He then berated his officers for being such poor fishing guides.

After dropping the tuna, Darrow grabbed a few beers from the cooler and tossed them over to the patrol boat. They reciprocated by tossing us a bottle of tequila, and we invited them to tie up alongside.

With our vessels lashed together, the men from the patrol boat came aboard, and we all introduced ourselves. "Where did you get those fish?" the police chief asked.

"*Cerca de Ensenada, Don Baylon,*" I told him. Near Ensenada.

"*Por favor, llamame Marco,*" Baylon answered, asking me to call him by his first name, putting us at ease by appealing to our American habit of informality.

For the next thirty minutes, I translated the conversation between Master Chief Darrow and the commander of Tijuana's police department about how to catch yellowfin. *Señor* Baylon was disappointed to learn that the harbor patrol vessel was not up to the task. "Maybe I need to buy myself a boat like this one."

Darrow shook his head. "Nah, they're a waste of money." He pulled a card out of his wallet and handed it to the man. "If you want to go do some real fishing, you call me, and I'll make sure you have a good time."

Baylon beamed, accepting the master chief's card and assuring him that someday soon, he would take Darrow up on his offer.

I continued translating for the time it took to exhaust our beer supply and their cache of tequila. After we were all quite drunk, we helped our new friends back aboard their boat, gave them one of our tuna, and sent them on their way.

Before leaving, Marco Baylon turned to me and, in nearly flawless English, said, "Thank you for translating for us. It still needs work, but for a *gringo*, your Spanish is very good. You need to spend more time in Tijuana to clean it up."

"You speak English?" I asked. "Why were you having me translate?"

"To be polite to my men, who don't speak your language very well. Also, I like Americans who respect my culture enough to learn Spanish, so I wanted you to look good for your boss. Like I said, come to Mexico and keep working on it."

I smiled. "I already spend a lot of time in Tijuana, *Don* Baylon."

"You do? Good! I hope to see you sometime down there."

"No offense, my friend, but my goal when I am in Tijuana is to have as little interaction with the police as possible."

Baylon laughed. "I don't blame you. That's a wise goal, *mi amigo*. I like you. If you ever find yourself in trouble in Tijuana, feel free to reach out to me." With that, the police chief shook my hand before I helped him back to his boat. I then assisted Miggy in casting them off.

"I don't want to tell you your business Brad," I heard Fitzpatrick say to my master chief once the Mexicans left. "But are you sure it's a good idea getting cozy with these guys? I know firsthand that the Tijuana cops are into some really crooked shit down here, and the higher up you go, the worse it gets."

"What're you trying to say, Fitz?" Darrow asked. "You think it'd be a better idea to tell them to fuck off considering that we're bobbing about ten miles deep into their territorial waters?"

"No, I'm just warning you that there are some seriously twisted things going on down here. I'm predicting that within ten years, Mexico is going to start making Colombia look positively bucolic when it comes to *narco* violence."

Darrow shrugged. "All the more reason to make some friends among the locals to help keep my business from being affected, isn't it?"

TEQUILA VIKINGS

*****

On Monday morning, I woke up completely refreshed. I had slept for nearly eighteen hours while on duty the day before, so I was out of my rack much earlier than usual. After a casual breakfast and my morning cigarette, I made my way up to the flight deck before anyone else and took in the crisp morning San Diego air.

Sand Dog, as we sailors called it, was beautiful on Monday mornings during the winter. Being a desert, it held virtually zero humidity in the air, so once cleansed of all the exhaust, it cleared up enough that you could see some of the mountain peaks in Mexico if you looked hard enough.

The flight deck of the *USS Belleau Wood* provided a great vantage point to take in the city. Towering several stories above the waterline, I could see the skyscrapers downtown, the Coronado Bridge, and the Mediterranean homes that looked down from the hilltops above. It was so alien from the Rust Belt urban decay of my home in Detroit that I never tired of seeing it.

Nor did I ever tire of looking over the 32nd Street Naval Station. It was thirteen piers full of haze gray maritime sentinels guarding America's sunset coast against the specter Karl Marx warned us about one hundred and fifty years before.

By 1992 however, the communists had defeated themselves. They crumbled not in the face of an unstoppable American military juggernaut but because, economically speaking, they could not manufacture anything of quality other than assault rifles, furry hats, and vodka. They could not even manage to make a decent pair of blue jeans.

The Soviet Union evaporated before our eyes in 1991. After that, I found myself in the most powerful military in history, with no real viable enemy to confront. Having lost the opportunity to quench our thirst for adventure in combat, many of my shipmates and I sought solace in alcohol-fueled mischief. In this, we were truly elite, a regular inebriate SEAL team. Tequila Vikings, we called ourselves.

As men started gathering around the flight deck to prepare for morning roll call, I made my way back to our mustering area. A few CSE people had already gathered in formation, like Rick Hammond, who was always early. This time though, so was ET3 Macklemore. I missed him the day before as

I was trying to sleep off all the drinking I had done on Saturday. To be honest, I had forgotten all about him.

Sighing and determined to get everything over with, I walked up to Warren and calmly called him to the position of attention. "You do everything I asked, Mack?"

Warren nodded. "Yeah. I think so."

Tempting fate, I leaned in and drew a deep breath of air through my nose. "Well, you smell pretty good this morning. You take a shower?"

"Yes, ET2."

"Good. Your haircut looks good. Your cover looks good. Good shave. Your gig line is straight. Your shoes are shined, and your name's stenciled in the proper places on your dungarees. How long have you been in the Navy, Warren?"

"Three years," Macklemore told me.

I was legitimately impressed. It seemed inconceivable that someone like Mack could have survived so long in any branch of the military. "Three years. When do they teach you how you're supposed to wear your uniform?"

"In boot camp."

"In basic training. That's right," I agreed. "Okay. Warren, did they teach you what shoulder your rank is supposed to go on in basic?"

I watched Warren swallow uncomfortably. "Yeah, I think so."

"Okay. What shoulder did the Navy tell you to iron your rank on, Mack?"

Pointing to his right shoulder, Warren asked, "Uh, this one?" It was a nice try.

"You trying to tell me I ironed my rank on the wrong shoulder? Did Hammond put his on the wrong shoulder too? What about Schiff?"

"I…uh…uh…I …" Macklemore was once again trembling.

"Did you ask anybody from Radar Repair for help? Like I told you to?"

"I…uh…no…uh… I'm sorry…"

"So, you did all of this yourself?"

"Yes, I…uh…" Macklemore hung his head. "I'm sorry. You're turning in the report chit, aren't you?"

TEQUILA VIKINGS

I nodded. "Yeah, I am. I'm going to turn it in tomorrow. Unless you can do better then than you did today. Your pants and boondockers look good. If you get assigned a working party, put on old dungarees, okay?"

"I can't. I threw them all away. They stunk."

You could have washed them. "Really? Okay. It's a good start. Look, pick your best set of dungarees and make it your morning muster uniform. Change out of it immediately after we're dismissed. Okay?"

"Okay."

"And pay attention to detail. How the hell do you iron your rank on the wrong goddamn shoulder after all this time? Jesus Christ. Other than that, though, you look good. And you're not odiferous. You've bought yourself another twenty-four hours as a third class electronics technician, Mack. Congratulations."

*****

CHAPTER
8

Lieutenant Howe, my division officer since I reported aboard the *Belleau Wood*, retired at the end of January. I always thought highly of him. He did his time, enjoyed a distinguished career, and, realizing that Master Chief Darrow had the CSE Division running seamlessly, left us all alone. Sometimes being a good leader simply required knowing when not to get in the way.

Mr. Howe's successor had little use for the subtle art of non-interference, however. Like Howe, Lieutenant Junior Grade Andrew Krause was also prior-enlisted, but unlike his predecessor, the new Electronics Materials Officer could not stop acting like a chief. He tended to leap into the minutiae of any initiative he pushed and was psychologically incapable of delegating anything to his senior enlisted subordinates. As a result, Krause got in his own way just as often as he got into ours.

Micro-management is hard enough to pull off for a capable officer. For one who has little idea what his men do for a living, it is virtually impossible. Krause spent most of his enlisted career as a boatswain's mate. He cross-rated to Data Systems Technician when he was an E-5. At the time, DSs were a hot commodity, and they fled the Navy in droves to take advantage of the premium pay they commanded in the civilian sector. There were so many open billets to fill that candidates could earn promotion just by spelling their names correctly on the advancement exam.

Krause made E-6 when he graduated from C School. As a result, he became the Leading Petty Officer of his division immediately after reporting to his first command in his new rate. Since LPOs are more managers than technicians, he never had the chance to learn his job before he rolled into the Enlisted Commissioning Program, and it showed. The lieutenant could barely keep up with the jargon of his DS techs and was hopelessly lost whenever an ET tried to explain equipment failures to him.

To make matters worse, our new division officer had a complex about his technical inadequacy. He compensated by directing his attention to the military aspects of Navy life, which he understood, to the detriment of the technical side of our work, which he did not. Instead of maintaining and repairing our gear, Krause had us spending most of our time cleaning spaces, shining shoes, and all the other mundane chores that were usually the bane of non-technical rates.

If the new lieutenant wanted his men to be all spit and polish, that was fine. LTJG Krause just needed to tell the chiefs what he wanted done and order them to make it so. Darrow and Ramirez could have found the balance between getting us to bend towards the lieutenant's predilections without negatively impacting equipment readiness. Our new EMO was just not wired that way, however. He needed to dog us personally, and if he felt it necessary to make his men miserable, he was not going to deny himself the pleasure of watching us suffer from a ring-side seat.

This became apparent the first time we met him. Krause was a severe-looking man and came to us in a uniform that was spotless, starched, and pressed with razor-sharp military creases. Even though the day was overcast and unusually dark for San Diego, the lieutenant introduced himself sporting the impenetrable sunglasses that became his trademark. He wore them both inside and out, and there were enlisted men who served through Krause's entire duration aboard the *USS Belleau Wood* who never actually saw his eyes.

As he approached our formation with the chiefs on his first day, Tony Bard did an about-face and called out, "Ah-teeeeeen-HUT."

Unlike in movies, very few sailors crisply "snap-to" the position of attention outside of boot camp. We generally straightened our postures, put our feet together, took our hands out of our pockets, and tried to look as if we were paying attention. This was not good enough for Mr. Krause.

"What in the world was that?" he asked as he stepped up to the formation. "Seriously? What was that? Do you men not know how to go to the position of attention? Pah-raaaaaaaaade REST!"

We all went to "parade rest" with feet apart and both hands pressed into the small of our backs. The division lacked parade-ground precision, but we got there.

"You've got to be kidding me," Krause muttered with exasperation. "AH! TEEEEENNNNN HUT!!!"

We all snapped to attention more or less in unison. Except for Macklemore. He was a full half-second behind the rest of us. "Come on, people! PAH-RAAAAAAADE REST!"

We snapped to parade rest. "AH! TEEEEENNNNN HUT!!!"

Back to attention. Back to parade rest. Back to attention. Back to parade rest. This went on for thirty minutes. As the rest of the ship's divisions broke formation and reported to their workstations, we practiced drill on the flight deck. "Wow," Krause said, shaking his head in disgust. "Just wow, gentlemen." Turning and taking a couple of steps towards Darrow, he asked the master chief, "Is that the best the men of the famous O-LONG-apo Earp can do?"

"I'll get them doing better," Darrow assured him.

"Well, they certainly can't do much worse." Krause turned his back on the chiefs and then strolled over to me. "Petty Officer…" the lieutenant paused to read the name stenciled on my dungaree shirt. "Murphy, is it? You one of the leaders of this rabble?"

"I'm the work center supervisor of Radar Repair, sir."

Krause perked up an eyebrow. "The guy with all the porn?"

"No sir, that's…"

"Don't lie to me. I already heard all about it. If you're the work center supervisor, how come you're not setting a better example for your men?"

"Sir, the porn is…"

"Forget the smut. I'm talking about your appearance. Your uniform. Why are you not setting the standard here?"

TEQUILA VIKINGS

I stole a glance down to make sure I had not accidentally rolled around in horse vomit without realizing it. "Am I in violation of something I'm not aware of, sir?"

"If you consider yourself a leader of men, petty officer, then you should be standing up here looking better than any of them." Krause scanned the formation until his eyes rested on Macklemore, who he called out to join us in front of the division.

Crusty Warren was on day twelve of showing up to muster on time and inspection ready, a personal record. Every morning I found something wrong with him, but it was getting increasingly difficult. That particular morning, Macklemore was the sharpest sailor in the division.

"Look at this man. Bright white cover. Fresh set of dungarees. Boondockers spit-shined. Military creases in his shirt. Have you seen this man's creases?" Krause asked me.

Yeah, I put them there teaching him how to work an iron without hurting himself. "Yes sir, they are exceptional creases."

"All of you! I want you to take a good look at this man!" As the lieutenant shouted this, I watched Darrow and Chief Ramirez facepalm themselves and start shaking their heads, knowing right where the new EMO was going. "You need to heed this man's example! I want you to look at him, study him, and I want you to *be* him! This is a man who obviously has himself together!"

I had to give the division credit for not bursting into laughter. It was something I struggled to do myself.

"It looks to me like you've been lacking some basic discipline, gentlemen. Let me assure you that this will not continue under my command. I expect...no...I demand that my division sets the standard for personal appearance! I demand that we have the cleanest spaces! I demand that we be the benchmark for personal conduct and integrity! Anything less will be dealt with severely! Is that understood?"

"YES, SIR!" we all shouted out.

"Are you sure?"

"YES, SIR!"

"Good! I will be touring the spaces first thing this morning. You're all dismissed. Get to your work stations and await my arrival."

After Krause cut us loose, the men scattered like cockroaches, hoping to get out of sight and out of mind before the new lieutenant realized he forgot to assign anyone to the daily working parties.

As a second-class petty officer, I did not worry about extra work details, so I took my time. Warren Macklemore, being used to hard labor, was not in any hurry either. "I'm sorry, Doyle," Mack said as he stepped beside me.

"Sorry? Sorry for what?"

"I didn't mean to get you in trouble with the new EMO."

"Trouble?" I had to think about it for a second, but then I laughed. Living dangerously, I swung my arm around Warren's neck and pulled him in close without taking a precautionary whiff of him first. "That wasn't trouble, Warren. That was just the new guy trying to show everybody his dick. I was far more pissed off about being mistaken for Palazzo than I was about your uniform looking better than mine. Mack, any time you feel like trying to get me in trouble by making me look bad in comparison to you, you go right ahead. Every time you succeed, I'll give you an amnesty day on the threat to turn in that report chit. Understand?"

"Sure."

I let Macklemore go and watched him scurry off. I was impressed. Warren still could not fix his gear or correctly remember and carry out a complex set of directions, but at least he looked good.

As I walked towards the island structure, I caught Darrow passing me from behind. "You know that guy, Master Chief? The new lieutenant?"

"Nope," Darrow answered.

"You sure? The way he called you 'Olongapo Earp'…it sounded to me like there was some bad blood between you."

The master chief agreed. "Yeah, I picked up on that. He bristled when I introduced myself this morning also. I got the feeling he's not a fan. I don't know the man, but I'm going to be making some phone calls tonight. I'm sure by the end of the day, I'll be getting to know him real good."

*****

Assuming a command and shaking things up is the norm in almost any military unit. The only thing that made Krause's inauguration as EMO extraordinary was its longevity. Two weeks into his tenure, we were still going through his motions just as hard as the day he first arrived.

On paper, there was no shop better equipped to deal with Lieutenant Krause than Radar Repair. Despite being lazy, insolent, and a mediocre radar tech, Palazzo presented himself very well in uniform. Every morning before roll call, we got dressed in our best dungarees and had him look us over before we marched up to the flight deck for muster. Krause could have found something wrong if he looked hard enough, but there were always others that looked worse to direct his attention elsewhere.

We also had Rick Hammond. Because of my arrangement with Rick to get him home early to his wife while we were in port, he repaid me by keeping our areas clean. With Macklemore assigned to Radar Repair, he had help. Our spaces were spotless before Krause reported aboard. After him, they resembled surgical suites.

At least to us, they did. To Krause, they were lairs of filth and disease. At one point, the EMO became so enraged at the state of the Radar Room One passageway that he made us deep clean it from overhead to deck three times in one day. The master chief conceded it looked no different after multiple field days than it did before them.

Going into our third week under Krause, morale plummeted, and degradations in equipment readiness started to show. We wasted so much time scrubbing already pristine spaces that there was little attention paid to our primary mission. The men of CSE Division were no longer technicians. We were over-skilled janitors.

Tempers started getting short as well. Bill Kramer, who was never a ray of sunshine to begin with, became intolerable. Kramer's relief valve, the man he used to take his frustrations out on, now worked for me. Since Bill no longer had a whipping boy accessible in Comm Repair, he started coming up to the 07 Level to blow off steam.

"Where is he?" Kramer growled as he pushed his way into my shop.

The door to Radar Repair tended to stick and needed a hard tug to get the latch to catch. It frustrated me that we could not get it fixed, and having people like Kramer barging into our space without a key added to my irritation. "Who?" I asked, though I already knew.

"Mack, goddammit! Where the hell is he?"

"What do you want? He doesn't work with you anymore."

"Yeah, well, then he needs to leave our fucking tools alone! I need a 3mm Allen wrench to perform checks on the WSCs, and I have everything BUT the fucking 3mm Allen wrench!"

In all fairness to Kramer, this was a classic Mack move. If he ever needed to pull a tool from our box to do a job, it would become lost almost immediately afterward. "How often do you have to do the check with the 3mm Allen wrench, Kramer?"

"A few times a week!"

"Is Mack still doing the maintenance on those?"

"No!" Kramer complained. "It was one of the few checks that were simple enough for that idiot to do on his own! Now I have to do it all myself!"

"Mack's been in Radar Repair for nearly a month now, Bill. If he's no longer assisting you in doing WSC-3 maintenance, that tells me either someone else lost the wrench, or you've been gun-decking your Preventative Maintenance Schedule checks."

"Gun-decking" was the Navy term for not doing the maintenance you were required to do but signing off the paperwork saying you did. It was a severe offense, and you would lose your rank over it. Kramer was notoriously lazy. I could envision him gun-decking his checks now that Mack was not around to do the menial work.

"So, which is it, Kramer?" I asked. "Did someone else lose your tool, or did you gun-deck your PMS? I suggest you go back down to Comm Repair before I start digging a little deeper into your maintenance records."

"I ain't gun-decking shit." With that, Bill slammed the door to the shop hard enough to finally get the latch to catch.

Since I did not hear Bill use the ladder to go back to the 06 Level, I assumed he went looking for Warren in our other spaces. I shook my head and turned to Palazzo, another notoriously lazy man, who was sitting in a chair reading a Penthouse Forum. "John, go down to Radar One and make sure Kramer's not causing any trouble."

"Why me?"

"Because you're an E-5. You outrank him."

"You're an E-5 too. Why don't you go do it?"

I felt my blood pressure spike. Gritting my teeth, I swung around in my chair and snarled, "Because I told *you* to!"

"I'll go," Dixie said, getting up out of his seat. "What the hell do you think Spanky's going to do about it anyway?"

That nickname always got Palazzo's blood up. "What did you just call me?"

Dixie slipped outside the door without answering. Palazzo got up to follow, forcing me to stop him. Kevin tended to forget that Palazzo outranked him. Considering how much stress everyone was under, I did not want Dixie crossing a line that Palazzo could burn him for, so I thought it best to keep them separated. "Where do you think you're going?"

Palazzo was incensed. "Did you hear what he called me?"

"I don't care! I told you to goddamn do something and you…!"

As I was starting to lay into him, Palazzo grinned like he knew something I didn't. "Don't you think you've got a bigger problem than me right now?"

"What? Wait…what are you talking about?" I suddenly felt that something was not right, but I could not put my finger on what it was.

Franklin was usually not my swiftest guy, but even he figured it out. "Hey, Doyle, do you think it's a good idea to let Dixie handle Kramer all by himself?"

"Shit!" Mixing Dixie and Kramer was far worse than mixing Dixie and Palazzo. Kevin had been looking for an excuse to bury Kramer for as long as he had been aboard. Putting those two within six feet of one another was lighting the fuse to a very big bomb. I bolted out of the shop to keep Dixie from getting us all into trouble.

When I opened the hatch to the radar room, I expected to find Kramer laid out on the deck and bleeding from a couple of orifices. To my surprise, though, Dixie was demonstrating uncharacteristic restraint while Macklemore was showing abnormal confidence. Usually, Warren would slink away from his chief tormentor with his tail between his legs. Mack was still petrified of Bill, but this time he was standing his ground.

I walked in just in time to hear Kramer indignantly ask, "What the fuck did you say to me?"

"Go find your own Allen wrench. I didn't touch it." Mack's eyes darted nervously to Dixie, giving away that he was drawing what little courage he had from Kevin's presence. He was banking on the hope that Dixie would not let Kramer get out of control.

Kramer was not used to having the division's pariah talk back to him. The color rushed into his face and, unable to check his temper, he reached out and grabbed Mack by the collar. "If you know what's good for you, you'll get your ass downstairs and…"

Mack swung his right forearm and broke Bill's grip. "Get your hands off of me!"

Kramer was stunned at first. Then he took a moment to look over Macklemore's shaking hands, his red face, and his quivering lip. He laughed. "Or what?".

Mack was trembling, but whether from fear or anger, I had no idea. I suspected that his fight or flight instincts were wreaking havoc on him internally as he tried to decide what he was going to do.

"Well?" Kramer laughed again. "What's next, you little faggot?"

"N-n-nothing," Warren stuttered. "Just go away and leave me alone."

"And if I don't?" Bill asked. He was enjoying himself. The scene playing out between Kramer and Macklemore was hard to watch for anybody who had ever attracted the attention of a schoolyard bully. I knew what Warren was going through and should have stopped it, but Bill had Macklemore cornered. Any cornered animal was dangerous, and something told me that Bill Kramer would be reminded of that very soon. It was what held me back.

I could understand why Bill did not see the potential of the situation. After breaking Kramer's grip, Mack took great care not to move in any way that Kramer could interpret as aggression. He was trying to respond to Bill but was so terrified all he could do was stutter.

"Spit it out, you pussy," Kramer barked. "What're you going to do?"

"I-I-I-I…" It began to look like Macklemore's flight instincts were getting the upper hand.

"You ain't going to do shit." To prove his point, Kramer reached out and lightly slapped Mack across the cheek. "You going to do anything about that?"

I took a step forward, but Dixie held his arm out to stop me. In the split second it took for me to push Kevin out of my way, I watched Macklemore pull back and throw a right hook at Bill's kisser.

It was poorly aimed. Mack's fist glanced off Kramer's shoulder before finding its mark, but when it hit home against Bill's chin, the blow was still powerful enough to wrench his head so far past his collar bone that the vertebrae in his neck popped. Dixie and I both dropped our jaws open. If Warren's momentum had not been interrupted by striking Bill's arm first, it could have been a knockout blow.

Bill was stunned, and his knees buckled. For a split second, I thought he was going down but at the last moment, he reached out and steadied himself on one of the SPS-40 cabinets.

When Kramer turned his head back to Macklemore, it was in disbelief and shock. Had Mack followed through right there, I was confident that Bill would have gotten his clock cleaned. Unfortunately, Mack was bracing himself for retaliation and trying to protect his body from the counterpunch. He lost the initiative and inexplicably ceded the fight.

Once he realized that Warren was no longer in the battle, Bill's disorientation turned to fury. Enraged, Kramer charged while Mack crumpled to the floor in the fetal position to weather an onslaught of body blows.

Before Bill could do any real damage, Dixie went into motion. He kicked Kramer behind the knees and dropped him to the ground. Realizing that Kevin joined the fray, it was Bill's turn to cower and prepare himself for a pummeling.

Before that could happen, though, I dove in between the two men and pulled them apart. Despite my best efforts, I got caught up in the moment and considered letting Dixie settle the Kramer issue once and for all. Then I remembered what we were all risking after what happened to Randy Green. When that realization set in, I got pissed.

I sent Dixie and Mack to the corner, then grabbed Kramer by the back of his shirt and dragged him to the exit. "When I tell you to go back to Comm Repair, I mean go back to Comm-fucking-Repair!"

Gasping, Kramer blurted out, "But Mack hit me!"

"Yeah? Oh well, you started it." I yanked Kramer up to his feet and threw him face-first against the exit hatch hard enough to make it ring. I then spun him around, grabbed him by the throat, and bounced the back of his head off of the steel even harder. It felt good. I nearly did it again. I wanted to in the worst way. I also wanted to knee him in the crotch, drive my fist into his gut, and smash my forehead into his mouth. It took incredible willpower on my part to keep my body from giving in to the urge.

Instead, I got into Kramer's face like Master Chief Darrow had at McDini's a few weeks before. "Stay away from my men," I snarled. "Stay out of my spaces. If you come up here looking for trouble again, Bill, I promise that you will fucking find it! Now get out of here or I'll turn Kevin loose on you!"

After Kramer stumbled out of the room, Dixie walked up and pumped his fist into the air. "Yeah! Fucking awesome! Just like old times!"

"Really?" I snapped at Dixie. I was furious. And frustrated. It was as if I was falling back into some addiction, or like a shark getting worked into a feeding frenzy after catching the scent of blood in the water. I desperately wanted to drag Kramer down to the Nixie Room and get medieval on him, but I couldn't. Nor could I place him on report. If I had stopped everything immediately after Kramer slapped Macklemore and wrote him up, Bill would have been an E-3 before the end of the week. If I did it now, he could counterclaim that we assaulted him in return, and every one of us would end up at captain's mast.

Unable to abuse Kramer, I turned on Kevin. "I'm glad you're feeling good about yourself, Dixie. Are you getting your thrills now by putting me in positions where I have to risk BOOST so that you can get your rocks off with Kramer? You trying to get me into another fight?"

"Hey, no, I didn't ask you to step in here! I had this all under control!"

"The fuck you did!" I yelled. "How do you think the captain's going to react after hearing of another Radar Repair beat down taking place right under his nose? He's going to think neither you, me, nor the master chief learned a goddamn thing after Green! He'll hang all three of us!"

I had not been seeing much of him then, but Dixie was the brother I chose, the closest friend I ever had. I knew he felt abandoned since I met Hannah, but I could see the last thing he wanted to do was put me at risk. He hung his head. "Doyle, I'm sorry, man..."

"I know, but you've got to start thinking, Kevin! Come on!"

"Doyle," Dixie pleaded. "Was I supposed to let Kramer beat up Warren?"

"That was my problem. I could have dealt with it," Mack said, puffing his chest out a little now that the danger had passed.

TEQUILA VIKINGS

"Like hell, you could have," Dixie retorted, pointing his finger at Warren's face. "And mark my words! Kramer's pissed about this. You know, if you'd went after his ass, you could have taken him. Now, he just thinks you got a lucky shot in. He's going to come back to finish this shit with you, Warren!"

Struck with an epiphany, I sized up Macklemore. "That was no lucky shot. Even with it broken up by Bill's shoulder, Mack still clocked Kramer hard enough to damn near knock him out. Dixie, feel his biceps. Warren, make a muscle for Kevin."

Kevin wrapped his fingers around Mack's arm and whistled in surprise. Mack had the dumpiest body I had ever seen on a military man. It was all because of lousy posture, though. Dixie found after squeezing Mack's arm that he was actually rock solid. "You been working out, Warren?"

"Yeah, he's been working out," I answered for Mack. "He's been taking the division's working parties for over a year now. That's hard physical labor. He's probably got the strength of a longshoreman but no idea how to wield it."

Dixie shook his head. "I've seen this boy run during the PT test. I don't think he's as fit as you think."

I pulled Mack's cigarettes out of his pocket and held them up in front of his face. "It's because of this. And the booze. You haven't been drinking much lately, have you?"

"Not with that report chit still hanging over my head."

"Is the chit the only reason you're off the sauce?" I asked.

Warren laughed humorlessly. "Look at me. You think I have anything better to do than stay drunk?"

I saw significant improvements in Macklemore over the past month, but nothing that suggested any fundamental shift in Mack's personality until now. I wondered why. "Warren, how come you stood up to Bill? Why now? Why not before?"

Mack shrugged. "Nobody ever had my back down in Comm Repair. I knew you guys were here to help me."

I let out a sigh and stepped closer to Macklemore to put my hand on his shoulder. "Mack, you've been doing good so far in the radar shop. As long as you carry your weight, which you have, we'll keep an eye out for you. Look, like with your uniform and stuff, we're not going to fight your battles for you, but I think Dixie here can teach you how to do it yourself. Do you think you can do that, Kevin? You think you can turn our boy here into another Tequila Viking?"

Dixie looked surprised. "You mean, teach him to fight?" he asked. "Yeah, I can teach him the mechanics, but I can't teach him to have heart. Mack, your problem isn't power; it's your head. You could have won that fight just now, but you gave up after one punch. What the fuck was that?"

Warren cast his eyes toward the floor. "I'm not a fighter like you guys are. I didn't want to get hurt."

"You weren't going to until you gave up!" Dixie snapped. "Dude, if you're going to hit a man, you better do it with the intent of putting the motherfucker down, not pissing him off!"

"Look," I said, hoping to stop Dixie before he went off on a tangent. "The boy needs some confidence. Do you think you can build it by sparring with him in the ring? By showing him what he's got?"

Kevin looked Macklemore over from head to toe. "Maybe. We can see." He sounded willing to try, but less than confident.

Still, I took that as a yes and ran with it. "Mack, Dixie's going to teach you to fight so you can handle Kramer. He's good at it. Even better than I am. I'm going to have Claude Metaire work on getting you into shape. You've got the strength, but you need stamina."

Confidence. Confidence. We need to instill him with confidence. If he doesn't believe in himself, it doesn't matter what we teach him to do with his fists. He'll never apply it. "We're not stopping there either, Mack. We're also going to work on your tech skills. I suspect you tugged on enough heartstrings that the instructors pushed you through ET A School even though you don't seem to have any aptitude for the job. How the hell did you test high enough on the ASVAB to strike as an ET to begin with?"

Macklemore shrugged. "I've always done good on tests. Even in A School. It's putting it to use that's always messed me up."

I was the exact opposite. I bombed enough exams to nearly get tossed out of ET School twice. I did well enough on the practical assessments to squeak through graduation, though. "Alright," I said, thinking on the fly. "Hammond is the division's best technician. He's going to work on at least getting you adequate on the gear. Palazzo's not good for much, but I can't knock him when it comes to uniform stuff. He's going to be in charge of keeping you presentable."

"What about Franklin?" Dixie asked, deducing that Macklemore was quickly becoming an all-hands effort. "What's he going to do? Give Mack dating tips?"

I grimaced. Sexually speaking, Todd Franklin was every bit as perverse as Palazzo. The man was shameless. The women he picked up were heinous, old, and alcoholic. There was no way I was letting him play the part of Macklemore's matchmaker.

But it put a thought in my head. A woman could do wonders for boosting a man's confidence. I wondered if Hannah knew any girls with really low self-esteem and weird fetishes for body odor and acne so severe it could be mistaken for larval-stage leprosy.

*****

Dixie and I were nearly to the shop when Palazzo stepped out of the door. Still stung over the "Spanky" slight, Gianni stuck his finger out at Kevin and snapped, "You and me need to talk! Get back to the Radar Room!"

Wanting to discuss my ideas about Macklemore with him, I patted Palazzo on the shoulder and said, "Give it a minute. I want a quick word."

"Doyle, you can suck my dick too and…"

That was enough. Still not entirely wound down from what just happened with Kramer, I exploded. Without even thinking, I bunched up my fist and sent it flying towards Palazzo's face. Only at the very last moment did I realize what I was doing and redirect the blow, punching the cover of the fuse box outside our shop door instead. It made a startling racket, sounding like a cymbal hit with a police baton. I then lunged at Palazzo and screamed, "IF YOU EVER FUCKING TALK TO ME LIKE THAT AGAIN…!"

Surprised, Palazzo jumped backward and slammed into the unlatched door of Radar Repair. It fell right open, sending him spilling across the shop floor, banging his head against the corner of the test equipment storage racks.

I burst into the shop right after him. Palazzo scampered across the deck like a drunken crab searching for safe haven while Franklin bolted from the room to avoid becoming a witness. He knew the drill.

"You want to go to war?!?" I yelled. "We'll go to fucking war! I'll start right now by writing you up for insubordination! Then we'll march on down to your locker to find your porn, and I'll write you up for disobeying a direct order from the fucking captain too! How do you think that will work out for you, you worthless wad of dick spit?!?"

I was raging. Part of it was the stress our new division officer was putting us under, and part of it was Kramer. A lot of it was just that I was sick of Palazzo, though.

"Who do you think is going to bat for you at captain's mast after I write you up?!? Let me spell it out for you! NO ONE! Master Chief and I both want you off the ship! We already took your job! We'll take your fucking chevrons, John! We'll take your career too if you don't watch your step, and after we make you a civilian, I'll hunt you down and kick the fucking shit out of you!"

Palazzo found his corner and had the sense to stay down and keep his mouth shut. I was able to straddle him but was careful not to make any physical contact whatsoever. I watched his false bravado melt away and saw how terrified he was, fearing he might reunite with Randy Green at Balboa Hospital if he made any misstep at all.

"Those two chevrons don't make you a tough guy, asshole. The men see right through that shit. How well do you think you're going to do if we take one of them away and make you junior to Dixie? Fuck, Spanky, you'll even be junior to Kramer!"

In frustration, I swiped a stack of technical manuals off the filing cabinet, sending them raining down on top of him. I then grabbed a chair and set it in the middle of the floor, facing my desk. Walking back over to Palazzo, I extended my hand and offered to help him up. He refused it and got to his feet himself. "Take a seat," I said, forcing myself to calm down.

I sat in my chair and faced Palazzo, lighting a cigarette and blowing the smoke towards the ceiling. "Are you alright?" I asked. When he fell through the door and into the equipment rack, he cracked his skull pretty hard. "Do you need to go to medical?"

TEQUILA VIKINGS

After Palazzo shook his head, I said, "Good. So what're our options here, John? Do you want to go to war with me? I'm perfectly fine with that. I'll win, and you know it. Is that what you want to do?"

It took a while for Palazzo to answer. I was sure he was trying to formulate a way to take me down for what just happened, but since I never actually touched him, he came up short. Finally, he said, "No."

"Well, I'm done settling things in the Nixie room, so my options are limited. Do you have any suggestions?"

I got nothing but silence and a look of contempt. "Okay," I said. "I guess it's up to me then."

What was good enough for Macklemore was good enough for Palazzo. Opening the bottom drawer of my desk, I pulled out the second report chit I ever had to fill out as a work center supervisor. Finally, that drew a reaction. "Please, don't," Palazzo begged. "I was out of line. It won't happen again. I promise."

"So what do you think we should do? How do we fix this?"

"I don't know, Doyle. Whatever you say. Whatever you want, I'll do it. Just don't write me up."

I sat there, glaring at him as if I had not already decided. "John, you have your strengths. You present yourself well right up until the point where you open your mouth. Your hair is always cut, you have the most squared away uniform in the division, and you know how to keep your rack and locker immaculate."

I paused to let the compliment sink in. "I think most of your problem is that you don't have anything to do here. You need a job. I'm going to give you one. Macklemore."

I expected Palazzo to protest, but he accepted it without a hint of resistance. "What do you want me to do?"

"I want you to switch racks with Franklin, so you're right across from him. You're to make sure he gets up when you do. I want you to make sure he showers, shaves, and brushes his teeth. Eat breakfast with him so he doesn't slop all over himself. Inspect him before quarters and have him corrcct whatever you gig him on. Make sure he immediately changes out of his inspection uniform before he goes to any working parties. Don't let him have his first cigarette of the day until then. Got it?"

"Got it."

"After work, look him over again at his bunk and give him the appropriate orders to make sure he remains squared away. Things like his laundry, ironing his clothes, or getting a haircut."

"Okay."

"You do what you have to do with Mack, John. If you need someone to ride, he's your guy. Your goal here is to mold him, though, to teach him and to guide him. You need to keep in mind that this isn't his punishment. It's yours. This one's off the books, but the next one is official. Is that clear?"

Palazzo nodded. "Yes."

"Now, I'm going to level with you. The men don't like you, and neither do the chiefs. The department head thinks you're an embarrassment. Even if I don't write you up, you're heading for a devastating performance review."

Palazzo's shoulders slumped. Trying to give him a little hope, I added, "We're going to start working on that too. I'm having all the guys work on Mack, so I'm going to have Metaire get you back into shape and have Hammond teach you 'trons.'"

"I don't think Hammond's going to like that," John said.

"You're right, Palazzo. He's not, and he doesn't deserve it. Consider that and adjust your attitude accordingly. Understand?"

"Yes."

"Do you have any questions?" I asked.

"No. Thank you. Once again, Doyle, I'm so sorry." I sensed sincerity in Palazzo's voice as he stood up to leave.

When he was gone, I took several deep breaths. I wanted to kick Palazzo's teeth in. I wanted to bust Kramer in the chops as well. I was ashamed to admit it, but there were times that I got so frustrated with Macklemore that I wanted to slap him too. Before Green, I might have slugged them all. Hell, even now, I found that I could still barely restrain myself sometimes.

I was trying to do better. After what happened to Randy Green, I promised that I would never raise my hand against another man ever again. Despite that, within the space of fifteen minutes, I came dangerously close to pummeling, not one, but two of my shipmates in short order. I knew that could not have been normal.

TEQUILA VIKINGS

I began to wonder how skewed my tolerance for violence was because of my childhood. I wondered if, possibly, it was military culture that cultivated my kind of casual aggression. Were servicemen just more likely to settle scores with their fists than people did in civilian society? I was not sure. I had seen, not to mention participated in, an awful lot of fighting in high school. Yet there were people in my division like Tony Bard and Chief Ramirez who went their entire lives without ever throwing a punch in anger.

I was curious to what extent fighting occurred in the other branches of the military. For that matter, was it just my ship that had a little more tolerance toward settling conflicts with our fists than other commands? Then again, was it only our division? I had a hard time imagining the Medical Department guys beating each other's asses in the fan rooms as often as we did. Or was it just the company I kept?

Ultimately, after I put a little more thought into it, I ended up wondering, *Or is it just me?*

*****

CHAPTER
9

Zone inspections were usually sources of major stress. These exercises started with the captain inspecting our uniforms at morning muster. They ended four to five hours later after the skipper finished touring the division's areas to ensure that the spaces were clean and the equipment in optimum working order. We used to spend a week working from dawn to dusk to prepare for the captain's scrutiny, but after Krause took charge, there was nothing more we could do for these evolutions that we were not already doing every other day.

Historically speaking, a pair of cement shoes could not sink a zone inspection faster than Warren Macklemore. There was one time when, despite spending an entire week preparing for it, Mack woke up late on the day it was held and forgot it was even happening. He showed up unshaven, brandishing that unmistakable Crusty Warren aroma, and wearing the same uniform he donned through four straight days of working parties. That was the closest I ever came to seeing Master Chief Darrow take a human life.

If we could have removed Macklemore from the zone inspection equation and put him on watch somewhere, we would have. However, Captain Fleming was wise to that trick, and Warren was such a high-profile dipshit that the skipper specifically looked for him to see if he was making any progress.

This time Macklemore looked sharp, though he seemed incapable of realizing it. The man was a bundle of nerves all morning waiting for the uniform inspection to begin. If there was an open mirror, he was searching for an odd hair he missed shaving, an errant smudge on his belt buckle, or a dangling thread popping out of a seam that he had not caught.

The crew noticed this and appreciated his effort. I heard several people tell Warren to relax and reassure him that he was looking great. Even Bill Kramer slapped Mack on the back at one point and said, "You're worrying about this way too much. You're squared away now, but if you keep primping yourself, you're going to mess something up."

Kramer nearly proved prophetic. Warren spent so long in the bathroom looking himself over that he lost track of time and ended up late for roll call. Tony Bard did not mark him tardy, but Mack barely snuck into the back of the formation just before the captain entered our field of vision.

"Ah!-TEEEEEEEN-HUT!!!" Master Chief Darrow shouted.

We all snapped to attention as the captain arrived, flanked by Krause and our department head, LCDR Barry Winston. Per usual, Captain Fleming was all smiles and acting as if inspecting our division was the highlight of his day.

As he went down the rows of men, the captain greeted each of us by name and asked how we were doing. On the rare occasions that he found something to gig us on, he took time to explain the discrepancy. He criticized constructively with the intention of teaching, not humiliating.

It happened behind my back, but I heard when the skipper got to Mack. It was no surprise that the captain would spend extra time on our division's problem child. "Nice shave, Petty Officer Macklemore. If I remember correctly, that was what got hit last time. Is that correct?"

"Yes, sir." That was one of them. There were others, but they were too numerous to mention.

"Great ironing job on your dungaree shirt. Your creases are very sharp. Anybody help you with those?"

I could hear the pride in Macklemore's voice when he answered. "No, sir. I did that myself."

"Good job, son! You know, I've seen you around the ship lately. You've been working hard, and it shows. I understand that you're in Petty Officer Murphy's shop now. Listen to that young man and I guarantee he'll take care of you. Keep up the good work!"

"I will! Thank you, sir." *Confidence.* I heard it in Macklemore's voice for the very first time.

The captain moved on to the rear of the formation to look at the last row from behind. That was usually very quick, but something caught his eye, and I heard Fleming gasp, "What the...?!?"

There was then some mumbling between the officers. I could not tell what was said, but none of them sounded pleased. The captain then stormed to the front of the formation, visibly angry. "Petty Officer Macklemore! Front and center!"

Warren inhaled hard enough for me to hear, and as he marched to the head of the formation, several other men had the same reaction. After Mack took his place in front of us, we all saw the bold black fingerprints smeared across his right shoulder with shoe polish.

Mack was at attention but trembling, thinking he had messed up once again. Seeing this, the captain patted him on the shoulder. "Relax, son. You're okay."

The skipper stepped between Mack and the division and took a good long look at the fingerprints. So did I, seething. When the captain turned around to face us, he must have seen something in my eyes that he did not like. Fleming pointed his index finger in my direction and said, "You need to settle down, son."

Addressing the division as a whole, Fleming asked, "Who thinks this is funny? Anyone? Let me tell you something, this isn't comedy. It's vandalism and cowardice. Want me to show you all how brave the man who did this is? It's easy. Whoever slapped Petty Officer Macklemore on the back with a handful of shoe polish, step up here right now."

As expected, no one budged. "Okay," the captain continued. "I stand before each and every one of you, and on my honor as an officer of the United States Navy, I swear I will grant you amnesty for this act as long as you step forward within the next ten seconds and reveal yourself. After that, when I figure out who you are, you'll be busted a paygrade, lose half a month's pay times two, and draw sixty days of restriction and extra duty. Any takers?"

Captain Fleming stared at his watch for a while before counting down. "…five…four…three…two…one. No deal. I'm hardly surprised."

The captain looked at the smudges once more. "Too bad we can't see fingerprints on that. Luckily, shoe polish doesn't wash off easily. Men! Hold out your hands!"

We did so with nearly as much precision as we snapped to attention, and the captain believed he found his man with the first hand he inspected. "Is this polish on your fingers, sailor?"

ET3 Bud Miles looked like he was ready to wet himself. "Yes, sir! But I didn't put those marks on Petty Officer Macklemore's uniform, sir!"

"Then how do you explain the staining on your fingers?"

"We have a zone inspection today, sir! I was shining my shoes!"

DS3 Nick Thomas was standing right next to Bud. Revealing the traces of black on his fingertips to the captain, he stammered, "I-I was shining m-my shoes also, sir!"

Fleming swore under his breath and returned to Macklemore. "Son, do you have any idea who did this to your shirt?"

Mack was already the division's outcast and our village idiot. He did not want the stain of being our snitch too. He shook his head, and when he answered, we all heard the sadness in his voice, his confidence rapidly deflating. "No, sir."

"Who slapped you on your shoulder? Who gave you an 'atta-boy!' this morning before inspection?"

"Lots of people, sir."

Fleming nodded. "Okay. That's the way it's going to be then. Petty Officer Macklemore, return to formation."

Mack saluted, then marched back to his place in the back row.

The skipper shook his head. "I've always considered CSE division one of the best aboard this vessel. You're sharp. You approach your jobs with the highest degree of professionalism, and it shows in our electronic materials' readiness rate. My only complaint is your tendency to be a little too enthusiastic in your approach to liberty. This stuff here is unacceptable, though. Especially from you."

Fleming let his words sink in for a moment before he went on. "This man has been working strenuously to better himself, gentlemen. He's striving to overcome his weaknesses, and here he is getting rewarded for his efforts by some miserable son-of-a-bitch trying to tear him back down."

The captain glared at us. "Right now, I'm speaking directly to the man who did this. *You* are not worthy of Petty Officer Macklemore. I don't know who you think you are, but you're not getting away with it. I'm canceling liberty for the entire CSE division for one week, excluding the officers, chiefs, and Petty Officer Macklemore himself. Heaven help you if your shipmates find out who you are now."

I was shocked, but it was not the collective punishment that surprised me. It was the tacit acknowledgment that if the men figured out who torpedoed our inspection just to torment Warren Macklemore, they were going to hurt him for it. The captain sounded as if he was encouraging our division to do what it took to unmask our vandal, then drag him down to the Nixie room to collect the debt of flesh owed to us in payment for our lost liberty.

Realizing that Fleming spoke in a moment of anger, I knew he would not tolerate another act of vigilante discipline carried out aboard his ship. I could understand how the rest of the division could come to a different conclusion, however. They never had the opportunity to discuss the topic one-on-one with the skipper as I had. As worried as I was that the men might solve the situation outside of proper channels, my level of concern was not even close to that of Bill Kramer's, though. Stealing a glance to my right, I saw he looked like a pet store rodent who knew he had a feeding-time reservation for a high-adrenaline tour of the python tank.

*****

No one in our division considered it much of a mystery who had ruined Macklemore's uniform, so if I wanted a piece of Bill Kramer's ass for it, I was going to have to wait in line. ET3 Stu Pulaski was particularly incensed. "My kid's birthday party is this weekend, you miserable cocksucker!" he spat. "Now, I get to spend it staring at your pathetic ass instead of being with my kids! This is fucked!"

TEQUILA VIKINGS

"I didn't do it!" Kramer's enthusiasm while voicing his innocence did little to make him more convincing.

"Bullshit!" shouted Darius Cleveland. "I heard you slap him on the back and say, 'Relax, or you'll mess something up!'" Cleveland and Sergeant Fordson were two men that Kramer could not intimidate physically. Either one of them could easily take him apart, and it looked like they were both getting ready to do so. So did Miles, Whitmore, and Willis. In fact, it appeared that the entire Comm Repair shop stood united against ET3 Kramer, except for Tony Bard. Our zone inspection was an unmitigated disaster on all fronts, and he was still dealing with the fallout in the EMO office. Had he been there, though, I had little doubt he would have some choice words for Bill as well.

"For Christ's sake!" Whitmore screamed. "We finally get Macklemore out of our hair, and you *still* found a way to make him our problem again! What the fuck's the matter with you?"

"I'm telling you, I didn't do it!" If Kramer was going to own up to his transgression, the time to do it was during the captain's window of immunity. To fess up now would have been fatal. He would get the book thrown at him at captain's mast and probably still get his teeth kicked in by his shipmates. He had no choice but to stick to his story.

"Who do you think you're fooling, you fucking prick?" Sergeant Fordson growled. "Do I need to beat the truth out of you?"

"Keep your hands off of him, Clay," I warned. "Despite what it sounded like on the flight deck, the captain personally assured me a couple of months ago that future blanket parties would end in court-martials."

"That fucking son of a bitch," Kramer whined. It began to hit him that Warren Macklemore no longer occupied the bottom rung of the division's social ladder. He now did. Bill was so mad that there were tears in his eyes. "I bet that piece of shit ruined his own uniform just to make it look like I did it!"

Several of us scoffed. "Nobody's buying that shit, Kramer," Fordson told him. "It's bad enough you don't have the balls to admit it, but trying to pin this on Mack only shows how pathetic you really are."

"Seriously! Guys!" Kramer pled. "Why are you so quick to take his word over mine? The guy's a fuck up! Don't you remember what he was like in here? He was the most worthless man in the entire division."

"The key word there is 'was,'" Cleveland corrected him. "He _was_ the most worthless man in the division."

Kramer scanned the faces of his shipmates, unable to believe they all turned on him. It was a harmless little prank. He did things like this to Macklemore for months, and no one ever objected. But then again, up until now, no one but Macklemore ever suffered from it.

Bill would never admit that he was wrong, not even to himself. I watched the wheels spin in his head as he rationalized how this was not his fault, twisting it in a way that he could blame it all on Macklemore. If Warren had been a little smarter, he would have known Bill was up to something and caught the smudges before the captain. If only Mack were not Mack, none of it would have happened.

When Kramer looked up at me, I saw his eyes begin to burn. He was furious, and he was going to find a way to take it out on Macklemore.

With nothing for me to do in Comm Repair, I smiled at Bill and walked out the door, only to see Dixie storming down the passageway. "Where do you think you're going?" I asked.

"To find Kramer," Dixie answered.

"For what?"

"What do you think? I'm going to kick his fucking teeth in."

"We've been over this. No, you're not. If anyone around here's going to be practicing any recreational dentistry on Bill Kramer, it's going to be Macklemore. You need to get busy molding that boy into a fighter."

Dixie stopped and stared at me. "You serious?"

"As a heart attack," I said. "Get him to the gym and get him into the ring. Kramer's coming for him. Not today, but eventually. When he lashes out, I want Macklemore to be ready for him."

*****

Balboa Park is a twelve-hundred-acre oasis in the center of San Diego. It boasts museums, gardens, theaters, and the world-famous San Diego Zoo. The Naval Medical Center also stands upon its grounds, near its southern boundary. This gives visiting family members of the hospital's patients, many of whom had severe medical conditions, something to take their minds off their loved ones' infirmities.

TEQUILA VIKINGS

Hannah loved it, though the koala exhibit set off pangs of homesickness. After the zoo, we visited the Museum of Man, then got something to eat before going for a walk through the Australian Garden. Hannah pointed out all of the exotic trees and plants that I would see when I eventually visited Oz with her.

"Balboa is amazing," she told me after we left. "I'm so glad we came."

"It's too bad we don't have more time. I've been coming here since boot camp, and I still haven't seen everything."

"We'll come back," she said. "We're going to have plenty of time pretty soon."

"What?" I asked. "What do you mean by that?"

"Lauren's hooked up with the drummer of some new British band. She and the kids are going to England to spend the summer."

"She's not making you go with them?" Based upon what I heard, Lauren Kale was afraid to be alone with her children for very long.

"She wanted me to," Hannah laughed. "But because of my immigration status, if I left the country, I wouldn't be allowed back in. Lauren didn't want to lose me, so she's giving me a four-month-long paid vacation. From May to the end of August. I've already talked to Cheri, and she's letting me live in the Ocean Beach house! It's going to be brilliant!"

We spent the next couple of hours strolling through Balboa, talking about everything we were going to do while Hannah was living in San Diego. Before we knew it, we walked the entire length of the park without realizing it. As we turned to head back, I heard a woman behind me ask, "Doyle? Petty Oppicer Murpee?"

Recognizing the voice, I spun around to find myself face to face with Rafaela Green and her son, Manny. "Oh my god! Rafaela!" I gasped.

I stepped forward to hug Randy Green's wife. She reciprocated, though reluctantly. When we separated, I introduced her to Hannah. I then squatted down to get eye level with Manny and asked, "How's your arm doing, little man?"

"It all better now!" he answered, eagerly wriggling his mended limb.

"Good!" I said, standing back up. "How are you doing, Rafaela?"

Crossing her arms, Green's wife shook her head. "Dey still treating Randy por da seizures. He no getting bery better, you know?" Rafaela paused for a moment to collect herself. "And dey gonna send him to jail, Murpee. Apter he get better. Maybe pive years!"

I nodded my head. "Yeah, that's about what you'd get for child abuse."

Rafaela sobbed. "He no getting pive years por hurting Manny, Doyle! He getting pive years por hitting you! We no can lib here pive years widout Randy! We hab to go back to Pilippines!" At that, Rafaela completely broke down.

Hannah tried to comfort her. "I'm so sorry, love. Is there anything we can do to help?"

Rafaela looked up at me with eyes pleading in desperation. "Doyle! Please! Do not press charges against Randy! Please!"

I shook my head. "The Navy doesn't work like that, Rafaela. As far as they're concerned, Randy didn't commit a crime against me; he committed a crime against the Navy. I don't get to withdraw charges. They're going to prosecute him no matter what."

"Den tell dem da troot, Doyle! Tell dem dat Randy only trying to depend himselp!"

"What?"

"Randy so scared op you, Doyle! He knew you going to hurt heem por what he do to Manny! He no sleep! He no eat! He just worry! All da time! He worry!"

"Rafaela, I…"

"You hurt heem so bad, Doyle! You break his arm! His reebs! His nose and his jaw too! You break his head! Now it no work right and he hab da seizures! He be punished por the rest op his life por what he do to Manny! Me and Manny, we get punished por what you do to him!"

Seeing how upset his mother was getting, Manuel started crying too and hugged Rafaela's leg.

"Doyle, ip Randy go to prison, I go back to da Pilippines! I hab to go back to working in da bars. Letting da men use my body…" Rafaela was nearly hysterical now. "Manny will grow up being da son op da whore, Doyle! He will neber get ober dat! Neber get good education! Always be hungry! Joining gangs! Going to jail too! I no want dat por my son, Doyle! Not my boy! Please! Tell dem da troot!"

What started as sympathy turned to anger. "Don't pin this on me! That man would have eventually killed you and your son! I know because I've been there! Randy broke your boy's arm *on purpose!* He should've been arrested for that, but you let him get away with it! If you'd protected your son and allowed the police to prosecute that man, he wouldn't have had to worry about me! Him being in that hospital over there? That's as much your fault as it is mine!"

Rafaela stood there bawling, shaking her head from side to side. "No. No, dat no right. You know da troot. Do da right ting, Doyle. Please. Help us."

I reached out to Hannah, placing my hand on her arm. "I can't do this. Let's go."

"Get your bloody mitts off me!" Hannah snapped, pulling away. I had yet to realize that I practically confessed to premeditating the attack on Randy Green. What actually took place in the Nixie Winch Room was crystal clear to Hannah Baxter, however. "You broke his arm? His...his ribs? His head! What'd you do? Crack his skull?"

My inability to answer told her all she needed to know. "Oh Christ, Doyle!" she spat out, beginning to cry herself. For the first time, she understood the full scope of what had happened. It was much more than the accident story that I had led her to believe. "What did you do?"

"Hannah, you don't understand! The man was an animal!"

"And so were you! What else could do that kind of damage, Doyle! What kind of rage..." Hannah paused as she made sense of the thoughts racing through her head. "It's rage, Doyle, don't you see? Rage! You couldn't control it! Neither could your father! That's why he did those things to your family!"

That was a punch to the gut that stole my breath away. "You think I'm like my father?" I asked.

"No, Doyle! But you're capable of it! God, it terrifies me that you can lose control so badly that you can do something like this! How could I possibly stop you if you're in that kind of state?"

I opened my mouth to say something, but it never came out. "What?" Hannah asked, ready to put the words in my mouth herself. "Are you going to tell me that you didn't lose control? God, Doyle! If you were in control of yourself and still did that to Rafaela's husband, it's so much worse! It makes you a monster instead of an animal!"

"Hannah, please!" I begged, reaching out for her. "You're taking the side of a child abuser over…"

"I'm not taking sides, Doyle!" Hannah stepped backward. "You may not be as evil as this Green bloke, but you're just as dangerous, and it scares me. Don't go to Cheri's tonight. You need to go back to the ship. You're spending the night there."

At that, Hannah grabbed Rafaela and Manny and led the two of them down the path toward the hospital. As they left me there, Green's wife turned around one last time. With tears streaming down her face, she begged, "Please! Please, Doyle! Tell da troot! It all I ask. Just tell da troot."

*****

CHAPTER 10

I wanted to drink. Dixie wanted me to drink too. Three days after running into Rafaela Green, though, my head was still reeling. I was in a dark place and knew better than to compromise my self-control. I had to maintain the appearance that all was right in my world while, in reality, I was falling apart inside. Not only was I sure that I had lost Hannah, but after listening to what she said to me, I was wondering if I really had inherited the rage that drove my father to murder my family.

That was such a horrifying prospect that, twice in the past three days, I had episodes triggered by nightmares of me murdering my loved ones. I had to stumble to my radar dome in the middle of the night, fighting to keep my composure until I had the privacy to get through my breakdown without bothering anyone else. Fearing alcohol would rob me of my ability to conceal my issues, I resisted Dixie's attempts to get me drunk at McDini's while we waited to meet Master Chief Darrow.

The master chief was not at work that day, but he left us a message to meet him at the bar. He arrived late, but he was all smiles and feeling no pain. He apologized for keeping us waiting, ordered a round, and asked us to guess where he had been.

I could smell the answer. "Went fishing, eh?"

Darrow laughed. "Yeah, I probably should've showered before I came here. Okay, guess who I was fishing with?"

"There's billions of people on the planet, Master Chief. Do you want us to go through them all?" asked Dixie.

"Chief Baylon," my master chief told me.

"No shit?" I asked. Darrow was indeed living dangerously. "How did that go?"

"Like any other charter. He had a good time. He's booked another trip for April to get into the yellowfin."

"Sounds like the start of a beautiful friendship."

"Who's Chief Baylon?" asked Dixie.

"The top dog of the Tijuana Police Department," Darrow answered. "It gets better. Guess who else I had come with us?"

"We have no idea, Master Chief," Dixie answered.

"ETC Frank Nelson. From the *USS Long Beach*."

That news perked my ears up.

"Who's that?" Dixie asked, lost once again.

I answered. "I don't know, but the *Long Beach* was Lieutenant Krause's last ship. You hear anything interesting?"

"A lot," Darrow said. "Frank knew Krause back when he was a first-class. Says he was a stand-up guy then. He's not making it as an officer, though. His instincts are all wrong. Worse, when he makes a bad call, he can't correct course. Like with all this cleaning shit he has you guys doing. Once he realizes he messed up, he tends to double down on the mistake."

The bartender knew Darrow and set a bottle of San Miguel down in front of the master chief without him even having to order it. "I probably shouldn't be telling you this, but both the captain and the department head lost their shit with Krause because of the zone inspection. He had you guys scrubbing our spaces down so hard we compromised the paint all over the place. The department doesn't have the budget to repaint all the CSE spaces, nor does the ship. Still, we can't leave them the way they are. I hate to break this to you guys, but you're all going to be shifting from cleaning to painting pretty soon."

TEQUILA VIKINGS

"Oh man," Dixie groaned. "That moron still has us constantly field-daying our spaces, though! This is never going to end! And we've got how many years with this guy?"

Darrow shrugged. "Maybe not as many as we think. We might only have a few more advancement cycles with him. He can't seem to make the jump to O-3. We did the calculation, and we're guessing that if he doesn't make lieutenant by next May, he'll lose his commission. He'll revert back to senior chief and be forced to retire."

"He can always turn over a new leaf," I said.

Darrow shook his head. "We don't think he can. Krause's making the same mistakes on the *Belleau Wood* that he did on the *Long Beach*. I've already learned that the most efficient way to mess with this guy is to do my best to help him. The man compulsively does the opposite of what I suggest every fucking time. He's got a thicker skull than Macklemore."

Darrow took a drink out of his beer. "Speaking of Mack, I have to say that I'm impressed with what you're doing with that kid. It looks like you're getting through to him."

I shrugged. "It's lipstick on a pig. Palazzo pulls him out of bed and stands over him while he showers. During working hours, we keep him busy so he doesn't get into trouble. After knock-off, Claude works him out in the weight room, then Dixie takes him to a gym in town to teach him how to fight. After that, he's too tired to do anything other than go back to his rack."

"Fight?" Darrow asked. "Why on earth are you teaching Macklemore to fight?"

Dixie swallowed his beer. "Sooner or later, Kramer's going to try to hurt him. Especially after that shit with the zone inspection. We'd like to get Mack to the point where he could turn the tables and whip Bill's ass instead. In self-defense, of course."

"Of course," Darrow smiled. "That'd be fun to watch. How's it going?"

"The results are a little mixed," Dixie answered. "Believe it or not, Mack's freakishly strong. After I taught him to keep his wrist straight so that it didn't snap when his punches connect, he developed quite a wallop. He's hitting the bag so hard it's lifting me off my feet when I hold it for him."

The master chief looked impressed. "You think he can plant one of those on Kramer?"

Dixie shrugged. "Sure. In fact, he's already done it once. The challenge is getting him to plant more than one. Macklemore doesn't do aggression. Only fear. He'll throw one punch and then freeze, bracing himself in anticipation of his opponent returning the blow. He surrenders whatever initiative he gains and lets his adversary have his way with him. Mack has the strength and the power to be a fucking beast of a brawler but no heart for it. He's too timid and submissive."

The master chief pulled another drink from his beer, pensively swishing it around in his mouth before swallowing. "You know what, gentlemen? I like the idea of what you're doing. I'm beginning to tire of our boy Kramer. We can fill a WSC-3 gap before we leave for Japan. He's not worth the conflict he brings to the division. I'd like to see Macklemore knock that punk right off of my boat."

Darrow slapped Kevin on the back. "Train Mack, Dixie. Make that man a fucking monster. When Kramer comes to get him, I want Mack to fuck that kid up. The captain already knows we suspect Kramer of that shit with Macklemore's uniform, so he'll barely get a slap on the wrist if he has to go in front of the old man. Kramer will get the book thrown at him, though."

"What if Mack loses?" Dixie asked.

The master chief shrugged. "Then he loses. A fight's a fight. It'll be all the excuse I need to give Kramer the boot. Mack kicking his ass is just a bonus." Turning and pointing his finger at me, Darrow added, "Whatever happens, *you* stay out of it! You don't have any wiggle room if you get written up after Green. If you lay a finger on *anybody* while trying to intervene, you'll probably end your Navy career. You understand?"

I nodded. "Yes, Master Chief."

"Good." Darrow flagged down the bartender and ordered three shots of tequila. After we downed them, he said, "Now, let's change topics. I'm sensing the division's leaders are suffering a real crisis in morale right now. I'm thinking we need to raise some spirits around here. What do you guys say about getting a group of us together and going to Vegas one last time before we leave for Japan?"

*****

TEQUILA VIKINGS

I intended to stay sober, but you simply do not refuse tequila shots purchased by a master chief in the United States Navy. You do not refuse shots of whiskey either. Nor rum. And damn it, if the master chief is buying shots, you better show him some appreciation by making sure he never has an empty beer in front of him.

Before we got too loopy, we settled on going to Vegas in the middle of March. We figured out the duty section and the invite list. Then the master chief decided we needed to blow McDini's and go where real men drank.

We ended up at one of Darrow's favorite haunts, a grungy, windowless dive called The Rusty Anchor. This was a chief's bar and designed to keep rowdy young sailors and the available young women who attracted them away so a more mature man could relax and enjoy a quiet drink. Though located relatively close to the 32nd Street Naval Station, one needed enough experience in the area to know where it was.

The Anchor kept the drink selection pretty basic. Beer in a can, straight shots, and drinks with one mixer, such as a rum and coke, was all you were going to get. The Bloody Mary was the singular exception. The owner made a point of keeping the Anchor just clean enough to satisfy the Health Department, and without exception you had to be at least twenty-one years of age to enter. That went for the songs on the jukebox just as much as it did for the patrons.

Both Dixie and I fell squarely within the demographic that was not particularly welcome in The Anchor, but Master Chief Darrow was a regular, so we did not draw too many dirty looks while walking in with him. It was a Tuesday night, so the three of us doubled the crowd of paying customers. Two retired sailors who had long ago crossed the threshold to clinical alcoholism were arguing with themselves on one side of the bar. On the other sat an ancient specimen either too full of experience or too lacking in idiocy to join them. "Oh boys, do I have a treat for you!" our master chief said as he led Dixie and me to the bar where the old man sat.

After ordering shots and beers for the entire place and contributing twenty dollars to something called "The Bucky Fund," Darrow told us, "Men, this here's Buccaneer Bill. Or 'Bucky' as we like to call him. That fund I donated to was to help make sure that this man never has to buy his own drink in here ever again. Bucky, you want to tell these boys when you joined the Navy?"

Bucky turned and gave us a wide grin. "I signed up in 1917. I was on my way to Canada to fight the Huns, but I only made it to Philadelphia before we done declared war on 'em ourselves. Ole' Woody Wilson saved me a trip!"

"Holy shit!" Dixie said. "That was before my grandmother was even born! You fought the Germans in World War I?"

"Nah. I was in two world wars and never fought Germans. I fought Russians. I was on the cruiser *Olympia*. We escorted troop transports to France, but in 1918, we went to Archangel to fight the Bolsheviks. Gawd, what a mess that was."

With a fresh beer in front of him, Bucky told us about how they had to get troops up the Dvina River on barges pulled by tugboats. The expeditionary force took about fifty men off the *Olympia* to help, one of whom was Bucky. "Feck. Trotsky had snipers all up and down them banks, and they took shots at us all the way up that ditch."

He then told us how they took the village of Seletsko but got flanked by the Soviets and had to retreat back to the coast of the White Sea on an armored train. Their ranks were decimated not only by communists and the cold, but also by a terrifying outbreak of Spanish Flu. "We lost a couple hundred of our boys there..." Bucky said, trailing off while staring into his empty glass of beer.

We discovered that Bucky worked like an alcoholic jukebox. As long as he had beer in his glass, he would talk about anything you wanted him to. He fell silent once he ran out of suds. To get him going again, you had to buy him another beer.

After we topped off his drink, Bucky went on to tell us about his tour across the Eastern Mediterranean after the *Olympia's* withdrawal from Russia. At one point, he had to go ashore on a landing party to separate the Italians from the Yugoslavians to keep them from going to war with each other over Dalmatia. He followed that story up with lurid descriptions of what he found in the bordellos from the Crimea all the way to Cairo.

"You boys ever seen a Moroccan girl?" he asked us at one point. After telling him we had not, he shook his head in sympathy. "They's heartbreakers, they are. Just beautiful. They have skin the color of caramel, straight raven-black hair, and gorgeous green eyes. They look like angels."

"You ever have a Moroccan girl?" Dixie asked.

"Nah…" Bucky answered, shaking his head. "They's just fer lookin at. The men there's pretty proud and not appreciatin' of us payin' attention to their lady folk. They'd slit yer throat jus' fer speakin' at 'em."

"How 'bout you, son?" Bucky asked me. "You ever seen a Moroccan girl?"

"I doubt it," Master Chief Darrow answered before I had the chance. "Doyle there's only got eyes for an Australian girl. She dumped him a few days ago. That's why he's looking so glum."

"Australian girl? Why you getting' glum over an Australian girl? I knowed a couple guys that had a thing for Aussie women. They think they's exotic 'cause of the way they talk an' all. I don't get it. They look just like our girls, but they sound like feckin' pirates if ya ask me. What'd she dump ya for?"

I told him about what I did to Randy Green and our encounter with Rafaela over the weekend. When I finished, he thought for a moment before sharing his take on it all. "Ya know, it sounds to me like you're both maybe tryin' to force somethin' that ain't meant to be. Now, I ain't faultin' her fer her views on fightin' an' I certainly ain't faultin' you fer what ya did to that fella fer hurtin' the boy. Y'all are just different, is all. Maybe this is fer the better. How old are you, son?"

"Twenty-two."

"Twenny two? Shee-it. You's a baby! Bradley here's tellin' me y'alls headin' to Japan in a little while. Take my word for it; you don't want to be tied down to no woman when you's goin' overseas that young. Hell, I didn't get hitched fer the first time until I's thirty."

"You found a woman prettier than the Moroccan girls?" Dixie asked.

Bucky smiled. "Yeah, I bought her in China."

"You bought your wife?" I nearly choked on my beer. "That's horrible!"

"She didn't seem to think so. I was poor's could be back in the states, but in China, I's a wealthy man when compared to the coolies. If I didn't buy her, she'd probably end up in a brothel or somethin'. She's right grateful fer what I done fer her. An' you know what? She was my one true love."

"What happened to her?" I asked.

"The feckin' Navy happened, that's what. I got sent back stateside from the Yangtze River in '33, an' the Navy wa'nt recognizin' no inter-racial marriages in them days. They made me sell her 'fore I left. I didn't keep no money from it though, I gave it all to her so's she could set herself up good if the fella who bought her wa'nt treatin' her well. He was a good man, though, and she had a daughter with him. She had a son with the man who bought 'er after that, too.

"By '33, I been overseas my whole life. I wasn't really American anymore, so I didn't stay long. I got back to China on the *Panay* in '36. I bought Jian back as soon as I'd found her, and boy did that cost me a pretty penny. In '37, though, the Japs overtook us, shot my first boat out from underneath me, and took Nanking. I never saw Jian or the kids again."

Bucky fell silent but this time not because he finished his beer. "Ya know, if I end up in Hell after I die, it's gonna be leavin' that woman and those beautiful babies behind that damned me. To this day, I wish I'd deserted and stayed behind to protect 'em."

"Doing that only would've added your corpse to the body count," Darrow said.

"Nah, I understand completely," I told Bucky. "I lost my family to a monster too. I was only thirteen, and if I'd been there, I probably would have been killed first. My dad hated me the most. Still, not being there to at least try to save them has tortured me my whole life."

"Your old man killed your family?" Bucky motioned for the bartender and bought a round of drinks for us instead of the other way around. He then made me tell him my story.

When I finished, Bucky shook his head. "Damn. Ya know, I understand this thing with the Australian lass a little better now. You ain't never really had a family, did ya? Sounds to me that you want one real bad. Son, don't force it. Get out in the world and get yer head straight. Get some shit done 'fore ya start gittin' ideas 'bout gittin' hitched. You got a whole lot of things to see 'fore you settle down."

To prove his point, Bucky told us about the time he spent in the Caribbean fighting the Banana Wars in the 1920s before going to China. He showed us a scar on his shoulder he got in Panama and told us how it was the closest he ever came to death. It was not the bullet that nearly did him in; it was the infection that followed it.

Bucky told us about patrolling off the coast of West Africa and meeting the handless men, mutilated by agents of the Congo Free State. They turned severed hands in for bounties, proof of amputations performed as punishment for not meeting rubber production quotas. After learning of this and other atrocities committed there, Bucky bitterly complained that King Leopold was always left off the list of history's butchers. "I ain't no Nazi but to tell y'all the truth, when I learnt that Hitler invaded Belgium, I thought to myself, 'Good. Feck 'em.' Nasty ass bastards."

He showed us another scar, one that ran from his right shoulder to his left hip. "Got that from a coolie pirate. We was fightin' 'em with bayonets an' he nearly took my head off with a sword. He just missed."

"A sword!" Darrow laughed. "A sword! Men, here it is in 1992, and you're sitting here talking to a man who fought against pirates with swords!"

"Did you get him with a bayonet?" Dixie asked.

"No, my buddy Arlo saw it and shot him in the back of the feckin' head before I got a chance!" Bucky then told us how after the Japanese sunk the *Panay* in Nanking, he transferred to the *Tutuila*. The Americans turned that ship over to the Chinese after the attacks at Pearl Harbor.

It took nine months for Bucky to get back to Hawaii, chased there nearly every step of the way by the advance of the Japanese military. He eventually ended up on the *USS Hoel*, which sank during the Battle of Leyte Gulf. Bucky was one of just eighty-six of the ship's survivors.

"After the *Hoel* sunk, I was feckin' done with the Navy. I'd had me enough. I needed to find my wife, though, so after the second war was over, I went back to the Yangtze on a PT boat. Never found so much as a trace of her or the kids. Feckin' Japs just killed 'em all."

Bucky left the Navy in 1950, settling in Subic Bay where he got married a second time. He had two daughters while in his fifties and moved to the US so they could get a better education. When his girls graduated, they wanted to remain in the United States, so he stayed with them, having lost his second wife in 1969.

By the time Bucky finished his story, I was in awe. I could not believe the things that he had seen and done. He lived the kind of life I was seeking when I signed up for the Navy.

Suddenly, I did not want to be an officer anymore, sending men into harm's way from the rear. I wanted to face the danger myself, to do things that other men would speak of when I was not in the room. I wanted people to tell stories about me like they did Master Chief Darrow. I was not going to get that from a college education and a commission.

As Darrow decided he was getting ready to go, we did one last shot together while I reassessed what I wanted out of my life.

To hell with BOOST. To hell with Hannah. This is what I want to do. Drink booze, fuck, and fight. I want to do what Bucky did.

Except get stung in the testicles by a Portuguese man o' war while skinny dipping in the Canary Islands. That's the kind of shit I can do without.

*****

Even though I did not want to drink, Dixie and I outlasted the master chief that night. He bought the bar one final round when he cashed out and stumbled to the door, bumping into a couple of old acquaintances on their way in. The newcomers shook hands with my boss and then made their way to the bar after a round of mutual backslaps, taking seats just a couple of stools down from me. Dixie was nearly catatonic, so I caught myself casually eavesdropping as they sat themselves down. "Who was that again?" the larger man with red hair asked.

"Brad Darrow. He was the enlisted guy who used to run the Armed Forces Police Department in the Philippines." The second man was older, grayer, and a little gaunt.

"Olongapo Earp?!?"

"That would be him."

Red looked back towards the door. "I heard that guy was a real head buster."

"He didn't take no shit, that's for sure."

"I heard he used to go overboard, though. Heard he really hurt some guys."

TEQUILA VIKINGS

The thin man shrugged. "Sure. But I was there a while with him. Ain't never seen him hurt no one that wasn't askin' to be hurt. Most o' the time, if ya did what ya were told, he just got ya home safe and had a buddy o' yours put ya to bed."

"I heard he ran the Philippine underworld while he was there."

"Well, I heard werewolves were running through Manila, too. Were you ever in PI when Darrow was runnin' the show?"

Red shook his head. "No."

"Then quit talkin' shit like ya was. You don't know nothin.'"

I felt a little pride as I heard those two men talk about Master Chief Darrow, realizing for the first time that the mythos of Olongapo Earp loomed just as large in the United States Navy as the legend of Hulagu did in Tijuana.

*****

CHAPTER 11

Darrow was long gone. Bucky was too old. All the other guys at the Rusty Anchor were too drunk. With no one at the bar able to give us a ride back to base, Dixie and I had to hoof it back to 32nd Street. It was not too bad at first, but as we approached Plaza Blvd, the fatigue factor set in. I suggested to Dixie that we should consider finding a place to take a break.

He agreed. "Where are you thinking? McDini's?"

I shook my head. "No, that's out of the way. Not to mention far too classy for a night like tonight."

"You're not considering…" Dixie vigorously shook his head. He knew what I was thinking.

"Of course, I am." I pointed up the road to a building with an outer décor that confirmed that the 1970s were the darkest period of American architectural history. "It's right there. Ten bucks says Franklin's still haunting it."

Dixie looked at his watch. "On second thought, it's almost 1:30 in the morning. Maybe we should just…"

"Cool! We can still make last call!"

TEQUILA VIKINGS

The Trophy Lounge was a 32nd Street legend. Located a hop, skip, and a jump due east from the naval station's Gate 6, it was packed with what we sailors called "WESTPAC Widows."

Every year the Navy's most awkward young men arrived in the Philippines during the annual Western Pacific Deployment (otherwise known as the WESTPAC cruise). They fell in love with the first woman they ever saw naked, despite the fact they paid a bar fine of thirty dollars to get her that way. Some of them married these girls and brought them back to the US. The overwhelming majority of these women were eternally grateful for being rescued from such a horrific situation and stayed faithful to their husbands. Others waited for their men to go back to sea then went to the Trophy Lounge in search of a better offer. These were the WESTPAC Widows.

Single women did occasionally end up in the Trophy Lounge. They were usually Asian ladies seeking American sailors, wanting to meet young men with a steady job and a future ahead of them. They rarely came back though, quickly discovering that the men who frequented that bar were not exactly the best the Navy had to offer either.

Take Todd Franklin. Like Dixie, Todd was on the shorter end of the height spectrum. Unlike Kevin, who was reasonably fit and trim, Todd was lumpy and out of shape due to too much drinking, chain-smoking, and letting women who were old enough to be his mother abuse his body in unspeakable ways. He was a Trophy Lounge regular.

It took some convincing, but I got Dixie to come to the Trophy with me. At 1:30 on a weekday morning, the couples that already hooked up were long gone. There was, however, a weird sort of sexual stand-off going on between a half dozen older men and women at the bar. This was a group of mutually unattractive people slowly realizing that if they did not start going home with each other soon, they would not be going home with anyone at all.

As I looked around, I spotted four or five women sitting at tables along the wall. They were significantly older than we were, but still reasonably attractive, but not even remotely attainable to the men who had already been there a while. A half-hour away from closing time, though, they considered Dixie and me fresh meat, and probably the last chance they had of getting lucky that night. They came at us pretty aggressively. I was startled when one of them snuck up from behind and slipped her fingertips just barely below the top of my jeans. "Doyle! What you doing here?"

I froze, instantly recognizing who the woman was. Her name was Lilly. I did not know her last name, nor did I care to. I met her at the Trophy when I was there with Franklin months before, and after getting nearly blackout drunk, I woke up in base housing with her, a potentially career-killing situation. "Why hello, Lilly," I said before I ordered Dixie and me a beer. "How are you?"

"Oh, you know, Doyle. Lonely." At this, I saw Dixie roll his eyes. Once he got his beer in hand, he walked away from us and headed towards the bathrooms.

"I'm sorry to hear that," I told her.

Lilly slapped me playfully across the shoulder. "Hey! How come you never call me?"

"Because you're married to a warrant officer and have two teenage children that wake up before their mother's booty call can sneak out of the apartment." That was awkward.

"I no gonna be married long. I gonna leave my husband soon." I believed her. Lilly and her kids were evacuated from the Philippines when Mount Pinatubo erupted, but her husband had to stay behind to keep Subic Bay running. From what Lilly told me, she found out that her husband started sleeping with their maid the moment she was out of the house, and I had the feeling that I was the little tryst she had devised to get back at him. I sensed the only thing keeping her from filing for divorce was needing to find someone else to pay her bills.

"That's too bad," I said as I looked around the lounge. I was just being polite, though. I could not have cared less about Lilly's domestic situation. To show that, I quickly changed the subject. "Lilly, has Franklin been here tonight?"

"He was earlier. He go home wit Lola." Lilly closed her mouth and puffed out her cheeks to imply that Lola was a large woman. "Are you going to buy me a drink?"

I grinned. "I can, but I'm not going home with you. I have a girlfriend." *At least I do as far as you're concerned.*

"You do?" Lilly puffed out her cheeks again. "I bet she fat. And losin' teeth. And ugly. Just like Lola."

TEQUILA VIKINGS

When Lilly mentioned missing teeth, an image formed in my mind, and I knew exactly who Lola was. I shuddered. The Olongapo skin trade had thoroughly corrupted that woman in both body and soul. She was hideous. I might have been more sympathetic toward her, but I suspected she had some poor cuckold at home who saved her from the fate of an aging Filipina prostitute, only to be repaid by her toying with the likes of Todd Franklin while he was away. Lola was the kind of woman that would make most men very reluctant to face their friends after having been seen leaving with her. Franklin, however, tended to celebrate such conquests. I had little doubt we would hear all about it in the shop the next morning after quarters.

"So, is she?" Lilly asked again, mercifully breaking my concentration and saving my mind from a mental picture of what Franklin and Lola were probably doing at that very moment.

"Is she what?" I asked as I caught the barmaid's attention and had her make Lilly whatever she was drinking.

"Fat and ugly? Your girlfriend?"

"Well, they can't all be pretty warrant officers' wives like you, can they?"

"Nope," Lilly said. "They can't. You need to drop her, Doyle, and get yourself an LBFM like me." LBFM stood for Little Brown Fucking Machine. It was not as insulting as it sounded and was a somewhat complementary, if vulgar, term sailors used to describe Filipina bar girls.

"Maybe I'll look for you here if things don't work out." I handed Lilly her drink just as the bartender shouted last call. I looked around for Dixie, but there was no sign of him. Nor was there any sign of him when the lights came on fifteen minutes later. I made one more pass around the building after the bartender herded us out, then I fought Lilly off me one last time before I gave up and walked back to the ship.

At the time, I figured Dixie assumed I was going home with Lilly and did not feel like waiting around.

*****

Alone and annihilated, it was a long walk back to the ship, but it gave me time to think. I had to admit it felt great to get Hannah, Rafaela, and everything else off of my mind for a while, but with every step I took, it all started flooding back to me. My momentary infatuation with Bucky's life rapidly melted away, and I knew what I truly wanted was my girlfriend back. It was breaking me to realize that I might not ever see her again. Even worse was the thought Hannah planted in my head that my father's rage issues might be hereditary. That terrified me. If true, I would never have a family of my own. I just couldn't ever bring myself to subject another human being to the misery of living with someone like my old man.

As exhilarating as Bucky's adventures sounded, I was craving a simpler life. I grew up in a constant state of violence, and it was sinking in that I wanted it to stop. I was longing for stability and needed a place in the world where I felt safe and had people that wanted me around. I was fortunate enough to have enjoyed five years of relative peace in foster care between my family's death and joining the military. Still, I was under no illusion that my guardians held any genuine affection toward me. We were just roommates. Once I aged out of the system, I never got so much as a postcard from them.

Whether in Brisbane or Baltimore, a simple life with Hannah was such an alien concept to me that it seemed even more exciting than fighting Chinese warlords along the Yangtze. I had it within my grasp but now felt as if I had lost Hannah before I had even met her, having preemptively destroyed our relationship when I crippled Randy Green.

When I got back to the *Belleau Wood*'s berthing area, I found Dixie's rack empty. I was curious about that but not concerned. Kevin was a competent drunkard who knew how to find his way home, even when inebriated to the point of psychosis.

I checked on him again the next morning and saw Dixon's feet sticking out of his rack's privacy curtains. His shoes were still on. Allowing him to get a little more sleep, I left him alone and took a long, hot shower. After that, I had a quick breakfast of fruit, milk, and aspirin. I made it to quarters just after Franklin, with about two minutes to spare.

Macklemore and Palazzo were there, looking sharp near the rear of the formation. "Warren!" I yelled as I walked towards Tony. "You're excused. Triple-time it down to the berthing area and get Dixie up here ASAP!"

"Who?" Macklemore asked.

TEQUILA VIKINGS

"Dixie, Mack! Dixie! Get down there and drag his ass up to the flight deck NOW!"

As Macklemore sprinted toward the island structure, I called out, "Todd! Franklin!"

"Here!" he yelled.

"You, sir, are one sick, sick man!" The division busted out laughing, knowing there was a story behind that and anxious to hear it. Franklin held his arms up in victory to a round of applause.

"You do a count yet, Tony?" I asked as I walked up on Bard.

"I got twenty-one heads. Now that you're here, everyone's accounted for except Dixie."

"He'll be here. Just have to hope he makes it before Krause."

We lucked out. For whatever reason, the lieutenant did not join us for morning muster that day. Master Chief Darrow was giving us our pass down, and he arrived at the same moment Dixie and Macklemore did. After leading Kevin to the front of the formation, Mack tried to jump back into ranks, but Darrow stopped him. "Macklemore!"

Warren executed an almost flawless about-face and went to the position of attention. "Yes, Master Chief!"

"Front and center! Get up here next to Petty Officer Dixon!"

Once Dixie and Macklemore were side-by-side, Darrow conducted an impromptu inspection on both. He looked Warren over and finished by saying, "Nicely done, Petty Officer Macklemore. I think you are the most put-together man in the entire division this morning. Congratulations."

"Thank you, Master Chief!"

Darrow then stepped over to Dixie and laughed. "Jesus Christ! I don't think I even know where to start. Your hair is hilarious, you smell like stale beer and my grandmother's perfume, and I don't think wearing lipstick to roll call is part of US Navy uniform regulations, son."

Dixie's eyes opened wide as the division busted out in laughter. He tried to wipe off his mouth, but Darrow corrected him. "It ain't on your lips, Dixon. Try your forehead. God damn! Your shirt is all untucked in back and your pants are all wrinkled. If I didn't know any better, I'd say you pulled these out of your dirty laundry bag. And then...JESUS CHRIST!"

Darrow physically recoiled. "Is that a hickey!?! Look at the size of that fuckin' thing! Good Lord, Dixie! Did you fuck a sea lamprey or something?!?"

Darrow leaned towards me. "What the hell did I miss last night?"

"I'm not sure," I answered. "I think Bucky got him drunk and took advantage of him. I lost him at the Trophy Lounge."

"The Trophy Lounge?!? For the love of God…"

Darrow spent a solid ten minutes embarrassing Dixie in front of the division. Kevin was not in any real trouble, though. Darrow and the chiefs had a little fun with him, pressed him for details on what happened, and eventually set him free.

After Darrow dismissed us, I went up to Dixie to figure out what happened, but he declined to go into specifics. "What did she look like?" I asked.

"Oh God, Doyle…Oh, God, no. I don't even want to go there. I feel filthy." Dixie then reached into his pocket and withdrew a pink piece of paper he pulled from the quarterdeck's message board. Stuffing it into my hand, he smiled and said, "I thought you'd like to see this right away."

Written by the petty officer of the watch, it read, "From Hannah Baxter. Call right away. Any time. She misses you."

*****

I desperately needed sleep, but my greater need was to speak to Hannah. When the announcement came over the 1MC to knock off ship's work for lunch, I sprinted down the gangplank to call her.

Hannah burst into tears the moment she heard my voice. She apologized to me over and over again. "I saw him, Doyle. I saw him."

"Who?"

"Green. Randy Green. I saw him, and I've been struggling with it ever since! My god, Doyle! What you did to him! It scares me. But what he did to that little boy…" Hannah broke down again.

"I'm sorry, Doyle. I shouldn't have treated you like I did. I saw how terrified Manny is of that man, and I saw how much that…that fucking arse hole hates that little boy. Like, if his arm had not snapped so easily, none of this would have happened."

TEQUILA VIKINGS

I heard Hannah blow her nose. "And Gawd! How his mother kept forcing that poor kid to hug the creep! She was trying to make it look like they were all one happy little family. It was sick, Doyle! That little boy doesn't stand a fucking chance with those people! I wanted to scoop him up and run away with him!"

Hannah sobbed again for a couple of moments before admitting, "I think you did save Manny's life, Doyle. Green needs to go to prison. They need to separate him from that poor little boy."

I heaved a sigh of relief, trying to keep from crying myself. "So now you understand why I needed to do it? Hannah, are we good?"

"No, we're not bloody good! Not yet! I want you to be honest with me, Doyle! What really happened that day?"

I did not want to go into this. Not on a public phone right next to someone who could overhear it and ruin me with a single call to the NCIS. If I could mend things with Hannah, though, I was willing to risk it.

Hannah did not understand military culture and would never condone the way Darrow had us occasionally settle problems off the books. I once feared Hannah would leave me if I came clean about what we did to Green. I now knew she would leave me if I didn't. "Hannah, he broke Manny's arm..."

"I bloody know that," she snapped.

"...and he got away with it. He was drinking more and more, and the fights between him and Rafaela were getting worse. We knew something serious was going to happen if nothing was done. So, Claude, Dixie, and I sent Green a message that if he laid another hand on Rafaela or Manny, we were going to break him. To punctuate our point, we meant to give him a preview of what he could expect if he fucked up again. Unfortunately, we...I mean I...lost control of the situation, and instead of giving him a taste of what was to come, I force-fed him the entire goddamn entrée."

"You're telling me that you didn't mean to cripple him?" Hannah asked.

I shook my head even though, over the phone, Hannah could not see it. "No, that wasn't intentional. Shit just got out of hand."

"How? I mean, how on earth did it get to that point?"

"Well, he hit me first..."

"Seriously?" Hannah blurted out, cutting me off yet again. "That was all it took?"

"You need to let me finish. No, that wasn't it. Hell, the hit barely hurt. It was the look on his face. Green wasn't scared, Hannah. He was pissed. He was angry that we had the nerve to interfere with what he was doing to his family. It was the same look my dad would get when social services came around to check on us growing up."

"What exactly did you do to him?"

"Whatever I could," I told her. "I broke his arm. He grabbed hold of the winch drum to pull himself up, so I stomped on it. His ribs? They probably broke when I jumped onto his chest. The rest was just from punching him over and over again across the face."

"Did Dixie and Claude hit him too?"

"No. Hannah, this whole thing didn't last more than a minute. Dixie was shocked by it and froze. Claude saw how bad the situation was getting and did what he could to pull me off of Randy."

"Is this kind of thing common?" Hannah asked. "Is this the way the Navy handles these people?"

"It's not unheard of, but I would not call it common. No," I answered.

"You'd done it before?"

"Not like that."

"Then like what?" I was finding Hannah to be a tougher interrogator than the NCIS.

"We smacked guys around. Open-handed. For mouthing off, not pulling their weight, or other minor offenses. It was an alternative to putting an official blemish in their service record."

"Do you like doing that sort of thing?"

I sighed. "No. I'd rather be goofing off in the shop."

"Do you regret it at all?"

I felt my hands shaking. For months, I told myself that Randy Green was a piece of shit who got what was coming to him. It was not that simple, though. Despite myself, I let out a single sob and turned my back so no one could see my face. "I do regret it. I may have paid him back for what he did to Manny and made sure he didn't get away with it, but I robbed him, too. I took away what little hope he had of ever redeeming himself. He'll never be able to change now. I crippled him and took away his ability to make amends for what he did. He'll never be able to overcome his demons now."

It stung to admit that out loud. Though I was hostile to the concept of organized religion, I still had sins I needed to atone for myself, particularly in regards to what happened when I was in El Salvador. Few things haunted me more than the prospect of going to my grave without somehow making up for that one day, and I was sure that Randy would never be able to right his wrongs after what I did to him. That was a horrible injustice, even for a man as repugnant as Randy Green.

"Are you going to do it again?" I heard Hannah's voice starting to soften.

"Are you kidding me?" I exclaimed. "The Navy will lock me up and throw away the…"

"I don't mean as a sailor, Doyle. I mean as a man. Has what happened to Green taught you anything about violence?"

I tensed up and did what I could to project my sincerity over the phone. "If Claude had not pulled me off of Green, I would have killed him. It would have been an accident, but he'd still be dead, and I'd be spending the rest of my life behind bars. I have no intention of ever getting into another situation like that for as long as I live, Hannah."

There was silence on the other end of the line for a while. Finally, Hannah sobbed, "I'm scared, Doyle! What happens if you get like that around me? How can I stop you?"

"It won't ever happen again, Hannah! I swear…"

"But your father! I keep wondering what your father was like when he met your mother. Was he like you? Was he funny? Was he adventurous? I can't imagine your mother falling in love with the bastard you knew, so what changed him? I keep wondering what could turn you into something like that."

There it was again. I did not know how to respond. "Honey…I…I…"

Hannah came wholly unglued on the other end of the line, "I don't care! I don't…you're not your father! If you tell me that you're done fighting, done with the violence, I believe you! Please tell me that you'll never do this again!"

My knees buckled, and I nearly fell to the pier, squatting down as far as the cord on the phone would let me. I pressed my temples with both hands, rocking slowly to keep myself from breaking down too. "I promise! I promise! I'll never get into another fight again! I promise!"

Hannah's crying suddenly became mixed with laughter. "Gawd, I love you!"

When I told Hannah that I loved her back, I did not say it lightly. I did love her. I loved her more than I ever loved anyone in my entire life. This was the very moment I decided that I wanted her to be my wife.

"I'm still moving to Ocean Beach, Doyle."

"Oh, thank God! When?"

"The middle of May. But I'm coming down to see you in a couple of weeks."

We talked until I had to get back to the ship. I hung up with a feeling of elation that would have lasted me all day. Then I started doing the math and stopped in my tracks when I realized I was going to Las Vegas with my master chief the same weekend Hannah was coming down to see me.

*****

CHAPTER 12

I was looking at Macklemore lying on the floor of the Radar Repair shop, passed out drunk on a weekday night. Shaking my head, I turned to Dixie and asked, "Was she hot?"

Kevin shook his head. "Of course not. This is Macklemore we're talking about. She looked like one of those *hyna* girls that the *cholos* hang out with in Barrio Logan. She was kind of fat, had on all this garish makeup, and dressed like she was going to play basketball. You know Mack, though. He didn't care what she looked like. He was just happy that a girl, any girl, was willing to talk to him."

"What on earth happened?"

"Man, Doyle, we had a good day at the gym. Mack was on point! He was being aggressive and coming out swinging. I'm telling you, Mack was a new man! He's ready for Kramer! That cocksucker doesn't stand a chance!" Dixie was smiling from ear to ear, beaming with pride in what he was accomplishing with Macklemore.

"Warren did such a good job that I offered to buy him a drink, take him out for a little while. He earned it. So, we come back to the ship to clean up, and you know, Mack bought himself some new clothes too. Doyle, the guy looked good, he smelled good, and he was carrying himself with a little bit of swagger even."

I cursed. "I wish I'd not been on Shore Patrol down in San Ysidro. I would've loved to have seen that."

"Doyle, you wouldn't have recognized the guy! Anyway, we get to this place downtown, and we're talking like he's normal. We're goofing off and legitimately having a good time. I leave our table to get another pitcher of beer, and next thing I know, there's this girl at Mack's table talking to him. I don't want to interrupt anything, so I pay for a pitcher and have a waitress send it their way with a couple of fresh glasses. Meanwhile, I hang back and watch from the other end of the bar."

"Does Mack have any game?" I asked, trying to picture the scene in my head.

"Oh, hell no," Dixie answered. "But it looked like the girl did. Mack was being Mack at first, but eventually, she got him to let his guard down. After a while, they looked like they were old friends, talking away at each other for at least an hour. They started getting closer, started touching each other, and I legitimately thought I was watching Macklemore getting ready to lose his cherry there. Then he got up to use the bathroom."

Kevin let out a long sigh. "No sooner had the door to the head closed behind Mack when this chick's lowlife boyfriend walks up next to her and they start talking. She was all giggles and smiles a second before, but she's all business now. Doyle, they were setting Mack up. They were going to lure him into the parking lot, beat his ass, and take his money. Sure as shit, when the dude goes back to his table, there's like four goons with him. It was a pretty bad scene."

Looking down at Mack again, I cursed his luck. "Goddammit. The guy can't ever catch a break, can he?"

Dixie shook his head. "Nope. Luckily, I'm in there enough that I know the bouncer. I let him know what's up, and we step in when Mack gets back to his table. Things get tense, the *cholos* start posturing, and the place calls the cops. Realizing that the jig is up, the chick is now talking all kinds of shit to Warren. She's laughing in his face and telling him he's the world's biggest moron if he thinks any girl would ever get with someone as ugly and stupid as he was. It was brutal.

TEQUILA VIKINGS

"So, when it's safe to leave, the two of us bounce out of there. Man, we barely got half a block away when Mack completely breaks down. The guy loses his shit and is just coming apart. He's talking about how worthless he is and always will be, how there's no hope for him, no one will ever love him, all that shit. Doyle, it's hard to explain to someone who wasn't there, but it kind of scared me, man."

I took another long look at Macklemore lying on the deck. "How did he get like this?"

Dixie shrugged. "The man was in bad shape. When we got back to base, I let him drink it off at the Enlisted Man's Club. I didn't know what else to do. Look, Doyle, Mack wasn't like, 'getting laid didn't work out, so now I'm sad.' This was, 'Man, _everybody_ wants to hurt me for some reason, so what's the point of living?' Doyle, I've never heard anyone talk like Mack did tonight. He also got this look in his eye like you get when you have those things, those episodes of yours. It's like he was kind of there, but somewhere else at the same time. That's why I brought him up here instead of taking him to the berthing area. If he snapped like you do sometimes, I didn't want everyone to see it."

Petty Officer Dixon was not one to exaggerate. He was concerned, and if he was concerned, so was I. "Doyle, I've got a feeling that what's eatin' Mack up inside goes deeper than an aversion to using the shower. I ain't sure that kicking Kramer's ass and learning Navy shit is going to fix this guy."

"Dixie, did he specifically say anything about hurting himself?"

Kevin considered it for a moment but then shook his head. "Specifically? No. He implied everything but, though."

I sighed and took a seat, wondering how to handle everything. Threatening suicide was another quick way a man could end up a civilian, second only to grabbing a master chief by the ass and slipping him a mouthful of tongue. Warren stopped short of that, leaving me in a state of uncertainty over what to do. If I over-reacted, Mack could end up out on the street with no resources, exacerbating the situation. If I under-reacted, he could end up all over the flight deck after swan diving from the top of the island structure. I was an electronics technician, not a psychologist. I did not know what to do.

"We need to keep an eye on him," I told Dixie. "Watch him close."

With all the stuff I had going on in my own head, I should have been better equipped to deal with a man like Macklemore. Unfortunately, that would not be the case. As inadequate as it was, 'keeping an eye on him' was the best I could do and was not even close to what Mack needed.

*****

Being spurned by a low life was all it took to undo months of work on Warren Macklemore.

The Monday morning after nearly being rolled by *cholos*, he once again showed up for muster able to aromatically part the CSE formation more effectively than Moses parted the Red Sea. Sober but dazed by a lack of sleep, Warren reported in a uniform that should have been retired, announcing to all of us that he officially stopped giving a shit again.

Knowing that Mack had a tough weekend, we let it go. We hoped that getting him into the groove of the workweek would bring him back on track, but we were wrong. Palazzo asked what he should do.

"You can only do so much," I told him. "Try to pull him back to the reservation. If he refuses to start putting in the effort again, it's on him, not you. You did what I asked. You're off the hook as far as I'm concerned."

Palazzo had come a long way as well. Having spent so much time with Macklemore, I sensed that John considered him to be a genuine friend, probably the only real one he had on the entire ship. He did not want to see Mack fail. "And what if I go back to forcing him out of bed and getting back into the program?"

"Then that's your initiative," I said. "You certainly won't be penalized for it. Just brace yourself for the possibility that it may not work out."

Some of the men were willing to kick Macklemore while he was down. Never one to pass up an opportunity to exert his inner asshole, Bill Kramer resurrected the idea of giving Mack the scrub with Deaver and Crowley. After Palazzo overheard them plotting it, the two of us marched to the EMO to report it to Master Chief Darrow.

"If Kramer wants to give Macklemore a GI shower, let him," Darrow said after hearing us out. "Isn't that what you're going for anyway? Giving Mack the opportunity to put Kramer's lights out?"

TEQUILA VIKINGS

"We're not just talking about Kramer here," I argued. "We're talking three against one. Kramer, Deaver, and Crowley. They're going to hurt that guy."

"Then they hurt the guy."

Palazzo looked perplexed. "What?"

"Look," Darrow said, turning around in his chair to face us. "I know you guys got this project going on with Petty Officer Macklemore right now, but at the end of the day, he still can't keep his shit together. A GI shower is probably what the son-of-a-bitch needs to get the point."

Darrow shook his head. "I'm NOT sanctioning this. If it happens, I will grab all three of those pricks and serve them to the skipper on a silver platter. If Fleming wants to make an example out of them, he might throw them all right out of the fleet. It'll be killing two birds with one stone."

I could see the master chief's strategy, but I did not like the idea of brutalizing Macklemore to get rid of Kramer and his gunner's mate buddies. "Master Chief, I..."

"Discussion's over. Let me spell it out, gentlemen. You are not to tell Macklemore what Kramer's planning. You're not to discourage Kramer from carrying this thing out. Once they start doing it, you're to stay out of the way and let it happen. Am I clear?"

"Aye aye..." answered Palazzo. I said nothing until Darrow slapped me across the face to get my attention.

"Am I clear, Doyle?" he growled.

"Yeah, you're clear..." I answered, rubbing my cheek.

*****

CHAPTER 13

L uckily, Hannah understood. I wanted to be there with her when she came down to San Diego, but there was only one weekend when we could get all of the division's key players together for a trip to Nevada, and that was the one she would be in town. She told me she would hang out with Dreadlock John and Space Kate, hoping that I would return soon enough on Sunday for us to spend time together.

Las Vegas is a twenty-four-hour town, but as late as we arrived, we had the bar at Harrah's all to ourselves. Once we dropped off our stuff, Darrow held court, and we drank ourselves stupid until well past dawn.

We did not wake up until the following afternoon. We prowled the strip for a few hours, but by the time the sun set, our group was splintering off in different directions. Stovic went where his luck was taking him. Fordson hit for a few hundred dollars on the roulette wheel, then he and Metaire disappeared with a pair of young women from Montreal.

We lost Dixie and our vehicle, leaving me with the suspicion that he ditched us to go to one of the legal brothels up north. Tony Bard hit it off with a waitress at the Mirage that Darrow kept calling "Stacy-cakes" and left with her when she got off work. De Alba struck out on both luck and love, so he bought himself a bottle of whiskey and went back to the room to get drunk and watch TV.

After Bard left, Darrow and I were by ourselves. We blew off the Mirage and started strolling the Las Vegas Strip.

"So, where are we heading to?" I asked the master chief as we walked, sweating profusely in the desert heat despite the late hour.

"I've got something for you," he said, leading us north for a few blocks. As we strolled up in front of the Circus Circus, Darrow swerved left and started making his way up the driveway. "You've been here before, haven't you?"

I shook my head. That was my third trip to Vegas, but I was under the impression that the Circus Circus was one of the more family-oriented venues. "No, Master Chief. I actually haven't."

"Seriously?" Darrow asked, surprised. "I thought you were a Hunter Thompson fan. I figured this place would be hallowed ground for you."

Thompson's *Fear and Loathing in Las Vegas* was indeed one of those books that changed my life. I read it at fourteen, and it showed me just how exciting bad behavior could be. It also piqued my curiosity into psychedelic drugs and ushered in a period where I sought ways to put the "fun" in "fungi."

I considered checking out the venue a couple of times to pay homage to Thompson's major opus, but I was under the impression that the place suffered from a chronic infestation of circus clowns. Few things could set my fight-or-flee instincts into overdrive quicker than a surprise encounter with a man in white make-up, so I thought it best to avoid the place while drinking.

"You've really never been here?" Darrow asked. After once again shaking my head, he said, "Well, let me show you around."

Having spent hours on casino floors by then, I was used to the din of slot machines, winner buzzers, laughter, loud conversations, and ice rattling around in cocktail glasses. Still, once they added carnival barkers and piped in animal noises, it added an entirely new dimension to the already over-stimulating Midway experience.

It was a lot to take in. I stood there with my mouth agape, wondering which attraction Raoul Duke would run screaming from if he were there to see it today.

Sensing that I was having a moment, Darrow set me down in a nearby chair and told me to wait while he got drinks. After he left, I sat there, staring wide-eyed at everything going on. I spotted a freakishly tall waitress stroll by in a chorus line outfit followed by two little people I first mistook for hotel employees. I later realized they were just tourists making unfortunate accommodation choices. They reminded me of an incident that took place in Tijuana during ET2 Jasper's discharge party, and I was on the verge of laughing out loud when my master chief returned.

"What's this?" I asked as I took a glass from him.

"Tequila and Squirt. A double."

I would have preferred water to rehydrate my chalky tongue, but if I could not have that, tequila and Squirt was a quenching substitute. I downed half of it in one swallow, took a breath, and tilted my head back to finish it off. It was during that second swig that I felt something alien enter my mouth and run down my gullet.

It caught in my throat, and I launched into a coughing fit, trying to dislodge it. Failing, I grabbed Darrow's rum and coke to wash it down. "Are you all right?" he asked as I tried to catch my breath.

"Yeah, man," I answered. "There was something in my drink. A piece of napkin or something."

"Or something." Darrow grinned.

"What?" I asked. "Was it supposed to be there? What was it?"

Darrow stuck his tongue out at me and showed me a small piece of paper, about a quarter-inch square, emblazoned with a picture of Bart Simpson on it. After slipping it back into his mouth, he cackled and said, "Just a little taste of that sunshine acid!"

*****

"You spiked my drink?!?" I exclaimed in disbelief. "Are you fucking crazy?!?"

Bradley Darrow was a master chief in the United States Navy. He spent over eight years assigned to law enforcement billets in the armed forces. Darrow was in his mid-forties and well past the age that he should be dabbling in psychoactive drugs. As a senior non-commissioned officer in the American military, the man was risking a thirty-year career by doing so.

He was also risking mine. I was furious. "What the hell happens if our numbers get called for a random drug test Monday morning?"

"Relax, Doyle..."

"Don't tell me to fucking relax, Master Chief!" I shot back, loud enough to attract the attention of passersby.

"Keep your fuckin' voice down!" Darrow snarled under his breath. "Even if they do pull our numbers, nothing's going to happen. They can't detect LSD on a random piss test. They can only detect it by a spinal tap, and they're not going to do a medical procedure on you unless they have a goddamn good reason to. So, if you can manage to keep your shit together and not give them that reason, we'll be fine."

"Keep my shit together?!?" I asked incredulously. "You want me to keep my shit together?!? Master Chief, I'm standing in what would be Dante's third level of Hell had Lucifer been a fucking Ringling Brother...*on acid!*...and you're asking me to keep my shit together?!? This has 'Baaaaaaaad Trip' written all over it!"

"You need to calm yourself down, or you're going to blow a circuit. Breathe. Purge yourself of all this negativity. Get your mind on a positive plane. Close your eyes and concentrate."

I shot my master chief a look that suggested I could not take him less seriously if he were tarted up in a leather negligee and wearing a Richard Nixon mask. In response, he yelled, "That's an order! Close your eyes! And concentrate!"

The Circus Circus casino was loud, full of all sorts of disparate noises. When my eyes were open and able to reconcile what I saw with what I heard, I knew I was in a carnival environment.

Once I closed my eyes and removed the visual component, however, I lost my ability of association. Screams of laughter became cries of terror. Popping balloons became sporadic bursts of gunfire. Roaring tigers became growling German Shepherds, and the rise of applause reminded me of boots running across cobblestones. I went from Las Vegas to Bergen-Belsen, literally within the blink of an eye.

Now, I knew from experience that LSD did not take effect that quickly, so I assumed whatever occurred was my brain's way of warning me what was in store if I stayed put. "Aw, fuck this," I said, doing a quick about-face and stepping into the Midway crowd. Hoping to follow them to the nearest exit, I lost myself in the passing throng before Darrow could stop me.

I chose poorly. The group of people I joined was going into the casino, not out of it, and before I knew it, I found myself deep within the belly of the beast. Casino architects made it as challenging to find exits as they did to find natural sunlight. It was a deliberate attempt to contain people with both disposable incomes and optimistic misinterpretations of the laws of probability. It was just as effective in trapping emotionally fragile seafarers seeking quieter environs before suffering a psychotic break born of Lysergic Acid Diethylamide.

I tried to calm down, knowing that the more distressed I became, the quicker my body would metabolize the chemicals in my bloodstream. The problem was, the more I tried to calm myself, the more agitated I got. It was not the drugs. It was anxiety, and I knew that if I did not get a handle on it soon, I risked slipping into another post-traumatic flashback, and that was NOT the frame of mind I wanted to be in when the walls started breathing. I picked up my pace, turning my brisk walk into a jog, and then…

…suddenly I was there. I was within the hotel, by myself in a hallway surrounded by rows of doors. The noise disappeared, as did the crowds. I could no longer smell popcorn and cotton candy, and I no longer seemed to risk running into any caged white lions if I took a wrong turn. Relieved, I took a seat on one of the hall benches and tried to see if I was ahead of the game or not.

I contemplated going to the hospital and saving my own ass in case the master chief was wrong about the drug test, but I quickly dismissed that thought. Darrow had connections. He had a LOT of connections, and it was not as if he had no dirt on me. Turning in my boss was not an option.

"Fuck!" I yelled in frustration. I then looked at my watch to see how much time I had before things started getting weird. And then they did.

I closed my eyes and put my face in my hands, taking advantage of being able to do so without the sensation I was being herded toward the gas chambers by festively attired National Socialists. When I opened them, though, I discovered I was not alone. Two muumuu wearing, morbidly obese women were making their way slowly down the hall assisted by walkers, heading right for me.

TEQUILA VIKINGS

They had to be sisters, judging by how similar they were in age and state of deterioration. Neither had more than a few thin wisps of gray hair coming off of their heads, and both wore similar styles of old-lady spectacles perched upon their tiny noses. Their lens prescriptions made their eyes look bigger than Macklemore's.

The women mumbled unintelligibly to one another as they meandered down the hall with squirmy, worm-like movements, panting and bickering with each other until they noticed me. That was when they both stopped, smiled toothlessly, and picked up their pace, visibly salivating.

They wanted me, though I did not know if for my reproductive potential or my nutritional value. I stood up and backed away slowly, not wanting to spook them with any sudden movement, hoping they would afford me the same courtesy. One tried to speak, but it came out in low-pitched barking noises that sounded more walrus than human.

Terrified, I turned and sprinted until I ran out of hallway, taking up a defensive position against a wall of elevators. The worm creatures continued their slow, but relentless, progression forward, lewdly barking their mating calls. I started punching call buttons, watching the worm-fiends getting closer and closer.

With a ding that announced my salvation, the elevator doors finally opened, allowing me to back in and press the lobby button. I kept my eyes locked on the larvae ladies. I did not even allow myself to breathe until the highly polished elevator doors completely closed, revealing an even more sinister beast getting ready to pounce from behind. I let out a blood-curdling shriek and threw myself against the only way out of the tomb, frantically clawing to get out so I could take my chances with the worm women. It was too late, though. I was trapped.

Overtaken with hysteria, all I could do was crumple to the ground and await my fate. I pled for mercy, hoping to strike a chord of compassion somewhere deep within that monster's heart. Having dropped two floors without being mauled, I turned to sneak a peek at the demon in the back of the elevator. I discovered that I was cowering from a giant poster of the clown host of the casino children's show. Not willing to let me savor my newfound sense of security, that was when the elevator doors opened, spilling me backward into the lobby.

It was a spectacular entrance, and any other patron would probably have been impressed by the world-class concierge staff who dropped everything they were doing to make sure that I was okay. For those of us who were tripping balls and reeling from having faced down a giant clown poster, however, it felt more like being bum-rushed. I leaped to my feet with my hands up in defense, yelling out, "KARATE! Don't fucking touch me! I mean it! Back off, goddammit!"

One of them closed in anyway, hunched over like he was preparing to wrestle an agitated alligator. This heightened the tension level, and I sensed it was in my best interest to defuse the situation before someone called the cops. Following my instincts, I tried to explain away my state with several layers of bullshit.

"Sorry, everybody! I know I'm a bit off! I've been awake for two days now, have consumed enough booze to kill a fucking Kennedy, and lost more cash than I can conceal from my ex-wife's accountant. I'm also extremely ticklish and dealing with an incredibly full bladder. I feel like nitroglycerin here, like if I'm moved the wrong way, something horrible is going to happen that I can't recover from. If I can just get back to my room at Harrah's, though, I'm pretty sure I can sort this shit out. All I need is a solid eight hours of sleep, a decent breakfast, and maybe a little bit of pornography. Could one of you people just show me where the fucking exit of this place is? It feels like I've been looking for it for hours."

An apprehensive young lady pointed to a set of doors to my left. I thanked her and made a break for them. No one pursued me, which I took as a good sign considering how notoriously trigger-happy the Las Vegas security apparatus was. I broke free with nothing more than a "Thank you! Come again!" from the doorman.

I yelled back, "Fuck you too!" then dashed out into the night.

*****

CHAPTER 14

Coming from a comfortably air-conditioned casino into the sweltering desert heat of The Strip was a shock to the system. It was like getting hit square in the face by the exhaust of a blast furnace, and with all my senses made hyper-sensitive by Master Chief Darrow's blotter acid, it felt as if it could sear my skin right off.

Then the lights hit me. The spotlights. The headlights. The lasers. The blinkers and the strobes. All of them so powerful I could hear them, even above the ambiance created by the people, the music, and the blaring traffic.

I left the casino convinced that Hunter Thompson never braved The Strip under the influence of high-powered hallucinogens. It was pure sensory overload, and any prolonged exposure to it would result in instant madness. The only way I was able to survive it was to put my hands over my ears while sprinting down the street, singing, "La! La! La! Laaaaaaa!" over and over again. I only opened my eyes wide enough to keep from stepping into the path of an oncoming airport shuttle bus.

Somehow, I passed Harrah's and kept on running, wandering for hours so far down Las Vegas Blvd that I could not even see the airport anymore.

The lights of The Strip were not even visible from my vantage point, though I could still make out their glow in the sky above them. That at least gave me the direction I needed to walk toward to get back.

I was in a sketchy part of town. There were no crowds of tourists, and there was very little traffic. The only people I saw were beggars who, I suspected, would resort to strong-arm robbery if I did not clear out of that area soon.

As if the vagrants were not enough, I spotted a rusty blue Ford sedan slow down and do a U-turn, pulling up to me from behind. In the front seat sat two long-haired tweakers who could have passed for extras in a horror movie, smiling at me as they rolled forward and offered me a ride. "No thanks," I said without breaking stride. "Just out getting some exercise."

"Here?" the one hanging out of the passenger side window asked. When he opened his mouth, he let his tongue roll out twelve inches down the door to remind me that the LSD was still going strong.

"Sure," I answered. "Why not?"

"Well, for starters, it's not very safe," the driver answered. "Judgin' by the crowd of misfits gatherin' behind ya, they's about to throw a stompin' down on yo' ass about any minute now. Jump in da ca' an' at least let us git ya to where da cops is patrolling."

I was turning around to see how bad the vagrant situation was when someone grabbed me from behind so violently that it knocked the wind out of me. The Ford's back door then flew open, and I was tossed inside, held face down into the rotting seat fabric. I heard the tweaker in the passenger seat scream, "Drive! Drive! Drive!" and then listened to the tires squeal as they peeled out back into the street.

There was not much room to fight in the back seat, and the man who was holding me down seemed bigger than I was. The only thing I could do was try to kick the guy, but I missed and hit the door, sending it flying open until it hit something, a car mirror, or a traffic cone that smashed it back closed again. "Hey!" cried the driver. "Watch my fucking ca'!"

To keep me from kicking again, the bruin I was struggling with released his grip to try to get a better hold. I capitalized on that by pulling my legs up underneath me. I then leaned back and pivoted them out in front, pushing off against the back of the driver's seat. I hoped that would send my assailant slamming into the passenger side hard enough to pop that door open again and throw him out into the street. My angle was all wrong, though, and all I did was send his head slamming up against the roof. That really pissed him off.

Trying to end my struggling, the thug punched me in the back of my head, and I retaliated by launching my right elbow into his face. I caught him just below the eye and heard him curse, "Goddammit, Doyle!" It was Master Chief Darrow.

The shock of that revelation made me hesitate. Darrow took advantage of that and slipped me into a chokehold that got tighter as I struggled to get out of it. "Shhhhhhhh," he pled. "Shhhhhhh. Everything's going to be alright."

"Ok, man," I heard the driver say as I tried to gasp for air. "Where to now?"

"The desert," Darrow answered.

"Where in the desert?"

"Anywhere! Just get on I-15 and take us someplace where nobody's going to bother us!"

Oh my fucking God! I thought to myself as the world started to go black. *He's going to fucking kill me!*

*****

"Oh, my God! What did I do? Oh my God! What did I do?"

That was what I woke up to, face down in the sand. It was still dark, but not as dark as it was when I got abducted. There was a slight chill in the air, but I was near a fire, so it was not as bad as it could have been. Darrow paced around our little patch of Nevada, freaking himself out. "Oh my God! What did I do? Oh my God!"

I tried to talk, but my throat was raw from the chokehold my master chief put me in. Still, something must have come out because once Darrow heard it, he ran over and hugged me hard. "Oh man! Doyle! Are you okay? Are you alright?"

I coughed. "I think so…" The colorful geometric shapes were back, and the scenery was shooting in and out on me, but otherwise, I was not any worse for wear. I would have thought that the trauma of being kidnapped would trigger another paranoiac episode, but to my surprise, I was calmer than I should have been considering the situation.

Darrow, on the other hand, was not. Once the tweakers had dropped us off, he couldn't revive me. Despite executing a hundred chokeholds while in the AFPD, the master chief thought this one went bad. "Oh man!" he said, back from the brink of hyperventilation. "I thought I lost you. Fuck. You scared the shit out of me."

"And you think you didn't scare me?" I asked, pulling away and dropping down upon my back. "I blacked out thinking you were dragging me out here to kill me!"

"What?!?" Darrow exclaimed, clearly offended. "Kill you? You're like a son to me, Doyle! How could you think that?"

"Well, for starters," I got distracted by a cactus that cut out on me, morphing into some sort of spiny peyote gremlin. It completely derailed my train of thought. "Fuck it. What are we doing out here?"

"Aw, man, I just wanted to show you something."

"Show me something? You choked me out to fucking show me something?!?"

"I'd been looking for you all damn night! After I lost you at the Circus Circus, I went back to the room, but you weren't there. I walked up and down The Strip searching for your dumb ass, and boy, let me tell you, was that ever hard on the senses! Finally, I had to pay a couple of junkies to drive me around until we crossed paths. You damn near killed me trying to push me out of that car. Fuck, man! That chokehold was self-defense. You just weren't listening to reason!"

"Master Chief, I thought I was going to end up raped in the desert by a trio of hillbilly speed freaks! I was fighting for my life! Or at least for my anal chastity."

"Dude," my master chief laughed. "I'd be fighting a lot harder than that if I thought hillbillies were trying to get up into my ass and shit."

"Fuck you. I did the best I could. What's so important to see out here?"

Darrow was completely not Darrow at that point. The man so accustomed to speaking in orders was now behaving like a Woodstock flower child. He and Hannah would have gotten along great.

My master chief led me east until we were beyond the heat of the fire and set me back down in the dirt, directing my attention to where the deep dark desert sky was just beginning to show hints of purple. "You ever see a desert sunrise before?"

Not long after graduating from boot camp, a couple of friends and I drove out to the Miramar Air Station to watch the fighter jets from the Top Gun school train overhead. Too drunk to drive back afterward, we camped out overnight, and, yes, I caught the sunrise while taking a leak. "Yeah, Master Chief. I've seen the freakin' sunrise in the desert."

"On acid?"

Nope. He had me there.

"When I got back from 'Nam," Darrow said. "I came to Vegas. I met a girl like Hannah, and we ended up camping around here for a few days, getting high and fucking each other's brains out. She would wake me up every morning with some weird-ass Indian ritual that she probably just made up, then we'd do drugs and make love while the sun came up. Sunrises out here on peyote are some pretty serious shit. Ever since, whenever I'm here, I drop acid and watch the sunrise. Usually, I'm alone..."

"Oh, thank God," I gasped. "For a second, I had the impression that you were expecting me to sleep with you while the sun came up..."

Darrow laughed. "That acid wasn't nearly that good. You know, I'm pushing fifty years old, Doyle. I think this is my last true Vegas visit. If I come back with my wife at some point, I'm going to be too old to party this hard. I'll just be one of those fanny-pack wearing lard-assed blue hairs grazing at the buffet. I wanted to pass the torch, and to be honest, you're the only person I thought that I could trust with this."

I was touched. "Me?"

"Look, I'm not big on dope. What we're doing here is for spiritual purposes. It's still illegal but...Ohhhhhhh! Look over there! Check it out!"

Darrow was pointing at the sky. The sun had not quite emerged from behind the mountain, but it was announcing its arrival with a symphony of color painted across the sky. Though impressive on its own merits, it took my breath away on acid. It was indescribably gorgeous, treating us to hues of blue, purple, pink, orange, yellow, and a couple of other colors that I am not sure I had ever seen before.

The hues were insanely vivid, enhanced to surreal levels by the chemicals still wreaking havoc within our skulls. It was so majestic that it was even accompanied by music, though not the type that we would recognize without the diethylamide. It was other-worldly, played by the angels within our heads and audible only to those of us blessed by the ergot fungus fairies. It was one of the most beautiful things I had ever seen.

I looked over to thank Darrow and saw him still marveling at the sky, tears streaming down his cheeks. "Jesus Christ…" I muttered. "Are you okay?"

Darrow shook his head, overcome with raw emotion. "No, no. Not yet. That was magnificent. One of the best there ever was. I just got this feeling, though…this feeling like…like I'll never see this again."

I understood. I sat there beside my friend in silence, allowing him to savor his moment. At least I did until the sun peeked at us from over the mountain, instantly ratcheting the temperature up ten degrees. "Master Chief," I asked. "How are we getting back?"

"Oh shit!" Darrow jumped up and started slapping the dirt off of his ass. The moment was over. "I forgot about that part!" He then turned and unceremoniously started walking away from the rising sun as if what we were looking at never happened.

"You forgot!" I yelled, jumping to my feet to catch up with him. "What do you mean you fucking forgot? How the hell could you just forget about something like that?!?"

Darrow shrugged. "I was on acid."

*****

Amazingly, we crossed paths with a taxi while walking down the interstate and got back to the hotel about 30 minutes before check out, which was just long enough to guzzle glassfuls of tap water, shower, pack, and meet the rest of our group in the lobby to leave.

Darrow and I were wrecked. Dixie was also, having spent most of the night sleeping on the hallway floor, locked out of his room. Tony was lip-locked with Stacy-cakes on one of the lobby couches, waiting for the rest of us, and he looked like he had not slept, either. Fordson and Claude were put through the wringer by their Canadian girls and could also have benefitted from a few more hours of rest. So could Darren Stovic. He had a productive trip and was returning $6,000 richer than he was when he arrived. Abel de

TEQUILA VIKINGS

Alba was the only one of us who got any shut-eye at all. We made him drive home.

As we were checking out of the hotel, Darrow and I found ourselves alone for a second. "Hey Doyle," he said. "I just want to apologize for what I did. I've been thinking about it, and I realize that it wasn't cool. I just need to know, are we good?"

Master Chief Darrow had kept me out of prison a few months before. It would take more than an involuntary acid trip to get me to turn on him now. "We're good," I answered. "But you owe me. I've got a chip to cash in with you, and when I go to use it, you'd better come fucking running."

I have to admit that I had mixed feelings about what Darrow had done. Despite what he told me, I was not entirely sure I was clear on the drug test issue and I wanted to deck him for putting me at risk. I probably would have hit him if I was not so wary of the damage he could inflict when he hit me back. On the other hand, after witnessing what I had seen in the desert, I also wanted to compliment him on having such a damn good dope connection.

On our way out of the hotel, Dixie excused himself to use the bathroom one last time before hitting the road. While we waited for him to return, I decided to lighten the load in my pocket by donating my coins to the bank of slot machines near the door. Trying to burn through my change before Kevin got back, I maxed out the bet and pulled the handle.

As if to demonstrate our acid still had some mileage left on it, the slot machine exploded into a kaleidoscope of light, accompanied by the deafening roar of air raid sirens. I threw myself to the floor and started screaming, trying to prepare myself for the platoon of Nazi stormtroopers I was sure would swarm in from the main entrance. To my surprise, though, I was instead helped up by a couple of floor bosses who informed me that I had just hit a progressive jackpot. The bastards then sent me back to San Diego with damn near $23,000 after taxes.

Before we even left Las Vegas, I had Dixie take me to buy Hannah's engagement ring.

*****

CHAPTER 15

Macklemore stumbled into the berthing area channeling old school Crusty Warren. If I had to guess, he last showered before we left for Nevada and had done little besides drink and sweat since. The boy was beyond ripe.

It was late, and for the most part, Macklemore got to his rack without attracting attention. It was not until he fell into it, passed out, and started snoring that I began hearing the first rumblings of discontent.

"Jesus Christ!" Kurt Dwyer, one of the FCs, complained. "I can't fucking do this again! This kid's going to make me puke! Is Petty Officer Bard here? Somebody's got to do something about this shit! I can't breathe!"

"Yeah, this is bullshit!" GM2 Fred Long added. "He smells like a fucking cadaver!" Warren slept through it all, oblivious to the racket building around him.

"Hey Fred!" came a voice from the other side of the berthing area. It belonged to DS3 Nick Thomas. "You want to keep it down over there? It's after midnight!"

"Fuck you!" Fred answered. "Come over here and smell this shit and tell me you'd sleep next to this asshole!"

Several men did exactly that to see just how bad it could be, and the consensus was that it was even worse than Fred Long had suggested.

"Gaaahhh!" yelled one of the younger aviation ordnance men as he passed by and got a whiff. He then ran around the berthing area like he was on fire. "Gah! Gah! Oh, God! Somebody help me! I think I got it in my mouth!"

Macklemore slept through that, too, but no one else did. Half of the Combat Systems Department seemed to wake up to laugh at the airman's antics. The other half woke up to tell him to pipe down.

Bill Kramer was in the latter half. He had the four to eight watch and knew that after being woken up, he would never get back to sleep. He was pissed, rolling out of his rack and charging the crowd making all the noise.

I am sure Kramer's first intention was to threaten the men responsible for the racket, but after realizing how outnumbered he was, Bill went for the source of the commotion. He reached into Mack's rack and ripped him out of bed by the scruff of his shirt, throwing him to the deck.

My first instinct was to break it up and send Mack to the showers, but as soon as my feet hit the floor, I saw Dixie roll out of his rack, all smiles. He mimicked some boxing moves to remind me this was what we were waiting for. It was showtime, the entire reason Kevin spent so much time in the gym with Macklemore.

"Get up!" Kramer barked at Mack. "Get your ass up off the floor! Now!"

I could judge by the pause that Mack was disoriented. He had no idea what led up to this and, since he could not smell himself, he could not even begin to comprehend how he had earned the ire of so many people while simply sleeping. "Wha?... Hey!...I...uh..."

Kramer reached down and pulled Macklemore to his feet by the hair. "How many times do we have to go through this with you!?!" Kramer screamed at him. "Huh?!?"

Mack howled in pain as he felt his hair ripped out the back of his head. "What!" he cried. "What'd I do!?!"

Hit him! I thought to myself. I was two rows of racks away from them. I could not see what was going on, but Kramer had already done plenty to justify a haymaker to the kisser from what I heard. *Hit him goddammit! Hit him now!*

"YOU STINK!" Kramer bellowed. "YOU FUCKING REEK!"

"I'm sorry!" Mack yelled back. "Let go of me! I'll shower! Let go, and I'll take a shower!"

"Fuck that!" Kramer retorted. "Mike! Get Crowley! It's time to teach Crusty Warren here how to clean his funky ass!"

The crowd around Macklemore's rack started turning into a mob. The immediate catalyst was frustration, stemming from the fact that Warren was compounding the crew's discomfort once again. That frustration was then amplified by anger because Mack was robbing us of sleep, a precious commodity in the military. The men were tired of Mack getting away with it. They wanted something done.

"Scrub that ass!" one of the junior men yelled. Then two others went to repeat the sentiment and said it in unison. From there, it became a chant. "Scrub that ass! Scrub that ass! Scrub that ass!" Men started getting out of their racks in a show of solidarity.

"No! Bill! Please don't!" Mack begged. "Please don't do this!"

Goddammit, Mack! Hit him! He's going to hurt you if you don't! I stole a glance at Dixie. He shrugged his shoulders at me in exasperation.

I heard Crowley and Deaver raiding the cleaning supply closet while Kramer struggled with Mack, ripping off his clothes. The chants went on. "Scrub that ass! Scrub that ass!"

Things were getting loud. I was expecting one of the senior petty officers to put a stop to it, but no one did. Looking at AO1 Healey's rack, I saw he had disappeared. GM1 Wegner's bunk was empty too. Senior petty officers were career men. They were not going to risk their futures participating in a GI shower, but they did not object to it going down. I guessed that they were all solidifying their alibis together so that they could plausibly deny knowing about it if something went wrong.

Considering the position I was in after what I had done to Green, I should have joined them, but I could not bring myself to leave.

"Noooooooo!" Macklemore screamed as Kramer dragged him to the shower, by now stripped to his underwear. "Please, Bill! Stop! STOOOOPPP!"

"Scrub that ass! Scrub that ass! Scrub that ass!" The mob followed them.

TEQUILA VIKINGS

Palazzo slipped into my row of racks between Dixie and me, grabbing his hair with both hands. "This is fucked up, Murphy! This whole command is fucked! Look at this shit! No one's even trying to hide it! It's like they know they're going to get away with it!"

After I got away with it, it's no wonder. I wanted to intervene, but with my very first step towards Macklemore, my mind flooded with what Master Chief Darrow said to me the week before:

Let me be perfectly clear to all of you, and especially to you, Doyle. You are not to tell Macklemore what Kramer's planning. You're not to discourage Kramer from carrying this thing out. You're not going to let on that you even fucking know what he wants to do. And once they start doing it, you're to stay out of the way and let it happen. Am I clear?

Mack finally fought back when they got to the shower room, but not against Kramer. He grabbed the doorway, struggling to stay outside. He was winning until Crowley punched him in the kidney and broke his grip. Warren was sobbing after that, screaming out for help. In response, Deaver grabbed the back of Mack's underwear and yanked it up over his head. It was an excruciating move the deck apes called an "atomic wedgie."

"Heeeellllllpp!" Macklemore cried out again as one of the men turned the water on at full steam. At that temperature, it could feel like your skin was melting away. As someone else ripped open a can of scouring powder and threw it at him, we heard Mack begging, "Pleeeeeeease! Someone! Heeeeeelp meeeeee!"

Kramer and his goons cackled mercilessly over the pain they were inflicting. "Make sure you get his armpits, Mike!" I heard Crowley laugh, followed by more screams from Macklemore as Deaver started scrubbing him with a wire brush.

"HEEEEELLLLLPPP! PLEEEEAAAAASEE! SOMEONE!"

From outside the shower room, the chants continued. "Scrub that ass! Scrub that ass! Scrub that ass!"

Closing my eyes, I put my hands over my ears to drown out the noise. That instantly thrust me into my underwater world, however.

I had a vision of my father holding me down on my parents' bed. He was bringing his belt down across my bare ass for what must have been the fiftieth time. I flinched as I felt the pain. It was as real now as it was when I was eight, and I could even feel the blood spilling out of my wounds to pool on the sheets beneath me. I was screaming for someone to help just like Macklemore, remembering how it felt when no one came. I had to force my eyes open to keep from slipping into a full-blown episode.

Snapping back, I heard Kramer demand that someone pass him a wire brush. "I'm going to teach him how to wipe his shitty ass!" he laughed.

"NOOOOO! NO! HEEELLLLPPPPP! DOOYYLLLLEE!"

"Jesus Christ!" gasped Dixie. "They're going to sodomize the guy!"

By the time Kevin said that I was already in motion, marching towards the crowd gathered outside the shower room door with clenched fists. "The fuck they are…"

*****

Airman Tyson stood about five foot six. He was a skinny guy, weighing about a buck twenty, but he was from the ghettos of Compton. He thought himself a pretty hard man. The airman played the part of a seasoned gangster, talking in street lingo and enjoying a reputation of being some sort of hoodlum enforcer. I had to hand it to him; he had balls. Tyson was not afraid to stand up to anybody. Not even me, despite being twice his size, outranking him by two pay grades, and knowing what I had done to Randy Green.

As I approached the shower room, the "Scrub that ass!" crowd parted to let me through. Except for Airman Tyson. He stepped directly into my path, putting himself between me and the door while flashing me a "bring-it-on-bitch" kind of grin.

In one fluid movement, I reached out and wrapped both of my hands around Tyson's scrawny little neck, lifting him clear off of his feet and over my head. I then smashed him against the bulkhead. The impact made a frightening sound against the fiberglass wall. In reality, it sounded worse than it was, but it knocked the wind out of the airman and gave him a compelling reason to mind his manners with me in the future.

When I entered the showers, Macklemore's tormentors panicked and scattered. Before I could get my hands on one of them, Dixie, Metaire, Stovic, and Sergeant Fordson were on top of me, taking me to the deck, knowing how much trouble I would land in if I hurt anybody.

TEQUILA VIKINGS

I screamed at them to get off but they refused, tightening their hold on me. Dixie put his mouth up to my ear and whispered, "Easy, Doyle. Easy. It's alright. They're gone. It's over. Mack's okay. You need to settle down…"

"NO!" I screamed back. "NO! LET GO OF ME! I'M GOING TO KILL…!"

"Sssshhhhhh…sshhhh. Easy, Doyle. You have to let this go, man. Let it go. We can't do this again. We're not going to let you. Settle down."

"GOD! God! Goddammit! Get off of me!"

"Sssssshhhh. We will. As soon as we know you've got control of yourself."

"Doyle, *mon ami*," Claude begged. "Doyle…*s'il te plaît…arrête*."

I could hear Macklemore bawling in the far stall, still under the running water. It was the only thing tempering my need to punish Kramer and his boys. "Okay! Okay! Let me go."

Almost at once, everyone released their grip, backing up to block my way out of the shower room in case I changed my mind about pursuing Kramer. As I caught my breath, I waved them off. "Go! Get out of here. Don't let anybody in. Not until I tell you. Dixie, go to Mack's rack and bring back his clothes."

Once everyone was gone, I made my way to Warren, relieved to see his physical injuries were superficial. Emotionally, though, the wounds were much deeper. I saw what Dixie meant about the look in his eye. Mack's body may have been in the Combat Systems berthing area, but now that the threat of physical danger had passed, mentally, Warren was being tormented elsewhere. I wondered if that was what I looked like during my episodes.

Mack was lying naked in the shower stall, shaking all over and sobbing. He could not even bring himself to turn off the scalding hot water. Seeing me standing above him, Macklemore started crying even harder. "Nooooo…Noooo…Joey…Nooooo."

"Joey? Who the fuck is Joey? Mack, it's Doyle."

I tried to reach out to him, to grab him by the arm and pull him back, but physical contact only made things worse. Mack recoiled, descending deeper into hysteria, withdrawing so far into his own mind that I was not sure if I could get him back out again.

When Dixie walked in with the clothes he fished out of Warren's dirty laundry, he was shaken by what he saw. "Is he going to be alright?"

"I don't know," I said, struggling to get Warren's skivvies on. It was difficult enough to dress a fully grown adult who is in no condition to cooperate with you, but it was even more challenging when no one thought to dry him off first. "I need to get him to the radar dome. I can work it out there."

We noticed that the more clothes we got on Macklemore, the more he responded. There was a point where he seemed to be half in both worlds where he brought up Joey again. "He's gone, Mack," I told him.

When we emerged from the showers, everyone was back in bed, though surely still awake. I was glad. The fewer people that saw the condition Macklemore was in, the better. We dragged him out of the berthing area and towards the mess decks to get to the catwalk.

"You want me to go with you?" Dixie asked once we finally hit the flight deck.

Mack was still in some sort of daze, but he was moving under his own power. I shook my head. "No, I got it. Go back below and try to get some sleep."

We crossed over to the island structure and then climbed the ladder to the platform that held the captain's gig, just outside the porthole to the EMO office. Up one more short ladder, and we were at the SPN-35 dome. Once inside, Macklemore collapsed onto the deck and broke down again. This time, he seemed more ashamed than traumatized.

"I'm sorry, Doyle. I'm sorry I didn't stick up for myself. Something happened when they started ripping my clothes off, and I didn't see Kramer there anymore. It was someone else and…and…I froze."

I knew what had happened to him. It was the same thing that I had to deal with, only set off by a different trigger. I shuddered, thinking about the kind of trauma that would flip that switch inside of Mack's head while Kramer's goons were forcibly removing his clothes. I did not want to know but could not stop myself from asking. "Was it Joey?"

Warren completely broke down, burying his head in his arms, hysterical again. "Oh, man! What did I say? Please, Doyle! Please don't throw me out! I'm not a fag! I was just a kid, and he made me! There was nothing I could do!"

TEQUILA VIKINGS

"Jesus Christ," I gasped, poorly equipped to deal with something like this. My knees went weak and I had to reach out for the workbench to steady myself. I did not want to hear any more than I already had, but once Warren started spilling his guts, there was no option but to listen.

Macklemore told me that his people were basically Alaskan hillbillies. When Macklemore's mother was in-between boyfriends, they lived in a shack out in the woods with neither electricity nor running water. Joey was someone that Mack's mother met who offered to take them in for a while over the winter.

Joey's house would not have passed muster as a garage anywhere else, but it had electricity, running water, and even cable television. By the Macklemore family's standards, it was the Ritz.

"We hadn't washed in weeks," Warren told me. "We were so nasty that even someone as sick as Joey wouldn't come near me until I took a shower. After I did, he..."

"Warren, I'm not a therapist," I interjected. "You don't need to tell me this."

Macklemore nodded and wiped his eyes. He kept talking anyway. "People knew about him. They knew we were staying there. They knew what he was making me do. I was now the town's littlest faggot. No one wanted me anywhere around them, especially their kids. The only time anyone was allowed to speak with me was when they were kicking my ass. I'm not queer, Doyle! I'm not!"

Things were different in 1992. Much different. It was not just religious zealots and political firebrands that believed homosexuality occupied the same moral plane as pedophilia. More often than not, those were mainstream views. The word "gay" was not an adjective. It was an insult, especially in the military.

"Please don't let them throw me out for this, Doyle! I swear I'm no fag! God! I want a wife! I want to have kids! I'd love them, Doyle! I just want somebody that I could give all of the things I never had! I'd do anything I could to make them happy, Doyle! Anything!"

Me too, Warren. Me too.

As Mack's state deteriorated, I sat down next to him and draped my arm over his shoulder, pulling him in close. "Warren, nobody's going to throw you out of the Navy for this. I'm telling you, though, man. If you backslide on all the progress you're making, you will end up discharged. You need to pull yourself back together."

I sighed. "It's not fair, Warren, but the world doesn't care what that fucker did to you. It's not going to change to allow you your place in it. To get what you want, you're going to have to be the one who changes. You know, people like Kramer see you as a victim, Warren. They think you're weak and easy to prey on. Part of that's because it's the same way you see yourself."

I pulled out a cigarette and offered one to Macklemore. After lighting them both, I said, "I've been through some pretty horrific shit myself. Yeah, I'm fucked up too, but I'm rising above it. Right hand to God, though, I don't think I would've survived what you've gone through. I would've ended up killing myself. I'm not even close to being tough enough to handle shit like that."

"I thought about that too," Mack confided in me. "A lot."

"Are you still thinking about it?"

Mack shook his head. "My little brother, if anything happened to me, it would kill him."

I patted Mack on the shoulder to show him I understood. "Well, we're going to make sure nothing ever happens to you again. We're going to protect you, but you've got to do your part. You need to get your shit together again and keep it that way."

I stood up and looked back down at Crusty Warren. "We need to start with this shower thing. I understand your issues with it. It all makes sense now. You've got to conquer it, though. It's the basic thing that sets you apart from everyone else."

"I smelled fine for that girl in the bar the other night. She didn't treat me the way she did because I stink. She did it because she probably sensed what I was."

"And what are you?" I asked.

"I'm this, Doyle!" Warren cried, holding his arms out. "I'm me! I'm ugly! I'm dirty! I'm stupid! I'm soiled! I'm fucking pathetic, man!"

"That shit show had nothing to do with you. Those were criminals in search of a victim, Warren. Put it behind you right now. Start realizing that you're not a victim. You're a survivor. Give yourself credit for that."

TEQUILA VIKINGS

I stole a glance at my watch. "We've got an hour before reveille. I'm going back below to try to get whatever sleep I can before that. You coming?"

Mack shook his head. "You mind if I stay here?"

"No. Not at all." I threw Mack what was left of my cigarettes and stepped out of the dome. After shutting the door, I turned around and was scared half to death by someone lurking in the darkness, standing by the ladder that led up to Comm Repair. I jumped in fright, and the squeal that escaped my lips hit an octave that I did not know I was even capable of reaching. It was WAY out of character. Palazzo would have found it hilarious had it happened some other time.

"What the hell are you doing here?" I whispered, keeping my voice low enough so that Mack did not realize we had company.

"I came up here to see if everything was okay," Palazzo whispered back.

"How long have you been up here?"

"Long enough," he answered, shaking his head in disbelief. "Jesus Christ."

*****

Darrow was so pissed that he hauled off and slapped me across the jaw again. "I gave you a fuckin' order!"

I remained at the position of attention and answered in the calmest voice I could muster. "You did, Master Chief. It was, however, an illegal order. It was an order to stand by and let a subordinate of mine get assaulted by three other sailors. Failure to intervene would have been a gross dereliction of duty."

Darrow smacked me again, but this time across the opposite cheek. "What the fuck do you think you are now? You a fuckin' attorney?"

"No, Master Chief, but if you disagree with my interpretation of the Uniform Code of Military Justice, I suppose that we can walk down to the ship's JAG officer and have him clarify it for us."

Darrow's face flushed red, and his hands bunched up into fists. I had the feeling that the next blow was not going to be with an open palm. "Do you really want to take this route with me, son? An order is an order! Yeah, you might think it doesn't pass your smell test, but you know what? It was given to protect your own sorry ass! It was given to keep you from doing stupid shit like grabbing one of the AOs by the neck and trying to throw him through the fuckin' shower room wall!"

"Airman Tyson was out of order and actively trying to prevent me from carrying out my duty as a petty officer of the…"

"I don't give a shit what he was doing!" Darrow bellowed. "I now have fifteen witnesses from combat systems that saw you assault this little prick and are willing to put you on report for it if I pursue any action against Crowley and Deaver for what they did to Macklemore! And I can't do a goddamn thing to Kramer without implicating those two ass clowns with him! So, you know what that means, Matlock? That means all that shit those men put Macklemore through was for nothing! NOTHING!"

"Master Chief, they were taking it too far."

"THAT WAS THE FUCKIN' POINT!" Darrow screamed. "If these cretins were going to go overboard on anybody, it was better to be on one of our waste cases!"

"Mack's not a waste case, Master Chief."

"The fuck he ain't!"

"Master Chief, he's got issues. He's got big issues. I can work with him, though."

Darrow shook his head. He was having none of it. "We've all tried working with him, Doyle! He's a waste of skin! An empty shell! We're sailors, Doyle! Not psychotherapists! He can't pull his weight so…"

"He was abused, Master Chief…"

"So fuckin' what! You were abused! I ain't never met anybody in my whole fuckin' life that went through anything as bad as what happened to you and…"

"Not like that, Master Chief. I was never abused like that."

I do not know if it was what I said or how I said it, but it took the steam out of Darrow's tirade. "What do you mean? Like what?"

"You want me to spell it out for you? Would you like me to give you all the gory details of why, in Macklemore's mind, a shower makes him feel dirtier coming out of it than he was going into it?"

"Oh my god. Are you serious?" After I nodded, Darrow started pacing around the EMO office. "Jesus Christ. That's awful. It's horrible."

TEQUILA VIKINGS

Darrow collapsed into his seat and lost himself in thought for a couple of minutes. I remained at attention. "Doyle, look, this takes a lot of the mystery out of Macklemore. It really does. It isn't our job to rehabilitate broken men, though. It's our job to defend the interests of the United States of America. That's why we're going to Japan. Macklemore does not help us further our objective. He hinders it. So does Kramer by compromising unit cohesion. This ship needs both of these men gone to eliminate the risk they pose to our being able to carry out our mission efficiently…"

"Give me a break, Master Chief. We're not going to Japan to go to war. We're going to Japan on a public relations mission…"

Darrow shot out of his seat again, freshly angered, "Don't you talk to me about war goddammit! I've been to war! You haven't! It comes when you least expect it, from a direction you never saw it coming from! When it happens, we'll be the first line of defense against it! That's what being forward-deployed means! When the bad guys come to wreak havoc upon freedom and stability, we good guys…"

"Good guys?!? We're the good guys, Master Chief? You know, I've seen our good guys at work. You wanna know what I saw the good guys do when I was in El Salvador?"

"You're acting like I haven't read your service record, Murphy. That's classified. I suggest you bite your tongue right about now."

I broke the position of attention. "Fine! Fuck El Salvador then! We'll come back to right here, right now. We're thugs, Master Chief. Thugs! Those guys were on the verge of shoving a wire brush up Warren's ass last night during that GI shower! How can we do that shit to people, *our own people*, and still consider ourselves the good guys?!?"

"What? What were they going to do?"

"You heard me."

"Bullshit."

"You don't get to doubt me on this, Master Chief!" I yelled back. "I was there! *You* weren't! And you know what? It stops here! No more! I don't care who it is anymore! I don't care if it's Kramer, I don't care if it's his goons, and I don't care if it's Lieutenant Krause. If anyone else wants to have a go at Macklemore, they're going to have to go through me first." I made sure that I was looking Darrow right in the eye when I snarled, "And that goes for you too."

I had never seen the master chief's face twist up quite like it did then. People did not challenge Bradley Darrow. They did not do it when he was an E-4 on the AFPD, and they certainly were not going to do it while he was an E-9. He stepped towards me, bringing his face to within inches of mine, and I saw him preparing his right hand to strike me again. "What the fuck do you think gives you the right to…"

"As god is my witness Master Chief, the next time you lay a finger on me, I *will* fucking hit you back."

I firmly believe that Darrow was capable of murder at that point, but after a few seconds of staring at me so intently that I could feel the heat radiating off of his reddened face, I watched his mouth twist into a wry grin. "You're going to hit me back? You think you're going to get away with that?"

"No. I'll hit you, you'll hit me. Chief Ramirez, who I'll bet is waiting patiently outside the door listening to all of this will rush in and break it up."

"You want to go somewhere off base and settle this where we won't get interrupted?"

"No," I answered. "But if that's what it takes to get you off of Mack's ass, I will."

"Who do you think is going to win a fight between the two of us, son?"

"I guess we'll find out soon enough, won't we?"

Darrow let out a laugh. A genuine laugh. "Take a seat, Doyle. We're not going anywhere."

I deflated in relief. I promised Hannah I would never come to blows with anyone ever again. She threatened to end our relationship if I did. I would never be able to hide a fight with Master Chief Darrow from her. Even if I won, I would walk away from it severely damaged. Hannah knew how I looked up to my master chief, too. She would think that if I could hit him, I could hit anyone. Maybe even her. She would leave me again.

As I sat down, Darrow fished a pack of cigarettes out of his desk and slid them over to me. "You've got balls. I'll give you that. You know what I can do, and you're still willing to risk going toe-to-toe with me over Macklemore?"

"He's a good man, Master Chief. He's a shitty sailor, but a good man. I'm not going to let the Navy destroy him. I would think you, of all people, get that. You went up against the frickin' NIS to keep the Navy from destroying me."

Darrow nodded. "That's loyalty, Doyle. I can depend on you, so I need to make sure you know you can depend on me too. You get the concept of loyalty. You're a bit misguided in where you apply it, but you get it."

Darrow took a long drag off of his cigarette. "If the shit ever hit the fan and you found yourself in a life or death situation, could Macklemore count on you to have his back?"

"Absolutely," I answered without hesitation.

"Of course, he could. But put the shoe on the other foot. If you found yourself in a life or death situation, could you depend on Mack?"

I let out a sigh of resignation. Mack was not a brave man, nor a capable one. Even if he somehow found the balls to help me in a critical moment, he would undoubtedly do more harm than good.

Darrow wanted to hear me say it. "Doyle, if you found yourself in a life or death situation, could you depend on Mack to have your back?"

I slowly shook my head. "No, Master Chief. I couldn't."

*****

CHAPTER 16

Hannah gasped, bringing her hands up to cover her mouth. "Oh my God…" she whimpered.

Dreadlock John looked even more surprised, his open jaw nearly landing in the sand. Space Kate gasped in shock and grabbed his arm, looking like she couldn't believe what was happening. Eddie Wayne appeared stunned while Lupe swiped her arm across her eyes. Warren Macklemore was spending a lot of time with me since his GI Shower, so he was there too, looking uncomfortable and unsure how to react.

I could not have cared less about how he reacted, though. I only cared about Hannah, and when she fell to her knees and buried her face in her hands, I knew things were going my way. "Yes!" she sobbed, falling into my arms beside the bonfire. "Yes! I will!"

With my own hands shaking now, I pulled the ring out of the box and slipped it onto Hannah's finger just before she tackled me and started smothering me with kisses in the sand.

Kate squealed and started clapping her hands. Lupe embraced her, and they both fell backward onto the beach. Eddie slapped my back to congratulate me while John stood up and announced to the crowd around us, "Hey everybody! I would like to be the first to introduce to you all the soon-to-be Mister and Missus Doyle Murphy!" The crowd responded with several scattered rounds of applause and a shower of full beer cans thrown in our general direction. It was perfect.

I could have proposed in Point Loma or Balboa Park or Sunset Cliffs while the daylight disappeared over the horizon. There were a million picturesque places to be found around San Diego that could have offered me the opportunity to pull off the perfect Hallmark proposal.

Neither Hannah nor I were those types of people, though. We enjoyed the company of the misfits of Ocean Beach. For me, the only place to propose was where we loved to be, surrounded by deviants while serenaded by the sound of the crashing surf in the darkness behind us.

Eddie, who dabbled in bartending so that it at least appeared like they had a legitimate source of income besides Lupe's pot-dealing, was not impressed by the beer thrown our way. "Good lord. Poor surfers have really shitty taste," he said, seemingly tempted to start throwing some of them back. "This won't do. We've got some champagne back at the Sand Flea. Why don't we go back there and let me treat you to some."

"That's okay, Eddie," I said. "You don't need to do that."

"Doyle, I'll be insulted if you don't let me. Come on. Follow me."

As we got up to leave, I noticed Warren was gone. "Where the hell did he get off to…"

"Mack? Don't worry about him, man. Hey Dino!" Eddie called out to the fire beside us. "Hey! If that funny lookin' guy comes back here, tell him to meet us at the Sand Flea. Alright?"

"Alright, bro!" Dino called back, flashing him a thumbs up. "Hey! Good luck to the couple!"

The Sand Flea was hardly the kind of place one would expect to find a bottle of champagne. It was basically a big shack built of weathered wood deliberately designed to look ready to collapse upon itself. It had just a couple of windows, and though there were a few stools against the bar inside, most of the seating was beneath several palm-frond *palapas* that backed up against the beach.

Eddie sat us down at a picnic table and went to see about that champagne. Before he could get inside, though, a loud ruckus erupted from within, and people started rushing out of the place as if someone pulled a fire alarm. I was astonished that little bar could hold that many people. I was even more surprised that they were all coming right at us.

It was dark, so they were hard to recognize at first, but once Chief Ramirez leaped over the table to hug me, I realized what was going on. Before I knew it, we were surrounded by Dixie, Claude Metaire, and Tony Bard. Rick and Melissa Hammond made it as well as Ramirez's wife, Elena. Behind them all was Warren Macklemore and Eddie Wayne, walking out with the champagne. Mack knew what was going down and arranged everything with Dixie and Ed as a surprise.

It was a big moment, but awkward that Mack was there for it while my best friend was not. Luckily, Kevin understood and still wanted to do something for me. "You're not mad about me putting together this shindig, are you?" Dixie asked as he handed me a bottle of mezcal from his pocket.

I grinned and embraced him. "Man Dixie, I was going to tell you, but getting plowed with you in Tijuana was going to be my backup plan if she said no."

"She wasn't going to say, 'no,'" Marty Pruitt said as he slapped me on the back. "If she did, Dixie had a plan for that too."

"Oh yeah? What was that?" I asked.

"Plan B!" Dixie yelled and then looked back towards the bar.

Through the front door of the Sand Flea strutted Master Chief Darrow and his wife, Jung. Jung was from Korea and in her thirties but looked no older than sixteen. She still got carded everywhere she went. Once outside of the bar with her husband, they unfurled a huge banner that read, "OUCH! Better Luck Next Time."

*****

"What's wrong?" I asked Hannah as she laid her head down into my lap. She had been giddy all evening after I asked her to marry me, but as things were beginning to wind down a few hours later, I sensed a wave of melancholy washing over her.

"Look at that poor guy over there," Hannah said.

We were lying in the sand on the beach. I was facing the bonfire, so I had to shift positions to get a better look at the Sand Flea. "Which one?"

"Macklemore. All those people over there having such a good time, yet there he is sitting by himself."

I squinted to see what I was missing. "Hannah, he's sitting at the same table as Dixie, Dreadlock John, and Space Kate."

"Who are all enjoying a great conversation between themselves. Warren is just sitting there, watching them all talk, with that goofy smile on his face. When you look into his eyes, though, you can see how sad he is. He so wants to be included, but never is."

"You can see that from here?" It was dark and we were pretty far away from the bar. Even with the crazy magnification effect Mack's glasses had on his eyes, I could not tell what he was feeling from that distance.

"No, silly, I saw it when I was over there. It's been like that all night. Don't you think it's sad that he doesn't have anybody?"

"He's got a brother."

"In Alaska. Here in California, he's all by himself. Can you imagine how lonely that must be? He's got no family here…"

I shrugged. "Few of us have family here, Hannah. I'm pretty sure Chief Ramirez is the only native Californian in the entire division."

"I thought he was from the Philippines."

"He was," I answered. "But he's been in the US since he was a kid. Master Chief has an ex-wife in California, as well as another back home in Arkansas with his two daughters."

"Brad has children?"

I nodded. "Yeah, but he hasn't seen or heard from them since the seventies. It was a nasty divorce."

"Where is Dixie from?"

"Ohio. I don't hold that against him, though. Rick and Melissa are from South Carolina, Claude is originally from French Guiana, but he grew up in New Orleans. And, like you said, Mack is from Alaska."

"I wonder what it was like for him, growing up in Alaska?"

"Well, let's ask," I said, picking myself up off of the sand and walking to the bar to bring Macklemore back with me.

I had only been bringing Warren out to Ocean Beach for a little over a week. He was a quiet guy for the most part, but when I thought about it, we hadn't ever really reached out for his point of view on anything. All it took was for Hannah to express a genuine interest in something Macklemore had to say to wind him up and get him going. Alaska was the perfect topic of conversation for him, too. It was a subject he was intimately familiar with, but one which few others knew much about at all.

It was surprising how eloquent Macklemore could be when he was in his element. We found he had a poetic cadence to the language he used, and I discovered that he might have been a little more intelligent than I gave him credit for.

"I hear that Alaska is a place for people who just don't fit in anywhere else," Hannah said to him. "Is that true, Warren?"

Mack let out that goofy laugh of his and nodded his head. "Yeah, look at me. Alaska's a great place to get lost in if that's what you want to do. You can even get lost in your own home town. There were times when I couldn't stand spending another minute with my mother, so I would just grab a fishing pole and a rifle and take off into the woods. Within an hour's hike, you're already so far out in the wilderness that you can't hear anything man-made. No cars, no radios, no machinery, nothing at all."

I could tell by the look in Mack's eyes that his mind was somewhere deep within the Pacific Northwest when he spoke. It was the place that had broken him, but there were at least a few people there that he could depend on to put him back together. He knew he did not have anyone like that in San Diego.

"I could stay out there for days in the summer," Mack continued. "There was a field way back in the forest that was overrun with fireweed, and in late July, when it blossomed, the entire place was covered in these bright pink flowers as far as you can see. Big Jim Akaluk lived around there. He was this drunk Indian guy…"

"An Eskimo?" Hannah asked.

"Naw, that's farther north. Way farther north. Big Jim was probably Ahtna or Koyukon or some tribe over by the Copper River. He was a misfit, too, so we got along pretty well. The two of us would hang out in that field forever, fishing, eating berries, hunting, and panning for gold. I was pretty good at fishing, so I kept Big Jim fed. He kept me drunk. He used to make his own wine out of wild berries, and he traded game meat for the harder stuff. He didn't care for people much, but he was always good enough to me."

TEQUILA VIKINGS

Macklemore then went on to tell us a long, but hilarious, story about a romantic encounter gone horribly awry when Big Jim Akaluk crossed paths with a bull moose during mating season. It had Hannah doubled over in the fetal position gasping for air. I knew Macklemore had won her over when she reciprocated by telling Warren a tale of a street brawl her father got into with a red kangaroo during a family camping trip. Her old man lost.

As the two of them talked, I got up and returned to the bar to refill our drinks. I got distracted by my friends and shipmates, and upon my return nearly an hour later, I found that they barely noticed I was gone.

It was the night that Hannah and I got engaged, yet my future bride was spending a large chunk of it ignoring me, devoting her attention to another man. I felt like I should have been a bit miffed by that, but I could not bring myself to feel cross at all. Not even a little. In fact, the more I watched them, the more in love with her I was.

Between his looks, hygiene, awkward demeanor, and total lack of confidence, Warren Macklemore's ability to repulse women was second to none. Hannah was being Hannah, though, and embracing the most hopeless man in our division, treating him as if he was the most important person there. She was building him up and feeding off of it, without even realizing it. I was not introducing her to someone I needed to consider a rival.

It was more like I had given her a human puppy to play with.

*****

CHAPTER 17

It was May when things started to get real. Our change of homeport to Sasebo, Japan, was only three months away, and the entire crew went into overdrive to prepare for it. The CSE Division spent most of the month painting all the spaces messed up by Krause's constant cleaning compulsion. Fortunately, May was mostly spent at sea anyway, so we did not lose much liberty doing it.

Hannah moved into Cheri's place at the beginning of the month, and I moved in with her. Macklemore and Dixie were out there so much there were times when it seemed like they lived there too. Hannah took Macklemore on as a hobby, and the two of them became close.

The friendship worked well for Mack. He did not want to wear out his welcome in Ocean Beach with his body odor, so he took the initiative to keep himself clean. Hannah also started grooming him, styling his hair, picking out his clothes, and changing his glasses. Before long, she had him shedding that aspiring vagrant look he had been cultivating his entire life.

TEQUILA VIKINGS

Even his acne showed improvement, though it remained disfiguring enough to be mistaken for some other medical malady.

It got to the point that Hannah started working on finding Mack a date. She seemed to feel that once he finally experienced a woman's attention, he would get the confidence he needed to make something of himself. Palazzo felt the same way, but had an entirely different idea of how to go about it. "I'm gonna get Mack laid," he announced one day when a few of us were hanging around the radar dome, trying to avoid Lieutenant Krause.

Franklin laughed out loud. "How're you going to do that?"

"When we're in Tijuana for your going away party, I'm going to take him to one of the cat houses down there."

Dixie laughed. "You think that's a good idea? Taking Mack to Tijuana? I've seen that boy get silly drunk. I'm not sure that's the place we need a zombie Macklemore wandering around." Kevin had seen Mack at his worst after the incident with the *cholo* girl. He did not come right out and say it, but I was sure that was on his mind as he contemplated dealing with something like that on the other side of the border.

"You guys are going to Mexico?" asked ET3 Steve Kent. Kent was Franklin's replacement and had just reported aboard the ship a couple of days before. From somewhere deep in the bible belt, Steve had led a sheltered life that often resulted in him being shocked by what he saw and heard around the ship. He did not seem offended by what the fleet exposed him to; he was just wildly out of his element. Kent was a decent enough kid and appeared to be a capable technician; he was just something of a mama's boy.

I shook my head. "No, we're going to Tijuana."

"Isn't that in Mexico?"

"Yeah, it's in Mexico, but it's hardly representative of what Mexico actually is. It'd be like visiting Disney World and thinking that people dressed up as cartoon characters all over America."

Our new guy looked nervous. Then again, he was a little overweight and sweated a lot, so he usually did look that way. "I heard it's really dangerous down there."

"It is," Dixie said. "Especially in the *Zona Norte*, where all the whore houses are." Turning back to Palazzo, he asked, "You're really thinking about taking Mack there?"

"It's not that bad," Palazzo said. "I've been there a few times."

"Do you think this is a good idea, Doyle?" Dixie asked me.

Before meeting Hannah, I practically lived in Tijuana, but I avoided *Zona Norte* like the plague. One could find trouble anywhere south of the border, but *Zona Norte* was where trouble found you. "It would be better if you stuck to Bambi's or Sans Souci on Revolucion. That way, you'd at least be closer to us if something went wrong. We're probably going to be spending a lot of time at Rio Rita's right across the street."

Palazzo shook his head. "I can try, but those places are on the main drag and always busy. The girls can be choosier. Let's be honest; if the girls are going to pass on someone, it's going to be Mack. Hell, the chicks at Bambi's even passed on me a couple of times."

I almost busted out laughing, but I did not want to hurt Palazzo's feelings. Mack was not the only person who had gone through something of a transformation since the GI shower went down. After discovering the type of abuse that Macklemore suffered as a child, Palazzo started showing some humanity. He was still lazy. He was still a pervert, and he was still less than proficient as a technician, but he was putting a lot of effort into mentoring Macklemore on some of the few things Palazzo was actually good at.

Mack and Palazzo seemed to be forming a genuine friendship, and as a result, the rest of our shop started cutting John some slack. Franklin even personally invited him to celebrate his discharge in Tijuana, and that was the first time since reporting aboard the *Belleau Wood* that Palazzo got invited to anything. He appeared sincerely touched by the gesture. I suspected that his decision to cure Macklemore of his virginity was his way of paying it forward.

Dixie was more apprehensive about Palazzo's plans for Mack than I would have thought him to be. He was no stranger to *Zona Norte* himself. "John, think about this for a second. Mack's not known for making the best decisions while sober. He really screws shit up when he's drunk. Warren also seems to be some sort of asshole magnet. If there's anyone within a ten-mile radius that needs a dog to kick, somehow he's going to find his way to Macklemore. Do you want to put this guy in a place like Bambi's or take him to *Zona Norte*?"

TEQUILA VIKINGS

"You know Kevin," I said while opening one of my workbench drawers to pull out a pack of cigarettes. "Mack's been getting a lot better about his drinking. He's been getting better about a lot of things lately. John, are you telling Mack that you're going to try to get him laid in Tijuana?"

"No," Palazzo answered. "I was going to let it be a surprise."

"Good," I said. Mack had been devastated by the way things turned out with the last woman who gave him the time of day. I did not want the guy getting his hopes up only to have them brutally dashed again. "Keep it that way until you have a woman who's willing to sleep with the guy. Just tell him you're going to watch them dance. I don't want to see him backslide after finding out you couldn't even get a hooker to touch him."

Dixie looked confused. "What? You're okay with this, Doyle? I thought you were fundamentally opposed to the skin trade."

I shrugged. "It ain't for me, but as long as the women are working voluntarily, I guess it's none of my business. Truth be told, if it wasn't for prostitutes, I don't see how a man like Mack would ever get lucky."

"And you think getting laid is going to solve all of Warren's problems?" Kevin asked.

I shook my head. "Oh, hell no. I don't see it hurting him, though. Not unless he ends up sleeping with a girl who has an Adam's apple."

"What's wrong with a girl with an Adam's apple?" Kent asked.

"It means she probably ain't a girl," I answered. Turning back to Dixie, I said, "If he gets a taste of what a woman can do for him, it might motivate him to try a little harder to impress one. That means keeping clean and gaining some ambition to get ahead in life. Is this a good idea? I'm not sure I'm willing to go that far. Is it a bad idea, though? Dixie, Tijuana just wouldn't be Tijuana if we went down there with any intention of exercising good judgment."

I lit up my cigarette and blew a lungful of smoke towards the top of the dome. "We've gotten into trouble in Tijuana before, but we've always managed to get everybody back across the border safe and sound. We're good at this, Dixie. If we could get everyone back after the Lilliput Riot that happened at Jasper's send-off, I'm sure we can handle this. If John's taking Macklemore down south to make a man out of him, I'd rather he did it while we're all down there in case something goes wrong."

"What was the Lilliput Riot?" Kent asked.

Franklin giggled. "You ever read *Gulliver's Travels*?"

"No. But I used to watch the cartoon all the time."

"Then you're aware of what Lilliputians are, correct?"

"Yeah," Kent answered. "They're those little people."

"You called them 'little people!'" Franklin said. "That's a good start! Well, if you ever wander into a bar drunk out of your mind and find it full of a dozen little people. Don't assume they're hallucinations."

"Yeah," Dixie chimed in. "Little people occasionally go out for a good time, too."

Kent looked confused. "Wait, are you talking actual Lilliputians or midgets?"

I shook my head. "Don't ever call them midgets," I told Steve.

"Or 'little critters.' They *really* don't like that," Franklin added.

I slapped Kent on the shoulder and pointed at Todd. "Pay close attention to that man. That shit there's good advice."

Franklin nodded. "And do not, under any circumstances, try to pet one unless they give you permission. And don't ask for permission, either. If they're into that kind of stuff, they'll bring it up themselves."

"Wait," Kent asked. "What happens if you try to pet one?"

"Exactly what you think would happen," I told him. "They'll beat your fuckin' ass. Look, you might be able to take one of them, maybe two if you know what you're doing. Three or more, though, well, nobody's that tough. Jasper found that shit out the hard way. There's nothing we can do for you if you're getting beat down by a dozen little people either, especially if you were being an idiot and deserved it."

"Well," Franklin corrected. "We can laugh at you."

"Yeah, I forgot about that," I agreed. "Yes, we can laugh. And we will. We laughed at Jasper until the day he got discharged. But first, we had to get his mangled ass across the border before the cops got him. We did it, but that was some high adventure shit. We almost all got arrested."

Franklin voiced a point of contention. "We would have been fine if we'd just gone home with Jasper. The cops were also looking for the little people, though, so Doyle had the brilliant idea of going back and helping them across since it was one of us that got them into trouble in the first place."

TEQUILA VIKINGS

I looked over at Dixie. "We got every one of them picked up and over to cross at Otay Mesa, where no one was looking for them. Kevin, if we pulled that shit off, we got nothing to worry about with Macklemore getting his cherry popped down there."

Dixie looked over at Palazzo and shook his head, prophetically saying, "I don't know, guys. I still have a very bad feeling about this."

*****

"Doyle, do you really have to go?" Hannah asked as she rolled herself a joint in bed. It was the night before Franklin's Tijuana soiree.

"Yeah," I answered. "It's a tradition. When a CSE guy comes to the end of his enlistment, we take him down to Tijuana and make sure we send him off with a night to remember. Todd's been aboard the *Wood* for four and a half years. He's earned his party. Besides, this trip is the end of it. We won't be able to do it anymore once the ship moves to Japan. This one's got to be epic."

Hannah sparked up her joint and inhaled deeply. While trying to keep the smoke in, she asked, "What's it like down there when you do these things?"

I smiled. "Mayhem. Complete and total mayhem."

"Do you guys get drunk?"

That was a stupid question. I laughed. "Like you wouldn't believe."

"Are there girls there?"

"Of course."

Hannah exhaled involuntarily. "Seriously? You're actually admitting..."

"I'm not admitting anything," I said, laughing again. "I'm not going to TJ to pick up chicks. Look, Hannah, when I wanted to go down and really have fun in Tijuana, I used to go by myself or just with Dixie. I speak Spanish, so I'm perfectly at home down there. When we're with this many people, though, my role is a lot different. I'm there to make sure everybody has a good time, but more importantly, Tony Bard and I are there to make sure all of our guys make it back in one piece. We're not there looking for girls."

"You mean you're going down there to babysit?"

I grinned. "You could say that. It's still pretty fun, but yeah, we're there to keep it all from going bad."

"Are you going to be drinking a lot still?"

"Not too much," I said with a shrug. "We're going to be too busy to get too drunk."

"What about fighting?"

"Not this time," I answered.

"What if one of the guys gets into a fight? How are you going to stop it without fighting yourself?"

"You know, Hannah, I was talking with the division's Marine, Clay Fordson, a little while back. That man has never been in a fistfight. The closest he ever came was wanting to pound Kramer for messing up Macklemore's uniform during our zone inspection. I figure if someone like him can go through his entire life without throwing a punch at someone, I can make it through one last trip to Tijuana."

Hannah stared at me for a moment, the look on her face telling me that she wanted to believe me but doubting I could really control myself. "And you're taking Mack down there too?"

"Yes."

"Doyle, how are you going to keep an eye on your men with Mack around? You know he's going to need most of your attention."

"Palazzo's going to watch him."

"Oh, God, no." Hannah recently met Palazzo while visiting me on the ship, and he tripped all of her warning instincts. "Doyle, that guy is so creepy. He's going to get Warren into some sort of trouble, I'm sure."

I was tempted to tell Hannah what Palazzo wanted to do but could not bring myself to go through with it. Mack was her pet project since she had moved to San Diego, and I did not want him tainted in her eyes.

"Hannah, Mack and Palazzo have actually become legitimate friends. It's been good for both of them since they're such outsiders. If either of them went down there without the other, they'd end up spending the night sitting by themselves. This way, I think they'll both have a good time."

Hannah shuddered. "What on earth could Mack and Palazzo be doing together? Watching smut all day?"

TEQUILA VIKINGS

"Actually, it's Star Trek. You know, ever since Palazzo's been working with Mack, I think his stress levels have been dropping or something. We haven't heard of the guy getting caught playing with himself in weeks."

"That man is so disgusting. Gawd, he looks at every woman like we're pieces of meat. And that laugh he does at the end of every sentence, that 'hehehehehe!' Does the bloke think he's that bloody funny?"

I laughed myself. "It's some sort of nervous tic. He does it all the time, but I noticed it gets worse in mixed company. The man doesn't know how to handle himself around women, well, normal women anyway, so it gets worse when he's around the wives." Something suddenly hit me, and I fell silent as I thought about it.

"What?" Hannah asked.

"You know, we were at the ship's picnic last year, and I noticed that Palazzo acted just fine around Rafaela Green."

Hannah gasped. "Do you think he was sleeping with…"

"Oh! No! Oh, God, no! Actually, I've got it from a pretty good authority that Rafaela was not messing around on Randy at all. Not with Palazzo or anybody else. Everything was just in his head. Rafaela was a prostitute in the Philippines, though. I was thinking that maybe the only women Palazzo's comfortable speaking to are hookers."

"That's so gross. Why do Navy men marry the bar girls in the Philippines?"

I shrugged. "They probably know they have no chance of marrying women that far out of their league back here in the States."

"There's that one guy from your ship, though, the other one who has a wife from the Philippines…"

"DS3 Thomas? Nick?"

"Yeah! Nick! His wife is Penny! He's a very good-lookin' bloke. Why did he marry a bar girl?"

"He didn't. Penny wasn't a prostitute over there. She was a nurse. Not all Filipina wives were once hookers. In fact, the vast majority of them aren't. You can usually tell that they were former bar girls more by the men they married than by the women themselves. If you see a goofy-looking Navy guy walking around with this gorgeous Filipina wife, then yeah, it's a pretty safe bet that he met her in an Olongapo brothel."

"I still don't understand how they could do that! No matter how ugly the poor blokes are! I could see how it would drive a man mad, always wondering what she's up to or if she's cheating on you. I'm not looking to excuse what Green did, but I understand what drove him that crazy. I mean, could you ever see yourself marrying a prostitute?"

I shook my head. "I don't use hookers, Hannah. I'm certainly not going to marry one."

"You think Mack could?"

I sighed. "If Warren Macklemore ever landed in the Philippines, I don't think it's just a possibility that he marries a prostitute. It's a probability."

"Oh, Gawd," Hannah groaned. "That'd be the death of that poor boy."

I shrugged. "Maybe. Maybe not. Look, those girls get a bad rap because of the few that hang around the Trophy Lounge. When I look around the base and see how many sailors married these women, I realize just how few of them are messing around on their husbands. I've heard both Master Chief and Chief Ramirez say the same thing. Most of those women got into that life because of some desperate situations. They're usually pretty grateful to the guys that get them out of it."

"Ugh," Hannah said in disgust. "Doyle, is the *Belleau Wood* going to the Philippines?"

I nodded. "That's the rumor. They're saying once we get to Japan, we're only going to be there a month before we go to shut Subic Bay down."

"When you get there, are you going to let one of those bar girls latch onto Mack?"

I shook my head. "Hannah, Mack isn't going to the Philippines with us. His orders were cut yesterday. When we stop in Pearl Harbor, he's cross decking over to the *USS Blue Ridge*. He's not even going to make it to Japan."

*****

CHAPTER 18

As I bit into a tortilla filled with zesty pork, ET3 Kent looked at me as if I were chewing on a rotten nipple pulled off the carcass of a decomposing wildebeest. "Aren't you afraid of getting sick?" he asked.

Tacos al Pastor were the second tastiest fare you could put into your mouth in Tijuana. We devoured them in ecstasy, entirely unconcerned that the owner of the street-side *taqueria* worried little about Californian cleanliness standards.

"If you're worried about getting sick," I told Kent. "Stay away from the mezcal. And trust me, if you're something of a lightweight who's prone to puking, you're going to want to eat a few of these first."

"Why?" Kent asked.

"Because dry heaving hurts your balls," Dixie said. "Besides, these things aren't bad coming up, either."

I ordered another taco and tried to give it to Kent. He refused. "Dude," I said. "If you go into this with an empty stomach, you're going to be passed out within an hour. I'm not carrying anybody home that early. Eat a goddamn taco."

"I'll catch something at a restaurant," Kent whined.

Dixie laughed. "You think the kitchens down here are any cleaner? Look, the food here's good, but you're not going to find anything in a restaurant that you can't get in Sand Dog. Eat the fuckin' taco. That's an order, booter."

Kent swiped the taco from me and, after way too much hesitation, took a dainty nibble out of it. His eyes opened wide as the flavor hit his taste buds. After ripping off and savoring a much bigger mouthful, Steve nodded his approval. "Damn, that's good!"

"Tonight, somebody's going to offer you a Danger Dog," I told him. "You're not going to be a bitch about it. You're going to take it with *pico de gallo*, mayo, hot sauce, and jalapenos."

"But I don't like…"

"You're already being a little bitch about it," Franklin snapped. "Just eat it. You're never going to be a Tequila Viking with that kind of attitude."

"Tequila Viking?" Kent had heard the term before but never knew what it meant. "What the hell is a Tequila Viking?"

Dixie laughed. "You ever hear of a berserker, booter?"

The new guy shook his head.

"They were ancient Norse warriors," Kevin told him. "The legends say that they used to get all fucked up before battle, then would rip off all of their clothes and fight naked. Just like Doyle. If you give him enough tequila, he'll strip down and try to beat you to death with his dick."

Kent turned to look at me. "You fight people naked?"

"Only on special occasions," I told our new guy. "Like when I get really drunk and go home with a woman only to have her husband walk in on us getting our freak on."

Steve laughed. "For real?"

Dixie answered for me, cracking up as he spoke. "For real. I had to pick the bastard up. This guy fucking gets into a knock-down, drag-out brawl completely in the buff. The fight starts in the second-floor bedroom, goes all the way down the stairs, through the living room, and out into the front yard. Doyle here finally knocks this girl's old man out on the sidewalk in front of all her neighbors. Just in time, too. The fight ended as the police sirens first started approaching. So, Doyle runs back inside, grabs his underwear, shoes, cigarettes, lighter, and wallet. He leaves his shirt, jeans, and socks behind. He then leaps out the bedroom window, on the second story, mind you, then tears through back yards until he hits the hills. That was when he went cross country looking for a payphone. He eventually found one and got in touch with me to come get him."

"No shit?" Our booter looked impressed. "That must have been terrifying."

"Terrifying?!?" Dixie scoffed. "It was EPIC! Dude, when I get to the cross streets Doyle told me he was lurking around, he's at the opposite corner. He breaks out of his hiding spot behind a gas station dumpster and sprints across the intersection in his tighty-whiteys! When he jumps in my car, he's laughing so hard he can't breathe! So, we buy another bottle of Cuervo Gold, drive to Sunset Cliffs, and drink all night."

I grinned at the memory. "At some point during the night, Dixie here came up with the term 'Tequila Viking.' We both loved it." I rolled up the sleeve on my left arm and showed Kent the tattoo I had on my bicep of a skull wearing a dixie cup sailor hat with Viking horns coming out from the top of it. Behind the skull was an anchor. Below it was a set of crossed booze bottles. Dixie followed my lead and showed Kent the ink on his bicep as well. "The first thing we did that morning was buy me clothes. The second thing we did was get this shit inked on our arms."

Franklin had one, too, and showed it off. He earned his by getting drunk and trying to escape arrest by diving into San Diego Bay. He was fished out of the sea by Harbor Patrol and got busted back to E-4 for his efforts. Metaire pulled his sleeve up and put his on display, awarded for sleeping with three women at once during Sea Fair in Seattle.

"Oh my god," Kent said after seeing how we were all branded. "What do I have to do to get one of those?"

"Something epic," Dixie told him. "Something *really* epic."

*****

Once everyone put away their share of tacos, I took them on a brief walk around the block to our safe house, the place we were to run to if we got into trouble. It was an apartment owned by a friend of Lupe Castillo, Javier Villa. Once we got there, I laid out the rules. "Any person who gets sick in

Javier's apartment and puts it anywhere besides the toilet owes him twenty bucks."

Hearing this, Javier rubbed his hands together greedily. I assured him I had every intention of making him a wealthy man by the end of the evening. I then took a collection from the group and paid him in advance for the use of his apartment.

With our sanctuary secured, we herded the crowd further south down the strip until we hit Rio Rita's. Rio Rita's was an underground bar in the most literal sense. The entrance to the place was just a lone doorway wedged between two shops. Once through the door, we had to descend a long narrow staircase straight down more than two stories to reach the lounge. The bar itself was unremarkable and reminiscent of any watering hole one could stumble into from Detroit to Dakar, but the drinks were cheap, even by Tijuana standards.

The seating area of Rio Rita's was not large, but there was little danger of it getting over-crowded before noon. If it did reach its capacity of forty or fifty people, there was a roll-down security gate at the back of it that, when raised, almost doubled the tavern's size. On weekend evenings, there was yet another gate that would open into a cavernous subterranean nightclub built to accommodate a few hundred more people.

As the bulk of the men started filing down the staircase, Palazzo grabbed Macklemore and dragged him across the street to Bambi's. Steve Kent went with them. Bambi's was not an outright brothel. It was a strip club, but one where prostitutes openly worked the crowd.

It was also a very rough-looking place, causing Kent to hesitate before walking inside. Steve was a man with deep anxieties about his own personal safety. You would not know it by looking at him, but apparently, the man had an awful lot to live for. Ultimately, though, his libido overrode his fear of being shivved, and he decided to keep Palazzo and Mack company.

There was little natural sunlight in Rio Rita's, making it difficult to keep track of time. Keeping track of how much we had to drink was not any easier. We walked into the place only intending to get a little primed. Before we knew it, however, we were getting up to use the head and discovered that our legs stopped working.

TEQUILA VIKINGS

In hindsight, I know our group never had a chance that night. There were too many unsavory elements at work in Tijuana who knew our sobriety was against their interests. Sober men did not give to beggars, succumb to the sex trade, or do things they needed to bribe their way out of. Drunks did all that and more, so everyone in Tijuana worked together to keep us smashed, and we did nothing but encourage the bastards.

The entire economy of Tijuana depended upon drunkards to grease its gears, and at its core were the same predator versus prey principles that rule every jungle. It was what made binge-drinking down there so damn exciting. There was always an undercurrent of danger charging the air, and anything could happen at any given time.

We could find ourselves amidst a paramilitary police raid by drunkenly stumbling around the wrong corner. We could pass out after our third drink and wake up in a tub of ice missing a kidney. Or onstage stripping next to an impressively aroused farm animal. Third World inebriates lived dangerously. The only sure thing about drinking in developing countries was that adventure awaited. You were either coming out of the experience with a good time or an epic tale of things gone awry.

There is just something about civil strife and insurrection that brings out the party animal in people. You had to embrace it.

*****

We were ninety minutes into Rio Rita's when the first signs emerged that we needed to pace ourselves. Having killed my fourth beer and a third shot of tequila, I was more of a mess than I was comfortable being that early in the day. Dixie was a beer and a shot ahead of me but had the tolerance to handle it. Metaire did not. Claude was not a regular drinker. He kept up with me beer for beer and shot for shot, but already reached the point where he had given up on English. Several of the other men were in similar states, which was distressing considering English was the only language they knew.

We needed a distraction, and it came at about one-thirty when Palazzo barged in and dropped into the seat beside me. There was beer on his breath, but he was among the few of us still sober. "We got a problem," he said.

I looked at my watch. "You know, I expected as much, just not so early. What happened?"

"It's more like what's not happening."

Dixon laughed. "Is Mack already too drunk to get it up?"

"No, man," Palazzo answered. "The girls won't touch him. They think he has AIDS."

I shook my head. 1992 was only about a decade into the HIV epidemic, and fear of the disease was pervasive. The women working in the Mexican sex industry had good reasons to be afraid, too. All things considered, though, military personnel were tested every six months for HIV, so Macklemore was a far safer customer than the other men they were servicing.

"Does Mack know the chicks won't go near him?" I asked.

Palazzo shook his head. "I'm not letting him know anything until I strike a deal. Just like you said."

"Good. Did you tell the ladies about the AIDS testing we go through?"

"Yes. They don't care. They're pretty sure our tests aren't working and they don't trust condoms will protect them from whatever it is they think Mack has. I get the feeling he may be ruining it for the rest of the military."

"Did you offer more money?"

John nodded. "Double. No go."

I took a final drag off my cigarette and stubbed it out in the ashtray. "Do you think more would help?"

Palazzo shrugged. "It wouldn't hurt."

"Okay." I stood up and asked everybody to contribute ten dollars each to a charitable fund to eradicate Macklemore's virginity. Nearly everyone believed it to be a worthy cause. Kramer refused to participate, but Franklin put in a twenty-dollar-bill to make up for it. As I handed the extra cash to Palazzo, I asked, "How's Kent doing?"

Palazzo let out the laugh that Hannah loathed so much. This time, though, it seemed like he found something sincerely funny. "He's going crazy over there, dancing with the strippers."

"Has he done anything with any of them?"

John shook his head. "No, I think he's trying to make up his mind on which one he wants." With that, Palazzo turned his back on me and took off up the stairs and back across the street.

TEQUILA VIKINGS

Once he was gone, Bard said, "I think it would be a good idea if we got these guys up and moving. Should we walk down the strip and try another place?"

I nodded. "Yeah, I think that would be a great idea."

"What time do we have to be at Las Pulgas?" Dixie asked.

I rechecked my watch even though it had not been 10 minutes since the last time I looked at it. "Three. In a little over an hour. Let's get these guys up and headed out the door."

We had only been in Rio Rita's for a couple of hours, but ascending the steps was far more challenging than it should have been that time of day. It took thirty minutes to get our boys out of the bar. Once we were back on the street, Bard led the group to Señor Frog's, a venue notorious for serving weak margaritas, while I headed across the street to Bambi's to let the others know we were changing locales.

Bambi's was old-school Tijuana. It was dark and full of smoke, claustrophobic, and suffocating. It was one of the few places on the main drag that drew in both Mexicans and Americans. Bambi's had three strippers taking their turns on stage, and once their set was over, they would disappear into some unseen back room. They were not for sale. There were, however, a half-dozen other women drifting from table to table plying their trade.

The girls working the crowd were pretty, yet at the same time soulless. They could flash a man a seductive smile, laugh at his crappy jokes, and make him feel as if they saw something in him other than money. The life had been sucked out of them by their addictions and their waning belief in their own humanity, though. Even they conceded that they existed only to be used and discarded. I often wondered where these women ended up when their earning years were behind them.

I caught sight of Mack taking in the show and was pleased to see him enjoying himself, sitting with a cold beer in his hand and a big goofy grin plastered on his face. If he knew Palazzo was finding it impossible to get him laid, he did not seem to be showing it. Beside him, Kent got pulled from his seat by one of the working girls, who led him towards the front door. Unlike the places of *Zona Norte*, Bambi's did not have rooms on the premises. The hookers had to use the hourly hotel across the street.

I was watching Kent and his girl making their way towards me when John snuck up from behind. "You looking for a progress report?"

"Not really," I answered. "Judging by the fact Mack's over there sitting by himself tells me the extra money didn't help."

Palazzo shook his head. "They won't touch him. I was getting ready to give up and go to Sans Souci."

"Okay. We're heading out of Rio Rita's. The plan is to hit Señor Frog's for a quick margarita…" I paused to keep from laughing as I watched the expression on Kent's face as his woman dragged him our way. He was so excited that he looked like a kid on a roller coaster, close to hyperventilating and sweating in buckets.

"You mean frozen fruit juice?" Palazzo asked.

I did not answer John right away; I was cracking up as I watched our new guy. "Yeah, weak drinks may do us some good at this point. After that, we're going to Las Pulgas. If you can, meet us there."

"We'll see," Palazzo said. "If I can't get someone to sleep with Mack at Sans Souci, I may have to take him to *Zona Norte*."

I winced. "Be careful." I pointed out Kent to Palazzo as the couple was almost upon us. John turned to look just in time to see our booter stop in his tracks with an expression of surprise and horror on his face. Steve's eyes then scrunched closed, his cheeks turned red, and he grunted loudly, looking as if he was desperately trying to hold something in.

Kent's girl suspected what was going on and looked very agitated. "Hey!" she shouted, loud enough to be heard over the music. "What you doing? Stop that! You no cumming, are you?"

Steve's face said it all. Leaning forward a little, Kent bit down on his lower lip and moaned, partly out of ecstasy, but mostly out of embarrassment. The girl let go of his hand and batted it away in disgust while Palazzo and I burst into laughter.

There was never a good way to discover you have issues with premature ejaculation, but finding it out in public must have been mortifying. Having it witnessed by two of your shipmates was even worse, as it had the potential to lead to long-lasting consequences.

And it did. As Kent stood there stammering, trying to figure out what to do with himself, I walked up and slapped him on the shoulder. "Better luck next time, Gonzales."

TEQUILA VIKINGS

"Gonzales?" Kent asked, bewildered and panting to catch his breath.

"You know," Palazzo told him. "Speedy Gonzales. The fastest mouse in all Mexico! Didn't you ever watch Bugs Bunny?"

The nickname stuck.

*****

An hour later, I jumped on a chair at Las Pulgas and yelled, "Hit it, Guillermo!"

The deejay answered, "You got it, *amigo*," then dropped a familiar tune by The Kinks.

Franklin sat in the middle of the dance floor, his back to Guillermo. As Ray Davies began singing about North Soho, a look of panic washed across Todd's face and he swung his head around to see what was sneaking up from behind. I yelled that there was no peeking allowed, but the music drowned me out.

Knowing what the Kinks were singing about, Franklin suspected that we had hired a transvestite to feel him up in public. He was wrong, but I could not fault his logic. Things like that were not without precedent in our division.

Before the Kinks hit the chorus, a door opened next to the DJ booth and out stepped Trophy Lounge Lola. The crowd erupted into applause, and Franklin fell to his knees, laughing hysterically at the sight of her seductively swaying towards him.

Unlike the Trophy Lounge, Las Pulgas was wide open to Revolucion Avenue and awash in natural light. It was the first time I got a look at the woman in all her glory. She was ghastly. I am about as enthusiastically heterosexual as a man can be, but I can honestly say I would have been more comfortable being felt up by a drag queen.

Franklin was shameless, though. He ran up to her, threw his arms around her shoulders, and stuck his tongue right down her throat. This set off another round of cheers and laughter. Lilly slid up beside me. "You owe me one por dat, Doyle. You have no idea how much I hate dat woman."

I put my arm around Lilly's shoulder to show my appreciation for her bringing Lola down. In return, she slid her fingertips beneath the waist of my shorts.

Reaching into my pocket, I pulled out the forty dollars I promised, thinking she would withdraw her hand to grab it. She did not budge. "Thanks for doing this for Todd, Lilly."

"I didn't do dis por Todd. I did it por you, Doyle."

"I told you I have a girlfriend. Actually, she's my fiancée now."

Lilly shrugged. "So? I have a husband."

Just then, I saw Metaire fall back in his chair. He hit the floor in a spectacular fashion, kicking over his table and sending drinks and peanuts flying in every direction. I stuck the money into Lilly's cleavage and rushed over to help. Dixie got there at the same time, as did a couple of angry waiters. We got the mess cleaned up, generously tipped the staff to keep them from calling the cops, and tried to assess how drunk Metaire was. The man was obliterated.

I reached into my pocket again for more cash, handing it to Dixie. "I'm going to see if I can get Claude to walk some of this off. Get Franklin and Lola a room across the street for an hour or so. I need you to get Lilly away from me too."

Dixie looked back and stole a glance at my former one-night stand. He then smiled and said, "No problem!"

"Kevin, she's the chick from the Trophy Lounge. She's married to a warrant officer."

Dixie only smiled wider. "Cool! I hate officers."

I was going to say something else but thought better of it. They were both adults and knew the consequences. "Whatever. Don't be an idiot."

We both grunted as we lifted Metaire to his feet. "You know, the best moments of my life generally have their origins in a monumental act of stupidity," Dixie told me. He then left to introduce himself to Lilly.

I got Claude out the door and walked him down the road past the jai alai stadium. When I finally got exhausted, I set him down, lit myself a cigarette, and realized Metaire had gone comatose.

I was an idiot. Knowing Claude was so wasted, I should have walked him in the other direction. When he finally gave out, we would have been closer to Javier's place, not a half-mile further from it. Since Las Pulgas marked the southernmost point where American tourists typically traveled to, we were also now beyond reliable taxi service. There was nothing for me to do but lift Claude as best I could and drag him back to one of the clubs.

It took nearly an hour to get Metaire to the north side of the stadium, and, as luck would have it, we got there as the food carts started showing up. I spotted one on the corner across Calle Galeana and was thrilled to see it selling Tijuana Danger Dogs.

Of all the words ever written extolling the virtues of Mexican cuisine, I have never heard anyone describe what I believe to be Mexico's most succulent offering to the world's culinary catalog. The Danger Dog was a grilled frankfurter wrapped in bacon and served on a steamed bun with jalapenos, onions, mayonnaise, hot sauce, pico de gallo, and mustard. It is to die for.

I have awakened out of a deep sleep with cravings so intense for this delicacy that I risked a Tijuana curfew violation to score one. They were exactly what I needed to ruin Claude's buzz, so I sprung for a half dozen of them. After eating two myself, I set to work getting the rest into Metaire's stomach.

It seemed to work. The smell of bacon alone brought Metaire back to the land of the living. After eating four hot dogs, he was still too far gone to talk to, but he could at least move under his own power. I had to remind him to keep walking, though. "*Marche, Claude. Vous devez marcher. Continue à marcher.*"

As we reached the Tequila Sunrise nightclub, I spotted one of our data systems techs looking off the balcony. Behind him was a couple more guys playing volleyball with a group of girls. Thrilled I did not have any further to walk to reunite with our shipmates, I turned to Claude and asked if he could get up the stairs. "*Pouvez-vous monter les escaliers?*"

Claude smiled, insisting that not only could he walk, he could dance.

That was a gross exaggeration. Metaire barely made it to the second floor, and once we got him into a seat, it was all he could do to keep from falling over. Bard strolled up once I got him settled. "You're a good man, Charlie Brown. You think he's done for the night?"

"Oh yeah," I answered. "I'm just taking a break. Once I rest, I'm going to get him to Javier's and dump him off." Looking around, I noticed our herd was thin. "Has the Palazzo posse made an appearance?"

Bard shook his head. "Nope. I did make a quick run to Sans Souci, but they weren't there. I'm guessing they headed into *Zona Norte*."

"Shit. Our three weakest guys, traipsing about in the one part of TJ where they're likely to get into the most trouble."

"If they do, our personnel problems might solve themselves," Bard told me, pointing out the silver lining. "How's the new guy? Kent?"

I told him about what happened to Steve at Bambi's. When I finished, Bard was roaring with laughter, wiping the tears from his eyes. "Oh God! He's going to fit right in with Mack and Spanky, isn't he? Was that enough to earn him a Tequila Viking tattoo?"

"Hell no," I told Tony. "You have to do something epic, not pathetic. It might be enough to make him the alpha male of that little group he's hanging with, though."

"You know, those two could teach him some bad habits," Tony warned.

"Nah, Kent's quirky but harmless. He'll be alright." As I said this, I saw Willis wobble on by. I shook my head. "Looks like Bo's getting a bit unsteady. I got Claude, Tony. If Bo passes the point of no return, he's yours."

"Roger that."

I looked around the club a bit. I did not see Todd or Lola. "Franklin never made it back?"

Bard shook his head. "Nope."

"What about Dixie?"

This caused Tony to sit up straight and look around. "You know what? He left with Franklin and that other girl to get them a room, and the son-of-a-bitch never came back. You think…?"

"Dude, I don't think. I know," I said, shaking my head.

Bard looked impressed. "For Christ's sake! They knew each other for maybe thirty minutes!"

"Her husband is a warrant officer who's still in the Philippines closing out the base. She's looking for some action and will take whoever's willing. Dixie's always willing."

"How do you know so much about that chick?" Bard asked.

"I woke up in base housing with her last year."

Tony let that sink in for a second. "Not bad. She's pretty hot."

"You should see her naked."

TEQUILA VIKINGS

Before Bard could ask for more details, Alex Schiff showed up at our table and let us know they were going to Rio Rita's with the young ladies they met. Bard offered to hang back and help with Metaire, but I waved him off. "No, you stick with the crew. I'll take care of Claude and meet you at Rita's."

Once our friends left, Metaire tried to stand but fell back into his seat. His second attempt was also unsuccessful. After his third try, Claude turned to me and said, "I need to use the bathroom. Can you help me up?"

"Okay." As I got Metaire to his feet, I saw his condition was deteriorating. He could barely stand, and I had to guide him to the restroom. Once inside, the attendant looked at him and shook his head, asking if Claude was alright. I told him if he wasn't, it was Tequila Sunrise's fault for making his drinks so damn strong.

The two urinals in the bathroom were side by side, separated by a metal divider. I pushed Metaire before the one on the left and took my hand off his back to see if he could stand on his own. He could, but it appeared to be all he could do. It was as if he forgot what came next.

"Claude," I told him. "I got you this far. This is as much as I'm willing to do for you, though."

"Oh," Metaire answered as he struggled to get his zipper down.

Looking to use my time wisely, I stepped up to the urinal on the right. A couple of seconds after I started pissing, I heard that Claude finally was, too. He was not hitting the urinal, though. He was pissing on the wall. "*Claude! Vous devez viser mieux!*" I yelled, imploring him to aim better.

The attendant stood up and protested, which was understandable considering he was the one who had to clean the place, but he startled Claude and only made things worse. Metaire tried to twist right but over-corrected, clearing the urinal on the other side. When he hit the gap between the divider and the wall, Claude cut into my space and put me in danger of taking on some serious splash-back.

To keep dry, I had to lean back but thrust my pelvis forward to make sure I was not adding to the mess. The attendant, sensing imminent disaster, shifted the tone of his voice from surprise to anger. Tijuana nightclubs do not tolerate disturbances of any sort and call the police at the first sign of trouble. I begged him to calm down.

"Amigo! Amigo!" I pleaded while pushing my body to its contortionist limits in a desperate bid to avoid getting wet. Offering to personally clean up whatever mess Claude made, I told him, *"Voy a limpiar todo, amigo! Todo!"* Then to Claude, I had to scream, *"Arrêtez de pisser Claude! À présent!"* trying to get him to stop urinating all over the place.

This set off a highly animated conversation between myself, Claude, and the attendant that spanned three languages and pushed way past the limits of my tri-linguicism.

While the attendant and I were yelling at each other, Metaire slowly started to lean backward. With both hands occupied in a futile attempt to improve his aim, he stiffened up and forgot to bend his knees. He keeled over like a majestic redwood felled by an expert lumberjack. Claude hit the ground hard and I shuddered at the sickening sound his head made as it bounced against the tile.

Both the attendant and I cursed in our respective languages and turned toward each other, wearing shocked expressions that could have only been borne by two people who never watched a grown man piss in his own face before.

*****

Getting a cab in Tijuana is usually no problem at all. If your traveling companion is bombed out of his mind and smelling strongly of his own urine, though, the difficulty increases exponentially. After seeing a dozen hired cars blow right past us, I stopped a trio of pretty college girls passing by and asked them if they would be willing to flag down a taxi for me. Within thirty seconds, one swerved onto the curb so hard that I wondered if it was trying to hit them.

Once the cab stopped, one of the young ladies opened the door, and I threw Claude into the back. He fell over sideways, leaving no room for me, so I shut the door, thanked the girls, and jumped into the passenger seat, giving the driver the address to Javier's place as I settled in.

The cabbie was not happy with the bait and switch, so he ignored me while he inspected Metaire. He then turned and said, "Your friend is all wet. Is he getting sick?"

I looked back at Claude myself. "No. He's sleeping."

TEQUILA VIKINGS

"I mean, is he going to get sick in my cab?"

"That depends," I said. "It's about seven blocks to the address I gave you. You think you can get us there before he blows?"

The driver shook his head. "You need to get him out of my taxi."

"Do you realize how hard he was to get in here? I think I slipped a disk getting him into the back seat. If you want him out anywhere besides our destination, you need to step on the gas."

The cabbie was getting ready to order me out, but before he could say it, Claude let out the wettest belch I ever heard. We looked back at Metaire, who sat himself up and showed us his chipmunk cheeks. He then swallowed whatever was in his mouth and smiled before exhaling a breath of foul, acidic air that filled the entire vehicle with a nauseating stench. I switched to Spanish and told the cabbie, "We're out of time, *amigo*! You need to go! Now! Now! Now!"

Our driver knew arguing was futile. He threw the car in gear, stomped on the gas, and sent us careening down Revolucion at what felt like three times the legal speed limit. The taxi pulled enough Gs to wreak havoc upon Claude's stomach, and I saw him struggling to keep his mouth closed while bouncing around the back seat. I started giggling as he furiously cranked the handle on the door to get the window open.

We were three blocks down Revolucion when Claude got the glass halfway down. He then let out another of those revolting burps, which caused my giggling to turn to outright laughter. The cabbie shot me a look suggesting he might slice me open once we stopped.

When we hit block four, the driver gagged, overcome with the bilious aroma drifting in from the back seat. This got me laughing even harder. On block five, I saw him gag again, and I lost complete control. In hysterics, I looked back at Claude. He was on all fours in the back seat. He stuck his head out the window while streams of thick saliva were peeled off of his lips by the wind. He looked like a large Guianan Basset Hound reveling in his wild car ride to the vet.

We got caught by the light at block six, and Metaire was no longer able to keep himself straight. He heaved once and launched the remains of four Danger Dogs into the lane to our left. This sent the occupants of the Ford beside us scurrying to get their windows closed in case Claude picked up more distance on his next round. I roared, writhing about on the passenger seat as Metaire heaved again and again as we waited for the traffic signal to turn.

When I caught my breath, I turned to the cabbie to apologize. I was horrified to find him too preoccupied to accept it, however. His cheeks were puffed out even fuller than Claude's, his eyes full of panic, and he was trying to roll the window down so hard he broke the handle right off the door. He was about to erupt himself, and now there was nowhere for it to go.

I stopped laughing, unable to appreciate the humor of the situation anymore. As the driver erupted into a horizontal fountain of Technicolor laughter, I threw myself against the passenger door in a desperate bid to keep myself unsoiled.

I had to hand it to Metaire. At least he managed to get sick outside of the vehicle. The driver, on the other hand, destroyed the interior, flooding out the dashboard, the windshield, the steering wheel, and his own seat. He was on his third heave when I finally pulled the door handle in the right direction, sending myself spilling out into the street. I took a roll, jumped up, and opened the back door, grabbing Claude by the ankles and pulling him out feet first. I then reached into my pocket and threw a handful of singles into the cab before fleeing around the corner. Metaire could not stop getting sick, sending people scurrying away from us everywhere we went.

I got Claude to Javier's and stayed with him until I was confident there was nothing left in his stomach to expel. I then sprayed him down with a garden hose outside and dumped him naked onto our host's couch before throwing Metaire's clothes in the dryer. I placed an empty garbage can by his head just in case.

With Claude finally tucked away, I stepped outside for some fresh air. It was still daylight, but I was exhausted. Leaning up against the wall of Javier's building, I slid down to take a seat on the sidewalk. I then pulled out a cigarette, finding myself a moment of peace to enjoy it in.

As I exhaled my first drag, I stole a glance at my watch and choked, discovering it was only six o'clock in the evening.

It was going to be a long, long night.

*****

CHAPTER 19

I doubted anyone ever used the word "courageous" to describe John Palazzo. Still, he was so determined to get Warren Macklemore laid he braved the notoriously volatile streets of Tijuana's *Zona Norte* to get it done. It was an uncharacteristically bold move.

Palazzo had been there before, but within a group from his old ship who could back him up if things went wrong. Mack and Kent were not men I would consider assets in a jam. They were liabilities and of little use when his luck ran out at the Miami Club, one of *Zona Norte*'s seedier establishments.

Exasperated by his lack of success on Macklemore's behalf, Palazzo sat Warren and Kent at a front table facing the stage and decided to indulge himself for a while. Within minutes of sitting down in a dark corner of the club with a beer in his hand, a lady landed on his lap and began rubbing his crotch while they negotiated a price.

Kent spotted them on his way to the restroom and, shouting encouragement, stepped over to give Palazzo a high five. "Good work, Johnny!" he slurred out. "She's SMOKIN' hot!"

J.E. PARK

Palazzo wanted to tell Kent to get lost but was not used to being complimented. "She is, isn't she?" he answered.

"Hell yeah!" Kent looked the woman over and whistled, marveling at how gorgeous she was in a tight purple dress.

"Choo like what choo see?" the lady asked, wriggling upon Palazzo's lap to accentuate her curves. She grabbed her breasts and lifted them in Steve's direction, squeezing them together. "When I finish with chour friend, maybe I come back for choo?"

Kent giggled like a smitten schoolgirl. "I don't know…"

"C'mon, what choo like best? My tits? My ass? How about my lips?" she asked, lifting her chin and blowing Kent a kiss.

Steve stopped giggling. "…your Adam's apple?"

"What?!?" Palazzo asked in terror.

"Dude," Kent called out. "The chick has an Adam's apple!"

Palazzo tried to get a better look, but his lady threw a hand over her throat while furiously shaking her head in denial. Unable to see her neck, Spanky jammed his hand under her dress and was horrified to discover extra equipment. Still, he wrapped his fingers around what he found and used it to pull the man off his lap. Palazzo was by no means a formidable fighter but fueled by rage, he then planted a right hook into the guy's eye and made sure it counted.

Things spiraled out of control from there. A couple of Marines saw what had happened and were about to get medieval on Palazzo for striking a lady. They only backed off when Kent shouted out that the woman they were so concerned about was actually a man. That changed the situation considerably and the leathernecks switched sides, cheering Palazzo on.

As Spanky fought his date, another cross-dressing hooker came out of nowhere and planted a high-heeled kick to Palazzo's head. Both of them then shed their effeminate façade and fought him just like any other guy would, albeit in fabulous makeup. As Master Chief Darrow pointed out to me once, gay people spent much of their lives under assault, and underestimating them could be a painful mistake, something Gianni Palazzo learned the hard way that day.

Kent attempted to stop a third man in drag from joining the fray but got himself dropped with a single blow. The Marines then stepped into the fight, against whom the prostitutes were no match at all. Neither were the trio of bouncers that rushed in to break it up. Seeing the Mexican doormen taking a beating, the Miami Club's local patrons joined the melee, which in turn attracted the American customers to even the odds.

The Miami descended into mayhem, engulfed in a free-for-all that spilled into the street and threatened to graduate into a full-blown riot. The police fell upon the club in force, which only escalated the situation. They ended up cordoning off the area and beating into submission anyone they could get their hands on.

That was about when I got there.

After dropping Claude at Javier's and checking on the guys at Rio Rita's, I tried to locate my missing men. Not able to find Palazzo on Revolucion, I turned onto Coahila and was already heading towards *Zona Norte* when I heard the commotion.

The cops were trying to contain the fight. This set off a stampede as people rushed the officers to avoid getting trapped on the wrong side of the perimeter. As there were too few policemen to hold the line, most of the men of this first wave escaped, and I found Palazzo among them.

At first, I was shocked to see him. With his face covered in blood, he looked seriously hurt, so I rushed him back to Javier's to better assess his injuries.

It took a lot of work, but we eventually discovered all the blood was coming from two wounds. One was hidden in Palazzo's eyebrow while the other was above his hairline. Both were insignificant but bled like hell. "John," I asked. "Do you still have the money you collected for Mack?"

"Yeah," Palazzo moaned.

That was too bad. I was hoping Warren at least got lucky before things went to hell at the Miami. "I need it. Give it to me."

"What for?" John was generally reluctant to hand over cash without getting anything in return.

I sighed. "For starters, we need to get you a baja and a t-shirt that's not drenched in blood. Other than your clothes, you look okay. Now, at the moment, the Mexican police have their hands full. Once they're done in *Zona Norte*, though, they're going to send cops to the border looking for people who got away. You need to get to the other side of the fence before they show up. Second, I need to figure out what happened to Mack and Kent and get them stateside. I need the money."

Palazzo grabbed his wallet and handed me more than a hundred dollars. Turning to Javier, I switched to Spanish. "*Amigo*, can you get him clean clothes and send his ass running for the border as quickly as possible?"

Javier nodded. "*Sí, amigo.*"

I gave Javier a twenty and slapped him on the shoulder. "Then do it. I have a feeling we're going to owe you big by the end of the night."

*****

I was back on the street, walking south down Revolucion, following the crowd. Things were getting busy as the streets filled with underage revelers yet to figure out how to hold their liquor. The tourists were long gone, as was everyone else who did not have every intention of getting irresponsibly inebriated that night.

Making my way back towards *Zona Norte*, I spotted familiar faces from Ocean Beach on the opposite side of the street. It was the group of SDSU hooligans led by the Hockey Mullet Frat Guy, and it looked like they were up to their usual mischief.

A half dozen of them took up the entire sidewalk, and as they marched down the street, they were practically daring people not to yield the pavement to them. Overtaking a couple of squids, the frat dicks rudely bumped them to the side as they passed. When the sailors protested the lack of tact, the entire group stopped and turned, challenging the pair to do something about it.

I would have stayed to watch how that turned out, but something else appeared across the street that caught my eye. It was a tall, shirtless Guianan man stumbling zombie-like up the avenue, heading north along the curb. My jaw dropped open, and I let out a litany of curses. "Claude!" I screamed. "CLAUDE!"

Metaire was out of it and could not even hear me. I caught up to him as he hit the corner of Calle Galeana, the spot where I had fed him Danger Dogs, a mistake that I would not be making again. Even face-to-face, Claude barely acknowledged my presence. "What the hell are you doing? Are you trying to get yourself arrested?" Seeing none of that registered, I repeated it in French.

"*Oui?*" Claude asked. He had no idea what I was saying.

TEQUILA VIKINGS

Luckily, Metaire was a compliant drunk. I spun him around and pointed him north towards the border. I could not sit on him all night, so I had to get him back to the ship.

As we walked, I patted Claude down and found he had the essentials: his wallet, cash, and military ID. I only needed to dress him. At the first open storefront we passed, I looked for a cheap t-shirt, finding one emblazoned with glitter and kittens meant for a geriatric white woman at least forty years Metaire's senior. It only cost five dollars and would probably disintegrate during its first wash, but it was worth double the price in entertainment value as I dressed Claude in it.

The trek north was slow but steady. It took us a half-hour to get to the spillway, where I heard a voice call out, "Doyle! Claude!" It was Dixie walking up from behind us with his arm around Lilly. Lola walked beside them, looking perturbed. Franklin, the evening's guest of honor, was conspicuously missing.

"Dixie!" I called out. "Man, am I glad to see you! Where's Todd?"

Kevin shrugged. "Your guess is as good as mine."

"Yeah," Lilly added. "He disappear a pew blocks ago."

"Shit!" I looked back at Kevin. "The *Zona Norte* is a mess right now. It's full of cops. If he went there, do you think he has the sense to come back?"

"Probably not," Dixie answered. "What's up with Claude?"

"Teetering on the edge of a tequila coma." Looking at Lilly, I said, "I still have a couple of guys lost out there. What will it take for you to make sure he winds up at the 8th Street Trolley Station?"

Lilly looked at Dixie. "Is he going to cause us any trouble?"

"No," Dixie answered. "You just have to lead him around like a big old drunk dog."

Lola giggled. "I like his shirt."

Lilly sighed, signaling she was reluctantly willing to help. "Okay." Turning back to Dixie, she pointed at him and added, "But you going to make dis up to me!"

"Oh baby, you KNOW how much I'm looking forward to that!"

Lilly smiled. "What I do? Just leave him at da station?"

"No," I said as I rifled through my pockets. "Has anyone got a pen?"

Lola reached into her purse and handed me one. I then pulled an old receipt from my wallet and wrote down the number to Cheri's place. "When you get to the other side of the border, call and tell Hannah I'm asking her to meet you to take Claude home. Have her put him up in the guest room."

Metaire was oblivious to our conversation despite standing in the middle of it. Once we made the arrangements, I lightly slapped Claude's face to get his attention. "*Mon ami!*" In French, I told him he was going home with the two ladies in front of him, which put a humongous smile on his face.

After repeating myself several times to make sure I was getting through, Dixie and I rushed to get Claude and the girls to the border crossing, hanging back to watch the three of them join the crowd returning to the US. Once we saw them clear the checkpoints, I turned to Dixie and asked, "So, you having fun?"

Kevin grinned. "Oh, yeah! That chick was a hoot!"

I shook my head as I walked back outside. "You're playing with fire, Dixie. I told you she's married to a warrant officer. You know, a prior-enlisted guy."

Outside of the building that houses the border crossing in Tijuana was a vast bazaar. It was a last chance open-air shopping center offering everything from massive cement lawn ornaments of Bart Simpson to velvet portraits of King Montezuma and Elvis Presley. Like San Diego, Tijuana sits in a desert with very little humidity. It gets chilly once the sun goes down. While there, I walked over to a vendor selling baja pullovers.

As I picked through the bajas, Dixon reminded me that I had slept with Lilly first. "You're also the one who got her to come down here. You know, she did this because she was under the impression you wanted her again."

"I was very clear that was in no way my intention."

"Yeah, your lips were saying 'no' Doyle, but your eyes were saying 'Yes! Yes! Oh my God, YES!'"

I laughed as I picked out a blue and gray baja. "You know, that's why I paid her forty bucks. To make sure she knew I had no romantic inclinations."

Dixie chuckled as I slipped on the pullover. "You gave her forty dollars! Dude! She hangs out at the freakin' Trophy Lounge! Cold hard cash is the

TEQUILA VIKINGS

Olongapo mating call! Giving her forty bucks is practically a marriage proposal! 'Romantic inclinations?' Dude, why don't you talk normal? Who the fuck uses the word 'inclinations' anyway?"

"You might want to think about improving your vocabulary, Dixie. Ten dollar words would go a long way in covering up that five-cent mind of yours."

As Dixie went on and on trying to justify sleeping with Lilly, I paid the vendor for the baja, having not the slightest idea of how thankful I would be in a few hours for making that purchase. As we left the border to descend back into Tijuana, Dixie gave me all the reasons he intended to see Lilly again, and he gave them in very explicit detail. For all Dixie's talking, however, neither of us would ever lay eyes on Lilly or Lola again.

*****

At about the time Franklin was wrapping up his tryst with Lola, Fred Baker got home from work. Finding his wife once again gone despite her assurances that she would stop fooling around, he snapped. His rage had been building for some time, and the day of Franklin's discharge party was the one when Lola's husband finally reached his breaking point. He started drinking whiskey on an empty stomach and three hours later stumbled towards his wife's favorite haunt with a .38 snub-nosed revolver in his pocket.

It was a long walk from the Baker house to the Trophy Lounge. Lola was probably crossing the border when Fred finally arrived, bursting through the door of the bar and demanding to see his wife. Fortunately for her, Lola was nowhere to be found.

In the pandemonium that followed, Fred squeezed off two rounds, both of which hit nothing but plaster. The bar emptied out into the street and the police were on the scene within a minute of getting the call about shots being fired. The ensuing standoff lasted three hours, with Fred inside alone and threatening suicide. Once the tear gas canisters deployed, though, he dropped his gun and gave up.

After that, Lola was no longer welcome at the Trophy Lounge. Once Fred was convicted of attempted murder, she lost her only means of support and ended up selling everything to move back to the Philippines.

None of this affected Lilly directly, but it opened her eyes to what she was doing to her family. She had two children with the man she married and wondered what would become of them if she pushed her husband past his breaking point as Trophy Lounge Lola had. She accepted one phone call from Dixie to let him know she was not going to see him anymore, then dropped off the face of the earth.

Looking back, we saved Lola's life by bringing her to Tijuana that evening. We were also the reason Fred Baker got five years in prison instead of thirty and why Lilly decided to salvage her marriage.

You would think that one of them would have been grateful enough to at least send us a thank you card.

*****

CHAPTER 20

Earlier in the day, I had looked over the women working the crowd at Bambi's. Knowing what a cruel life that was, I wondered where Mexico's bar girls went after they lost their desirability. At about eleven that night, I found out.

It started with the Hockey Mullet Frat Guy crew from Ocean Beach. They were hogging the sidewalk, coming straight for Tony Bard and me as we approached the Hard Rock Café. When they got to the venue's doorway, a Marine stepped through it right into their path. True to form, the mullet mob practically bowled him over, laughing as they passed.

Had they apologized, nothing would have come of it but some smart ass in the gang shouted, "Get the fuck out of the way!" and sealed their fates. The Marine cranked back and landed a haymaker to the jaw of the closest punk he could reach. The blow was so hard, the sound that it made echoed off the buildings around us as it connected.

Heads turned towards the Hard Rock to see the frat hooligan's legs collapse beneath him as his lights went out. The Marine was now between a half dozen belligerents and their incapacitated comrade. He seemed entirely unconcerned about that, however.

The boys from SDSU were not so nonchalant about the situation. "What the fuck is your problem?!?" Mullet Man yelled. "You looking to get your ass kicked?"

"You looking to kick it?" the Marine asked with a Texan drawl, sounding less than impressed with the quality of his opponents. When the frat boys charged, he seized the opportunity to knock another one of them senseless with a single strike.

Now, no one ever goes to Tijuana alone, and this Marine was no exception. While the frat hooligans were so focused on him, they overlooked his friends inside the doorway. Right behind them, trying to get out too, were AG2 Ben Gott, Marty Pruitt, and, unbelievably, my boy Gonzales. My workshop neighbors bumped into Kent along Revolucion and, recognizing him as our new guy, invited him to tag along.

As the frat boys went after the Marine, they were set upon by a horde of leathernecks rushing out of the restaurant. Pruitt joined them, always up for a fight. The odds went from six against one to nine against six before the louts knew what was happening.

The college kids never stood a chance. By the time sirens could be heard in the distance, two frat boys were unconscious, one was nearly choked out, and two more were pleading for mercy. The rest fled with their clothes as tattered as their egos. There was not a single injury among the military men, who scattered with far more exuberance than the mullet man crew.

Gott and Kent, not wanting to be mistaken for combatants, ran too. Luckily, they bolted right towards Tony and me, allowing us to intercept them. To get us all off the street, we pushed our guys through the black bed sheet covering the doorway to a place called Chutey's House of Beer. That is how I found out where Tijuana's fallen women eventually ended up.

Chutey's was surreal. Before you can adjust to the darkness, you're struck with an overpowering sense of dread and desperation. It was not a happy place. My first instinct was to turn around and walk back out, but the bedsheet over the entrance proved a horrible sound barrier. The racket outside on Revolucion convinced me to stay put.

I could hear the police rounding up the pair of frat boys who were too hurt to run. The *gringos* protested their innocence, claiming they were the victims of the assault, not the perpetrators of it. When they resisted being handcuffed, the cops beat them worse than the Marines did.

TEQUILA VIKINGS

As things came into focus inside Chutey's, I found myself being stared at by a line of frightening people seated at the bar. They were all women, and they showed every minute of the abuse their profession subjected them to. Years of smoking had weathered their skin into thick, furrowed leather. They bore scars and teeth lost to neglect, drug use, and violence. I counted at least two glass eyes among them. They looked more like pirates than prostitutes.

My three shipmates took a table in the back. As I marched towards them, I felt like a debutante braving a construction site gauntlet. I was groped, grabbed, whistled at, and propositioned in ways so obscene I still blush when I think of it.

Before I could sit down, a short old woman with more wrinkles than a dehydrated Shar-Pei blocked my path. Speaking in a voice that reminded me of a female Louis Armstrong, she asked, "Whassa matta wich choo faggots?!? Choo no lahk mah goorrrrlls?"

I took another look at the women along the bar, then turned back to the madam. "Ma'am, we didn't know women were on the menu here. The sign outside said Chutey's House of Beer, not Chutey's House of Heartbreakers." I stuck to English because I wanted to be very diplomatic. The last thing I wanted to do was to offend someone in Chutey's. They would make us all bleed.

The madam was not impressed. "Choo goin' to fuck or not?"

"Not," I said. "We have girlfriends." Hit with an evil spurt of inspiration, though, I pointed at Kent. "Except for the chunky guy. We call him Gonzales. I don't think he's ever been with a woman before. He says he has, but none of us believe him."

The ladies at the bar heard this and slithered their way over to Steve. I looked back at the madam and asked, "Choo going to serve us beer or not?"

When I got to our table, a woman older than Kent's mother was trying to slip her hand down his shirt. He was fending her off with a hilarious combination of fear and shame. She was particularly unkempt, making no effort to make herself presentable. She did not even try to cover the track marks on her arms. Judging by the look on Kent's face, premature ejaculation was not going to be an issue at Chutey's. "So Steve," I asked him as he squirmed. "What the hell happened to you after the Miami Club?"

"I ran," he started to say as he pulled the woman's hand out of his pants. "I was lucky because I was close to the door. It was tough, though. The Mexicans were pounding on every American they could get their hands on."

I had little doubt that the Americans were doing the same to the Mexicans. "Did you see Mack?"

Kent shook his head. "He was deeper inside the place, closer to the stage. He would've had to fight through a lot more people to get out than I did. You know, once the cops got there, they were picking everybody up who even looked like they were in a fight."

"They still are," Gott added. "Marty and I were up at Margarita Village and some *federales* walked through scoping the place. They found a guy who looked like he got popped in the eye. They asked him a couple of questions, then yanked him outside."

"You think Mack could've been arrested?" I asked Steve.

"I don't know, Doyle. When that place erupted, I took off. I did not want to be there when the cops showed..." Kent was interrupted as his suitor started fumbling with his zipper.

Gott, Bard, and I exchanged disapproving expressions. Steve Kent's stock dropped significantly among the three of us. Our expectations of Palazzo were already low. We were not surprised he left Mack and Kent behind when the train flew off the rails at the Miami Club. He got cut some slack because he was injured, though. Granted, his wounds turned out to be nothing, but with the amount of blood pumping onto his face, it was understandable how he could have concluded otherwise.

Kent was not hurt. He looked fine. Hanging back to help his shipmates should have been instinct, but it appeared Gonzales thought only of himself. None of us said anything, but we all questioned his dependability in a clutch situation. His standing had not sunk to the depths of Bill Kramer's, but he was not getting off on the right foot either.

When the noise outside died down, I saw the sheet near the door open up as a police officer stepped through it. We were the only customers there, so he walked directly to our table. The woman who was trying to feel Kent up backed off and returned to the bar.

TEQUILA VIKINGS

"*Buenas noches*," the officer said as he approached. After we returned the greeting, he commented in English, "This does not look like the kind of place I expect to find *gringos* like you in."

"It's not the kind of place I would have expected you to find us in either, *señor*," I answered. "It just seemed safer to be in here than out there for the time being."

The policeman leered at the women seated at the bar. "You sure about that?"

Giving the ladies a second look, I smiled. "Well, now that you mention it…"

"Did you see the fight outside?"

I nodded. "Yes, *señor*. We saw the whole thing."

"What started it?" the officer asked.

"The way I saw it," I said. "Was that seven guys tried to beat up a single Marine…"

"And why would they do that?"

I shrugged. "The chickenshits seem to have a twisted sense of entertainment."

"You are all in the military too, yes?" It was not a hard deduction to make. With our haircuts, sideburns, and mustaches, military personnel tended to stand out. "You wouldn't lie to protect your fellow Navy guys, would you?"

I shook my head. "Those dudes were Marines. No, we aren't going to lie for those pricks." That was blatant bullshit. The Navy and the Corps always enjoyed a healthy rivalry, but we would do what we could to protect them.

"Were you guys fighting?"

"No, *señor*."

"Are you sure? Do you want to stand up for me?"

Though I knew I did nothing wrong, my heart skipped a beat. Still, I did what the officer asked. Once on my feet, the policeman inspected me, looking for blood splatters, torn clothing, or bruises. After shining a flashlight on my knuckles, he told me to take a seat at another table while he handed me my beer. He then repeated the process with the rest of the group. I held my breath when he inspected Kent. I did not know if he would present any evidence of his role in the Miami Club brawl.

Satisfied we were not involved in the disturbance outside, the officer asked where we went that night. We rattled off all the bars we visited but made no mention of *Zona Norte*. "Did anyone see the fight at XS?" the officer asked.

"No," we all answered.

"What about the one at Señor Frogs? That was a big one." Again we said we missed it. "The Miami Club?" No. "It must be a full moon. There are a lot of fights going on tonight. You boys stay out of trouble, okay? And stay out of places like this. Nothing but trouble to be found in here."

*****

At that point, it seemed like there was nothing but trouble to be found anywhere. The entire vibe of Tijuana had gone sideways. The fight at the Miami Club was so big it had a domino effect on the rest of the city. Too many people on both sides of the fracas escaped. As they crossed paths in other parts of town, the violence would flare up again and draw even more people into it. By midnight, fights were breaking out all over Revolucion and the police responded with heavy-handed tactics that only aggravated the situation.

It was Mexicans versus Americans at XS. It was sailors against Marines near the jai alai stadium. It was cops against civilians at La Estrella, a Mexican venue off of the Revolucion strip. We heard the crowd had turned on the officers there and sent a few of them to the hospital. Tijuana police officers were never famous for exercising restraint. After that though, the brutality they used to pacify suspects increased exponentially. What was already a tense situation threatened to devolve into a full-blown riot. I had been going to Tijuana for years, and never had I seen anything like it.

Tony Bard and I decided to get our guys off the street. We had already sent Metaire and Palazzo across the border. We got word from Javier that Franklin had crossed too. He told us that Todd had jumped on stage at one of the gentlemen's clubs and, stripping down to his underwear, made more tips than the ladies had. They were not pleased and voiced their displeasure with their fists. Todd was able to get his pants and shoes before fleeing down the street in his tighty-whiteys, but left his shirt behind. He bolted to our safe house, hoping to score another. That worked out well as Javier sent him back to the border wearing the one Metaire left behind. While there, Franklin told our host he spotted Macklemore on Revolucion, though from a distance. I was relieved to hear that at least Warren was not in jail.

"Why didn't Mack come to Javier's?" Tony asked as we set out to find him. The question was obvious.

So was the answer. "Because he's Macklemore," I said. "Nothing gets through that thick skull of his until it's told to him twenty fucking times. I guarantee you that he just can't find the place. Hell, if he's had enough to drink, he's probably forgotten about it completely."

When we got Kent to Javier's, Kramer was already passed out on the couch. We stationed Dixie there to watch them and dropped off a couple of cases of Pacifico beer to make sure no one else left.

The rest of our group was still at Rio Rita's. A few decided to get hotel rooms with the girls they met. The others called it a night and returned to the safe house. That left only Warren Macklemore unaccounted for, and I was worried. We got word from the bouncer at Bambi's that he was still out on the street, but besides Franklin, none of us had laid eyes on him since the Miami Club brawl. Mack was ill-equipped to navigate Tijuana alone after dark. Hell, he was hardly equipped to navigate it in broad daylight.

Bard and I patrolled Revolucion time after time searching for him. We stopped in every bar along the way, speaking with the staff and describing whom we were looking for. Fortunately, Macklemore had a unique look to him, one that people tended to remember. Having him stroll into your bar was kind of like having an unexpected encounter with a masturbating Sasquatch. He was not something you went looking for, but once you saw him, he left a pretty big impression on you.

We could not cross paths with Warren Macklemore no matter how hard we tried. It seemed like we were running into what remained of the Hockey Mullet Frat Guy's crew every time we turned a corner, though. At a different point in my life, I would have relished mixing it up with that group, but I made Hannah a promise. It ran counter to my instincts, but whenever we saw them coming, I led Tony across the street to get out of their way. It was evident they were looking to take their frustrations out on someone. I did my best to ensure it was not us.

Around one o'clock, Tony Bard gave up. He was exhausted, but as the crowd finally began to thin, I decided to make one more pass by myself. I finished going up the west side of the street, past Las Pulgas, then crossed over and made my way back one last time.

It was then when I heard a commotion break out at the Toucan Club about a block or so ahead of me. At that point, I bore witness to so many fights I was getting bored with it all. Then I spotted a figure burst onto the sidewalk with the Hockey Mullet Frat Guy hot on his heels. As police sirens fired up in the distance behind me, I caught myself getting excited. Watching the *federales* knock the block off the Mullet Man would have been the highlight of my evening. I picked up my pace to avoid missing anything.

I was not expecting to see a trio of police officers on foot beat the patrol cars to the disturbance. By the looks of it, neither were the frat punks. Taken by surprise, the thugs broke off the attack and dashed back into the tavern. The officers charged in after them with batons out and swinging. As the vehicles pulled up, they unloaded an additional two pairs of cops. Half of them immediately set upon the poor guy on the sidewalk. They surrounded, cuffed, and roughly stuffed him into a squad car, then rushed in to help their partners get the other hoodlums out of the bar. I started walking even faster.

Though still too far away to clearly make out what was going on, I had no problem hearing the ruckus. There were yells, screaming women, and the raised voices of policemen trying to exert their authority. I got to the scene in time to watch a pair of *federales* haul the Hockey Mullet Frat Guy out. The officers each pounded him with several blows to the ribs, then threw him into the other police car. As they turned around to help their friends get the other two, a lone beer bottle sailed out of the club. It caught a sergeant square in the nose, knocking him right off of his feet. He landed on his back, sprawled across the sidewalk and clutching his face in his hands.

For a split second, everything went quiet. Everyone in the vicinity realized what happened. That was a direct assault upon a Tijuana policeman, an affront that would not go unanswered. We all knew the *federales* just got the justification they needed to escalate the situation dramatically. The momentary silence was everyone bracing for what came next.

TEQUILA VIKINGS

The stricken sergeant was not a large man, only standing an inch or two above my shoulders. He appeared fit for a guy who was probably in his mid-thirties, but he did not look particularly strong or athletic. Just vicious. As he writhed in pain along the sidewalk, his partner rushed to his side. *"¡Sargento Martínez! ¡Francisco! ¿Estás bien?"*

The sergeant screamed out in pain and rage. He then let out a litany of curse words that far exceeded the Spanish skills I needed to fully appreciate them. He leapt to his feet, far angrier than wounded, and charged back into the bar with his nightstick drawn. His partner took a split second to call for backup, then ran in after him. I decided it was time for me to bounce.

Avoiding the bar's entrance, I jogged out into the street to go around the squad cars. As I passed, I glanced inside to see the unlucky bastard in back, stopping in my tracks. It was Macklemore.

At first, I stood there reeling. I had been coming to Tijuana for a long time. I had seen some pretty bad situations down there, yet this was among the worst. The cops were busting heads, and I could already see that people were going to get hurt.

Macklemore often got abused by his own shipmates. Even when cleaned up and sober, he effortlessly drew ridicule and hostility from complete strangers. I could not even comprehend what was going to happen to him in a Mexican jail cell. I could not let him go.

What got into me then, I have no idea. It was not like I had a plan or anything; my instincts just took over. I reached down, pulled the door handle, and to my surprise, the damned thing opened right up.

I discovered the hard way that leaving valuables in an unlocked car was an excellent way to lose a wallet. It turned out leaving a police vehicle unattended in the wrong part of town was an excellent way to lose a Macklemore. Considering that these were cops I was dealing with, they should have known better.

I took a quick look around to make sure the coast was clear. The officers were still fighting in the bar, so no one was watching. I reached into the back of the squad car and grabbed Warren by the collar of his shirt, yanking him out into the street.

"Doyle!" Mack gasped, tears still running down his face. "What...!"

I pulled off the baja I bought at the border and threw it over Warren, hiding his handcuffs. "Shut up and start walking! Now!" Leading him away from the car, I tucked the sleeves into the front pouch of the pullover. That made it look like Mack's hands were in his pockets instead of shackled behind his back.

"Hey! What about me?!? Get me out of here!" the Hockey Mullet Frat Guy screamed as we passed his car. In response, I lifted my middle finger and pressed it up against the glass.

"Fuck you!" he screamed as we left. "I swear to God, I'll find you! You fucking pricks! I'm going to kill you! I mean it! Get me out of here goddammit!!!"

I considered springing the mullet man so I could kick the snot out of him later but remembered the promise I made. I also remembered processing Corey Baker aboard the ship months before. The *federales* brutalized that guy just to ease their frustrations after losing a suspect in a foot chase. I could only imagine what they would do to the HMFG after losing a suspect from the back of a cop car.

I almost considered hanging around to watch it live.

*****

CHAPTER 21

"**S**top it," I told Macklemore as he sniffled again. "If you don't pull yourself together, you're going to get us into serious trouble."

We were a few blocks off Revolucion now, heading north. It was a rougher part of town where "*¡Bienvenido!*" was often expressed through rape and strongarm robbery. The area was dangerous enough that even police officers tended to avoid it at that time of night. Considering my companion was wearing handcuffs, I felt safer braving *cholos* than *federales*.

But not if I couldn't get Mack to stop sobbing. "I'm not kidding, Warren. This is the kind of neighborhood where you want to look tough. Crying isn't making us look like guys you don't want to mess with."

"If I knew how to look like a guy you didn't want to mess with, don't you think I'd be doing it by now?" At that point, Macklemore was close to ugly crying. "What is it that makes everyone want to fuck with me all the time? I was minding my own business in that bar, trying to figure out how to get home. I wasn't doing anything to anybody! The minute those guys walked in, they started messing with me for no reason! I tried to leave, but they wouldn't let me! I didn't do anything to them! I didn't even look…"

Warren was getting loud, so I cut him off. Broadcasting that voice through that neighborhood *en ingles* was like blood in the water. "I've told you before, Mack. A coward tries to make himself look tougher by messing with weaker men. I've seen those guys in Ocean Beach a million times. They travel in packs to have strength in numbers. Individually, there ain't one of them worth a shit. People like that pick fights they know they can win, and Mack, you carry yourself like the perfect victim. That's why these punks fuck with you. They know they can get away with it."

"I can't keep living like this," Mack cried. "It's like my entire purpose in life is to be a punching bag for someone else…"

"Because you let them, Warren. We've been over this, man. You're a strong guy! Stronger than I am. You can knock the shit out of a punching bag. If you took it upon yourself to actually hit these fuckers back, you'd see that you're not nearly as weak as you think you are."

"But…"

"But nothing! Warren! If you're going to get your ass kicked anyway, what the hell do you have to lose? Get pissed and take a couple of the fuckers down with you!"

Even in the darkness, I could see a lightbulb go off in Macklemore's head. It was finally computing. If he was going to get beat up anyway, he had nothing to lose by fighting back. Nothing to lose. *Nothing to lose.* He was having some sort of epiphany and suddenly stopped sobbing. "How much longer before we get to Javier's place?"

"A block or two." I was banking on our route being deserted that late and it paid off. Whatever the *barrio* malcontents were doing, they were doing it somewhere else. We made it to Javier's without being accosted by cop or crook. I got away with breaking a man out of a goddamn police car. I enjoyed some epic adventures down in Tijuana but never had I done anything that brazen before.

Once inside and off the street, I allowed myself to relax. I grabbed a beer, lit a cigarette, and told the men how I sprung Macklemore. They could not believe it and asked me to tell the tale again, but I had to refuse. "There's no time for that. We need to get ready to make our way back to the border. Javier, do you have a hacksaw?"

TEQUILA VIKINGS

"A what?"

"*Una sierra para metales...*"

"Ah! Yes! *Sí, yo tengo…*"

It turned out Javier had a very dull hacksaw. It worked, but it took forever to get through the handcuffs. As Dixie worked on cutting off Warren's shackles, I once again imposed upon our host. "How about scissors? Do you have scissors? *Tijeras*?"

"Scissors? What do you need scissors for?" Macklemore asked.

"We're shaving your head."

"What?!? Do you have any idea how goofy I look without hair?!?"

Do you have any idea how goofy you look WITH hair? "Look, we don't want to take any chances running into a cop who thinks you look familiar. It's best if we make you look as little like yourself as possible. Would you rather be ugly and free or have a fabulous looking mug shot?"

Of course, Javier's scissors were no sharper than his hacksaw. After our first go at Macklemore's coif, he emerged looking as if he had survived an assault by an escaped lunatic with a set of electric gardening shears. It took three more passes to get it short enough to shave, but once we did, we were happy with the result. Warren was not, now sporting a look inspired by disfiguring misadventures in chemotherapy.

"What do you think?" I asked Dixie.

Kevin shrugged. "If this doesn't work, at least you did everything in your power to make sure he doesn't get raped in prison."

With Mack's hair finished and his cuffs removed, we did some wardrobe shifting so Warren was not in the same clothes he was picked up in. By then, it was seven in the morning. The curfew was over, and it was time to start filtering people back into the United States.

We sent Kramer and Kent over first. Dixie shadowed them to make sure the coast was clear. When Kevin returned, he reported it was like any other morning we crossed after staying out all night. The streets were deserted with only the trinket vendors milling about. There was not a police officer to be seen anywhere.

"Those guys had a long night," Dixie said. "I'm thinking they're taking a well-deserved morning off."

I agreed but wanted to be sure. We sent Bard and a couple of the Comm Repair guys next. Again, Dixie trailed them, and again, he came back giving us the all-clear. The next batch went the same way. By the time it was our turn, it was going on ten in the morning. I was positive the officers involved in Mack's detention finished their shifts hours before. I shook Javier's hand, slipped him another twenty dollars for his help, and headed out to go home.

The walk back was as uneventful as Dixie said it would be. For all the sin that took place in Tijuana at night, Mexico was still a Catholic country. Sunday mornings were for church. There were hardly any cars on the road, and as far as I could tell, there were only a half dozen of us walking toward the US.

I started getting worried once we got to the home stretch. That was where things always went wrong. "It would be a good idea if Dixie went ahead of us," I told Mack. "When we get to the bazaar in front of the crossing, I want you to do about thirty seconds' worth of shopping. Give me a chance to get through first. If I see anything suspicious, I'll back out, and we'll hire a cab to Otay Mesa. Understood?"

"Okay."

"And Mack, there's usually a lone police officer inside the building. Don't panic if you see him. Keep walking normally and smile. If something does happen and you need to make a break for it, go for the turnstiles. That's the finish line. You clear those turnstiles, and you're safe at home. That's the United States."

For once, Warren followed my directions to the letter. He fell behind to shop for trinkets while I entered the border station. There was nothing to it. The lone police officer was there but so engrossed in his newspaper that he did not even notice me pass. Fifty steps later, I walked through the turnstile and was safe on the right side of the frontier. I spotted Dixie ahead of me, already talking to a border agent. Instead of joining him, I held back to wait for Macklemore.

Twenty seconds later, Warren walked in and, just like me, breezed past the cop without a second glance. Seeing me waiting for him, he allowed himself a little smile, and I could see him walking with a bit of extra swagger. He survived his first trip to Tijuana and could now claim fame as the man who got busted out of a *federale* police car. Macklemore earned his first bona fide sea story, and it was going to be shared with relish when we got back to the ship. Hell, in his head, he might even have been thinking himself worthy of one of our Tequila Viking tattoos.

A door opened to my left, and two more police officers stepped through it. My heart stopped, and I caught myself focusing upon them as they stepped into the corridor. Both of them looked at Warren, but instead of doing anything alarming, they cracked broad smiles.

Macklemore was not a handsome man. While shaved clean and beaming that goofy-ass grin of his though, he was a scream. The two cops both looked at me and flashed expressions that seemed to say, "Whoa! Check out that funny-looking guy over there!"

I had to laugh, shrugging my shoulders at them to say, "I know, right?" Then the yelling started.

"That's him! The tall dude in the baja! That's the son-of-a-bitch that broke that guy out of the police car!"

I lifted my head and saw the Hockey Mullet Frat Guy pointing his finger at me. He emerged from the same door as the policemen I was watching, but I was too focused on the officers to notice. Accompanied by his lawyer, the college boy was furious. He looked intent on getting me arrested despite his escort urging him to shut his damn mouth.

When Mullet man outed me, I was leaning on the turnstiles. That was within reach of the officers, so I jumped back and took a couple of steps deeper into American territory. I made sure to backpedal away from Warren, keeping everyone's attention on me. To help, I yelled accusations back at the frat dick. All Mack had to do was keep pace, and he would have been fine. Instead, he panicked and ran to the turnstiles, just like I told him to do.

Warren was not on anybody's radar until he broke into a sprint. Once he took off, the officers charged to intercept him. As Macklemore leaped over the barriers, the *federales* plucked him out of the air and spiked him to the turf.

"NOOOOooooooo!!!" Mack screamed as he hit the floor and struggled with the two cops putting handcuffs on him. "NO! NO! NO! Oh, God! Oh, God! Please don't! *Please don't!* DOYLE! HELP ME! PLEASE!"

Instinctively, I took a couple of steps forward as I tried to figure out what to do. As I did so, the officer reading the paper approached me from the other side of the turnstiles. "Hey, *amigo*! Aren't you going to help your friend? Come on over! It'll be okay. Give your friend a hand!"

"Please," I begged. "This is all a big misunderstanding. He didn't do anything. I swear! What'll it take for you to let him go? I got money!" I pulled out my wallet to show him and then realized I had barely enough cash on me to buy a trolley ticket.

"DOYLE! DON'T LET THEM DO THIS TO ME! PLEASE! HELP ME!"

"*Por favor amigo,*" I said, switching to Spanish. "I know the chief of police in Tijuana! He said if I ever got into trouble to let him know..."

"Really?" the officer asked. "Who is this chief you know?"

Between the excitement and the months that passed since I had met the man, I momentarily drew a blank on what the chief's name was. It eventually came to me, though. "Marco! Marco Baylon!"

The police officers seemed to settle down. "You know *Commandante* Baylon?" one of them asked.

"*¡Sí! ¡Sí, conozco al jefe!*" I exclaimed.

The three officers exchanged puzzled looks and loosened their grip on Macklemore. "That changes things. I think we need to see him to get this straightened out. Come on, *amigo*. We'll go straight there."

I exhaled in relief, thankful for my chance encounter with *Don* Baylon while fishing. I was about to hop back over into Mexico, but an American border guard brought me back to my senses. "Don't you even think about it, kid!" he called out from behind me.

Realizing what I nearly had done, I began to shake.

"Aaaaaaaahhhh," one of the officers laughed, wagging his finger at me. "We almost had you!" To punctuate his point, he hauled off and punched Macklemore in the side. Warren erupted into a bloodcurdling scream that was cut short by a blow to the gut that took his breath away. The police struck him several more times as they dragged him through the door they had emerged from.

The third officer approached me one last time. "If you change your mind about coming to help your buddy, he'll be down at the jail. When you get there, ask for *Sargento* Francisco Martinez. He'll be very happy to help you."

TEQUILA VIKINGS

My head started spinning as my thoughts turned to Macklemore's arrest at the Toucan Club. I remembered the beer bottle getting thrown from the bar and catching the policeman in the face. I recalled his partner running up to him. *"¡Sargento Martínez! ¡Francisco! ¿Estás bien?"*

Sargento Francisco Martinez.

A conversation I had with Lupe Castillo several months before then popped into my mind.

"He's a narco. He provides security for the Arrellano-Felix brothers. Los Hermanos. No, I don't know him. I hope I never know him. I know of him. Everybody on the street in Tijuana does. Sargento Francisco Martinez of the federales. He's a real bastard, that guy. You never want to get to know someone like that."

My heart sank. Not only had I broken Mack out of a Mexican police car, but I had stolen a prisoner from Hulagu himself. And not the fake one every crooked Tijuana cop pretended to be, either. I put Warren on the wrong side of the real fucking deal.

I went numb, sinking into a trance under the realization of how far out of our depth I had landed us. The Hockey Mullet Frat Guy broke my reverie. As his lawyer pulled him past me, he stuck up his middle finger and shoved it into my face as I had done to him a few hours before. Had I not been in shock, I would have killed him for that, but at the time, I was too despondent to care.

*****

CHAPTER 22

Dixie practically had to carry me to Master Chief's door. My legs refused to work. It was not out of fear, though. Hell, I would have run to Darrow's door had I any realistic expectation that he would put me out of my misery. I could not walk because I was overwhelmed with guilt and grief. It took everything I had to stand under my own power when Jung answered the door. Once Darrow stepped up from behind his wife, though, I fell apart.

Both men carried me to the couch. I tried telling Darrow what happened, but all I could do was sob and babble. We must have been there ten minutes before I was able to say, "I fucked up, Master Chief. I fucked up bad."

Tired of trying to get it out of me, Darrow finally turned to Dixie. "What the hell's going on?"

"Mack got arrested. In Tijuana."

Darrow looked unsurprised. "For what?"

"Fighting. Originally, anyway."

"I saw it, Master Chief," I told him, pulling myself together a little. "He wasn't fighting. He got attacked. He didn't do a goddamn thing!"

Looking at Dixie, Darrow asked, "What do you mean by 'originally?'"

TEQUILA VIKINGS

I answered for Kevin. "I didn't think he could survive a night in a Tijuana jail cell. When no one was looking, I opened up the door of the police car and pulled him out of it."

"*You did what?!?*" Darrow exclaimed.

I explained the opportunity that had presented itself and how I seized it. I then managed to get out how we cut off Mack's handcuffs, shaved his head, and changed his clothes. Finally, I described how it all went wrong at the final moment.

My master chief listened to the whole thing with his mouth agape. "You fucking idiot," he growled when I finished. Standing up to pace, he said, "Mack was picked up for fighting. Guilty or not, it happens twenty times a night in Tijuana. We would have just marched down there, paid a hundred-dollar fine, and brought him home! Do you realize what you've done? You got Mack to commit a felony! Doyle, he's probably going to jail for a couple of years now!"

"I know! I know!" I cried, sliding off Master Chief's couch onto my knees. "What can I do? How do I make this right? This is my fault, not his! I'll trade places with Mack if they'll let me! Tell me how to arrange it!"

Darrow brushed me off. "They're not going to let you trade places with Macklemore, Doyle. If you go down there, they're going to put both of you away."

"That's what I have to do then! I can protect him in prison! He's in serious trouble, Master Chief!"

"No fucking shit, Murphy!"

Shaking my head, I said, "No! It gets worse!"

"Mack's looking at serious time in a Mexican prison! It doesn't get much worse than that!" Darrow yelled.

I got back up and reclaimed my seat on the edge of the sofa. "It does, Master Chief. It does. I didn't know it, but I broke Mack out of Hulagu's custody."

"Hulagu?" Darrow let out a chuckle, but it was without humor. "Hulagu's a myth."

"Most of the time, yes. There's a real Hulagu, though. He works as muscle for one of the drug gangs down there."

My master chief's face betrayed his skepticism. "How the hell would you know that?"

"I got people too, Master Chief."

Darrow growled and dropped onto the couch beside me. "Jesus Christ! This is fucking up on a biblical scale. Mack's fucked, Doyle. Fucked! And you are too! When the captain gets wind of this, he's going to burn your ass!"

"I don't care what happens to me. How do we get Mack out?"

In frustration, Darrow turned and started jamming his index finger into my forehead. "Apparently, I'm not getting through to you! We're not getting Macklemore out of a Mexican prison, Doyle!"

"But we have to…"

"We can't!"

I dropped my face into my hands and sighed. I stayed that way for a long while, shaking my head and trying to work up the nerve to change tactics. "Master Chief, you said you owed me one for what happened in Vegas. I'd like to cash that in now. I need you to contact Marco Baylon and have him help us."

"Are you out of your fucking mind?" Darrow exclaimed. "That chip is nowhere near big enough to get me to coerce the chief of the Tijuana Police Department to free a guy like Warren Macklemore! This Hulagu guy you're talking about? Fuck! For all I know, he works for Baylon! Those guys are dirty, Doyle! They're dangerously dirty! The last thing we want is to be owing people like that favors!"

"You have to…"

"I don't have to do a damn…"

"…because if you don't, I'll come clean about Randy Green."

Dixie's jaw dropped open while Master Chief's face flushed a deep shade of red.

You did not try to blackmail a man like Olongapo Earp. I regretted my words as soon as they had crossed my lips. Still, I could not take them back. "I'll tell them you knew all about it. I'll admit how you suggested I take care of the others too. I'll even let them know that the captain was aware of it, and taking care of Green the old way may even have been his idea. I have more than $16,000 left from what I won in Vegas. I'm willing to use every penny of it to get Mack back."

TEQUILA VIKINGS

Master Chief's eyes narrowed, and the look he gave me put ice crystals in my veins. I was playing with fire. "You'd do that to me? To *me*? Doyle, I've treated you like a son. Would you really sell me out?"

I buckled. Breaking down, I fell forward off the couch again, resting my forehead on the floor. It was an empty threat. Even if I did go to the NIS and come clean, it would do nothing to get Macklemore out of Mexico. It would only land more of us behind bars. "No," I sobbed. "I don't think I can. I'm desperate. Please, Master Chief! I'm begging you! Please! I can't live with this! Help me get Mack back!"

Darrow sighed, shaking his head. He then got up and walked towards the kitchen, where the telephone was. "I'll see what I can do."

*****

Dixie and I spent the next four hours in Darrow's back yard. We chain-smoked and wrung our hands while our boss pulled every string he could to get Marco Baylon to work with him. It was not an easy process, nor was it for the faint of heart.

My own ticker nearly gave out when Darrow floated an initial offer of only $5000 to spring Warren. I lost my mind and almost sabotaged my master chief's efforts by raging about it while he was still on the phone. Luckily, he stopped me with a "shut-up-or-I'll-rip-your-throat-out" look before I did any real damage. After chewing me out boot camp style, Darrow explained he had to lowball the initial offer. He knew the Mexicans would demand more money. If he started by offering all we had, there was nothing left to counter with.

It was approaching dinner time when my adrenaline finally wore off. Having now been awake for more than thirty hours, I felt myself starting to slip. That was when the master chief emerged from the house to let us know where we stood.

"You were right about this Hulagu guy," Darrow told us. "When I mentioned the name Francisco Martinez to Baylon, he got very serious. Baylon is the head of the Tijuana Police Department. Martinez is a *federale,* so Marco has no real authority over the prick. I get the impression they're both in bed with different groups that don't play well with each other. He told me Martinez is a severe individual, and even approaching him to negotiate was going to be tricky."

"I don't get it," Dixie said. "You saying the chief of police does not have any pull over a lowly sergeant of another organization?"

Darrow held his hands up, indicating he did not understand it either. "All these guys seem to have dual loyalties, Dixon. Their rank in the police department is one thing. Their standing in whatever cartel they're serving is more important, though. I get the feeling Baylon might be some sort of passive participant in this stuff. He's probably just getting money to look the other way where illegal activity is concerned. Martinez sounds more active in it, though, guarding contraband, eliminating threats, that kind of shit."

"Oh, Christ," I moaned, dropping my head into my hands again. "Hulagu's going to fucking kill Mack, isn't he?"

"No. Not for something like this. If Mack stole dope from them, yes. For this, Martinez is going to make an example out of him. Luckily, Macklemore is being held in the local hoosegow. That's Baylon's jurisdiction and works in our favor. The chief has physical custody of him."

"So he can get him out?" I asked.

Darrow nodded. "He can, but not without kissing some ass. If he springs Mack on his own, Baylon risks open conflict with this Martinez guy. It's a delicate situation, apparently, and all about street cred. At first, he would not even consider approaching this sergeant to suggest we talk."

"Not even for money?"

My master chief shook his head. "Not even for money. I had to call in a favor with the 32nd Street Command Master Chief to threaten to put Tijuana off-limits for all military personnel. That would eliminate half of everything spent down there and put Baylon in a rough position with the business owners who support him. I used that, took the position that you were trying to help a man who was being unjustly arrested, and the offer of cash to get him to change his mind."

"So he can do it?" I asked.

Darrow nodded. "We got it done. I think. You need to bring $15,000 down to Marco."

Dixie shook his head. "No way. I wouldn't put it past these people to kill Doyle for having the balls to bust Macklemore out of a cop car, let alone to take fifteen grand away from him. It sounds like a setup."

Our master chief agreed. "Yeah, I'm not letting him go without assurances either. Baylon has a nephew who's a cop down there, too. He's coming north to sit with us while Doyle goes down to get Mack. I made it clear that whatever happens to Doyle while he's in Mexico will happen to his nephew before we send him back. Marco's sending one of his guys to meet you at the border crossing at Otay Mesa with Mack to make the trade."

"It's going to be $15,000 total?" I asked.

"Yeah, I saved you a grand. Don't spend it, though. When this is over, you're going to pay for a fishing charter to thank Master Chief Cairns for throwing his weight behind the threat to close the border."

I nodded. I knew I was going to end up owing some favors. "So it's done then?"

"It's done."

"Good. Can I use your phone?" Darrow nodded and motioned for me to grab the one in the kitchen.

Once inside, I dialed up Cheri's place and waited for Hannah to answer. "'Ello?" she said as she picked up, her voice heavy with worry.

"Hi, Hannah…"

"Doyle? Where the hell are you? Do you have any idea how…"

"Honey, please…"

"What?" she asked, concerned about my tone of voice. "Are you alright?"

"Hannah, I…" I paused, trying to keep my voice from cracking. "Hannah, I don't know when I'm going to be home. Honey, I really fucked up…"

*****

"You get busted for drugs?" Though Macklemore was the only American in the packed cell, there was at least one other man there who spoke English.

"No," Warren answered, shaking his broken head as best he could.

"Seriously? Then what does Hulagu want with you?"

"Who's Hulagu?"

"You don't know who Hulagu is?" Mack's cellmate laughed. "Man, he's the guy who beat your ass, Holmes!"

Mack was at one of the lowest points he had ever been. He had been abused by his family, his shipmates, and even random strangers on Revolucion Avenue. Now a psychotic Mexican police officer wanted him to suffer as well. It seemed as if this was what his entire life was destined to be.

Warren could at least understand his shipmates' animosity. They knew him. The rest were baffling. It was as if Macklemore drew the attention of every beast needing to satiate a lust for random cruelty. Mack did nothing to the Hockey Mullet Frat Guy and his friends, yet they zeroed right in on him as soon as they walked into the Toucan Club. He never threw a punch nor even spoke to the men who assaulted him, yet they attacked him anyway. When the police arrived, they were equally unforgiving. It was not fair.

Macklemore did not think his second arrest was fair either. Sitting in the backseat of a police car was the last place he wanted to be that night—still, the thought to escape never crossed his mind. Had I asked his opinion, Mack would probably have opted to spend the night in jail and get bailed out in the morning. I never offered him that option, though. I just opened the door and yanked him out.

Warren only did what I told him to do. When I ordered him to get out of the car, he got out of the car. When I commanded him to run away from the Toucan Club, he did. When I directed Mack to walk faster to get off Revolucion Avenue, he never questioned me. He let us shave his head because I said so. He even charged the turnstiles because I told him that was what he needed to do if things turned sour.

Warren Macklemore's trust in me earned him a cold hard bed on the concrete floor of a Tijuana jail cell. And the beating of his life. The cops roughed him up a little at the border. For the most part, though, they saved him for *Sargento* Martinez. He and a couple of other *federales* showed up in the evening and pulled him into the corridor. There, in full view of the other prisoners, they thrashed the living shit out of that kid.

TEQUILA VIKINGS

Martinez did not speak much. He let his fists do his talking. There was nothing Hulagu wanted out of Macklemore other than to see him get hurt for having made him look like a fool. Warren sensed Martinez knew he was not the mastermind of his own escape. I was. Since Doyle Murphy was not within his grasp, he did to Warren Macklemore everything he wanted to do to me.

Hulagu was reaching his stride when one of the jailers interrupted the assault. "What?!?" Martinez screamed, angered at having his momentum disrupted.

"You need to take a break, Sergeant!" the officer told him. "We were contacted by city hall. Apparently, that other *gringo* actually does know *Commandante* Baylon."

"I don't care if the *gringo* knows President Salinas himself," Martinez barked. "I don't work for Baylon."

"Well, we do, *amigo*," the officer told him. "We need you to get off the prisoner."

"Fuck you."

"No, fuck you," the guard answered. "You're in our house, Francisco."

Martinez stood up, looking like he was about to direct his venom toward the jailor. One of the *federales* stepped between the two men to prevent it, though. "Come on, Francisco. Not here. Not now. We'll come back." Leaving Macklemore balled up and whimpering on the tiles, the *federales* walked away.

When they were gone, the two guards who interrupted the beating reached down to pick Warren up off the deck. "I don't know what the hell you were thinking, *gringo*," one of them said in English. "But of all the policemen you could have pissed off in Tijuana, you messed up picking that one."

"I think you made him a little mad yourself..." Mack answered, blood spilling out of his mouth.

"Yeah, and let me tell you, I'll be watching my back when I go home tonight. You watch yours. We've been told not to let that guy back in here. They're working on getting you to a safer place. The problem is this guy has a long reach. Keep your eye on the other prisoners. If one of them starts making you uncomfortable, you let me know."

"Thank you," Macklemore groaned. "Who are you?"

"Guerrero. Ask for *El Jefe*. That means 'the boss.' That's me. I'm in charge of this bloc."

Macklemore spent the evening trying to sleep on the floor; he wasn't tough enough to fight for one of the seats. Besides pain, Warren endured brawling inmates, lights that never went out, and the incessant shouting of the guards. It was the longest night of his life, especially with no word from anybody about what was happening to him. He had no idea what anyone was doing to bring him home until the next evening when Guerrero was back on duty.

Sometime after dinner, the bloc captain called for him to step out into the corridor. Warren could barely move. Between the beating and twenty-four hours spent lying on a concrete slab, he was stiff from neck to ankles. He needed help to walk but got none until the guards placed his hands back in cuffs and led him to the rear of the jail.

"Where am I going?" Mack asked his guards.

"To see your friends," Guerrero told him. "They're coming to get you at the Otay Mesa crossing."

A wave of relief hit Macklemore so hard his legs nearly gave out. The two men who were steadying Warren had to almost carry him. He was not able to support his own weight until he was outside and standing before a couple of jeeps. Blinded by the glare of headlights, Warren asked. "Who are they?"

"Your ride, motherfucker!" Sergeant Martinez shouted. Hulagu then took his nightstick and pummeled Mack in the gut with it so hard that he vomited.

*****

CHAPTER 23

Withdrawing fifteen grand in cash turned out to be harder than I thought. Pulling out that much coin raises red flags as bills left no paper trails. Large withdrawals were more likely to go towards nefarious purposes that banks did not approve of. I suspected paying off corrupt police officers fell under that category and was probably frowned upon by my credit union.

To avoid the hassles that the truth was sure to raise, I told the teller I was buying a car. I then had to listen to them try to convince me to use a Navy Federal car loan instead. It took me more than two hours to get out of the bank with my own money.

It was easier to set up an appropriate place to hang out with Marco Baylon's nephew. For obvious reasons, we could not bring him on base and the master chief did not want this guy knowing where he lived. Darrow once again leaned on his connections in law enforcement to secure a rundown apartment in southern San Diego. It was in Nestor, which was a very rough neighborhood, but Darrow got the place for a couple of hours off the books.

Once we got there, I found it hard to believe that the apartment was ever on the books. Most of the building's other residents were squatters judging by the lack of handles on the doors. Luckily, our place did have a handle, as well as a virtually indestructible steel door. It also had a functioning lock, power, and even a working telephone, but it was ransacked and dirty. The place looked like the perfect locale to shoot someone in the head without attracting much attention.

I suspected that that was the impression that my master chief wanted to convey. Darrow did not know the man he was going to host there. To ensure they did not run into difficulties, he corralled a collection of "Old Navy" types to help us. He picked men that he could trust to bend the rules, or at least keep their mouths shut if the master chief did.

Claude Metaire, now cured of his hangover, was one of these men. The division's Marine, Sergeant Fordson, was another. Joining them was a shady older policeman who worked with Darrow in the Philippines. He declined to introduce himself. We were also joined by a sketchy private investigator who was even more evasive about how he knew our boss. Dixie was going to be my ride to the border.

Darrow went to San Ysidro himself to collect the police chief's nephew. Noel Dominguez was younger than we expected, and if he was nervous about the Nestor safe house, he did not show it. He was jovial, relaxed, and more concerned with putting us at ease than worried about his own safety. "So, who is the man who is actually going to Mexico with the money?" Noel asked in perfect English.

I stepped forward and allowed him to shake my hand again. "Are you nervous, *amigo*?"

"Of course," I answered.

Dominguez smiled. "*Amigo*, I'm in a room surrounded by six men who are going to hurt me very badly if anything happens to you. I'm not nervous at all. You know why? Because this is going to be a piece of cake!"

I knew Dominguez was trying to soothe my nerves, but he failed. "Look, *amigo*, when you get down there, you're going to meet a very good friend of mine. His name is Jaime Serrano. He's a tall guy and very skinny, with a thin mustache. You can't miss him. He'll be wearing a polo shirt and a sport coat. You'll be very easy to pick out too. There aren't many lone *gringos* carrying duffel bags across the border at Otay Mesa. Especially ones looking like they're very uneasy about meeting someone."

"Is he a cop too?" Darrow asked.

Dominguez nodded. "Yes. Jaime used to be my partner. He's a good guy—someone we can trust. You're going to put the duffel bag with the money in the trunk and get into the passenger side. When you get to the jail, they're going to put Macklemore into the back seat. Once he's inside with the door closed, you will push the button in the glove box that opens the trunk. The guards will take the duffel bag and open the gate for you. Jaime will drive you back to Otay Mesa, and you'll cross the border. That's all there is to it! You come back here and Bradley gives me a ride home."

Master Chief turned to Dixie. "You keep your eyes on him for as long as you can. If there's anything that looks like it deviates from the plan, you call back here right away and let us know."

Dominguez nodded. "Your boss is right. You see anything that looks strange, you need to call us right away and tell him."

Darrow scowled at Noel to remind him he was not the one giving orders. Noel held his hands up, gesturing he meant no offense. "Aside from your man who's carrying the money, I have the most interest in making sure this goes smooth as a baby's bottom."

Turning to Dixie, Dominguez made sure he got the basics. "Remember, he leaves with a tall, thin guy only. If there is anyone else with them, call us. They're leaving in a light brown Ford sedan. If they get into any other type of vehicle, you let us know. If there are police there, dark uniforms are okay. Those are our guys. The lighter gray or green uniforms are *federales*. Those are not okay."

"Do you have any of your guys watching?" It was one of Darrow's civilian friends who asked.

Noel shook his head. "No, the fewer people involved, the better. Martinez's people are always watching us. Our people are always watching them. To be honest, we spend more resources keeping tabs on each other than we do watching criminals. It's sad, but that's our reality. It's why we need to know very quickly if there's anything unusual happening. We need to expect the unexpected and react accordingly. Does anybody have any questions?"

After we all indicated we did not, Dominguez turned to Darrow. "Before they leave, I need to call in and make sure everything's still going according to plan. Do you have a telephone here?"

Darrow stepped out of Noel's way and motioned towards an old rotary phone sitting on the floor next to the couch, ancient technology even in 1992. Dominguez dialed the numbers to *La Ocho*, as the Tijuana jail was known by the locals, and waited for someone to answer. When they did, he said, "Let me speak to Officer Guerrero, please."

*****

There was not a lot of foot traffic going across the border at Otay Mesa. In fact, there was not a lot of anything going south other than big rig trucks that late in the evening. Otay Mesa is a commercial crossing. There were few pedestrians, which meant I was easier to pick out, both for Officer Serrano and Dixie. Kevin kept an eye on me from the American side of the fence through a pair of Darrow's binoculars.

Jaime Serrano was not nearly as cheery as Dominguez was. He looked as if he did not laugh often. Serrano was polite enough when we met, but I got the impression there were other places he would rather have been. "Is everything still alright?" I asked him in English, deciding it would work to my favor not to let on how much Spanish I understood.

Serrano shrugged. "Do you have the money?"

"Yes."

"Then things are about as good as they are going to get."

It was not the way that I would have inspired confidence. With the benefit of hindsight, I now know it was the officer's way of ensuring that I put my guard up. Asking me to follow him, Serrano led me to the parking lot behind the customs building. As we walked, Jaime asked, "The *gringo* on the other side of the border with the binoculars, is he yours?"

Nodding my head, I said, "Yes."

"Good. Give him a wave to make sure he still sees you. Try to look concerned when you do it."

"Concerned?" I asked. "Why? Do I have a reason to be concerned?"

"We both do, *amigo*."

TEQUILA VIKINGS

Without needing to ask any more questions, I turned and waved to the parking lot where I knew Dixie was watching. Unfortunately, I did not look concerned enough. Kevin did not pick anything up and never raised the alarm.

"I don't understand," I said after my wave. "Dominguez checked with the jail before I left. Everything was supposed to be alright."

"When Noel talked to the jail, everything was alright. Now, not so much. Somehow, the *federales* got your friend out of jail, and now *they* have him, not us."

"What?!?" I gasped. "Shouldn't I be going back then until we can get this straightened out?"

Serrano shook his head. "No. The *federales* are at the border. They watched you come in. If you try leaving without permission from *Sargento* Martinez, they'll arrest you."

"Shit." I cursed. "Shit! Shit! Shit! What are we going to do?"

As we approached Serrano's Ford, the passenger door opened and a smiling *federale* stepped out to greet us.

"We do whatever that fucker tells us to do," Serrano told me.

I turned my head, wondering if Dixie caught sight of our unexpected guest. All I could see was a hedge and a tractor-trailer, though. My view of the parking lot on the American side of the fence was completely blocked. It was safe to assume that if I could not see Dixie, he could not see me.

We were on our own.

*****

At first, Macklemore thought they had put a hood over his head to prevent him from seeing where they were going. Before long, he realized that it was to prevent him from seeing what was coming. At random intervals, a blow would strike him without warning. The first one took him between the legs. While Warren gasped for air, everyone else laughed. Then they went back to their unintelligible conversations for a while longer. When it seemed they had finished with him, someone else would throttle him across the cheek. There was no way for Macklemore to brace himself for whatever came next.

"Please!" Warren begged after taking a debilitating shot to the ribs. "Please, stop. I'm sorry. I'm so sorry. I didn't mean it. I was scared. When the door opened and I was pulled out, I didn't know what to do. I went along with it because once I was out, I was afraid to go back. I didn't know what to do. I didn't know what…"

"You know, *gringo*," Martinez said in English. "Maybe you didn't know what to do. By the time this is over, though, you will know for sure. When the *federales* arrest you, you stay arrested. Man, you almost got away with it. If you'd just been a little bit quicker, you would've been over that turnstile and out of reach. You'd be standing there on the safe side of the border mocking us. If that happened and word got around, all you fuckin' *gringos* would have been trying to get away with that shit. We can't have that."

The car had been on some sort of highway but turned onto what Warren could tell was a dirt road. "You see what happened when we picked your sorry ass up at the Toucan Club, *gringo*? One of you *pendejos* hit me in the face with a beer bottle. You bastards came to *my* country, *my* town, broke *our* laws, and then attacked *me* when I tried to do *my job* to keep the peace! Then some prick breaks you out of one of our police cars? Who do you think you are?"

The Ford slowed to adjust to the state of the road. It was crawling when Martinez asked, "Would you have pulled a stunt like that back in San Diego? Of course not. And why? Because you respect the police there. Well, we're going to show you that you need to respect the police in Mexico too."

The sedan stopped. "We have a dangerous job, *gringo*. Much more dangerous than the cops do in California. We have criminals down here that are more powerful than the police. Those guys, they give us a choice, *plomo o plata*, silver or lead. We take their money and do as they say, or they kill us. We have to look out for other cops who might be working for other gangs too. Sometimes we even have to look out for our soldiers. All these guys are bad *hombres*. What if we let a puissant little *gringo* like you get away with what you did? We'd look stupid. We'd look incompetent. We'd look weak. We'd lose the respect of the street."

Martinez sighed. "When we lose the respect of the street, we die. I ain't losing the respect of the street, *gringo*. No, not because of some pathetic punk like you. Nope, you *pendejos* ain't going to be braggin' about how you were clever and escaped from the police in Tijuana. No, you're going to be talking about how your dumb asses gambled and fucking lost, Holmes!"

The sedan's doors opened, and Martinez kicked Warren out of the car. He landed on his side in the dirt. One of the officers then ripped his hood off and carried him out to the middle of the road. There, they placed him on his knees under the glare of the headlights. Woozy from the beatings, Mack could not keep his balance with his hands bound behind his back.

"Un-cuff him," Martinez told one of his men.

"You sure that's a good idea?" the officer closest to Warren asked.

"Where do you think he's going to go?" Hulagu pulled his pistol out of its holster and pointed it at Mack's head. Switching to English, he asked, "You going somewhere, *gringo*?"

"No!" Macklemore cried. "No! No! I ain't going anywhere!"

"I didn't think so." Switching back to Spanish to address his men, he reiterated his order. "Take his cuffs off and get him on his knees with his hands behind his head. Those guys will be here any minute. When they pull up, I don't want them to think we already killed his ugly ass."

*****

Heading east out of Tijuana, things got remote rather quick, and I had a bad feeling about the drive.

This is exactly how it happens. It was a momentary lapse in judgment, something so trivial in the moment, but with monumental consequences. That's how people get themselves killed.

We drove eastbound along Highway 2 towards Tecate, but I doubted we were going all the way there. There was plenty of empty desert between the two cities. The *federales* did not need to go far to find a secluded place where they could do whatever they were going to do to us.

It's not even about the escape anymore. It's all about the money in the bag. People get murdered down here for far, far less than fifteen grand. Hulagu wants it all. That's why he's going to kill us.

Both Serrano and I were in the front seat. The unwelcome passenger was in the back. That way, he could put a bullet in the back of our heads if we deviated from his script.

I'm so far out of my league here. I can't even begin to think of what I can do to get out of this. I then remembered my conversation with Macklemore as we walked back to Javier's house. *Nothing to lose.* If it got to the point where I knew I was going to die, I decided to go for Hulagu. I knew what he looked like now. He was the cop who got hit with the beer bottle. If I was going to die, I was going to take that son-of-a-bitch with me.

"Slow down, Serrano," the backseat *federale* told my escort. "It's coming up on the left. Go through the break in the median and head back west. There will be a dirt road a couple of hundred meters after that. Turn right onto it."

They don't care if I can see where I'm going. I'm probably not coming back from this. "Shouldn't you put a hood on me?" I asked, hoping to get a clue about what my fate was.

The *federale* laughed. "What? Do you think I'm taking you to our super-secret headquarters or something? There's nothing for you to see, *gringo.*"

He was right. All there was to see was a bluff, a thirty-foot tall mound of dirt, rocks, and desert scrub. At the west end of it was a trail that was all but invisible to any vehicle traveling by at highway speed. After a hard right turn and a bumpy fifty-meter downhill trek, we were completely hidden from the road. It was almost too convenient. Less than sixty feet from the highway, they could do anything they wanted to us and nobody would ever be wiser.

Two vehicles were facing us. One was a squad car with a pair of officers resting against the hood. The other was a Jeep. A *campesino,* a rather rough-looking peasant, sat in the Wrangler's driver seat. Two other policemen were milling about nearby. I suspected that once they shot us, the peasant would be the guy who dug our graves. In the middle of us all was Macklemore, on his knees, fingers locked behind his head, quietly crying as blood dripped from his face. They had messed him up pretty bad.

"Get out," the *federale* in the backseat told me. "Take your money with you."

I did as ordered. When I emerged from the car, there was another officer carrying a pump shotgun in front of me. "You know who I am?"

TEQUILA VIKINGS

I nodded. I saw him at the Toucan Club. "Sergeant Francisco Martinez."

"You know what they call me?" the officer asked.

"Hulagu," I answered.

The *federale* smiled. "You hear about me?"

I nodded again.

"So you heard about me, and you *still* decided to pull this motherfucker from the back of my car?"

I inhaled deeply. "At the time, I didn't know…"

Martinez lifted his shotgun and smashed the butt of it into my face. The blow knocked me to my back, and I dropped the duffel bag.

Serrano stepped forward to intervene, but two officers by the Jeep warned him to stand down. "Hey! Hey!" Jaime yelled. "Knock it off! Noel Dominguez is north of the border with the *gringos*!"

"Baylon sent his nephew north as a hostage?" Martinez laughed. "The man is more stupid than I thought." The sergeant stepped over to the duffel bag. "How much money are these *pendejos* bringing him? It must be an awful lot if he's risking his nephew."

"There was no risk until you got involved," Jaime answered.

"No risk? This was my prisoner. You think you're going to profit off my prisoner without cutting me in and not have any risk?" Hulagu started counting the money in the duffel bag.

"That's bullshit," Serrano quipped. "Baylon was giving you an equal share."

There was a pause while Martinez finished his tally. "Equal share? Baylon was giving me $5000. That's a third of what's in this bag."

"$5,000 for you. $5,000 for the prison staff that has to do the paperwork. $5,000 to split between him, me, and Noel to get this done. You got the biggest share, Francisco."

Martinez shrugged. "Maybe I did. Maybe I didn't. Something's still fishy here. $15,000 is a lot of money, but not enough to send his nephew north to allow this deal to go down. What else is going on here?" Hulagu walked over to me. I still had my face cupped in my hands and was writhing on the ground, wondering if he had broken my nose. "What about you, faggot? You know what else is going down here?"

"No," I said.

Hulagu cranked his leg back and kicked me in the gut. "Bullshit!"

"I don't know…" He kicked my hands that were still covering my face, snapping my head back so hard that my neck cracked. "I swear! I don't…"

Martinez dropped his shotgun and leaped upon me, punching me in the ear. Then the eye. Then the cheek, then, I don't know. It was blow after blow after blow after blow. "You fucking prick!" He screamed. "Who the fuck do you think you are?!? Huh? You think you're something? Huh? You think you're better than me, motherfucker?!?"

"Get off of him, Martinez!" Serrano screamed. "You made a deal!"

Hulagu stopped to respond to Jaime. He climbed off me and swaggered over to the only person in my corner. "Deal? Yeah, I made a deal. I made a deal for that pathetic little bald fucker over there. Go ahead, take him. Put him in the car. This man, though? I didn't make any deal for this man. This is the guy who broke that shit stain out of my car. This one's all mine."

To punctuate his statement, Martinez pulled his pistol out and pointed it where I lay. In one fluid movement, he then pulled the hammer back and squeezed the trigger. What he did not do was aim. The gun went off and the ground exploded next to my head, sending rocks and other debris tearing through my scalp.

The *federales* all jumped at the shot and drew their weapons, pointing them at Serrano. Jaime drew his and aimed at Martinez. The *campesino* stood up in the Jeep and started yelling something, but I was too rattled to understand what it was. Having the slug from a .357 pass within an inch of my melon had wreaked havoc on my foreign language skills. Ultimately, whatever the peasant was babbling about did not matter because Martinez was ignoring him anyway. Confident his men would drop Serrano before he could fire, Francisco took more careful aim before he fired his second shot at me.

Nothing to lose. I've got nothing to lose. Not wanting to give Martinez a stationary target, I rolled to my left as the gun went off. The dirt erupted precisely where my head had been. I then went right and got to my feet. I was groggy, though. My movements were slow, uncertain, and predictable. Still, I charged.

I was not nearly fast enough. As I lunged, I watched Hulagu bring his weapon up and point it right between my eyes. To put myself at even more of a disadvantage, I stumbled and lost my ability to dodge out of the way. I was looking Martinez right in the eye at that point, waiting for him to fire.

TEQUILA VIKINGS

Then I saw his head lurch forward as he dropped to his knees. At first, I thought he got shot, but once he hit the dirt, I saw Macklemore fall on top of him. Crusty Warren was not bracing for retaliation this time, though. He was pummeling Martinez with everything he had.

The first punch Macklemore landed was so brutal Hulagu had to struggle to stay conscious. He was left with little ability to fight back and Warren took full advantage of that. He landed one devastating blow after another, all to the officer's face. Warren loaded each strike with retribution for every injustice he ever suffered in life, delivering each of them with crippling force.

The abuse Warren endured as a kid split the sergeant's lip wide open. The ostracism he suffered due to what Joey had done to him parted the skin above his eyebrow. The bullying he had survived in the military crushed Hulagu's nose. I guessed that Kramer's nonsense was the uppercut to the jaw. The fight at the Toucan Club hurtled towards the *federale's* throat. Only a nightstick cracked across the crown of Macklemore's head prevented it from landing.

I tried to jump up and help him, but I had two guys on me before I moved six inches. The remaining *federales* were bludgeoning us all seconds after that. The only two people not in the fray were Martinez, who was rolling around spitting blood into the road, and the peasant at the Jeep. The *campesino* watched it all unfold in a state of mild amusement.

Eventually, the *federales* beat the three of us into submission and Martinez came back to life. "Oh, man," he groaned as he struggled to get up on his feet. "Oh, man! You fucking dare…!"

Hulagu looked around the ground until he discovered where he had dropped his pistol. After picking it up, he stepped over to Macklemore and pointed it at his head, shaking with fury. "You think you can get away with…!"

"Stop it!" Serrano screamed. "Baylon's going to have your ass for this, Martinez!" Mack cried out in anticipation of the gun going off and I started shaking, knowing it was all over.

"That's enough!" I heard someone say at the very moment I expected to hear a gunshot. All the *federales* stopped and looked up at the peasant driver who was walking toward us. "Let them go! Stop this shit now!"

Martinez was aghast. "But that son of a whore…!"

"Hey! Francisco! If you play with people, you have to expect that sooner or later they're going to play back. I let you have your fun, but now this shit's getting out of hand. You fucked up your *gringos*, and you got your money. It's getting late, and we have shit to do. Play time's over."

"I can't let them get away with this! I'll lose face if I let these fuckers walk now!"

The peasant gestured over the three of us. "Let them walk? These poor guys can barely crawl. You made your point. It's time to go."

Martinez rubbed his hand across his face. He winced in pain from the damage Macklemore had done. "And how do I explain this? Huh? Do I just tell everyone that…"

"And what is Baylon going to tell everybody about you getting his nephew killed? If I let you slaughter these guys, that's what's going to happen. You're not the only one with face to save, Francisco. If you kill these men and something happens to Dominguez, what do you think Baylon's going to do? He's going to declare war, that's what."

"Fuck Baylon. We'll win that war."

The peasant shrugged and took off his cowboy hat. "Maybe we will, maybe we won't. The only thing I know for sure that will result from a war against Baylon is that business will suffer. We're making a lot of money right now. Baylon's making a lot of money right now. Fuck Francisco, *you're* making a lot of money right now. I'm not letting you start a war over $15,000 and some silly-looking *gringo*. I'm not telling you again. Let them go."

Unable to bring himself to give the order, Martinez turned on his heel and stormed off towards his car. With a single nod from the *campesino's* head, it was up to the rest of the *federales* to let us fall forward into the dirt. Though they were not happy with the verdict, they obediently got back into their vehicles. The *federales* drove off without another word to us, leaving the duffel bag full of cash behind. I was wrong. That whole thing had almost nothing to do with money. It was all about street cred.

Battered so badly that I could not walk, I crawled to where Macklemore was lying. Reaching out and putting my hand on his chest, I whispered, "You okay, Warren?"

Macklemore shook his head and moaned. "No."

TEQUILA VIKINGS

I grinned. "You son-of-a-bitch. Do you realize…ugh...do you realize what you did tonight?"

"I saved your life," Mack answered weakly. I could barely hear him.

"Yeah. You saved my life. You know what else?"

Warren groaned. "What?"

"You…you just fucking kicked Hulagu's ass," I told him. "If that don't rate a Tequila Viking tattoo, I don't know what does."

*****

CHAPTER
24

Dominguez went completely white when Mack and I walked back into the apartment. Darrow went completely red. "What the fuck happened?!?" he snarled, glaring at Baylon's nephew.

"We got our asses beat," I mumbled. "I…"

Before I had a chance to get another word out, Darrow slugged Dominguez across the jaw. The master chief's officer friend then grabbed one of the Mexican policeman's arms. The private investigator seized the other. Darrow then reached behind his back and drew a government-issued .45, pointing it right at Noel's face.

The beating the *federales* inflicted on us was savage. When it was over, Macklemore, Serrano, and I had lain in the road for a couple of hours, unable to move. For all I knew, Serrano was still unconscious behind the wheel of his Ford in Otay Mesa. We were all messed up. Still, I found the energy to jump up and grab Darrow's arm. "Don't! Don't do this, Master Chief!"

"Don't do this?!?" he spat back at me while ripping his arm from my grip and sending me falling back to the floor. "No! These sons of bitches aren't getting away with this shit! If we let them, it's going to be open season on our boys down there! No, if they want to put our guys in the hospital, we'll put theirs in the fuckin' morgue!"

"Please, Brad! Don't do this!" Dominguez begged. "This wasn't us! I swear it, man!"

"Dammit, Master Chief! Put the goddamn gun down!" I yelled, struggling to get to my feet. Instead of going after Darrow again, I stumbled to Noel and put myself between him and the master chief's pistol. That made it the second time I had a gun pointed at me that day.

Now, I knew there was no way my master chief would ever shoot me. Still, there are few things more unnerving than staring down the barrel of a .45 automatic. It took a conscious effort to maintain bladder control. I did not blame the police chief's nephew for all the shaking he was doing behind me. "It wasn't Noel or Baylon who did this to us!"

"Yeah? Then who was it?"

"People who want to hurt them, that's who! This was Martinez!"

Darrow looked even angrier. "You turned them over to fucking Martinez?!?"

"No! No!" Dominguez shouted. "We didn't turn anyone over to anybody! Trust me! My uncle and Martinez are NOT on friendly terms! My uncle is the reason we're dealing with a Sergeant Martinez instead of a Lieutenant Martinez! If Francisco got his hands on your man, it was not because of us!"

Darrow lowered his pistol, but not his temper. Placing his weapon back into the small of his back, he lashed out again, trying to get to Noel through me. Before we knew it, all three of us were wrestling around on the floor. Metaire and Dixie tried to weave through the mess to separate us. It nearly killed me. Every square inch of my body was writhing in agony over what they had done to us in Mexico. I was in no shape to take on my master chief now. After our men pulled us apart, all I could do was lay on the floor and gasp for air. "Let him go," I pleaded to Darrow. "It's over. We got our guy back."

"No! It's a long way from being over, *amigo*." Officer Dominguez hissed while pointing his finger at Darrow. "This is just the beginning! Do you know this guy, Hulagu? Do you know what kind of man this guy is? This is the man who cut a child to pieces in front of his parents to send a message from the cartels. He once kidnapped and sold a courier's eleven-year-old daughter to a brothel. He did that to recoup the cost of the coke her father had to ditch to avoid arrest on your side of the border. Do you know what he does for fun on the weekends? He arrests cute college girls. He likes blonde-haired, blue-eyed *gringas* and offers to turn them loose if they'll fuck him. Or sometimes he'll plant dope on their boyfriends and exchange sex for their freedom. He's a monster, Brad. And we couldn't touch him."

"Couldn't touch him? Why the hell not? He's a fucking animal!" Darrow snarled.

"He's got connections! He had friends in the DFS, the *Dirección Federal de Seguridad,* our CIA. They use him because he's willing to do things a lot of people won't."

"The DFS was disbanded," Darrow's private investigator said. "They were too corrupt even for Mexico."

"They weren't disbanded." Noel countered. "They just changed their name. Now they're the *Centro de Investigación y Seguridad Nacional.* It's the same nasty guys. Bradley, these two boys, if Martinez had them and was willing to beat them like this, they should be dead right now. Beating them, killing them, the message is the same."

Dominguez turned to the men holding his arms and asked to be let go. Noel knew he would be punished harshly for doing anything stupid. After Darrow nodded his permission, his pals released their grip.

"Brad, these boys were nothing. This should have been a little sideshow for Martinez. He has much bigger things to do than deal with shit like this. He went to Revolucion the other night because it looked like we could have a riot on our hands. He went because it sounded like fun to go around and bust some *gringo* heads. Having Doyle spring this other boy from his police car was embarrassing, though. My uncle thought a few thousand dollars would be more than enough to make it right."

Dominguez shook his head. "My uncle believes Martinez is too much of a loose cannon to hold a high position in our community, and the DFS agreed. Martinez was an asset on the streets, but his instability could be a liability in a position of command. He always resented my uncle for that, and doing this to your men was a direct challenge to him. Still, I don't know why Martinez let them live."

TEQUILA VIKINGS

"He was going to kill us," I said, still lying on the floor. "Some older guy stopped him, though. A *campesino*. He looked like a farmer. I thought he was a driver or something at first."

Dominguez shook his head. "No, no, the *federales* don't have drivers. If he was not in uniform or in a suit, he was a cartel guy."

Dominguez paced a little bit as he thought but took care not to walk in the master chief's direction. "I'll be blunt. Two criminal organizations share Tijuana's drug trafficking. One has people in the *federales*; the other has people in the Tijuana Police Department. It's no secret Martinez does not want to share the business anymore. He wants it all. *Los Hermanos* have had to hobble him more than once to keep him in line. He's proved a little too ambitious on several occasions."

Noel waved his arm over Mack and me. "This beating, this was his attempt to make my uncle look weak. Maybe he was trying to announce that now was the time for war, time to take control of all the dope. The guy who stopped Hulagu from killing you? I'm betting he thinks now is not the time for war. I'm thinking he's getting nervous about how ambitious Martinez is becoming. That's why he stopped the man from killing you. This could be an opportunity for us."

"There is no 'us' here, Dominguez." Darrow stepped forward to close the gap between them. "We're not getting involved in your bullshit south of the border. We expect you guys to make this shit right, though. I want this fucking Hulagu guy."

Noel nodded. "Yes, Bradley. I know. You may not believe this, but we want him even more than you do. And I think now we may finally be able to get him."

*****

Balboa Hospital diagnosed me with a major concussion and a couple of cracked ribs. Besides that, I got more than seventy stitches in various parts of my body. There was also a lot of swelling and some gruesome bruising. The final word was that there was no permanent damage, though. I got off easy.

Macklemore's diagnosis was a little more severe. He had fractured ribs, missing teeth, and a broken nose. His jaw was also cracked enough that the doctors considered wiring it shut. Warren was relieved when they decided against it. He also snapped some fingers while pummeling Hulagu across the chops, but that was pain that he savored. Balboa admitted us for a few days of observation while the doctors marveled at our ability to take a punch.

My first visitor in the hospital, arriving just before lunch, was Captain Fleming. He was not happy. "I told you I did not want to hear about you taking center stage in any more epic sea stories," the skipper said when he saw my condition.

"I didn't mean to, sir." It was customary to stand at attention when the ship's captain enters a room. Military protocols did not apply in hospital settings, but I at least tried to set myself up straight.

Even while angry, Fleming was concerned about my discomfort. "No, no, relax. Get your rest. I'm here to see for myself how bad this was."

"And how bad is it?" I asked.

"It's pretty bad." The captain let out a long sigh. "By all reports, Saturday was quite a night in Tijuana. I heard our guys were right in the thick of it too. The *Belleau Wood* got everybody back, though. I hear that was mostly thanks to you."

Fleming shook his head. "I don't know whether to commend you or throw the book at you, son."

"Well, sir, if you're looking for my vote on which way to go, I'd say…"

"I'm not looking for your vote, Murphy. This isn't a joke. You nearly got yourselves killed down there. I'd say that was a serious lapse in judgment. Serious enough to be fatal for your BOOST application. It's off the table."

I dropped my chin down onto my chest. "Yes, sir."

"If it didn't mean we had to put Palazzo back in charge of Radar Repair, you'd be on report right now too. Krause wrote you up this morning, but your department head dismissed it. Had Winston endorsed the charges, I'd have busted you back down to E-4. I'll have you know, though, Krause is furious about the CSO not passing the chit up the chain. I expect he'll be aiming to make your life even more miserable than he already is. And to be blunt about it, son, you earned everything that man is going to throw at you."

"I'm not getting busted for this?" I asked, surprised.

"As it stands now, no. I've told Darrow to put in for an E-6 when he requisitions the next replacement for your shop. When that happens, you'll step down as work center supervisor. Understood?"

"Yes, sir." The captain was effectively firing me. I felt a lump in my throat.

"Once that situation sorts itself out, the next time you mess up, I will bust your ass right out of the Navy. Understood?"

"Yes, sir."

"You want some advice, Petty Officer Murphy?"

I nodded. "Sir, I think I'm at a point right now where I could really use your counsel."

Fleming squinted at me, trying to gauge my sincerity. "Too bad you're not making a habit out of acting upon it. Well, in case you decide to follow through this time, I'm telling you to finish your enlistment and get the hell out of my Navy. You've picked up some nasty habits from your master chief. If you think you're going to get away with stuff like he did, you're in for a rude awakening. Murphy, if you had any other captain on any other ship, you'd be going straight from the hospital to the brig."

He was right, which once more raised my suspicion that Darrow must have had some sort of dirt on him. Fleming was a Boy Scout, yet he was sticking his neck out for me again. It was driving me crazy trying to figure out why. "Sir, I don't know how to thank you for all you've done."

"Thank me by getting your act together."

"I will, sir."

"You better." The captain sounded as if he did not believe me. "I'm getting tired of visiting my sailors here after they've gotten their asses kicked."

I nodded. As Fleming said that, I realized I had not heard anything about my Nixie Room victim in quite some time. "Do you know if Green's still here, sir?"

Fleming shook his head. "He's long gone. It's been a couple of months by now. Green and the Navy reached a deal. He agreed to divorce his wife so he's no longer a threat to her. He also had to absolve the Navy of any responsibility for his medical condition. In return, we agreed not to prosecute him and to let him go with a general discharge. He's back in whatever backwater spawned him, and his wife went back to the Philippines."

After a few more minutes of small talk, Captain Fleming left me to see how Macklemore was faring.

When the captain departed, I was surprised by how much losing BOOST affected me. I went back and forth about whether I wanted it or not, but with it withdrawn, I felt as if I had failed. I had no family or anything to fall back on once I left the service. I needed every opportunity I could get, and now I had one less option at my disposal. When Hannah showed up to see me a couple of hours later, I felt as if I might lose one more.

When she saw me, Hannah covered her mouth with her hands as if she was trying to stifle a scream. "Oh my god, Doyle! What did you do?"

I could see how torn she was between wanting to know if I was okay and wanting to walk out the door. To her, this looked like the result of one of my violent episodes. I tried to set that straight right away. "Hannah, I didn't do anything! This was not a fight! I took it all. I never threw a single punch."

"You let them do this to you?" Hannah sobbed. "And you never fought back?"

"I did nothing, Hannah! Nothing! I never even bunched up a fist."

Hannah rushed in to hug me, but every touch sent bolts of agony ripping through my nerves. Giving up, she kissed me on the forehead. "And Mack? How is he?"

"Same as I am. He broke some stuff, though." I caught myself laughing a bit. "He broke 'em beating the piss out of the most notorious cop in Tijuana! Can you believe that shit? Macklemore!"

"Mack did? Mack hit somebody?!?" Hannah's eyes were wide with surprise. "What on earth got him to do that?"

"That cop I told you about on the phone was going to kill me, Hannah. He pulled out his gun and fired it at my head. He barely missed. He was aiming the next shot when Warren knocked the shit out of him from behind."

Hannah lost her composure when she heard how close I came to being killed. She was also furious about how casually I dropped it on her. Once I got her calmed down, though, she voiced her surprise over what

TEQUILA VIKINGS

Macklemore did to Sergeant Martinez. "Doyle, the man will not raise a finger to defend himself. Yet he took on a policeman with a pistol for you?"

"I know."

"Have you seen him?" she asked.

I shook my head. "Not since we got here."

Hannah nodded and then looked around the hospital room. "Doyle, are you in any trouble for this? It seems like kind of a big deal."

"It is," I told her. "And I don't know. The captain's withdrawing his BOOST recommendation. He told me he's going to fire me as work center supervisor and advised me to leave the Navy when my enlistment's up. He didn't come right out and say it, but the implication is that my Navy career's over."

"Really?" Hannah tried to sound sympathetic, but her voice betrayed a bit of relief. "Are you okay with that?"

I thought for a moment before answering. "I would have been more okay with it if I had money in the bank. I still had to pay the Tijuana cops for Mack. My cash is being divvied up between a bunch of Mexican policemen right now."

"You lost it all?"

I nodded. "I've got a thousand left, but I'm going to blow it repaying some favors Darrow cashed in for this shit show."

"We can still do it, you know," Hannah said. "I've got some money put aside. It's not as much as what you had, but it'll get us started."

"Started with what?"

"Our life! Get out of the Navy, Doyle! We can go somewhere...like Bali! Where it's beautiful and cheap! I've always dreamed of living there! We can leave all the stuff that's been haunting you behind! We'll live on the beach and open up a surf shop or..."

"I'm not good enough at surfing to..."

Hannah's face lit up. "But you dive! You scuba dive! We can open up a surf and a dive shop! It won't take much money! We'll start small and..."

"Bali?" I asked. I'd never seen it for myself, but Darrow told me Indonesia was a fascinating place. "You ever been there?"

"Of course I have! Bali is to us Australians what Cancun is to you Yanks. It's where we all go to surf, party, and cut loose! Doyle, it's so different from here. It's so different from Australia too. It's the perfect place for you to forget everything you've been through! It'll be just me and you, Doyle! In Bali!"

She was serious. Dead serious. Hannah made perfect sense, though. I had nothing in the US except bad memories. There was no reason I could think of not to try to build myself a brand-new life somewhere else. Why not Bali? Especially if it would make Hannah happy.

"You know, after we get married, my pay will almost double. I can bank all kinds of money between then and my discharge."

Hannah beamed. "So you're getting out then? Out of the Navy for good?"

I thought about it for a few seconds. Then, I committed. "I'm getting out. I'm leaving the Navy. I'm marrying you, moving to Bali, smoking dope, surfing, and growing dreadlocks just like John."

*****

Warren smiled through his broken lips. "Never been better..." he groaned, answering my question.

Macklemore's room was a few doors down from mine. Once visiting hours were over, I wanted to make sure he had someone checking in on him. "You're a liar," I told him.

"Am not." Even through his disfigured face, I could see he was pretty pleased with himself. "We made it. I didn't think we would."

"I didn't think so either. If you hadn't clobbered that prick, I'd have ended up in the ground."

"If you hadn't shown up down there with all that money, I'd have ended up in prison. I wouldn't have survived that. You saved my life too." Mack swallowed and grimaced, showing that even that was painful. "I'm going to pay you back, Doyle."

"You already have…"

"No. I'm going to repay you every bit of that money. You were willing to give everything you had to get me back."

"If it hadn't been for me, you wouldn't have been in jail in the first place."

"If it hadn't been for me, there wouldn't have been an arrest to escape from. Doyle, you've done stuff for me nobody's ever done before. Hannah told me it cost you BOOST, your job, your career, and fifteen thousand dollars. I can't do anything about most of it, but I can do something about the money. I'm paying you back, Doyle."

I studied Warren's expression for a moment. "Mack, are you smiling? Your face is pretty fucked up, but it looks to me almost like you're smiling. I don't think you have much to smile about."

"It felt good, Doyle."

"What?"

"Beating that son-of-a-bitch. That cop." A tear rolled out of Macklemore's swollen eye, but for once, it was a tear of joy.

I had to grin myself. "I bet it did. Mack, have you given any thought about what you're going to do after all this? After you leave the Navy?"

Warren nodded weakly. "My brother will be out of school by then. I'm going back to Alaska. I'll get a job at one of the fish processing plants. I may not know anything about electronics, but I know how to cut fish. I can do that shit all day. The pay's pretty good too. That's what I'm gonna do."

It sounded like a bleak future to me, but Mack seemed to relish the idea. "You know, Hannah and I talked earlier. When I get out, we're moving to Indonesia. To Bali. We're setting up a surf and scuba shop. I want you to know if things aren't working out for you in Alaska, you can try your luck over there with us. You'll always be welcome."

Mack looked touched. "Thanks, Doyle. I'll keep that in mind. I want to be close to my brother, though. Once I get out, I don't ever want to be this far away from him again. I'm staying wherever he lives."

I nodded. "I understand. Once I get a family, I don't see myself ever leaving them either."

I had not been in Macklemore's room for long. Still, the effort was exhausting. I needed to get back to my bed and catch some sleep. Before I left, I had one more question. "Warren, what possessed you to attack that guy? What the hell were you thinking?"

Despite the discomfort, Macklemore smiled even wider. "I was thinking if we were going down, I wanted to take that asshole with us. I was thinking we had nothing to lose. Just like you said. Nothing to lose."

*****

Warren Macklemore was proud of himself when he graduated high school. He was even prouder that he completed Navy boot camp. He was prouder still when he finished ET A School, especially considering that he had come close to washing out of it so many times. I could relate to that one, having barely made it through the program myself. The feeling of accomplishing those three things combined, Warren told me, still paled in comparison to the pride he felt after getting the Tequila Viking tattooed on his arm.

We were a couple of weeks out of the hospital when we took Mack to get his ink. Until that point, I had no idea how coveted that little piece of body art was among the men of the CSE Division. All of us who had one, Dixie, Metaire, Franklin, and myself, went with Warren to the studio. So did Tony Bard, John Palazzo, and Steve Kent, none of whom ever expressed a desire to get tattooed before. I was surprised to hear all three of them say that they would love to get the Viking themselves, were they ever deemed worthy of the honor.

It amused me to hear that from Bard and Palazzo. Both of them were career Navy men expressing an interest in getting an insignia permanently inked upon their shoulder earned by a spectacular act of misbehavior. That was not exactly the "New Navy" attitude.

As the artist at OB Inkslingers pulled out the design we had on file there, Mack looked it over and then turned to me. "Doyle, do you think I could change it up a little?"

With a shrug, I said, "Sure, it's your arm. What're you thinking?"

"I want to replace the anchor in the background with one of those old-fashioned helm wheels," Macklemore told me. "Anchors keep you stuck somewhere. The helm lets you steer your way into uncharted territory."

I grinned. "I like it. Go for it."

Mack did not do us very proud in the tattooist's chair. He was not a big fan of needles and looking at his face while he was getting inked, one would have thought that he was having a limb sawn off. He got through it, though, and truth be told, with the helm behind the skull, I liked his design better than ours.

I can honestly say that the man who got out of that chair was not the same person who sat down in it. Mack now stood with a straighter back. He made eye contact when he spoke to you. I even detected a hint of swagger in his step despite the limp he still had from what happened to us in Mexico. Mack was no longer the scared little boy who believed his sole purpose in life was to be abused by others. He was now a Tequila Viking. Warren Macklemore had earned his stripes, and with them, the genuine respect of his shipmates. At least he had the respect of those of us who took him to the tattoo parlor, anyway. That was good enough for him. As far as Macklemore was concerned, we were the only ones who mattered.

After we walked out of OB Inkslingers, the four of us who were already branded took a swing at Macklemore's arm and punched him as hard as we could where the fresh ink was most tender. We then hugged him and welcomed him into the fold. I went last, hitting him the hardest and hugging him the longest. "You saved my life, Warren," I told him.

"And you saved mine," he told me back.

From Inkslingers, we all walked down to the Sand Flea where we pounded down several shots of tequila and a half dozen beers apiece. After that, Bard, Metaire, Palazzo, and Kent went back to the ship. Dixie, Mack, and I made our way to Cheri's place, where we found a party already in full swing when we got there. Besides our usual friends, Hannah was also hosting some new faces this time, including a Romanian nanny she had recently met named Oksana Popescu.

Lupe Castillo was there and had gotten her hands on some epic herb out of Oaxaca. She got Hannah absolutely baked off of it. "What are those guys celebrating?" Lupe asked my fiancée as we walked into the house, already smashed out of our gourds.

"They got Mack one of those tattoos the guys have on their arms. Apparently, you've got to do something monumentally stupid while drunk to get one, and Warren earned his in Tijuana."

"Is that how they got hurt? I thought Doyle said they got into a car accident."

Hannah smiled conspiratorially. "Yeah, Doyle said that to keep it on the down-low, but they actually almost got murdered down there by some dirty cop. Warren clobbered the prick as he was trying to shoot Doyle in the head."

"Oh my God!" Lupe gasped. "Was that Hulagu?"

Hannah's face lit up. "Yeah! That was 'is bloody name! Hulagu!"

That was right about the time that I walked up.

"That was you?!?" Lupe Castillo exclaimed to me. "You were the guys who fucked up Martinez?!?"

"You heard about that?" I asked.

"Doyle, that's the biggest story in Tijuana that's not in the newspapers! Word on the street down there is Hulagu's in serious trouble now. He had to disappear because even his own people turned on him. They're saying he almost got the police fighting each other! That would have been embarrassing for the government. Especially while they're promising everybody to clean up the corruption. I even heard there's a price on his head!"

"Oh shit." I thought of something that gave me pause. "If we were the spark that lit Hulagu's ass on fire, you think he might come this way looking for us?"

Lupe shook her head. "He's more concerned with keeping himself alive right now than settling a score with you. If he survives this, though, yeah, I'd be worried. He'll come after you, Hannah, your children, your pets, anything you care about."

Hannah and I exchanged looks of concern, psychically conveying to one another that we should keep our plans of moving to Indonesia to ourselves. I figured that by the time the dust settled in Tijuana, I would be in Japan and Hannah would be back in Australia. Both were far beyond Hulagu's reach.

The Romanian nanny turned towards Macklemore. In halting English, she asked Warren, "You...you deed these? You safe heem?"

Oksana was not an attractive woman but Mack was no looker either. I saw an opportunity and ran with it.

"Yes," I told her, speaking slowly so she could understand me. Slapping Mack on the shoulder, I said, "This is the bravest man I ever met. What he did down there...I can never repay...I owe him my life."

Everyone in the room took the cue. They all made a point of paying Warren the reverence due a proper hero. They also made sure to show Oksana how much esteem we held him in whenever she was paying attention. It was beautiful.

Of course, Macklemore was still a man with no game. Had he been talking to a woman who spoke adequate English, he would have blown his chances several times over. At best, Oksana was only comprehending

TEQUILA VIKINGS

fifteen percent of what Warren was saying. His awkwardness went entirely unnoticed. It also helped that Ms. Popescu was not a woman accustomed to enticing much interest from men. Finding herself the object of Macklemore's undivided attention, though, she was forgiving him his trespasses.

Oksana and Mack talked on the couch for an hour. Then they moved to the patio for a little privacy. After the sun went down, I noticed that they had shifted from there as well. Concerned, I got up and asked Hannah if she knew where they were.

"Don't worry about it," she told me. "They're both adults. They don't have a curfew and they don't need chaperones."

"Hannah, Mack's busted up worse than I am. If he walks out too far, he might not be able to get back."

"I'm sure they're fine. If it makes you feel better, though, we can take a walk down to the ocean and see if we can find them."

They were easy to spot. Macklemore was a trooper, but he could still only walk so fast. We found them strolling down the boardwalk holding hands. I caught Hannah smiling from ear to ear. "You did this on purpose, didn't you?" I asked her.

"Maaaaay-be," she sang back. "I thought I'd see what happens if I put the two of them in the same room together. I think we're getting some promising results so far."

The results were promising. They were entertaining, as well. At one point, Mack got his courage up and went in for his first kiss. Unfortunately, he found the logistics of it a little much. They were too far away to see for certain, but it looked like he poked her in the eye with his nose. It reminded me of the time I watched a Jack Russell terrier trying to hump an unattended Cabbage Patch doll. He desperately wanted it but had no idea how to go about having it. Fortunately for Mack, Oksana had a better grasp of these things. When she returned the gesture, she executed it with far more grace.

Hannah squealed in delight as their lips met. She jumped up and down, clapping her hands excitedly. "Did you see that! Did you see that, Doyle! They kissed! We did it! We…"

Hannah paused as she looked up at me. "Oh my god! Doyle! Doyle, are you…? Are you crying? Your eyes are all…"

"Black. My eyes are black, Hannah. I'm not crying."

"You are too! I can even see it in the dark. Your eyes are all wet and glassy!"

"Hannah, my eyes had the shit beat out of them, yeah, they get glassy from time to time, but I'm not…"

"Bullshit. You're crying like a little bitch." She leaned in, wrapping her arms around me. "It's okay, Doyle. I've got a shoulder for you to cry on."

"Goddammit. I'm not cry…"

"Save it, you pansy. I'll take this over that hoodlum you can be any day of the week. I can't believe you went through all that in Mexico and never lost control, never fought back. I think you did it, Doyle! I think you conquered your demons. If they're gone, there's nothing that can stop us. It's going to be you and me forever."

*****

CHAPTER 25

One of the benefits of youth is the speed with which you heal. By the second week of June, Mack and I had recovered to the point that our injuries were barely noticeable. I was back up on a surfboard before the schools got out on summer break, though admittedly, it was against my doctor's advice.

Things were going well. They might even have been going a little too well, considering what happened in Mexico. With that in mind, I was not surprised when Darrow called me down to chat about developments south of the border. As I took a seat in the EMO office, my master chief asked, "Guess who I saw last night?"

"Marco Baylon," I answered.

"Yeah, Baylon," Darrow looked disappointed that I always guessed that, but I have no idea why. Marco Baylon was the answer every single time he asked that question.

"You take him fishing again?" I asked. "In Mexico? You sure that's a good idea after you stuck a pistol in his nephew's face?"

"Yeah, he wasn't too happy about that," my master chief told me. "We settled it, though. We made nice."

"You talk about Hulagu?"

Darrow nodded. "That's all we talked about. He got some intel I thought I should share with you. Apparently, Martinez is up against the ropes down there. He doesn't have many allies, and even his friends are beginning to realize he's a lost cause. The only people he can count on are the guys who were in so thick with him that their fates are tied directly to his.

"He's beginning to realize how hopeless his situation is. He's going down, and he's starting to lash out. He even clipped a couple of guys in his own organization. One of them was the bloc captain at *La Ocho* that gave up Macklemore, some guy named Guerrero. Marco was pissed about Hulagu getting to that motherfucker before he had a chance to. He also took a shot at Noel and one of Marco's girlfriends. They missed Dominguez, but Baylon's girl took a bullet in the gut. She'll live, but there's going to be a lot of permanent damage."

I winced. "Shit. If you see Marco again, pass on my condolences."

"I will. Doyle, Martinez also put out some feelers to get a line on you and Macklemore."

I felt my face go white.

"Marco was clear that Martinez is impotent at this point. The likelihood that he can get to you is very low, but it's not nonexistent. He told me what you or Mack could expect if he gets his hands on you. It was pretty horrific. Even worse is what he would do to Hannah. What are you planning for your leave period?"

The USS *Belleau Wood* was ready to depart for Japan. I was on the eve of my thirty-day pre-deployment furlough. "We're staying in Ocean Beach. We were going to hang out and surf."

Darrow sighed and shook his head. "This guy's no joke, Doyle. We can't underestimate him. Don't stay in Ocean Beach. Take Hannah and go somewhere. Don't tell anybody where, just go. By the time you get back, we'll be ready to leave. Maybe the Mexicans will have him by then. Until that happens, though, you need to keep your head on a swivel."

I sighed. "Master Chief, taking off for a month would have been an option before this Tijuana thing. I can't afford to travel for thirty days now."

Darrow looked me straight in the eye. "You can't afford not to. I'm serious. Baylon told me some of the stuff this guy has done. Martinez castrated the grandson of a man who refused to join up with *Los Hermanos*. He did it himself and even the people he worked for were disturbed by it. And those are the guys who tortured that DEA agent to death in Guadalajara a few years back. Martinez is a fucking psychopath, Doyle. You don't want to be rolling the dice with this guy."

Darrow was right. I didn't want to roll the dice with Hulagu, but I did not have the funds to flee. I was broke, which weighed heavily on my mind that night as we sat around our bonfire in Ocean Beach.

I was okay until I spotted a Hispanic man leaning up against the wall separating the beach from the boardwalk. He was staring at us a little too long and abruptly walked away after seeing me take notice of him. This made me take a closer look at everyone else around us.

Being surrounded by Latinos in OB was not unusual. In fact, it was the norm. It never bothered me. After my conversation with Darrow, though, I realized how vulnerable we were. If Hulagu's people came after me while I was in my element, they would blend right in without even trying. They could stick a knife between my ribs, and I would never see them coming.

"Doyle, are you OK?" Hannah asked me, catching how intently I was studying the crowd.

I smiled at her and lied. "Yeah, I'm fine."

"You seem a little quiet today," Dreadlock John said.

I shrugged. "I got a lot on my mind right now, that's all. A lot of work stuff."

"Work stuff?" Macklemore asked. He was lying in the sand while Oksana rested her head in his lap. "You're getting ready to go on leave. You shouldn't be worrying about work."

"I have a lot of things I need to get done before I go," I said, staring at Lupe.

Lupe.

The circles Lupe moved in south of the border were connected to Francisco Martinez. She got her grass from there. She could lead Hulagu right to us. *She could make some pretty good money telling Martinez's people where we were.*

I felt my pulse quicken. Lupe could lead that son-of-a-bitch right to our front door. I watched her cracking up at one of Eddie's jokes. She was a smuggler, but small time. Lupe was far from being a hardened criminal.

She was just a girl who knew a few tricks about getting small amounts of marijuana over the fence. Lupe was a friend of ours. She would never do that to us. Not for money.

But what if she talked to someone down there? I felt myself sweating now. Word on the street was currency within the underworld, no matter what level you worked at. What if she bragged about knowing the people who knocked the legendary Hulagu down a notch? And then what if they told someone else? And then that person told another person who then told someone who knew Martinez?

I closed my eyes and saw myself and Hannah in bed. In the dark. I felt someone clasp their hand over my mouth to keep me from screaming. Hulagu stood beside Hannah, grinning at me to broadcast what he planned on doing to her. He said something to me, but it was hard to understand. It sounded like we were underwater.

Underwater!

I forced my eyes open, hoping to keep myself from slipping into an episode while I tried to suppress my shaking. *Lupe isn't stupid. She's too street smart to say anything. She wouldn't do that to us. She's a friend of ours. A trusted friend of ours.*

A trusted friend. As that realization hit, I felt my anxiety start to wane. We had nothing to fear from Lupe. She was firmly on our side.

But what about that Hockey Mullet Frat prick? The man who gave Mack up at the border? I saw him all the time around Ocean Beach. What if he saw me too? Hulagu had him in custody. What had he told him about us? The Hockey Mullet Frat Guy was not our friend. He was an asshole that would get a thrill from knowing Hulagu's goons had gotten their hands on us. *Fuck!*

I was slipping underwater again. My heart was racing. I was panting, trying to catch my breath, and no matter how hard I tried, I knew that I would not be able to control my shaking.

"Jesus! Doyle! What's the matter with you?" I heard Hannah call out.

I could not answer, only whimper and shake. I was slipping.

"Oh, my God!" I heard Kate say, just before her voice transformed into my mother's. "Doyle! Doyle!"

"Is he having a seizure?" Lupe asked.

"No," I heard Hannah answer with confusion in her voice. "I think he's having a flashback!"

"Oh no!" someone who sounded like my dead sister gasped. "My old man had those! From Vietnam! I didn't know Doyle was in combat!"

"He wasn't!" I heard my fiancée scream. "His fucking father did this to him!"

*****

When I snapped out of it, I was lying on the living room sofa at Cheri's place. Hannah squeezed between me and the couch's back and wrapped both of her arms around my chest. Kate had one of my hands clasped in hers. "You back with us?" she asked.

I was so embarrassed. "I'm sorry. I'm so sorry. I…"

"Shhhhhhh. It's okay, Doyle. I used to go through this all the time with my old man. Everything's alright."

I then noticed everyone from the bonfire gathered around me. "Hey, I…"

"Shhhhhhh," Kate whispered. "We don't care, Doyle. We want you to relax. Calm down."

"I am calm. Now."

"You know what the trigger was? There's usually a trigger." Kate was doing all the talking.

I nodded. I knew exactly what set off my episode.

"You want to tell us about it?" she asked

I shook my head.

Kate took her hand and put it on my cheek. "Okay then, you don't have to," she said. Space Kate understood.

"Thanks." I turned to Hannah. "I'm sorry. I guess this is…"

"You didn't hurt anybody, Doyle. You didn't threaten anybody. This wasn't anything. I watched Kate bring you back. I think I know what to do when this happens. This is what you were telling me about, isn't it? Your episodes? This is something we can deal with. You need to get help, though, I think…"

"I think we need to get out of town for a while." I interrupted. "You ever been to the Grand Canyon?"

*****

Hannah and I went to that big ditch in Arizona. We took my motorcycle, and it was amazing. We also saw Las Vegas, where we dropped acid and watched the sunrise. We then rode north through Oregon, Washington State, Idaho, and Wyoming. We discovered that the entire state of Utah could have been a national park. We would have spent more time there had it not been so hard to find a place to drink.

The trip exhausted everything I had left in the bank and came close to maxing out my credit limit. From a piece of mind perspective, though, it was money well spent. I returned refreshed and encouraged by word out of Tijuana that the noose was tightening around Hulagu's neck. It did not appear that he was going to be much of a threat to us.

That left me free to be more concerned with other news. Hannah and I were still unpacking when Macklemore arrived, acting very, very agitated. Mack wholly transformed himself after Tijuana. He was sober and doing everything the Navy expected from him without being hounded. Warren was making it to quarters on time and even showering on his own. The only thing he was still struggling with was his technical abilities. He was making progress there but still had far to go. For the first time in his life, he felt a sense of belonging. And he was about to lose it.

Mack's transfer to the *USS Blue Ridge* had been set in stone for months. There was nothing anyone could do about it now. To further complicate the situation, Macklemore had a girlfriend. Oksana was the first girl ever to show any interest in Warren. She was the first young lady he ever held hands with. She was his first kiss and the woman he finally lost his virginity to. When we left San Diego, Macklemore would be leaving her too. "I can't lose the *Belleau Wood* and Oksana, Doyle. I can't." He was distraught.

"How much time do you have left on your enlistment?" I asked him.

"Three years!"

That was a long time. Despite knowing better, I said, "Mack, if this was meant to be…"

"Don't give me that. I've only known Oksana a month. I don't know if this is meant to be or not. I want the chance to find out, though!"

TEQUILA VIKINGS

"What are you thinking of doing?" Hannah asked.

"I'm thinking of proposing to her."

I let out a long whistle. "That's a big step, Warren."

Mack dropped his head into his hands. "I know, I know. And I know that neither one of us is ready to take it yet. Doyle, this has been the happiest month of my life, and I don't think I'll get this chance again."

"Don't say that, Warren," Hannah told him. "If this doesn't work out, there'll always be someone out there for you. You have a lot to offer and…"

"You're right, Mack." I interrupted. "You might not get this chance again. You've got to make a decision here."

"Doyle!" Hannah exclaimed.

"No, hear me out. Oksana's good for you, Warren. When you ask her, tell her you know it's a little early for this, but she makes you very happy. Tell her that you want…no...tell her that you *need* to know if this will work. Ask her to marry you and follow you to Hawaii so the two of you can find out together."

Macklemore shot me his goofy smile. "Thanks, Doyle. I …"

"But Mack, you have to put yourself in her shoes. She barely knows you. She might not be ready to make such a big leap in such a short amount of time. To be honest, few rational people would. It's a big risk for her. If she says no, it's not about you, Mack. It's about not having had the chance to get to know you yet. You can't fall apart on us like you did after that girl tried to set you up to get rolled. You have to brace yourself. Okay?"

Mack's head bobbed up and down nervously a couple of times before he exhaled and said, "Okay. Can you help me pick out a ring?"

"Not really," I told him. "Have Hannah help you. She's much better with jewelry than I am."

*****

"You're shaking," Hannah told me as we sat around our bonfire on Ocean Beach. "I don't think you were this nervous when you asked me to marry you."

I smiled at her. "I guess I was more confident that you would say yes than I am about Oksana saying it."

"Really? And what made you so certain that I was going to agree to marry you?" Hannah asked.

"Well, I'm startlingly good-looking for starters. Not to mention something of a sexual dynamo…"

"Oh, bloody hell…"

"When are they supposed to be back?" Kate asked.

"Whenever they get here," Dreadlock John answered. "It's their moment. Let them savor it."

Lupe lit up a joint and started passing it around. "Here. This will help kill time."

I laughed. "For you, it might. I have to sit here watching you all get stoned?"

"Don't you always?" Dreadlock John asked sarcastically before taking a super big hit off of Lupe's dope.

"Hannah, do you know when you and Doyle are getting married?" Kate asked.

My fiancée shrugged. "Whenever the *Belleau Wood* makes it to Australia, I guess."

Lupe turned towards me. "Are you going to Australia?"

I took a drink out of my beer and nodded. "The US Navy does a WESTPAC exercise every year. Australia is always a port call at some point. If I had to guess, we'd end up down there next spring."

"That's almost a year away," Kate said. "Why don't you both go to Vegas and get hitched before you leave?"

"My visa," Hannah confessed. "I've overstayed my tourist visa by almost two years now. If I register to get married, I'm going to pop up on someone's radar. I'll get my bloody arse deported."

We talked about Hannah's immigration status for almost half an hour. Then we argued whether Nirvana or Alice in Chains was the best band out of the Seattle scene. Finally, we were trying to decide if Ted Kennedy or Boris Yeltsin would be the better drinking companion when Macklemore snuck up from behind. He screamed at the top of his lungs and scared us out of our wits, ruining our buzzes. Warren then collapsed into the sand and roared with laughter as we tried to regain our composure. He was plastered.

"Well?" Hannah asked, slapping Warren across the back a couple of times.

TEQUILA VIKINGS

"Well, what?"

"C'mon Warren!" Kate yelled at him. "We've been waiting here for hours to see what happened! What did she say? Where is she?"

Mack waved his hand towards the direction of one of the beachside convenience stores. "She's over there trying to call Romania on the payphone. She said, 'Yes!'"

The crowd around the campfire erupted into cheers. As Lupe had him wrapped in the tightest hug she could give him, Mack called out and asked, "Hey Doyle! Can I bum a cigarette off of you?"

Considering Mack walked over from a convenience store, I should have been irritated he did not buy himself a pack while he was there. I was too happy for him to be cross, though. I gave him my last smoke and threw the empty box into the fire. I then stood up to brush the sand off my legs.

"Where you going?" Hannah asked.

"That was my last cigarette. I'm going to go get more."

"Hey! You better not be puttin' your hands on my girl while you're over there!" Mack joked as Eddie passed him a bottle of beer.

Walking away, I heard Hannah call out, "He wouldn't dare! He doesn't want to be sleeping on the couch tonight and miss out on what I got planned for him!"

I turned around to her and held up my hand, "Don't get too smug, honey! You may be outstanding in bed, but don't underestimate the competition you face from my left mitt and an overactive imagination!"

Those were the last words I ever spoke to Hannah Baxter. Had I known, I would have told her something more profound. I would have told her how much I loved her. Or I would have let her know how sorry I was about what was going to happen next. I certainly would have made sure that the last thought I ever conveyed to her was not about my proficiency in masturbation.

*****

I was walking backward when I made my little joke. Between that and the dark, I did not see the group of men coming up from behind me. When I turned back around, I ran right into one of them, knocking him off his trajectory. Before I could excuse myself, one of them planted both of his hands into my chest and shoved me onto my ass. "Watch where the fuck you're going, asshole!"

I could have let it go, and I would have had it been some random group of beach dicks. I recognized the voice, though. I heard it at the border crossing a couple of months before.

"That's him! That's the son-of-a-bitch that broke that guy out of the police car!"

He got a haircut. I might not have recognized him had he not opened his mouth, but it was the Hockey Mullet Frat Guy. "Hey!" I yelled out, grabbing his attention.

The whole group, all five of them, stopped at once and turned to face me. Mullet Man himself then stepped forward. He wore the cocksure grin of a young man who rarely suffered the consequences of bad decisions. "What? You have a problem?"

"You don't remember me?" I asked as I stood up and dusted myself off.

"Should I?"

"Yeah, you probably should. I left you in that police car so you could spend the night in a Mexican jail a couple of months back."

Mullet Man laughed like someone who was very confident of his advantage in numbers. It was five against one. I was a pretty good fighter, but there was no way I was good enough to take them all on at the same time.

What Mullet Man failed to realize, though, was that I did not care. He was the guy who attacked Mack and got him arrested. He was the reason I felt I needed to spring Warren from the back of a police car and the reason we did not get away with it. He was the man who had exposed us at the border. He was the person who nearly got us killed, who got us beaten within an inch of our lives. This man cost me fifteen grand, my BOOST recommendation, and my ability to reenlist. He caused Mack and me a lot of suffering. Not only did he not regret any of it, but I could tell by the way he smiled that he was proud of himself for what he had done to us.

I knew there were going to be consequences for what was going to happen. This kid's father was in a position of authority. I knew there were good odds that I was going to spend the weekend in jail. I would probably land myself in front of the captain on Monday morning and get busted back down to E-4. Mullet Man owed me for what he had done, though, and I needed to make him pay up.

The frat guy was oblivious to this, still thinking I lacked the guts to do anything to him while he was surrounded by his boys. He casually closed the gap between us, intending to prove how little he feared me. He did not realize that I was waiting for him to get within reach. Hannah did, though. Looking back, I vaguely remember hearing her call out something to the effect of, "Doyle! Don't do it!" At the moment, though, it did not register in my head at all. I was focused on the mullet man—nothing else.

"So, how'd that goofy lookin' fucker like it when he…" *CRACK!*

Mullet Man took that first blow squarely on the nose. It exploded into a geyser of crimson droplets that would have looked horrific in daylight. I would have followed it up, but I walloped him so hard that he flew backward out of range. The college boy howled in shock and pain as he crashed onto his ass in the sand. My instinct was to leap on top of him and keep going, but I heard someone charging from behind.

The first of Mullet Man's friends to leap into the fray was a big guy wearing an Oakland Raiders football jersey. Caught off guard too, he came at me without much of a strategy. Oakland looked as if he intended to body check me to the ground instead of hit me, so all I had to do was jump out of his way. This threw him off balance and, confused, he stopped.

Before Oakland could get his bearings, I reached out and grabbed a handful of hair on each side of his head. Using his coif as handles, I drove his face down into my knee, not once, but three times. It felt like the first hit crushed his nose just like Mullet Man's. The second ripped his lips wide open and cracked a few of his teeth. The third broke his jaw. The lummox hit the ground shrieking.

Before my friends around the fire could get to their feet, I was down to fighting only three of them. If they decided to bum rush me, they could have taken me down. The losers hesitated, though, looking at one another as if they were figuring out whose turn it was to go next. I decided for them.

The kid closest to me was tall, skinny, and scared. I threw my foot out and kicked him in the crotch as hard as I could, sending him to the ground, hunched over and gagging. I then turned to the other two punks, who both developed a change of heart and decided to run. I was impressed with myself. Within a few seconds, it was down to only the Mullet Man and me.

And maybe Oakland. When I turned back around, he was getting up. I dropped him with a blow to the temple that probably hurt me more than it did him. Still, it sent the message that if he had enough, he needed to crawl away from the fight, not walk.

I was not giving Hockey Mullet Frat Guy that option. By the time I turned my attention back to him, he was up and running, trying to get away. I chased him down and tackled him not far from our bonfire.

"No! Please! Stop!" he pleaded. "I'm sorry! I…"

SMASH! I struck him in the eye so hard all four limbs shot out spastically from his body. "You son-of-a-bitch!" I screamed. SMASH! I hit him in the other eye, causing him to scream out too. "You nearly got us killed!"

Mullet Man was crying out loud now. "Help!" he pleaded. "Someone, please help! I'm sorry! I …!" SMASH!

I socked him so hard that he went silent and limp. He was helpless now, unable to defend himself. The fight was over. For him it was, anyway. I, on the other hand, was just getting started. With strength fueled by rage and adrenaline, I kept hitting him as hard as I could. I throttled him time after time after time. One horrendous blow I landed cracked my knuckles. With bolts of excruciating agony shooting up through my wrist, I jumped off of my victim and screeched. Then I started using my feet.

"You still think you're a tough guy?!?" I roared as I kicked the mullet man in the gut. I then sent another foot to his crotch with enough force to crush his testicles and shouted, "HOW ABOUT NOW?!?"

Though not even conscious, the mullet man's hands dropped to protect his groin. That left his head exposed again and I fell back upon him. I could not stop myself.

"Doyle!" Dreadlock John yelled. "DOYLE! STOP!"

I ignored him. Oddly enough, this was not one of my episodes. It was all rage and hatred. I *needed* to hurt this kid.

"Stop it!" Eddie shouted out. "You won, Doyle! Let it go! We need to get the fuck out of here before the cops show up!" I kept going though, throwing punch after punch.

TEQUILA VIKINGS

It took Macklemore to pull me back from the brink of committing murder. He tackled me and took me down into the sand. I screamed out in unbridled fury and tried to hit him too, but Dreadlock John grabbed my arm. Then Eddie clutched the other one. I screamed out again, bellowing long and hard.

"STOP IT!" Mack howled back. "STOP IT! HANNAH! SHE'S…"

All it took was Hannah's name to hit me with the realization of what I was doing. "Hannah!" I shouted out. She was gone. "HANNAH!" I looked at my hands. They were covered in blood. So were my clothes. So was Mullet Man. Hannah saw what I had done. She now understood what I was and knew the entirety of what I was capable of.

I knew Hannah had gone back to Cheri's, so I tried to get my friends off of me to go after her. It was no use. Lupe tried to calm me down. "Don't, Doyle! Don't do this! You need to settle down!"

"No! I need to see her! I've got to explain! That prick was the reason we…"

"IT DOESN'T MATTER!" Lupe screamed at me, mainly to get my attention. "Doyle! Jesus! Look what you did! Look!"

Glancing beside me, I looked at the mullet man again. His face was reduced to a bloody pulp. As my head started to clear, I realized how bad I had hurt him. I tried reaching out to see if he was even alive, but Mack held me back, thinking I was going after him again. "No more, Doyle. We can't have another Green!"

I stifled a sob, fearing that we already did. As we fled the scene of the fight, I turned to Lupe with tears in my eyes. "Hannah…It's…it's bad, isn't it?"

Lupe nodded, opening her hand to show me what she was holding. It was Hannah's engagement ring. "Yeah, Doyle. It's bad."

I have no idea what happened to Mullet Man that night. I knew I had hurt him worse than Hulagu hurt Mack and me in Mexico, but judging by the lack of police activity afterward, I can only assume he fared better than Randy Green had. Still, my bonfire friends were worried enough about being implicated in what had gone down that they didn't feel comfortable gathering around our Ocean Beach fire pit again until long after I left for Japan.

Oddly enough, I was not worried about the police at all. I should have been. If they had any idea who had beaten that kid like that, I would have been looking at a significant prison sentence. Still, that specter did not cause me even a hint of anxiety.

In the frame of mind I was in, the prospect of doing a few years of hard time was nothing compared to the thought of spending the rest of my life without Hannah Baxter at my side. The only thing I could think about was how to get her back.

*****

CHAPTER
26

Consuming alcohol was strictly forbidden aboard US Navy warships. A week after my fiancée broke off our engagement, though, I could not have cared less.

After six days of trying to reach her by phone, I rode out to Cheri's place to talk to Hannah in person on Saturday morning. She had already packed up her stuff and moved out, leaving my things piled in a stack near the front door. I loaded what I could onto my bike and sought out Dreadlock John.

By nature, Dreadlock John was an optimistic man. He told me that Kate had been in contact with Hannah, and she was as distraught as I was. At first, he tried to tell me he thought I had a chance at reconciling. When Kate joined us later, though, she was clear that she did not share her boyfriend's opinion.

We were sitting outside at the Sand Flea, crowded around one of the *palabra* picnic tables. "Can you just tell me how to get hold of her, Kate? I need to speak to her. I need to…"

Kate shook her head. "No, Doyle. She won't talk to you. Not yet. You have to give her time."

Frustrated, I lost my temper and slammed my hand down on our tabletop. It was loud enough to stop every conversation taking place around us. It startled both John and Kate as well. "I don't have time, Kate!" I exclaimed, a little louder than I meant to. Lowering my voice, I then said, "I'm leaving in less than two weeks! Please! For Christ's sake…"

Kate lowered her eyes and stared at our drinks. "I'm sorry, Doyle. I can't. I promised."

"Look, Doyle," John said. "This is a tough break, but think about this for a minute. You two were good together, but, man, you have to think hard about who she is. She's all peace and love and…"

"It's not even that." Kate tore her gaze off of the table and looked me in the eye. "Doyle, she's a lovely girl. I can't think of a single negative thing I could ever say about her. She was a hell of a catch. She's not had to experience a lot of adversity in her life, though. And, Doyle, this thing you're dealing with…these flashbacks…I went through this with my old man. They're no joke. To be honest, she'd never be able to handle that. Not over the long term. It's better you figured this out now, before you had a couple of kids together, which would really complicate everything."

I dropped my head into my hands and sat there for a moment, trying not to cry. I'd almost had it. I was so close, and I did not even let it slip through my fingers. I crushed it with my own two fists.

Kate reached over the table and squeezed one of my hands. "Hey, Doyle. This will stop hurting. It's going to take a while, but it will end. One day you're going to meet someone that can handle you, a great girl who's probably been through some shit herself. The two of you will make each other very happy. In fact, when you're done with the Navy and find yourself back in these parts, come look me up. I can think of a dozen girls that I would love to introduce you to."

I nodded. I did not believe her bullshit but humored her nonetheless. Kate always had the best of intentions. I reached into my pocket and pulled out a letter I had written. Sliding it to Kate, I asked, "Can you at least get this to her?"

Kate took it but told me, "I don't think she's going to read it."

That hurt. "She hates me that much?"

Kate reached over the table and took my hand again. "Noooo. No, Doyle. She doesn't hate you at all. She loves you. She loves you more than she's ever loved anyone before. She just knows she can't do this and has to get out while she can. She's terrified that if she talks to you, she'll end up coming back. She won't chance letting her heart overcome her head."

That sounded pretty final, but I could not give up. "Please, get that letter to her. Tell her that we're leaving in just over two weeks, on August thirty-first. That's a Monday. If she changes her mind, tell her to get in touch with Oksana, and she can come see me on the pier with her and Mack. She can come to me any time before that, but that's our last chance. That's our very last chance. After that, we'll be gone."

There was nothing more for me to say. I stood up, hugged both John and Kate, and thanked them for everything. I told them that I would miss them. I then went back to 32nd Street, smuggled a bottle of mezcal aboard the ship, and got sloppy drunk alone in my radar dome.

*****

I was awakened by a slap across my face and opened my eyes to the sight of Master Chief Darrow standing above me. He was in civilian clothes and waving my empty bottle of Monte Alban in front of my face. "What the hell do you think you're doing? Do you want to get your ass busted?"

"I don't care anymore," I said, trying to drift back to sleep. "If you want to have me busted, go ahead and bust me."

Darrow smacked me again, this time much harder. He then grabbed me by my shirt and wrenched me up to my feet. Throwing me up against the wall of the dome, he yelled, "Goddammit! You don't get to do this! I got plans for you, you son-of-a-bitch! I'm not letting you sabotage what's left of your military career!" He tapped me on the head with the empty mezcal bottle, not hard enough to do any damage but enough to certainly hurt. "How drunk are you?"

"I don't know. What time is it?"

"Five o'clock."

I was confused. "In the morning?"

"No asshole," my master chief barked. "It's seventeen hundred."

"No shit? What day?"

"Sunday."

I did the math. I knew that I had been drinking late but was still surprised that I had slept through an entire day. "I don't think I'm drunk anymore, just really hungover. And hungry."

"And you smell like Macklemore. Jesus Christ, there is no sicker stench than the reek of stale tequila sweated out of a man's pores…"

"It's not tequila," I countered. "It's mezcal."

"Which is rotgut tequila. Go below and get your ass cleaned up. I'll get you something to eat on the way."

"On the way?" I asked. "Where are we going?"

"You'll find out when we get there. Now hurry your ass up! I've been looking for you all fuckin' day for Christ's sake!"

Unfortunately for Darrow, I was in no shape to hurry for anybody. Not even him. I took a long Hollywood shower while he got rid of my empty booze bottle. When I finished, I met him in the EMO office. From there, he took me out to eat *carne asada* at Adalberto's on Rosecrans. That was across the street from the Recruit Training Command, where I had gone to boot camp. It was also near the marina where Darrow kept his fishing boats in Point Loma. I lived on Adalberto's when I was going to BE/E School but had not eaten there in ages. It was glorious.

As I ate, my master chief tried to tell me that Hannah would be little more than a distant memory within a couple of months. "I know you don't want to hear this now, but you're going to end up with more tail than you can handle once we get overseas. You don't want to go into your first deployment tied down to anybody, Doyle. Hell, you don't want to go into *any* deployment attached to anybody. That's why I've been married so many fuckin' times."

Darrow was right; I didn't want to hear that. I didn't want to talk about it either. To change the subject, I asked, "You want to tell me where we're going now?"

"We're going for a boat ride."

It was a little late to go fishing. "To Mexico?"

Darrow nodded. "To Mexico."

"You think that's a good idea?"

Darrow shook his head and looked me right in the eye. "Not at all. It'd be a far worse idea not to go, though. Baylon asked us to meet him. He says he has something for us. If he's on the level, this could be good. If he thinks we're a loose end that needs tying up though, well then, things could get very, very bad for us."

"And you're willing to take that risk?" I asked.

Darrow finished chewing his food, washed it down with a gulp of soda, then cleared his throat. "We don't really have a choice. I have my wife's family here, not to mention the family of another ex-wife. They know how to get to my daughters back in Arkansas. Once we leave for Japan, they won't be able to get to me. They'll have to get to me through them. No, if I have a debt to square with the house, I need to make sure I'm the one who pays it. Not them."

"I don't have anybody here in San Diego anymore. Hell, I don't have anybody anywhere, so…"

My master chief scowled at me. "Well, you're the one who got me into this shit, so you're going to pay your share."

Fair enough. I did not care, anyway. Between having lost Hannah and my biblical hangover, I was as miserable as I had ever been. Having Baylon and his boys blow my brains out would have been a relief.

Darrow and I did not talk much more until we reached the boat. After we were on our way to the Coronado Islands, he broke the silence by pulling out a pair of .45 automatics. He slipped one beneath his belt at the small of his back and passed me the other. "These both yours?" I asked.

"In a sense. The one that you have was stolen from the armory by a dipshit that used to work for me back in Olongapo. We busted him but never officially recovered the weapon. The prick sold it to a Filipino gang leader for dope money. Rico Tejada, a friend with the Philippine National Police, eventually confiscated it. By the time he turned it back over to me, though, it had already been stricken from service. So, for all practical purposes, it no longer exists."

"And yours?"

"It fell from a Master-at-Arms' holster while he was scuffling with a drunk Marine on the bridge out of Subic. It got kicked to the side and fell into the Shit River. That's some nasty-ass water. There's always a gaggle of kids hanging around it that will dive in after coins sailors flip into it. After the weapon was removed from the registry, I offered thirty bucks to whoever could dive in and find it. The damned thing was in my hands inside of an hour."

"They're both untraceable?"

Darrow nodded. "Yep. Completely."

That did not surprise me, but I was curious. "Why do you feel the need to collect untraceable firearms?"

Darrow shrugged. "You know, I caught a lieutenant commander messing around with little boys in Pagsanjan. That place is a real Sodom and Gomorrah. You can get anything there. It's near the river where they filmed the movie 'Apocalypse Now,' but that's beside the point. I didn't catch the guy in the act, but I was onto him, and he knew it.

"This shit bird was married too. He had a beautiful wife who was a real sweetheart. She knew he was queer but had no idea he was into such sick shit. She married him because she thought it was wrong for the Navy to discriminate against homosexuals. She got an opportunity to see the world and he got some cover to keep his career safe. Anyway, she'd been seeing this helicopter pilot, a really nice guy out of Cubi Point, so now things were getting complicated.

"So, this lieutenant commander knows I'm onto him and feels like he really needs the cover that having a wife provides. He's never had a problem letting his wife do her thing, but once I'm onto him, her affair is getting tricky. He knows he's under scrutiny and he's scared because his wife is getting serious with this flyboy. The commander starts putting real pressure on her to end her fling with the pilot."

Darrow paused to light a cigarette. "Anyway, long story short. The guy comes home, finds the pilot there with his wife, and she asks him for a divorce. The lieutenant commander senses that even if we can't prove he's molesting little boys, we're going to find out he's queer. He may escape prison but the divorce is going to end his career in disgrace. The fucker snaps and assaults the pilot. Realizing he's losing the fight, he pulls his weapon and ends up getting shot with his own gun during the struggle. He didn't make it. He died right there in his kitchen."

Darrow scanned the stars to get his bearings. "Now this pilot's a great guy, but he's fucked. On the outside, it looks like this lieutenant commander came home, caught the flyboy putting it to his wife, and then got murdered by his old lady's lover. I knew better but didn't have the proof I needed to exonerate the poor guy. Even if I cleared him of murder, the pilot's career is still over. He'd likely end up prosecuted for conduct unbecoming an officer.

"Luckily, the lieutenant commander lived out in town because he couldn't get away with his lifestyle on base. The Philippine cops got there first. We used a lost .45, just like one of these two, to shoot the lieutenant commander again in the same wound. The forty-five is bigger than the 9mm. As long as we got the trajectory right, it now looked like he was killed with a stolen weapon rather than his personal sidearm."

The master chief took a drag off his cigarette and thought for a moment, wondering if he should be trusting me with this kind of information. He must have figured it was too late now.

"I turned the 'official' murder weapon over to the Flips. They 'recovered' it shortly afterward during a raid against some local gang members that went awry. They then pinned the murder to one of the thugs killed in the shootout. The official story was the lieutenant commander was shot during a home invasion. The murder weapon was a pistol recorded as destroyed, but sold to some local hooligans."

I shook my head in disbelief. That was some real gangster shit. "What happened to the pilot?"

Darrow shrugged. "He married the widow and enjoyed a long and prosperous career in the United States Navy. He went on to command the *USS Belleau Wood*. He owes me a few favors that you've had me cashing in fairly regularly lately."

I had to laugh. I knew Darrow had something on Captain Fleming.

"Look, Doyle, what we're going into tonight, it could be nothing. It could also be that this Hulagu fuck somehow got the upper hand. Baylon keeps telling me that they're on top of this guy, that he's run out of friends, and that they'll have him any minute. Somehow, though, this asshole keeps not getting caught. That makes me suspicious and sounds like they're stalling for time. Shit down here in Mexico, it's always fluid, you know? Alliances are always shifting, the situation is always changing, and you never know who's on top.

"If Baylon's being straight with me, this'll be nothing more than a business meeting. If he's not straight with me, this is going to be some big-league shit. Stuff that's way over anything that I've ever had to deal with before. It'll be combat, Doyle. There won't be any time to question my orders, to decide for yourself what's right and wrong. If I tell you to shoot, you need to fucking fire. You think you can do that?"

"Yeah, no problem." I was oddly alright with it, actually. I was more concerned about what kind of business deal Master Chief Darrow had with a man like Marco Baylon.

"No problem? You ever point a gun at someone before, Doyle?"

"Nope, but I really wanted to once. In El Salvador. Unfortunately, I didn't have one at the time. They only sent me down there with a couple pieces of test equipment."

Darrow chuckled. "Okay, I told you one of my secrets. Why don't you tell me one of yours? What happened in El Salvador?"

I had little expectation of surviving a gun battle with Mexican police officers, so I did not see much harm in talking. "I was sent there to set up the land-based version of the SPN-35 radar at this remote base in the Salvadoran jungle. Well, as remote as you can get in El Salvador anyway. The country's so tiny that you can't twirl a monkey around by its nut-sack without sending it through customs. I'm down there with an Army Special Forces guy, a *bona fide* Green Beret named Sergeant Finnegan. He's kind of shadowing me while I'm working, making sure I don't trip over my own dick while I'm setting this thing up.

"Anyway, me and Finn are getting along pretty good, and we're partying with the local grunts after hours. It turns out my Spanish is better than his, so I'm doing a pretty good job at the 'hearts and minds' part of the Special Forces mission. We're getting pretty crazy with these soldiers we're drinking with. Eventually, we're all shit-faced, and the locals suggest seeking out some action with the ladies. Me and Finn are thinking they're talking about going to some bar in a nearby village or something. They were actually talking about just going back to their barracks, though."

Taking a deep breath of salt air, I said, "You know these guys we're drinking with? It turns out they're from a nasty unit down there called the Atlacatl Battalion. Apparently, they massacred a village nearby and brought back a couple of 'prisoners.' They were young girls they were keeping for entertainment. The soldiers liked us so much they decided to share one of them with us."

Darrow shook his head in disgust. Knowing how far beyond my moral tolerance that went, he said, "I'm kind of surprised you lived through something like that. I figured you'd get blown away trying to beat some ass."

I nodded. "It was close. Shit went down. Punches were thrown. A weapon or two were drawn. Finn had some pull, though. He got me out of there and assured me he'd correct the situation while I was confined to quarters. It was a tiny base, so I was not far from the commander's tent. I heard a lot of shouting and cursing. I could tell the commander was far more upset that his men showed us the girl than he was about what they were doing to her. I heard him tell them to get rid of her.

"An hour later, after one last hurrah, I heard her crying as they led her off somewhere. A little while after that, I heard a single gunshot ring out from the same direction. The fuckers killed her. Finn stuffed me into a helicopter the first thing the next morning and sent me back to the states."

I could have used a drink right about then, but I knew my stomach would not be able to handle it. "You know, I like Marco. I don't see him as the type of guy that would sell a ten-year-old girl to a brothel or rape college students like Hulagu, but he's part of the same system that lets people get away with shit like that."

The more I thought about it, the angrier I got. "Martinez is a proper villain, no doubt. The man's a monster. These guys, though? Our 'friends'? They don't want to kill Hulagu for all the heinous shit he's done. They're hunting him only because he tried to hurt *them*. That's it. They don't give a shit about what Martinez did. They only cared about it when he wanted to do it to them."

I lit a cigarette and leaned back in my seat. "I hope it doesn't come to that, but if those guys draw on us, I'll shoot Marco. I'll shoot Noel, too. No problem. I'll murder all those fuckers. I'll do it in the name of that poor girl I got killed in El Salvador."

Besides, I've got nothing to lose.

*****

I was expecting a scenario out of the movies. I thought we were going to pull up alongside the harbor patrol boat with a dozen heavily armed cartel enforcers roaming the decks. Instead, we rendezvoused with the *Loma Linda*, Master Chief Darrow's other fishing vessel. As we tied up alongside, I saw only three people aboard: Marco Baylon, his nephew, and whoever drove the boat. The *Loma Linda* was big, though. There could have been another half-dozen people waiting to ambush us from below.

"So?" Darrow asked Baylon once I fastened the boats together.

Marco walked to the side of the *Linda* and looked down on us. "It's nice, Bradley. She runs very well. My man says she's in good shape, has been well taken care of. She's not as lucky as the *Pescado Grande,* though. We didn't catch shit out there."

"That's not the boat's fault," Darrow laughed. "Knowing where the fish are is the captain's job."

Baylon nodded. "Yes, I'm sure that's the problem. You sure your men don't want to stay on and work for us?"

"I'm sure," Darrow answered. "They don't want to get mixed up in any trouble down where you guys are operating from. They're out."

Marco looked disappointed, but he understood. "I don't blame them. Is that Doyle with you?"

"*Sí, Marco. Es bueno verte de nuevo.*"

"It's good to see you too, *amigo*. I appreciate the respect you show me by speaking in Spanish, but English is fine! It would be rude for us to speak in front of your boss in a language that he does not understand. Bradley! Can we come aboard?"

Darrow gave me a sideways glance telling me to keep my eyes open. "Of course! Come on over."

"Okay. Take our luggage first."

With a nod of his chin, Darrow directed me to the side of the *Pescado,* where Noel tossed a duffle bag to me. It was far heavier than I expected. At first, I suspected it was full of dope, but I could feel the bundles inside. It was stacks of cash. Lots of them. "Hey, Doyle!" Noel called out. "Drop that. I have another one for you."

I caught the second bag and tried to check my surprise. "Take those below," the master chief told me.

When I returned, both Noel and Marco were aboard our boat. I held my hand out to Noel, but he refused it, insisting on hugging me instead. While doing so, one of his hands brushed my piece. "You know those aren't allowed in Mexico, my friend."

TEQUILA VIKINGS

"That's a lot of money." Master Chief told him. "It's in case we run into pirates."

"Besides," I added. "Considering what happened to me the last time I was down here, I wasn't coming unprepared."

Noel smiled and slapped me on the shoulder. "You saved my life, *amigo*. This time I'll let you off with a warning."

I scoffed. "I hardly saved your life, Noel. My master chief wasn't going to pull the trigger."

"Doyle," Chief Baylon said to me. "I've been a policeman for three decades. When angry men pull out firearms, people die. It happens all the time. Your boss may have regretted it later, but it could have happened. It took a lot of balls to put yourself between my nephew and Bradley's pistol. That is an act of courage that will not go unrewarded, my friend."

I turned to Noel. "And you don't have any hard feelings about my boss cracking you in the jaw?"

"Huh," Baylon grunted, answering for his nephew again. "Bradley told me that whatever shape you came back in was the way he was going to send my nephew back to me. We all knew this before you came down. We were just overconfident that there wouldn't be any trouble. Thanks to you, Noel got off easy. Let me tell you, Doyle, I like you. Had the shoe been on the other foot, though, I would have killed you if what happened to you had happened to my nephew. Make no mistake about that. Don't tell me your boss would not have pulled that trigger."

"Yes, I'm afraid we are still in your debt on that," Noel added. "I should have returned to Tijuana looking like you and your friend. We'd like to settle that debt now if you please. May we invite you to the *Loma, amigos*? We have something for you."

It was an invitation that felt like a trap, but it was one that we really could not refuse. Our boats were tied up together, so there was no way to escape. We needed to stay alert. Following Marco and Noel back to the *Loma Linda*, I heard Noel call out, "*¡Hombres! ¡Llévalo a la popa!*"

I could see Darrow tense up. "What does that mean?"

"Take it to the stern," I answered. "Or him, maybe it was take '*him*' to the stern." As we climbed aboard, I saw two men emerge from below, dragging someone to the back of the boat.

When we caught up to them, we got a better look at their captive. He was in rough shape, bloodied, broken, and wrapped in the thick chains used for towing vehicles. I guessed these were more to weigh the man down than to restrain him. One of Marco's men shined a flashlight in his face, showing us what they had done to him. They had taken one of his ears, an eye, and nearly all his fingers. He was barely alive.

"You know who this is, Doyle?" Noel asked me.

The man was unrecognizable, but I had a pretty good idea of who it was. "It's Hulagu."

"Yeah," Noel said. "Good guess. My apologies, but I owed my old friend Jaime the pleasure of doing most of this. I asked him to save a little bit for you."

"How is Jaime?" I asked.

"He's good now. He recovered nicely, like you." Noel reached out and one of his men passed him a revolver, which he placed in my hand. "We decided to let you have the honor of sending this piece of shit to hell. We thought it would be a nice touch to seal the deal of Marco buying your boss's fishing business."

I was caught off guard and not sure what to do. I looked over my shoulder at Darrow for guidance. He shrugged. "He's a dead man no matter who pulls the trigger, Doyle. And if there's anybody on the planet who has it coming, it's that motherfucker."

Marco stepped over to me and put his hand on my shoulder. "I want you to know that he was trying to get to you. That's how we caught him. He was reaching out to some people to cross the border. He was going down, he knew it, and he wanted to make sure that he took you with him."

"Were we in danger?" I asked.

"Of course, you were," Marco answered. "Had he got to the right people, you'd be missing body parts too before you died. Lucky for you, he got to the wrong people. He got to our people."

I looked down at Hulagu. He was mumbling to himself, sounding like he was chanting a constant stream of Hail Marys. *"Hey, Puta. ¿Me recuerdas?"* I asked him if he remembered me.

"Sí, Sí. Hago," Martinez answered quietly.

"Are you ready to die?"

TEQUILA VIKINGS

Martinez shook his head and sobbed. He then looked at me in pure terror. It was not the look of a man who was afraid of the pain of death, though. This was the horror of the Catholics, the realization that he was facing a state of eternal damnation. "Please," he whined pathetically. "Can you get me a priest? I've not had confession."

Noel laughed. "There's plenty of priests in hell, Francisco. Look one up when you get there."

I raised the revolver and put it between Martinez's eyes, holding it there while I stared at him.

"Go ahead and get it over with," Darrow told me when he realized I was not pulling the trigger. "At this point, you'd be doing him a favor."

He was right; I would be. Martinez was spent. My guess was that if I walked away and left him alone, he would be dead within the hour. It was a horrible way to go, what they had done to him, but Hulagu had earned every bit of it. I would be lying if I said I was sorry for what they had put him through. He personified the evil that men of authority could inflict upon the powerless.

But I was not powerless anymore. I was standing there, pointing a revolver between Martinez's eyes. I held the power of life and death in my hands. They were allowing me to set things straight, to avenge Hulagu's victims by blowing his brains into the Pacific. It would be a chance for the cosmos to at least begin correcting what it had done to us.

I would have paid a fortune for the opportunity to have had my father in Hulagu's position once. I would not have hesitated, and I knew that killing him would have saved the lives of the three people I loved the most. Liam Murphy was killed by the police, though, forever robbing me of the ability to collect what my father owed me.

Francisco Martinez was not my father, though. He was worse. Knowing this, I pulled the pistol's hammer back.

I did not doubt that I could kill a man if I needed to. I would not have joined the military otherwise. What gave me pause before pulling the trigger on Martinez was the realization that I could so easily kill someone when I did *not* need to.

I could justify the shooting of Francisco Martinez as justice. I could even accept it as an act of vengeance or plain old karma. He was defenseless, though. Chained up and bleeding on the stern of the *Loma*, he was no threat to me. I started to realize that though I was the kind of man who could kill such a vile person in cold blood, I did not want to be. I did not want the act of taking a life to be so easy. I lowered the revolver's hammer and passed the weapon back to Noel. "I'm not going to do it like this."

Dominguez looked surprised. "Is there another way you'd like to do it?"

Shaking my head, I said, "Not while he's defenseless."

"Well, *amigo*, he's never going to be any less defenseless than he is right now."

"I know."

Noel nodded in understanding. "Okay then." Using his right foot, Dominguez unceremoniously shoved Martinez into the water. There were no screams and no drama. The chains dragged him to the depths so quickly that there was the sound of a little splash, then he was gone forever. Just like that.

Francisco Martinez was the first person I ever actually watched die. It was anti-climactic. I felt almost nothing about it. No shock. No satisfaction. No regret. No glee. Not even the same sort of morbid fascination you get when driving past a bad traffic accident. It was almost a non-event, a stark contrast to the deaths I would be involved with later in life.

Marco solemnly nodded as I approached him on my way back to the *Pescado*. "I can respect that, Doyle. There's no shame in not being a killer."

The police chief reached into his jacket pocket and pulled out what looked like a bank book. Handing it over to me, he said, "Have you ever been to Panama, Doyle?"

I shook my head. "No."

"When you get out of the Navy, take a trip down there. Go to the capital and find the main office of *La Banca del Istmo*. Give a teller the safety deposit box number and passcode in that bank book. In return, she'll give you the money that *Sargento* Martinez left for you. It's compensation for the harm that he caused and the reward for protecting my nephew. There's $50,000 in there. We found a lot of his money when we got him. Enough to buy your boss's fishing boats even. Bradley! Are you sure you don't want us to handle your money in Panama too?"

TEQUILA VIKINGS

Darrow shook his head. "Thanks, but I've been hiding cash from divorce lawyers since the 1970s. I'll use my own people."

"Suit yourself," Marco reached out and took my hand, shaking it. "Please accept my sincerest apologies for what happened to you and your friend. I find you to be a very interesting young man, Doyle. I regret that I will probably not ever get to know you better. I hope you do not think it's because of any bad feelings on my part when I tell you never to come back to Mexico again."

Smiling, I shook my head. "I don't, Marco. I understand."

"Good," he said as he patted me on the shoulder. "Enjoy your life, my friend."

*****

CHAPTER
27

You sold your business to Baylon?" I asked my master chief as we made our way back to San Diego aboard the *Pescado*. "You know, when Hulagu was beating the shit out of me in the desert, he insisted there was something else going on. He told me there was no way Baylon would send his nephew up as a hostage for a lousy $15,000. He was right, wasn't he? Did Marco send Noel up to protect this business deal?"

My master chief nodded and grinned. "Yeah, he told me it was time for him to get out of the police racket. He's hoping to retire to the life of a sportfishing captain."

"You believe that?"

Darrow shook his head. "Nope."

I thought for a moment as I lit a cigarette. "You think they're going to run dope in these boats?"

"For a little while," Darrow answered. "Until they get caught, I guess."

"Didn't you tell me it was a bad idea getting too involved with these guys?"

"I did. And it is," Darrow answered with a shrug.

I exhaled a lungful of cigarette smoke. "Then why did you do it?"

TEQUILA VIKINGS

My master chief sighed, "You know, I don't speak much Spanish, but I do know what the phrase '*plomo o plata*' means. Do you?"

"Yeah. It means 'lead or silver.'"

"That's what it translates into. Do you know what it means, though?"

"It means you're being offered money or bullets." Mack told me all about what Hulagu had said to him.

"Shit, you really do know everything, don't you?" Darrow grinned. "Yeah, if these guys come to you proposing a deal, you can take it and get rich, or you can refuse it and get dead. Doyle, you got me into bed with these guys to get Mack out of Mexico. Your fifteen thousand dollars was a distraction for Hulagu. The real deal was me selling my business to Baylon. That's what got Macklemore back. When they offered me twice what it was worth, I saw a way out, and I took it. I'm going to Japan now free and clear of any entanglements with these people. So are you."

"They paid you in cash?"

My master chief nodded. "Just the part that was way over what my business was worth. The rest will be paid the normal way when our lawyers work out the transfer. That's the part my wife will know about."

That piqued my interest. "You're hiding money from your wife? You planning on divorcing her or something?"

Darrow shrugged again. "Planning on it? No. Let's just say, though, that being forward deployed has historically been a little hard on my marriages. I don't do well around temptation. You want some advice?"

Since I knew that I was going to get it anyway, I said, "Sure."

"Never tell women overseas how much you're worth. If you decide to marry one of those girls in the Philippines…"

"I'm not marrying any bar girls, Master Chief."

Darrow grinned. "You say that now Doyle, but..."

"Jesus, after what Rafaela did to Green, you think I'd…"

My master chief shot me a scowl. "She did nothing to that piece of shit. She was a good girl, Doyle. She was a good girl forced into a horrible situation. Most of them are. Our boys have married thousands of those women and brought them back here. Most of them have made great wives. You're painting the lot of them based upon the same couple of dozen ungrateful bitches you've seen at the Trophy Lounge."

Darrow reached into the cooler and pulled out a couple of beers, handing me one of them. "Another piece of advice is to give a girl a chance. Play the field all you want. If you find someone you like, don't dismiss her because of what she's been forced to do to survive. Give them a little latitude."

I nodded at Darrow to humor him, but there was no way I saw myself getting romantically entwined with a woman I would meet working in a red-light district.

"My final piece of advice is to get to Panama as soon as you can and move that money to a different location. Don't put it in any American bank account, or any bank account for that matter. If you do, it's going to throw out all kinds of red flags. And Doyle?"

"Yeah?"

"Whatever you do, don't claim it on your fuckin' taxes, okay?"

"Okay." That seemed like common sense.

"And one more thing…"

"What?" I asked, a little more terse than intended. The master chief was starting to sound like an overprotective parent.

"You didn't pull the trigger, and you didn't kick Martinez into the drink, but you'll want to keep this stuff to yourself. As far as the law's concerned, we're both accessories to murder right now if anyone ever finds out about this shit."

*****

August 31st was a busy morning on Pier 2. It was flooded with both civilians and military personnel milling about while a brass band played in the background. Even the local news crews were there to see us off. The pier was packed with hundreds of sailors in their dress whites saying goodbye to their loved ones. It was a month-long journey to Japan and they tried to make every minute count. I was on the pier myself, desperate to say goodbye to someone I loved, too.

I spent more than an hour weaving through the crowd, hoping against hope to catch sight of Hannah's face. I did not sleep the night before, fantasizing about how I would spot her in the mob on the pier. I pictured a perfect Hallmark moment, where we saw each other through the throng and ran into each other's arms. I would drop to one knee, pull the ring out of my pocket, and once more ask her to marry me. After she accepted, we could run off to live happily ever after.

When I caught sight of Mack and Oksana, my fantasy crumbled. They were by themselves and Oksana bore an expression of deep sympathy on her face. As she approached, she put a letter in my hand. "I sorry, Doyle," she told me. "I very so sorry." Macklemore could not even make eye contact.

I took the envelope and tried to make small talk but had difficulty expressing anything intelligible. It was evident I was not going to be happy with whatever Hannah wrote to me. Leaving them, I retreated to a quieter part of the pier before I opened the letter.

Dear Doyle:

I am writing to you in the hope that you will forgive me for leaving you the way I did. No words, no explanation, just running away without ever speaking to you again. You deserve better than that. But that was the only way I could do it.

You see, Doyle, I still love you. I will always love you. I just can never…

That was as far as I could get. I crumpled up the letter and envelope, pitching both into the bay. To relieve my frustration and anger, I then threw a quick succession of punches into the air. When I finished, I dug through my pockets for the engagement ring and launched that into the bay too. It was then that Dixie appeared and grabbed my arm, leading me back towards the gangplank. "Come on, Doyle, that's enough. Let's get back to work."

"It's over, man," I blubbered. "She's gone for good."

Dixie nodded in sympathy. "I know, Doyle. I know."

We crossed the quarterdeck, but instead of going to the shop, we stepped over to one of the mooring line stations. From there, the two of us looked over the crowd one last time. I spotted Macklemore and Oksana from above and watched as they mauled each other while sitting on one of the unused bollards. Their passion was so intense, it was hard to believe that they were planning on reuniting in just a couple of weeks. They were acting as if they would never see each other again.

Dixie noticed them too. "You know, it probably doesn't help you feel any better right now, but what you did with that kid is a fuckin' miracle.

He's cleaned himself up, gotten himself some swagger, and really turned himself around. The guy got himself a girlfriend even! Can you imagine that? That goofy-looking son-of-a-bitch got himself a lady!"

I wiped my eyes and took another look at Mack. I was pretty proud of the way he had turned out. "Yeah, he's going to be okay, I think. Fuck, he better. Keeping him out of trouble cost me BOOST, my chances of reenlisting, my fiancée, a pretty bad beating, and damn near my life."

"Not to mention fifteen grand…"

I never told Dixie about the money I got from Baylon. I was not going to either, so I went with it. "Yeah, and fifteen grand."

As I watched the pier, I spotted Kramer and his cronies coming towards the ship. They were swaying as they walked, still boozy from the drinking they had done the night before. One of them caught sight of Mack and Oksana and cruelly burst into laughter. Even from where we were, I heard them call out some snide remark about how ugly their babies were going to be. I was sure Mack heard it too, but he let it slide. I made a mental note to talk to Kramer in the Nixie Room sometime before we reached Pearl Harbor.

Emboldened by Mack's lack of action, the trio of drunks became even more brazen about their jokes. Not wanting to chance Oksana's feelings getting hurt, Macklemore decided to start making his way onto the ship. He kissed her goodbye one last time and walked to the gangplank. Unfortunately, the drunks were at a bottleneck in the crowd. Oksana had to weave through them to get off of the pier. When she passed, Crowley reached out and pinched her backside. I saw it, Dixie saw it, and tragically, so did Macklemore.

The executive officer did not. All he saw was Macklemore walk up to Crowley, whistle to get his attention, then lay him out with a single thump to the eye. Two of the television news crews covering the *Belleau Wood*'s departure from San Diego saw it too. They even got it on tape.

Sailors fight. It happens. Had this taken place in private, deep in the bowels of the ship or somewhere out in town, we might have been able to smooth things over. Macklemore knocked Crowley out on television, though. *On television*. There was nothing we could do. The captain had no choice but to make an example out of him.

TEQUILA VIKINGS

Warren Macklemore, the last thing I thought I had salvaged out of my final few months in San Diego, was finished as far as the US Navy was concerned.

It felt as if I was finished, too. BOOST. Hannah. Hulagu. My career. All of it laid waste by pulling Mack out of the back of that police car, a single act born of good intentions.

As a couple of SPs seized Macklemore and took him to the ground, I looked away towards the open ocean. In a little over an hour, we would be underway, steaming across the entire expanse of the Pacific to a land completely alien from anything I had ever known. It was the perfect opportunity to start over, but this time while embracing who I was.

Fuck the New Navy, I thought to myself. I wanted to follow in the footsteps of seafaring giants like Buccaneer Bill and Master Chief Darrow, sailing across the Far East, taking in new experiences, and seeking adventure in exotic locales.

And like both of those men, I had every intention of doing it all naked and drunk as often as I could. There was no use trying to resist the pandemonium anymore. I was who I was. I was a Tequila Viking. If I could not escape it, I might as well enjoy it.

THE END

Next in Series – Olongapo Earp (May 2021)

Author's Note –   Did you enjoy this story? If so, I invite you to *please* leave a review on Amazon.com! Good reviews not only raise the visibility of an author's work; they massage our fragile egos. It keeps us from priming our muses with absinthe and psychosis.

Acknowledgments

No great task is ever undertaken alone, and this was certainly no exception. There were plenty of people who offered me their encouragement and support in getting this, and the subsequent books of this series, written.

The first people I have to thank is my family. This has been a LONG effort, more than three years in the making. There was a lot of time taken away from my wife and children to get this done. So, to Patrina, Regan, Mason, Carson, Fairen, and Linden, I love you and thank you for your patience, your enthusiasm, and support.

Second, I have to thank the men I served with aboard the *USS Belleau Wood* in the early 1990s. The *Tequila Viking* series is absolutely a work of fiction, but it was inspired by the diverse cast of colorful characters I was in the Navy with. They were, and are, the finest people I could have ever served with, and I miss them every day.

In that same vein, I need to send accolades to my brothers from another mother, Ritch and Matt Shefke. Most of the Tijuana storyline in *Tequila Vikings* was inspired by the trips I took south of the border with these two guys, both of whom I have been friends with since high school. Without Ritch, I would not have gotten into half of the trouble I got into in Mexico, and without Matt, I would not have gotten out of it. I'm still kind of surprised that we never ended up behind bars down there.

For her early encouragement, I would like to thank author Mary Sojourner, who, after seeing me write something about the Philippines on an internet forum, contacted me and pushed me to consider writing a novel. For early encouragement, I would also like to thank Tim Mucciante, the first person I sound off on during the creative process. He has seen and endured plenty of my early efforts that were certainly not fit for public (or anyone's) consumption. I applaud his strong stomach.

I also need to thank the authors of the Grand Blanc Authors Meetup, who have continually read, critiqued, and listened to my work for three years now. Doug Allyn, Boyd Craven, Gloria Goldsmith, Brenda Hasse, Stephen Foster, Richard Drummer, Mike Asselin, Kathleen Rollins, Jo Macek, and anyone I may have missed, THANK YOU!

TEQUILA VIKINGS

And finally, my beta readers! Beta reading is no easy task. It is a HUGE undertaking and requires a lot of time and effort to do. It also requires commitment. You really have to be dedicated to the project to see it through. There is no such thing as casual beta reading and these people are an author's most valuable asset in cultivating a story. So, Rich Sorgenfrei and Tim Geniac, thank you so much for your help and invaluable assistance in helping me get this done.

And, of course, to you, the reader, thank you for taking a chance on an unknown author and reading this work. I hope you enjoyed it enough to continue on with the following books in this series.

Appendix I
Slang and Abbreviations

1MC -	The ship's public address system.
Aft -	In the direction of the stern of a ship.
AFPD	Armed Forces Police Department – An American military law enforcement organization tasked with keeping order in Olongapo, Philippines
Airedales -	Sailors assigned in roles to support air operations.
A School -	Navy school that teaches a recruit how to do their job.
BE/E School -	Basic Electricity and Electronics School. This is the first phase of training for US Navy electronics rates for ET, FC, ST.
Blanket Party -	(or "Bosun Locker Counseling Session" or "Fan Room Counseling Session") Unauthorized, and illegal, disciplinary action involving violence to adjust a crew member's behavior or mete out revenge if a man could not be held accountable through normal channels.
Booter –	Green, new sailor. Fresh out of boot camp or A School.
Brig -	The ship's jail.

TEQUILA VIKINGS

Bow -	The front of a ship.
Bulkhead -	A wall on a ship.
Captain's Mast -	Non-judicial punishment for relatively minor (misdemeanor) offenses. Sentences can range from restriction, loss of pay, confinement with bread and water, or discharge from service (known as Article 15 in other services).
C School -	Technical school that teaches a sailor how to perform a specific task or repair a particular piece of equipment. Training that allows a sailor to become a specialist within their rate.
CIC -	Combat Information Center. The place on a ship where the crew monitors the radar, sonar, and other detection systems. It is a dark room with a lot of electronics gear.
CSE -	Combat Systems (Electronics). A division of the Combat Systems Department in charge of maintaining radar and communications equipment.
CSO -	Combat Systems Office -or- Combat Systems Officer. Is used interchangeably as a space or a person. The CSO person is located in the CSO location.
CO -	Commanding Officer.
Deck -	The floor or the ground on a ship.
Deck Apes -	Boatswain's Mates, sailors assigned to the Deck Department charged with maintaining the appearance and working order of ship's surfaces.
EMO -	Electronics Materials Office -or- Electronics Materials Officer. Is used interchangeably as a space or a person. The EMO person is located in the EMO location.
Field Day -	Deep cleaning of a ship's spaces.
Fore -	In the direction of the bow of a ship.
Gedunk -	Junk food.

GI Shower -	(or "The Scrub") When the sailors pull a crew member with hygiene issues into the shower to clean him up with wire brushes, scalding water, and industrial abrasives.
Gundecking -	Signing off work as complete despite not actually doing it.
Head -	Bathroom.
Helm -	The wheel used to steer the ship.
IC Line -	Ship's internal telephone system.
JAG	Judge Advocate General – A Navy lawyer
Ladder -	Stairs.
LBFM -	Little Brown Fucking Machine. Slang for Filipina bar girls (not derogatory. It is a complimentary, if vulgar, term – bar girls would often refer to themselves as an LBFM).
Liberty Drip -	Venereal Disease.
Master-at-Arms -	Navy version of an MP (Military Policeman).
NIS -	Naval Investigative Service. The US Navy's version of the FBI. At the time of this story, the NIS had just been renamed as the NCIS (Naval Criminal Investigative Service), but the change was new, and the sailors of the fleet still usually referred to it by its old name.
OOD -	Officer of the Deck. This is the watch that controls access to the ship and is in charge of the quarterdeck while in port.
Overhead -	The ceiling on a ship.
Passageways -	Hallways on a ship.
Pecker Checkers -	Hospital Corpsmen, the ship's medical personnel.
PI -	The Philippines.
PMS -	Preventative Maintenance Schedule. This dictates the frequency and timing of equipment maintenance tasks.
POOW -	Petty Officer of the Watch. Mans the podium on the quarterdeck while in port, armed with a

	pistol. Makes the announcements over the 1MC, logs activity about the ship.
Port -	The left side of a ship when facing forward.
Rank -	Paygrade of a sailor, his place in the command hierarchy.
Rate -	The job a sailor is trained to perform aboard a ship.
Sand Dog -	San Diego
Scuttlebutt -	A rumor or a drinking fountain.
Shellback -	A sailor that has gone through the Shellback initiation ritual while crossing the equator – a tradition hundreds of years old.
Skating -	Avoiding work, goofing off (also skylarking).
Space -	A room or a compartment on a ship.
Snipes -	Engineers. Sailors charged with the propulsion of ship and essential services such as electricity, water, and fuel.
SP –	Shore Patrol. US Navy version of MP, but composed of duty personnel, not professional military police personnel.
Starboard -	The right side of a ship when facing forward.
Stern -	The back end of a ship.
TJ -	Tijuana, Mexico
Trons -	Electronics
Twidgets -	Technicians, sailors working in technical rates.
UCMJ -	Uniform Code of Military Justice. This is the list of laws and regulations that apply to military personnel, violations of which can be punished under a Captain's Mast or court-martial.
Wog -	A sailor who has never crossed the equator and has not taken part in the Shellback initiation rite.
XO -	Executive Officer (ship's second in command).

Appendix II
Rates and Rank

Officers

Naval officer ranks are straightforward, progressing from the lowest officer paygrade (O-1) to the highest (O-10).

O-1	Ensign (ENS)
O-2	Lieutenant Junior Grade (LTJG)
O-3	Lieutenant (LT)
O-4	Lieutenant Commander (LCDR)
O-5	Commander (CDR)
O-6	Captain (CAP)
O-7	Rear Admiral Lower Half (RADM)
O-8	Rear Admiral Upper Half (RADM)
O-9	Vice Admiral (VADM)
O-10	Admiral (ADM)

Enlisted Rates and Rank

Rank

Enlisted ranks are among the most complicated of any US military branch. A typical enlisted rank consists of a two or three letter rate designation followed by letters or numbers that identify a sailor's paygrade. For instance, the rank "ET2" means that a sailor is an E-5, a second-class electronics technician. The "ET" signifies that the sailor is an Electronics Technician. The "2" indicates that their paygrade is E-5. An ETSN would be a junior Electronics Technician whose paygrade was E-3. An ETCM would be a Master Chief Electronics Technician (paygrade E-9).

Junior enlisted ranks are identified by hash marks on the right arm, the color of which designates which general function of the ship's contingent they work for.

Seaman (White Hash Marks) – General seamanship duties
Airman (Green Hash Marks) – General aviation duties
Fireman (Red Hash Marks) – General engineering duties

E-1	Seaman / Airman / Fireman Recruit (SR, AR, FR)
E-2	Seaman / Airman / Fireman Apprentice (SA, AA, FA)
E-3	Seaman / Airman / Fireman (SN, AN, FN)
E-4	Petty Officer Third Class (PO3)
E-5	Petty Officer Second Class (PO2)
E-6	Petty Officer First Class (PO1)
E-7	Chief Petty Officer (POC)
E-8	Senior Chief Petty Officer (POCS)
E-9	Master Chief Petty Officer (POCM)

Rates

AC	Air Traffic Controller
AG	Aerographer's Mate
AO	Aviation Ordinanceman
BM	Boatswain's Mate
DS	Data Systems Technician
ET	Electronics Technician
FC	Fire Control Technician
GM	Gunner's Mate
HM	Hospital Corpsman
MA	Master-at-Arms
MS	Mess Specialist

J.E. PARK

OS	Operations Specialist
QM	Quartermaster
RM	Radioman
SK	Storekeeper
ST	Sonar Technician
SM	Signalman
YN	Yeoman

Author's Note –

The Engineering Department is grossly underrepresented in this story. This is only because it is told from the viewpoint of an Electronics Technician. ETs tended to work near the top of the island structure on an amphibious assault ship, several stories above the waterline. The snipes worked deep within the ship's bowels, well below the surface of the ocean. The two groups did not mix much, served different duties and watches, and rarely crossed paths anywhere but on the mess decks. On the occasions I did run into an engineer shipmate out in town, ninety-five percent of the time they did not even look familiar to me, nor I to them. Mad props to the snipes, though – they worked insanely hard at a dirty, demanding job. Without them, a navy ship goes nowhere. - JEP

About the Tequila Vikings Series

Tequila Vikings is a four-part series chronicling the story of Doyle Murphy as he seeks his place in the world and a way to overcome the trauma of his childhood while serving aboard the *USS Belleau Wood*.

Book One –   Tequila Vikings (Feb '21)
Book Two –   Olongapo Earp (May '21)
Book Three –   Neptune's Martyrs (Aug '21)
Book Four –   Darien Gap (2023)

Next in Series – Olongapo Earp

As the US Navy closes its base in the Philippines, Doyle Murphy tries to protect his master chief from vendettas spawned by past sins committed while serving on the Armed Forces Police Department. In the meantime, he feels compelled to help a young girl he has befriended avoid the fate of her mother, a Filipina prostitute that Murphy finds himself reluctantly falling for.

About the Author

J.E. Park grew up near Detroit, MI, where he spent much of his gloriously misspent youth seeking misadventure within the Motor City's punk rock scene. After high school, he joined the Navy and spent several years bar brawling his way across the Far East, experiences that formed the bedrock of the *Tequila Vikings* novels. He currently resides in a suburb of Flint, Michigan.

Made in the USA
Monee, IL
30 November 2020